MILT MAYS

THE GUIDE

DEDICATION

To my wife—my soul mate and light in the wilderness.

ACKNOWLEDGEMENTS

There are so many people who deserve thanks for their help in the making of this book.

My first reader and editor has been my wife, both in writing and in life. Without her encouragement, I would have never taken off two years from medicine to enjoy my dream of writing and becoming a fly fishing guide in Rocky Mountain National Park. Thanks, Babe. Thanks also to my children and grandson for putting up with me closing the door to my den and writing. Your encouragements in my endeavors have been inspiring as well.

My critique group has helped me grow as a writer, helped improve my writing from its lowly beginnings to what hopefully will be appreciated by many. Thanks to Jane Boch, Jean McBride, and Beth Eikenbary. Also thanks to fellow writers from Pikes Peak Writers and Rocky Mountain Fiction Writers, most especially, Julie Kazimer and Anne MacFarlane, for their encouragements in this novel.

Thanks to special readers for their help with medical aspects and other concerns: Sandra Guidry, M.D., Lee Evans and Trishia Bowden.

My editor, cover designer, and designer, DeAnna Knippling, has been fabulous. Her expertise and gentle prodding, despite my stubbornness, helped make this novel a more readable and attractive novel.

There have been numerous fly fishing clients and friends over the years who aided in the reality of this story. The beauty and wonder of the Rocky Mountains continues to enthrall me.

And a special thanks to all Vietnam veterans, for all your sacrifices, both in the war and after. In my practice, I learn lessons from you every day.

There's more I'm sure I've missed. Thank you so much. Now, I'm going fishing.

PROLOGUE—JUNE 2007

Who's there?

Farrah thought she'd seen a familiar face, but couldn't be sure. She lay on the hospital bed and lolled her head side to side, squeezed her eyes shut, and opened them. An inky haze stared back. Disjointed thoughts rode on a magic carpet, soft and multicolored—dreamy, oh so dreamy. She wanted to close her eyes and enjoy the feeling.

But she kept her eyes open. Where did the face go? Was it Roman?

A reading light by her bed twinkled and refracted through the IV fluid in the colors of a rainbow. The song came back to her and she wanted to sing along with Dorothy. *Somewhere over the rainbow...*

But this wasn't Oz.

She stared at the IV, forcing her mind to focus. *Drip, drop. Drip, drop.* Each plink was a rainbow of poison—chemotherapy, controlled poison.

That's what Roman had said last week. This final treatment was to remove the bad part—he'd called it something else, but that's how she remembered it—remove the bad part so tomorrow her body would accept the new part. The bone marrow transplant.

She touched her scarred and empty left chest. Remove another part?

How did she get two cancers? First breast—now this?

She recalled Roman's answer to that one: "You're lucky I treat cancer." That was no answer. And there was something else—the way he said it, the way he glanced away, as if there was something he didn't want her to see.

Sure, she'd been lucky for a respected cancer doctor like Roman to marry her. As a "domestic worker," she normally never would have even bumped into him in a town the size of Loveland. But to be a volunteer at the hospital in Loveland, all you had to do was fill out some paperwork. If you wanted to work in a particular area, they usually let you. So why not? Help out a rich doctor. He wasn't bad looking. She had applied to help in his clinic, and did. Maybe she'd flirted a little. Maybe a lot. One thing she'd always had was a great body. He'd asked her to clean his house. Man, what a mansion. So she'd cleaned his house, and a lot more. He was an animal in bed.

If only she'd got that boob job after the mastectomy. Shaking two in his face like the old days. That would get him hot again. In the end, sex was what he wanted, right? It's what all men wanted. That was okay. Love was overrated. She gave; he gave—money, oh yeah, lots and lots.

Something else nibbled at her, though, an ant crawling around, hinting she'd left sugar in the wrong place. Something about the timing of the cancers. If she could only think. Her brain was encased in Jell-O, each thought a bubble that got stuck in goo before it could pop.

Pieces came back. One seemed important. Over a year ago, before they'd whacked her boob, she'd wanted to surprise him, going to the best diamond dealer in Denver without him ever knowing. He loved her to look sexy, and she knew jewelry did it. The necklace had thirty flawless diamonds, perfectly clear, cut so well her cleavage had glowed. Yet when he'd seen the necklace his eyes turned to dark pools.

What had he said?

She blinked hard, trying to remember his words: "A patient died." He despised losing patients, but this one must have been very important. He'd never been the same.

And neither had she. First the mastectomy. Then the leukemia.

Okay, yes. Her gooey brain fit them together: diamonds, bad day, mastectomy, leukemia. What did it mean? There was something she wasn't putting together.

She choked: saliva thick, lips slow. Something was wrong. She could barely cough, barely breathe. *Push the call button.* But her hand fumbled; her arm had become an iron log. Why couldn't she move?

The face drifted in again and floated away into the black void, beyond the light.

Maybe this was all a dream.

She bit her tongue, gritting down. At least her jaw worked. The pain seared her tongue; the copper taste of blood was real. This was no dream.

But if it was real, the face had been real. Roman *was* here.

A band of steel constricted her chest. She could not catch her breath.

Why was she afraid of him? He was her husband, a respected doctor. He helped people every day. Yet the thought of him being here?

Get out now!

Her lips were as flaccid as raw steak, her body a slab of granite.

The door opened. *Oh Christ oh Jesus!*

A nurse bustled in, along with the aromas of alcohol and feces. Farrah breathed easier. She could tell the nurse. But her hand was lead; her wooden lips only twitched. The blood pressure cuff squeezed her arm.

Any second the nurse would surely look at her, see the panic in her eyes, and help.

Like Jake. He'd always helped her. Jake. Where was he? His kind eyes could see inside, caress her fears. Warm, gentle hands that felt…like a fairy tale. Like his very touch could heal.

Not Roman. He wanted it rough: slaps and screams and drill it hard. How she had loved that. Then.

The *snick-snick* of the nurse's shoes faded out the door. She'd never even looked at Farah. Never noticed the bathroom door was closed. Only looked at the damn machines. Too busy.

She tried to scream, *No, stay! Look in the bathroom!* No sound came from her mouth.

The door to her room closed.

She had to get a grip. Roman was a doctor, for Christ's sake. He must have ordered a drug to relax her, help her deal with tomorrow. He was a good person. Just like her niece, Carrie. Donating the marrow was so heroic. She deserved a big thank you. Maybe a new car. A pink Lexus convertible. Carrie would wet herself.

That was better. Even thinking about spending money was like Valium. She breathed in. Out. Okay. Much better.

Roman's face loomed.

She tried to jump, but nothing moved. She stared, her thoughts as paralyzed as her body.

His face spread into The Winning Patient Smile. It sent creeping ants into her spine. This special smile—he actually called it The Winning Patient Smile—relaxed patients, inspired trust. The first time she'd seen it, she'd actually relaxed, felt soothed…for one single second. It was after he'd had a bad day. He had seemed jovial, his words touched with a nasal, New England sneer.

"I dispense poisons in smallish increments. Too much will kill you. Too little will be a wicked pissah but not even come close to killing the cancer. It has to be," he'd pinched his forefinger and thumb, "just the right amount."

Then he'd shown her The Winning Patient Smile. That had been the single second she had felt soothed by that wicked grin.

He added in a JFK twang, "And I have that power. Every damn day."

Ice ran up her spine. *Oh my God. What kind of doctor was he?*

Maybe it was a joke because he'd had a bad day.

A joke. Had to be. Yet after that, every time she saw his Winning Patient Smile, it made her cringe.

Now that terrible smile loomed over her, and a thought, too terrible, too insane, a thought that had been unable to fully form due to her hazy brain, was finally crystallized by his Cheshire grin: those gleaming teeth; diamond-cold eyes.

The timing hit her again: diamonds, bad day, mastectomy, leukemia.

Her eyes widened. She slammed them shut and held her breath. *No, no, no, no!* He'd see inside and know she knew.

All her troubles with cancer started with—his nose touched hers—the necklace. He'd hated that she'd spent all that money on a diamond necklace.

She must make him believe she still wanted him, still adored his rough sex. She opened her eyes and forced a bedroom look. Desire. He would trust that.

The Winning Patient Smile twisted. The sparkle in those hazel eyes, the very sparkle that exuded confidence to patients, cracked and poured out a black river of hate.

He knew.

Scream! Run!

Her lips and body ignored her.

"Today's the day, you know." His words sounded so kind. "I've been giving you a little something to relax you. Don't be concerned if you can't speak. It works that way."

At the edge of her vision his hand pulled something from his pocket: a syringe.

"Yes, today's the day, Sweetheart." His voice was sweet and loud, his diction upper-crust Boston, all a show for any nurse listening. Then he capped it with a working-class whisper, "Or should I say *bitch*?"

Surely, Jake would come in, any moment now. *Please!*

Then she remembered: Jake was gone for three days. "But Roman will be here," he'd said. "After all, he's your husband. He'll make sure everything is absolutely perfect."

Absolutely perfect. She held her breath for an instant. Another light dawned. Roman never had a partner until Jake Roberts. She always wondered why, out of the blue, he chose Jake. Now she knew. Everything would appear above reproach: ethical. Jake had started the chemo treatments, not Roman. Jake had witnessed Roman do everything possible to help her. Absolutely perfect.

Roman had planned everything. She knew that now. He loved his money and loved to brandish it. And if he gave, that was fine. But she'd *taken* when she bought that lavish necklace without his okay. That had been the beginning of her problems.

Yet, was that possible? Could he have actually given her breast cancer and leukemia? He was an oncologist, not a wizard.

Roman stuck the syringe into the IV port and pushed the plunger. The pretty, prismatic dripping stopped. Something crawled on sticking, pinching legs through her vein, up her arm.

The brain goo was gone. Her thoughts raced and beat frantically against a stone mask. She felt as if her entire body was made of concrete, unable to even twitch.

She could breathe, but only if she concentrated.

Yet her eyes saw and her ears heard. And though she could not move, she could feel. Everything. A pull on strands of her hair. The grating sound of scissors and the pull let go. Had he cut off a lock of her hair?

His guttural whisper tickled her ear. "Don't worry…*Dear*. You will get exactly what you deserve. You never wanted my love, only my money."

He stared into her eyes.

"It will only hurt for twelve hours. You won't be able to tell a soul. It will be agony. It will burn and twist inside you like a thorny worm wriggling in your veins, your heart, and finally, your brain. It will suck your life inside of it, savoring every morsel."

He turned on The Winning Patient Smile and pushed the plunger all the way down. Her eyes closed against her will. She could breathe and think. And she screamed, over and over inside her head.

But the stone mask made no sound.

CHAPTER 1

Eighteen months later.

The excitement in Loren's eyes made Stony want to run outside the fly shop, pump a fist at the azure Rocky Mountain sky and scream *Yes*! He wanted everyone in Estes Park, all the tourists toting shopping bags up Main Street, all the shop owners, the campers up the road, even the bear and elk high up in the Park to hear him.

Loren was totally hooked.

As a fishing guide he lived for moments like this: a twelve-year-old girl bubbling over with joy after a morning catching a Rocky Mountain Grand Slam—brown, rainbow, cutthroat, and brook—a feat most took years to accomplish. Loren had done it in four hours—her first day fly fishing, too.

Yet his smile faded. There was one small, nagging detail. Technically, the brook trout *was* a catch—she'd got it in close enough for him to touch the leader. *But man, if I could have only netted it.*

Loren, in her crisp denims, tan plaid shirt, and black Converse tennis shoes, ran across the shop from her dad and jumped at Stony, throwing her arms around his neck and hugging him. "Thank you so much, Stony. You were the greatest."

"Sure. No problem. But you caught all the fish." Even though it embarrassed him, he had to wrap his arms around her to keep from falling forward. One carrot-colored pigtail rubbed his cheek. It smelled of peaches. His face felt as warm as the beginnings of a good drunk. He gave her a tentative squeeze, eyeing her dad's glare from across the store.

She kissed his cheek. He set her down on her feet and gently unhooked her arms from his neck. She stood close, her freckled face upturned, beaming bright with sunburn. "You taught me. Someday I'm gonna be a guide, too."

He looked at the floor. It was great she was thankful. But Loren could do much better than being a fly fishing guide. He wiggled his toes in one boot. A blister burned. He should tape it.

He looked back at her, those bright blue eyes and smile as brimming with life as the first minute he'd seen her. "Thanks, Loren. First, you get good grades and finish school." He made sure it was loud enough so her dad—"Daddy," as she called him—could hear it.

She frowned, but Daddy's glare was gone now.

"Promise me."

"Okay." She walked back to Daddy, a little dejected. Not exactly what she wanted to hear.

At the front of the store, Daddy paid the owner of the shop, Bob, for the balance of the trip, then shuffled around, not making eye contact, easing toward the door, wanting to leave and get on with whatever important events he'd interrupted to be with the bubbly, giggling Loren: his daughter.

Yeah, but he'd done his "Daddy" thing for the summer.

Memories assaulted Stony of rough knuckles to the face, steel-toed boots to the groin, vomiting, and wishing his own father would never come home again.

Stony tucked the errant side of his tan Simms shirt into his sky blue, beltless Columbia pants and ran fingers through his thick shag of black hair, smoothing it back over his ears. The gray was creeping in more each month. Distinguished. Right.

He let a deep breath flow out through his nose, slow and easy. Loren's dad was nothing like his own.

Still, how could Daddy read a book the whole time Loren fished, only glancing up with a token smile when she screamed in triumph, holding up another fish? What about the gin-clear river full of fish, and—oh yeah—the doe and fawn and hawks? *Missed those didn't you, Daddy?*

Stony shook his head and walked to the back closet. He didn't own the shop but everything had its place. He kicked the edge of the closet lightly with his Merrel hiking boots, visualizing Daddy's head at his toe. Just a light bump. That's all. He moved the hung waders over to add Loren's to the rack.

That's when he saw them.

On the floor under the waders sat two empty cans of Bud and a roach clip pinching a tiny twist of paper. One can was on its side, amber liquid on the linoleum. The sour-sweet beer smell did not enhance the faint aroma of weed.

Stony wanted to crush the cans on either side of Caleb's head, the young guide who'd probably left them. He'd been covering the shop all day until a few minutes after Stony had come in from his trip. Bob had come in a few minutes after that.

Stony had wondered why Caleb had given him the eye as he left the shop. Now he knew. Caleb hated that Stony got the choice trips and great tips.

Stony looked up to make sure Loren or Daddy hadn't seen. This was the second time in the last week Caleb had used the shop as party central. Luckily the owner was preoccupied with his big date tonight and hadn't seen it yet.

He'd blame Stony if he did.

Didn't matter that Stony'd been sober and drug-free for years. It would be the end of his guiding. Was that Caleb's plan, or was he merely doing what Stony had done when he was a kid: believing that his youth protected him from misery and guilt? Stony would have to sit him down. No threats. Just the facts, the scars, the pain. History. Let him make up his own mind. That's what a man had to do—if Caleb wanted to be a man.

Bob caught Stony's eye, pointed at the cash register, and hurried to the bathroom up front. Stony smiled, trying not to look guilty. He always felt guilty when the subject of drugs or alcohol came up. The past still had a noose around his neck.

The bell tinkled at the front door. Stony's heart raced. He moved the waders back over the evidence. The door was probably the town sheriff, David, wanting his new fly reel. Bob had said he was coming by. Great timing.

Stony stood, trying to look relaxed but holding in a breath, knowing his guilty eyes would bring the sheriff back here, curious.

A rangy man wearing a light olive western shirt, black jeans, plain brown belt, and matching Danner boots strolled in and began perusing the flies.

Not the sheriff. Stony let out his breath.

Over by the fly rod display, Loren tugged at Daddy's sleeve, pointing at a rod, the same one she'd pointed out before they'd gone on the trip that morning. She was persistent.

The rangy guy glanced at Stony; his blue eyes said, *I'm patient, take your time.* Then he went back to picking over the flies.

Maybe the sheriff wouldn't come in. Stony's heart rate returned to somewhere between full sprint and jog. He reached for the beer cans.

The bell tinkled again. Stony jumped and nearly tipped over the other can.

Daddy was sidling out the front door, with effervescent Loren in tow. Hadn't even left a tip.

Stony raised his middle finger to the closing door, murmuring in his Mississippi drawl, "Keep your money, asshole. You might need it for another paperback at the airport."

Then he shook his head. He breathed in. Out. *Chill, dude.* At least Loren wouldn't see this crap back here. And her dad actually did *do* a *Good Daddy* deed. Anyhow, no one knew the big picture. On Daddy's plane ride back to Houston, he'd probably text Loren how much fun he'd had. He had to have a good side. Stony's dad had taught him fishing and hunting and love of the wilderness. A good man down deep. Loren's dad was, too. Had to be. For her sake.

Loren would be someone important. Stony was sure of it. When she went back to Mommy in LA, she'd remember this adventure on a pristine mountain river and grow up to be the mayor and clean up that cesspool of pollution and asphalt.

If not, there was always Stony's original plan: a nuke on the San Andreas Fault, and throw a rosary at the city of angels as it sank into the Pacific, pissing on the last crappy skyscraper.

He grinned. Yep, that was him: The Grumpy Guide. New title. He'd hang the sign outside the shop. The Grumpy Guide. Unique, primitive, and a curiosity. Tourists would swarm like mosquitoes on a baby.

Jesus, he thought. *Give it up.* He remembered his dad's funeral. A day as bright and hot as any in a Mississippi August. The sweat dripped and his tears flowed. Forgiveness does that.

The odor of the river's damp moss and the fishy hint of the day's catch hung in the air, overcoming the beer. He breathed deep. The river smell seeped in and tightness flowed out.

How could you hate someone you love?

Bob was out of the bathroom, spiffed: hair gelled, wearing a black, long-sleeved shirt, new Wrangler jeans, and a wide, black belt with turquoise buckle. He hustled out the front door. "It's all yours, Stony. See you Monday. If David comes in, his reel's under the register."

The front door slammed and the bell jangled like a hammer hit it. Bob was in a hurry. Saturday night, tequila, and a babe. Stony eyed the roach clip. Good thing.

"I'll be right there," he said to the guy who was still concentrating on the fly bin.

The man held up a hand, but kept looking at the flies. "No problem."

Stony snatched the beer cans and clip, and in a five-count had them in the trash, bag cinched and tossed into the dumpster out back. The cans clinked a few times. Thankfully, the afternoon breeze blew from the front to the back of the store. Pine trees grew out front, and their smell was a relief.

He grabbed a paper towel and wiped up the beer, then made two quick sweeps with the big broom, getting out the back door most of the river gravel traipsed in from a day full of clients. A lot of gravel for the first of October. Another reason for Bob to be happy: money in the bank.

Five o'clock Saturday night, and here Stony was…in the fly shop. Again.

He could call Summer, though he was still uncertain about her. What did he actually know about her? She was beautiful, smart, liked older men. And he hadn't felt this way in over thirty years. But she had unusual…desires. A little "out there" for him, but…why not?

He picked up his cell phone to call, then remembered he had a customer. The guy was inspecting fly rods.

Stony walked over and nodded. "Sorry for the wait."

The guy looked up. "End of the day. You're a busy guy. Good thing the owner has you." He held out his hand. "I'm Jake Roberts. You do guided trips?"

His gaze was steady and deep, his eyes as clear and warm as a spring day after a hard winter. You could always tell a man by his handshake. Jake had an iron grip, but smooth hands. No calluses. There was something else: like his gaze, Jake's handshake made Stony relax.

"Name's Stony. What kind of trip you have in mind?"

"Stony, huh? That's a cool name. Nice to meet you. Well," and his eyes shifted ever so slightly, "I really want to hike into a remote area and catch cutthroats."

Stony's favorite trip. Day hike at altitude in the Colorado high country got the blood pumping before the adrenaline surge of catching the big cutts. Good for the heart, soul, and what ails you. Or hasn't yet.

He studied Jake. Why had his eyes shifted? Stony didn't share a backcountry trip with just anyone, not like the ordinary day-clients— mostly fat, out of shape flat-landers aching to be as cool as Brad Pitt in *A River Runs Through It.* Or maybe parents who could care less about fishing, punching a family-outing ticket with their kids.

Yep, the Grumpy Guide. Add Pessimist, too.

Jake definitely wasn't an ordinary day-client. He was tall, with a chiseled face, eyes like pieces of sky, and so easygoing. Hell, Stony was ready to take him to dinner and chat.

Right. Chat. The sign out front would be the envy of the other guides. Stony: The Grumpy Guide, Pessimist and Chatterbox. Impressive.

"You after camping overnight, or just hiking for a day?"

Overnight would pay for a new Sage four-weight rod. Pricey devil, but sweet casting. This would probably be the last chance to earn it, so late in the season.

"Overnight?" Jake smoothed an eyebrow slowly with two fingers. "Yeah. Matter of fact, that sounds great. Maybe we could even stay a few days and hike into real wilderness."

"Sure. We could hike in ten miles or so. A few days? Like two or three?"

"How about five or six?"

He said it fast, so fast that Stony wondered if that had been the plan from the get-go.

Stony squinted, inspecting Jake more carefully. Nice clothes and boots: he could probably afford the trip. Clean-shaven and new haircut: no slob. Long legs and no gut: probably in shape. Could be a smoker, though.

"Any health problems? You in shape?"

"Oh, sure. Look at me." Jake put his hands out, palms up. "I'm a lean, mean fighting machine." He chuckled, free and easy.

The way he held his hands, the rising tone of his voice...

A memory flashed that had been buried deep: a sunny day in a jungle so green it made Stony ache to go back, all the while running to get away, running as fast as he could. Outside a no-name village near An Loc, he'd asked the mamasan if there were any VC in the village. She'd held up her hands and shaken her head, as innocent as a two-year-old. So he'd trusted her. And lost three friends.

But this wasn't Nam, and Jake sure as hell didn't have enemies killing his family. He probably wanted to escape from work problems, family difficulties, the droning gray noise of everyday America. Stony'd heard every reason before, and had faith the wilderness and fly fishing could heal Jake's small problems. After all, it had saved Stony's life. That and a woman as beautiful as an Alaskan spring and hard as the winter. It had taken him a long time to meet another like Sonja. Summer was the same but different. Good, he guessed.

Why the hell was chatting with this friendly guy bringing up all this bad history? Stony forced a cheery face. "When you looking to go?"

"Day after tomorrow."

Stony frowned, trying to appear friendly and not scowl. He had a trip scheduled tomorrow, and he'd need at least a day to get the food and everything ready.

"Monday's a little quick. How about the day after that? Say Tuesday the fourth."

Jake dropped his head and looked at the floor, as if he didn't want Stony to see his eyes. "Gee, I was hoping to get going earlier. But…sure, that'll work."

"Okay. I'll see you Tuesday morning 'bout seven. We'll plan on five days. Make sure you have good socks and hiking shoes." He handed him their standard list of items to bring. "That's a summer list. You'll also need a fleece top and bottom in case it gets cold. For a five-day trip, you'll have to carry a light pack. I ain't no mule. Think you can handle that?"

Jake nodded and signed the standard waiver that said if he got hurt or died on the trip it wasn't the shop or guide's fault. He bought two pairs of socks Stony recommended. That was a good sign: the guy listened. Stony ran Jake's Visa card, they shook hands again, and Jake left.

Pretty simple. Guiding usually was.

Stony locked the door and peered out the window.

The feeling when he shook Jake's hand lingered: warmth and something else. A banana plant waved in the winds of his mind, and black smoke snaked around the leaves. The smell of rice paddies and gunpowder unsteadied his legs. A woman with blue eyes and a scarred face stared deep into his eyes, and a wolf howled in a cold Alaska night. He started to lose his balance and caught himself with his hand and leaned against the wall.

Jake got in his Outback and drove away.

Stony watched the car, then the wind blowing the pine trees, then the clouds floating across the sky. He walked back inside and called Summer. His cell phone read "No Service." Maybe that was good, a sign he shouldn't get involved.

He finished sweeping; wrote down the final money count and locked up. On the walk home, he thought about Jake, Summer and a past he thought he'd left buried.

CHAPTER 2

Roman pulled the sleeve of his crisp white lab coat up enough to see his watch for the second time in ten minutes. The last patient of the day, six p.m., and he still hadn't been able to locate Jake. Mondays were always busy and tomorrow looked almost as bad. But the rest of the week he was off for two reasons: Find Jake. Kill Jake.

The elderly man caught Roman's eyes and asked, "Do you need to go, Dr. Johnson?"

Roman gave the man his Winning Patient Smile. "As soon as we're finished, Mr. Randal. Your getting energy back after the chemo is great. Your blood count looks good. I suspect your remission is in the bag. Why don't I see you in another month and check your blood count again? Enjoy your great-grandson." Patients who appreciated Roman got his best, and he made sure they lived longer.

Finished with patients, Roman strode into the crisp October evening to his midnight-blue Mercedes. The navy-blue Brooks Brothers wool suit kept him warm, and he still felt as professional as he had this morning, in his red tie and gray, pin-striped shirt. He started the car and sat back, waiting for the diesel to warm up. The front of the newly-built hospital entrance with its new, burnt-orange brick veneer and white colonnades stared at him through the windshield and made him yearn for the old days.

The good old days of medicine had been like sweet apples falling right into his lap. Patients came to his office; he diagnosed their ailments, prescribed treatments, and gained their trust. Most of the time nature healed them, not anything he did. But he took the credit, their trust, *and* their money. Why not? He had to admit, though, they rarely died. He was too good. And he always made special efforts for patients like Mr. Randal. They were a pleasure.

His photographic memory had served him well, both in school and in remembering patients' personal details. Especially the powerful ones. They enjoyed the extra time he took with them, showing them he was a caring doctor. Yet they preferred to think of him as their friend. They were the ones with the power. They could help him out with his practice.

None of them were like Mr. Randal. They wanted power over Roman. Not the way it would be. Ever. But he knew how to play along. Even in medical school at Colorado University. He'd always said, "I want to help people." Interviewers for his residency ate it up. The professors marveled at it, especially coming from a guy so damn smart. The thing was, he really did like helping patients—the ones like Mr. Randal. They really, truly loved his help.

But the others? The ones who tolerated Roman, or came to him out of necessity but really thought Roman a mere pawn in their game of money, money, money? What they didn't know couldn't hurt them. And his side practice of oncology? Wonderful to have that power over death. And life.

The cash flowed in. Certainly he helped many patients. Put on The Winning Patient Smile and quote the latest medical study, and they believed. He was smarter than all the local quacks, but he had always enjoyed the business of medicine more than the patients. And he hated sharing. So as an internist dabbling in oncology, solo private practice proved quite satisfying and lucrative.

Time passed. HMOs paid for nothing. Malpractice costs skyrocketed. Patients believed they could diagnose and treat their illnesses better than he could. That was after they got their degree on the Discovery Channel and their residency from Fox News. Somehow it didn't matter anymore that he was the doctor—the one with eight years of postgraduate training and twenty years of private practice.

Jake should have understood, as a fellow physician. And Roman's partner.

Jake had even used brain implants to help his patients. Brain implants were the cutting edge of pain relief. A local neurosurgeon used deep implants to help Parkinson's patients. Deaf patients could hear again with cochlear implants. Jake had worked with the local neurosurgeon to help pain in cancer patients, help rehabilitate those with brain cancer and stroke-like symptoms. They'd found it even helped other cancers in ways they didn't understand. It caused personality changes—perhaps the depression would leave, a better attitude, positive thinking. No one really knew. But it was cutting edge. And cutting edge always meant HMOs did not pay. Ever.

But good old Jake kept hoping, spending his own damn money to help the patients.

One side of Roman's lips rose. That's why he'd hired Jake: naïve as snow was white.

Now Jake had been gone for days. Him, his wife, and daughter—vanished. Roman didn't care about Jake's hag of a wife. How Jake stomached her was beyond him. But his daughter, Summer? Quite another story.

He pulled out of the parking lot and called his office manager on his cell.

"Amy, have you heard anything from Dr. Roberts?"

"No, sir. Is there something wrong?" Every time she spoke, her soft voice reminded him of her legs. Almost as long as Summer's.

"No, I have a surprise for him and was hoping he'd called in. Never mind. Oh, did you get with Dr. Ahmad about covering my practice for the week?"

"Yes, sir. Dr. Ahmad said he would take your calls from tomorrow evening until Sunday night the tenth at eight p.m."

Ahmad was pretty smart for a Pakistani. But he'd been drooling over Roman's choice patients. Probably couldn't wait to tell them how much better he would treat them. Couldn't be helped. Take care of Ahmad later. First Jake.

"Okay, I'll see you tomorrow. Don't worry about Dr. Roberts. I'll find him." Damn right. He glanced in the rearview mirror and ran manicured nails through his slicked-back, mousy-brown hair. First Jake, then he would concentrate on Amy, her legs, lips, and—

"No problem, sir. Oh, almost forgot, workman's comp called to remind you about the deposition on Mr. Farnsworth next Wednesday at one p.m."

"Yes. I remember. Thanks."

He ended the call immediately. His feelings about Farnsworth were not for Amy's ears. She must continue to think he was sad about the poor man. Farnsworth. Fucking scammer.

He laid the Palm Pilot smartphone on the seat beside him and looked in the mirror, smoothed an errant patch of hair, showed his teeth, and rubbed coffee off them with a finger.

Farnsworth. He'd finally be done with him. A year and a half but well worth the wait.

That day was etched in his memory—that glorious, wonderful day he was reborn as a doctor. A month after getting rid of The Bitch, he'd had the epiphany. He, Roman Johnson, MD, was the cure for modern medicine: the dreaded workman's compensation patients, HMOs and their denial of payments, and so much more. His entire life up to that moment had been preparation. The dabbling in oncology had paid off, finally.

Yes, Roman was the cure, and he would find that idiot, Jake Roberts, and show him what happened to people who got in Roman's way. Smart always beat stupid.

He put the Mercedes in gear and drove to the local McDonald's. He was hungry, but mostly he needed to think, and Mickey D food always helped both. After getting a quarter-pounder with cheese, chocolate shake, fries, and a hot apple pie, he parked in the McDonald's lot and savored every morsel. Not like the three-way he'd grown up with—thin-cut roast beef with mayo, James River barbeque sauce, and American cheese, but it would do. He'd always eaten anything he wanted. It was his right, being of sound mind and body with normal cholesterol, low blood pressure, and normal weight, not to mention hypnotizing hazel eyes. He was handsome, but not distinctively so. His mousy hair and weak jaw had once disappointed him. But they had turned out to be good things. The right nondescript clothes and he could melt into any crowd. Who said genes didn't matter? He was a testament to how little nurture meant.

Wouldn't Aunt Gladys agree? After all, she always told the truth. And whipped it into Roman, her fat arm as heavy as oak, the belt removing sin and drawing blood from his naked ass. She said she did it because she loved him.

The bloated woman's sweaty face and hungry eyes broached the surface of Roman's subconscious. Maybe nurture did have a tiny bit of influence. Though perhaps Roman's genes had a flaw or two. He chuckled. Good old Mom.

Jake would feel the full force of Roman's nature and nurture very soon. The strong conquered the weak.

While he ate, a detail about Jake bubbled up: fly fishing. Maybe Jake had gone on a fly fishing trip.

He grabbed his Palm—then choked. He coughed and wheezed. He breathed in slowly then coughed forcefully. *Shit!* Now his crowing breath was barely audible and his chest felt like a belt had tightened around it, keeping him from inhaling. He could barely move any air.

He coughed again. A dislodged piece of french fry hit the dashboard. His chest heaved in deep breaths, several until he could think again. How stupid was that? When he got excited it always happened: he inhaled the food. Asinine.

He must be calm about Jake. He took a drink of shake and a few deep breaths. That was better.

He queried his Palm for the nearest fly fishing shop, *Flies Are Us,* in downtown Loveland. He called and a woman answered.

"Hello, I'm Dr. Johnson," Roman never used his first name when talking with potential witnesses. There were lots of Dr. Johnsons. "I'm trying to locate Dr. Jake Roberts. I think he came to your shop a while back. One of his patients has a problem and I need to talk to him as soon as possible. It is really a matter of life and death."

"Oh, yes. Jake Roberts. Bought a rod here. Nice man. Stopped in a week or so ago wanting to go on a backcountry trip. We don't do those types of trips, though."

"Backcountry? Where would that be?"

"The closest would be up in the Park. But we could give you a great trip right on the Thompson through our shop."

"Did you not hear me? Life and death. I need to find Dr. Roberts." His tone shut her up.

He waited, letting guilt squeeze her itty-bitty mind.

"I'm sorry, sir."

If she could only see his Winning Patient Smile, her sudden anxiety at being totally irritating would be dissipated immediately. The tone of his voice would just have to work. He would employ his best bedside "smoothie," a tone of voice that always won patients over to consider chemotherapy right after he'd told them they had a few months to live. "When you said the Park, did you mean Rocky Mountain National Park?"

"Yes, sir. This time of year, a hiking trip to one of the high lakes might be fun." She was tentative. Extra polite. That was better.

"Hiking trip, huh? Who would take him on one of those?"

She gave him the name of the fly shops in Estes Park. He thanked her, hung up, and stared at the golden arches.

Had Jake already spilled the beans? Was he trying to hide?

No, Jake wouldn't tell. He was a coward, like all the gutless doctors who could never bring themselves to report a colleague. There were thousands of drug-addicted doctors, well known to their colleagues, and no doctor ever reported them. None of them had the guts to do what Roman had done with Farnsworth.

What was Jakey-boy thinking, anyhow? He could never hide from Roman.

Another, more ominous, thought struck him.

Could the Farnsworth hearing be more than routine? Maybe those workman's compensation idiots knew.

CHAPTER 3

After walking home, Stony got the grill going on the small patio and put the steak on. He went back inside to get a drink. There were two photos on the kitchen counter, the only reminders he'd kept of a time before everything went to hell. One was of Sonja, a compact woman with raven hair, the snowy Alaska Range in the background, her iceberg-blue eyes staring into the distance, most certainly at wolves. *Her* wolves. A pack she'd studied and followed near Forty Mile Park. She had saved him. He looked at the other photo—saved him from what had happened *there*. It was his unit in Vietnam, a scraggly bunch holding beers and one lean youth in a white tee-shirt, smiling, holding a roach, front and center: Stony. Reminded him of Caleb.

They'd had a party that day, the evening after his deed. They were inside their hooch, a homey hooch with footlockers for tables, a tin bucket of iced Schlitz in the front. They all held cans of Schlitz, wearing green fatigues or green tee-shirts. Except Stony. He'd changed and showered off the blood and put on a white tee. He was The Main Man that day. A celebration.

He shook his head and glanced back at Sonja.

Beside the photos sat a bottle of Corona, his favorite—or had been. Sweat dribbled down the side, amber liquid beckoning.

AA had helped, but there was something about those confessions, the God thing, and complete abstinence. To have a taste of beer once in a while… He was trying this new system: moderation. Have one, that was it. Like a normal person. Summer said it worked with a few people she'd known. She sounded convincing—though how would she know? Then again, she could be a drug treatment counselor for all he knew.

Sonja had been his first true love. There had been women since, but none like Summer. She brought back feelings he thought he would never have again. He called her, got voicemail. "Hey, Summer. Just wanted to talk." He paused, thought about saying more, then pushed *End*.

He rummaged through the drawer, grabbed the bottle opener, popped the top and took a long guzzle.

What the hell?

He ran out the back door and smashed the bottle on the grill. The golden hops ran down the side, sizzling.

He knew right then that the moderation system was not for him. *Sorry, Summer.* One bottle, and the five more waiting in the fridge would go down after it. Way too easy. Where the fuck would he be if he did that? Nam and square one. Add a little Oxycontin and it would have been a real party. Stony and Daddy's ghost, dancing in the grave.

More like wallerin' in it.

Although with all the damn zombies around lately he might get bit, or ate, or whatever zombies do when you get down in that grave with them. Call NBC. Another great story. Could zombies even live above eight-thousand feet? Wouldn't their eyeballs pop?

He chuckled. The Corona tasted like piss anyhow.

He went to the fridge, took the five remaining Coronas and emptied them one at a time into the sink, staring at the two photos. Nam had started it. Sonja had ended it. He wasn't going back.

He tossed the bottles into the recycle bin, then went to the grill, forked out the medium-rare cube steak, and shut the back door with his foot on the way to the kitchen. He turned on Lynyrd Skynyrd and let go of the past. Songs about the South still did it.

—

The next day was Sunday, a day of worship. Stony had a good trip with the skinny dude from Boulder. Or rather, the transplant from Ireland. Stony could listen to the guy talk all day, loved that brogue. The guy was odd, though. Even on the stream, he took a flip pad from his shirt pocket and carefully jotted every one of Stony's pointers. Flattering, but strange. That was guiding. Got some weird ones every now and then. At least the guy tipped.

After the trip, Stony probably should have gone to AA. Instead, he grabbed two granola bars, an apple, and water, and hiked to Lily Lake. Could have hitched a ride, but it was just over the hill and he felt like walking. He caught fish, released them, watched the sun go down. There were no candles or prayers. No shouting, guilt-inducing preacher, either.

Monday morning he scrambled eggs and watched the cow elk outside his back door. Behind her, two calves chewed their cud. Aspen leaves flittered in the breeze like gold coins tumbling in water.

The photos on the counter hadn't moved and wouldn't. They reminded him of the battle he'd won and his vow to Sonja. Every damn day.

He called Summer. No answer again. He left another voicemail. Why had she not called him? Maybe he should have gone along with handcuffing her like she wanted, but it rubbed him against the grain. And when she wanted to blindfold him? Nope. He didn't want to risk going off on her. Hopefully she understood.

Nguyen called him Monday afternoon. He'd made a new special—Bánh Mì—pork and vegetables and a crispy baguette. Would Stony try it? Damn straight. And it was damn good.

Nguyen's talent for Vietnamese food endeared the people in Loveland, and he'd done well since Stony brought him over in '88. There were a lot of Nam vets around, and seeing a friendly Vietnamese face and tasting that food brought back the good memories about the war instead of always the bad ones.

Stony laughed at one of the compact man's frequent jokes. Nguyen's daughter, Kim Lyn, laughed loudest.

Strange, though, how Nguyen's mahogany eyes held none of the sadness of the boy in 1969, clutching his dead father's head, tears streaking his dirty cheeks, cleaning off war like fingers of purity.

Now Nguyen always tried to make Stony laugh. After all, Stony had been a soldier back then, and those things should be forgotten because things like that were okay when done by a soldier, in war.

Right.

It could have gone different: Vietnam, Alaska, after. Way different. Stony had never made much money. But he'd saved enough to help Nguyen start his restaurant and fund Kim Lyn's college. Her giggle still echoed in his mind as he'd chased her around in the early days of Nguyen's restaurant, pretending to be a bear when she was five. Stony would never see his own daughter, but he couldn't be sad about that. Not now.

Kim laughed hard at another of Nguyen's jokes, her black eyes brimming with as much emotion as intelligence. Stony could watch her every Sunday. This and fly fishing: better than any church.

That night Stony got ready for the trip with Jake Roberts, and wondered about his new client. He was forty-five. Maybe a little old for packing in. But Stony was nine years older, and could out-walk every guide in the Park. Jake looked pretty rugged, like he was in shape. Evasive, though. And there was the other thing.

Stony shook his head like midges swarmed his ears. Let those dogs sleep. Right now he had to finish packing. The TV blared the weather forecast: chance of snow next week. They always said that this time of year. Anyhow, the forecast in the high country past two days was worthless. Like throwing dice, only worse odds.

"No one knows the big picture," he muttered. It didn't really matter. He was ready. Besides, this was Colorado, not sub-zero, hurricane-force-wind Alaska. The purple and green curtain of the aurora borealis folded in his mind, and he heard Sonja's scream echo through the cold cabin on that last night. There are things a man cannot prepare for, but still survive, and live stronger. She'd helped him learn that.

The phone rang. It was Summer.

"How are you, lady?"

"Fine. Going to be out of touch for a few days. Family problems."

"Wanna talk about it?"

"I can handle it."

"Okay." He paused wondering if she was pissed because he'd asked to help. She had this "me woman and strong" thing going.

"Are you upset because I wouldn't, you know—"

"Not a bit." Her words were still short and he didn't know if he believed them.

"Right. I'll be on a backcountry trip for about five days anyhow. Talk to you when I get back."

The line was quiet, but he could feel her still there. Finally she said in a tone of weakness he'd not heard until then, "I'm sorry. My dad is... Never mind. Have a good trip." She hung up, the last words in her usual "hard-woman" talk.

She was tough, though not like Sonja. Hadn't been kicked around as much. Maybe that was good.

He sighed, finished packing, and went to bed early.

Next morning he put on clothes, all polyester or Lycra-blends that would dry quick if sweaty or wet: gray undershirt and shorts, a fresh Simms beige, long-sleeved shirt with vertically zippered breast pockets—his favorite for long trips—and olive pants, convertible to shorts with a zipper at the knee. A frog-green nylon belt snugged them nicely. For the feet, liner socks to wick sweat and avoid blisters. Smartwool hiking socks over those. Then came his best partners: the good old Gore-Tex Merrels and the beige, stained, and torn Simms ball cap, his good luck cap.

He got to the shop a half-hour early at six-thirty to pick up more flies, tippets, and freeze-dried food—a few last-minute things. He twisted the key. The deadbolt wouldn't open. He tried again. The other keys on the ring rattled against the door. The lock wouldn't budge.

Was this the way it was going to be today?

One slow breath and one more twist, and the lock clicked open. Easy. Jake pulled into the parking lot.

Stony chuckled as Jake walked over. Probably couldn't sleep. Some people were like that—got all nervous the night before something new. Not Stony. Once, he'd slept through a grizzly ransacking the camp. He might have been a little drunk that night. *Yeah.* A tad.

"Morning," Stony said, "Couldn't sleep, huh?" They shook hands.

There it was again, the vice grip and the other feeling.

"No, I slept great. Thought I'd come early to see if you needed help."

"I'm good. Grab a few things and we're outta here." Sure as hell, Jake didn't look anxious. Not like the others. He was wearing what Jake had suggested, too: gray Simms shirt, beige pants, a navy-blue baseball cap with a Royal Wulff dry fly embroidered on the front, and well-worn Danner hiking shoes. Looked like he hiked a lot in those.

Stony snapped his fingers. "Hey, Jake. Maybe I forgot to ask. You got any health problems?"

Jake grinned; black pupils sparked against baby blues. "Like I said. Look at me. I'm the picture of health."

Stony smiled, but it felt weak. Why didn't Jake just say *no*? Now Stony would have to use his Doctor McCoy Star Trek health scanner. Yeah. Wouldn't that be nice? Shit! If Jake wobbled, burped wrong, or breathed too hard hiking the first quarter mile, it was over. Forget the fee. Not worth it. Stony had never lost a client. Not about to.

He remembered the time Sonja had asked for his promise. He'd said *yes.* She'd mouthed *thank you*, and gripped his hand tight. Then her hand relaxed and the light went out of her eyes. The snowy wind had slapped hard against the Alaska cabin, clapping the shutters, an echo as fresh as yesterday. He rubbed his thumb on his fingers, unable to rub off the tacky feel of her blood, though it had been gone for thirty-two years.

Whatever Jake needed, Stony would give him. Fly fishing in the wild changed people. Sometimes it saved them.

The drive to the trailhead featured a family of foxes, a buck deer, and small talk that kept Stony guessing about Jake. When they unloaded, another surprise smacked Stony off-balance. Jake needed no help getting his pack cinched and settled. An experienced hiker was nice, but Jake had seemed green at the shop.

The first ten minutes they walked up a steep grade without conversation, Stony catching his breath with the heavy pack and wondering why Jake was so quiet. Usually the client was curious about where they were going, what to expect. After all, they would be together five days in the wild. This time of year, middle of the week, even camping this close, people would be sparse. Ten miles in, there'd be nobody.

"So," Stony took in a labored breath, "how far you want to go?"

Jake appeared comfortable, hiking easy, breathing heavy but not as bad as Stony.

Stony did have a few years on him. And he was carrying thirty more pounds in his pack. And the first mile gained eight hundred vertical feet. Stony was no slouch, but he had to admit Jake was in okay shape. This could work.

"Oh, I suppose," Jake said, "like you said yesterday. Ten or fifteen miles. You know, put some distance between us and anybody else." He chuckled. "I'm surrounded by people and civilization every day. Maybe that's what this trip is all about. Get away from it all."

Stony eyed Jake sideways. Jake's breathing had slowed, his stance was straight and tall. Stony shrugged into the pack, tightened up the straps, and strode forward so quickly he only narrowly avoided a pile of horse manure in the path, which made him think about his own childhood.

"Yeah, I hear ya. Nice to get away from all that shit—back to Mother Nature."

At least they had good weather today.

The day Stony had left his home in Natchez it was raining, had been all week. It was the day after his eighteenth birthday—September 12, 1968. The rain felt like an omen, then. The feeling had been accurate. Hitching rides to Dallas was a soggy, frigid mess. Each time a car passed his outstretched thumb and splashed icy mud up to his waist, he'd thought about going home. He'd shivered, wiped off the mud, thought about his burned-out alkie father and worn-down mother in a no-win life, waiting to die. He'd stuck his thumb out again.

When he got to Dallas, he'd decided to stop hitching and buy a Trailways bus ticket to Denver, then work his way to Alaska. Might take him all winter, but once in Alaska he could wait tables and rent until he could get a good down sleeping bag and a tent. He'd be okay.

And he had been, for a while.

Stony high-stepped through a rocky part of the trail and was about to hike further, but Jake hadn't answered, and his footsteps were absent. Stony stopped and looked back.

Jake was leaning against a rock on the side of the path, staring out over the cliff.

Damn. Stony walked to Jake. "Sorry about the crass language. Kind of a guide thing."

Jake flinched and jerked his head up, eyes wide, as if Stony's voice had spooked him. Then he relaxed, motioned with his eyes at the view. "No. You hit the nail on the head. It is a bunch of shit sometimes, maybe even most of the time—trying to get the job done, make the boss happy, make some more money, please the…customer, all the while rushing through real life without much sleep, breathing polluted air, eating cancer fuel, ignoring what counts. But this?" He spread his arms out toward the valley. "This is why I'm here."

They both surveyed the glacier-lined canyons chiseled into the twelve-thousand-foot mountains, salmon-pink with the first sun. In the verdant valley below, the lazy, gun-metal river snaked through a meadow while antlered elk splashed through on their way to better grass. Above, a golden eagle circled for breakfast.

Jake sighed deeply and looked at Stony. "I'm holding you up."

Stony planted his butt against a rock. "Nah. We could sit here all morning if you like. I love it, too."

Jake followed the eagle for another moment. "I really want to catch some of those cutthroats everyone keeps talking about."

"'Nuff said."

Stony got his ass back in gear. They had to get moving anyhow. Flat, dark clouds were already gathering to the west.

CHAPTER 4

After another busy clinic on Tuesday, Roman left at four p.m. and drove home, getting angrier and angrier at Jake's sudden disappearance. The groveling little ass had been very secretive since he left the practice six weeks ago. Maybe he'd rethought last December.

Roman loosened his tan and red striped tie, and for the first time in years wanted get out of the gray Calvin Klein suit quickly, get into jeans, and leave town. He should have never let Jake cover his patients that cold, pre-Christmas day. He'd thought Jake would make cursory rounds because he had to go to Summer's medical school graduation. But the next morning, the nurses reported that Mr. Casper had required extra attention, and Jake had spent a lot of time with him and his chart. When asked, Jake had given Roman The Look before averting his eyes. "He had a few problems, but everything turned out fine." Only a few seconds, but it was the same look that Roman's mother had given him: suspicion and disgust after hearing about local pets burning to death in trash cans. Roman had said to her, "Why would you think I did that?" But The Look said she knew. She would tell.

Death comes in many forms, but suffocation? Terrifying and lasts forever if you know what you're doing. And no one ever suspected. According to the coroner, Mommy Dearest died in her sleep, lucky old woman. Buried her right next to Auntie Gladys, fat whore. It had been Roman's ticket out of South Boston: finally got all Mom's money, including land outside Denver her uncle had willed her.

After Jake gave Roman The Look, he became more and more distant. But Roman had covered his tracks well.

Given that, and given that Jake was an idiot when it came to money, he was still a doctor, and had proven himself smart enough to get this far. If he delved into the wrong places he could ruin it all.

Ruin it all? On second thought, highly unlikely. Roman was a successful oncologist, savior to many. The community loved him. Jake had no proof, only suspicions, and was a coward like most doctors: he would not confront a colleague. Yes, Jake had never said one word to anyone. Eventually he seemed to forget the incident. Trust in Roman returned. All was well.

He even left his insulin in the office fridge.

It had taken six months of poisoning Jake's insulin for his bone marrow to succumb. His white cells were resilient, but eventually Roman's superior poison won out. Leukemia.

Who better to diagnose and treat Jake's leukemia than the best oncologist in town? Humans were such trusting animals. Roman became Jake's oncologist and treated him with his own special chemo, laced with marrow poison.

But Jake wouldn't die, even after a month of tainted chemo. Merely a little ache in his bones. That wasn't right.

After another month, Roman took it to another level. He feigned sorrow and depression over his wife's death, saying he missed her so much, especially their weekly trips to the movie theater. In reality, the last movie they'd gone to was when he'd started poisoning her, The Bitch. He asked Jake's daughter, Summer, if she might accompany him to a movie, to assuage his deep sorrow. The deepest.

"Sure, Doctor Johnson." She was always so quick to please. Just like Daddy.

Roman was the consummate gentleman. He even bought her popcorn.

After, he took her home. She had been living with her parents for the last month, waiting for a new apartment to open up. Jake opened the door and frowned at them.

Roman put his arm around Summer and kissed her on the cheek. "Thank you, dear. I had a great time."

Then she did something that surprised even Roman.

"You're welcome, Roman." She kissed him on the lips, and went inside.

Jake's eyes got wide.

Roman smirked, and raised his eyebrows. Then he gave Jake The Winning Patient Smile. Summer would be all Roman's if Jake said anything about Casper.

Jake got it. His look said it all. Now *that* was real pain.

Pain was exactly what Roman wanted. Cancer responded to the psyche, as proven over and over with breast cancer support groups. The psychological stress made Jake's system less resistant. The special chemo started working, and a few more weeks would have done it. But Jake had stopped getting treatment and left the practice. Then he completely disappeared last week. He must have something more than suspicions about Casper. And without the weekly infusions of poison, he might actually improve. If he brought in the authorities…

Roman scratched his inner forearm through the gray suit coat. Eczema had plagued him from age two. He scratched harder, wanting it to hurt.

Dammit! He stopped and peeled back the coat and shirt to bare skin. His forearm was red and a bead of blood oozed. He touched the blood and licked his finger. It kept oozing, so he repeated the touch and lick twice more. He let out a deep breath.

He would get Jake.

After that, he would concentrate on Summer and her long legs. He'd perused her Myspace site for several weeks, found she liked older men. *How wonderful.* God, she had a tight ass. He wanted to masturbate in the car. No one was looking.

He started to unzip his pants, then zipped them up.

Jesus. In the middle of town? He was losing it.

At the red light, Roman rolled his head around. His neck loosened; he opened his eyes and concentrated on the red light, breathed in and out twice, three times, then a fourth. He could do this.

He started calling the fly fishing shops in Estes Park. No answer at the first two. On the third he got the owner.

"Hello. I'm Dr. Johnson and I'm looking for Dr. Jake Roberts." Roman's voice was as polite as any he could muster. "I believe he came to your shop for a backcountry trip. There's been a problem with one of his patients, and I need to talk with him." Yes, charming was better. Nastiness was more memorable, and the less these idiots remembered, the better. No "life and death" scenario this time. Emergencies always got people asking too many questions.

There was a pause.

"Yeah, let me see here. That name seems to ring a bell."

Shuffling of paper in the background.

"Oh yeah. Jake Roberts. You say he's a doctor? Huh. Doesn't say that on the paper here. Maybe it's a different guy?"

Roman wondered how many Jake Roberts went through a goddamn fly shop each year. Jesus, this guy was a dunce. "Did he give his address as 6231 South Steele Street, Loveland?"

"Yep. That's it, all right. Must be him. He left with Stony this morning. They went on an overnight. Three, maybe four-day trip, hiking to high mountain lakes."

"Oh, a hiking trip. Any way to contact him? You guys carry walkie-talkies or long-range radios or something, right?"

Roman heard a muffled chuckle. There was a pause, as if the hick needed to compose himself from whatever humor he saw in Roman's question. "No. There's no way to contact them without someone hiking to find them. A ranger might go if Stony was in the Park, but I doubt it, them all short-staffed with the cutbacks and such. If it's an emergency we could send a helicopter. Someone would have to pay for that. Ain't cheap neither." The man paused again. "Besides, I'm not even sure where they went. Stony don't tell me or the other guides where he goes. Kind of a trade secret, you know."

Roman frowned at the phone and breathed hard through his nose, holding back his desire to scream.

"Isn't that dangerous? I thought it was some kind of law that a guide had to post his hiking route in case he didn't come back or there was a true emergency."

The man on the other end huffed in the phone, seeming frustrated with Roman's ignorance.

"Not a law, nope. Good idea, sure. But see, that's the thing about Stony. He don't particularly care for that idea. Does pretty much what the hell he wants. Ordinarily, I would never let a guide do that. But clients keep coming back, request him. He helps out a lot at the shop, too. Plus, he's getting a little older. So, I give him a little leeway."

Roman squeezed his eyes shut and gritted his teeth. This was getting nowhere. He relaxed the tightness in his shoulders, unhinged the spasm in his jaw, and opened his eyes. If he spoke when he was stressed, his Southie accent came out, and he hated that, hated the fact that he had grown up with so little money. And he certainly didn't want this guy to remember his accent. He stared coldly at the wall and poured on the charm. "Well, shoot. Do you have any idea where they might have gone? I was thinking about taking a hike to stretch my legs. You know, we doctors need to practice what we preach. Might be nice to take a few pictures of the aspen changing."

Another pause. He could feel the man thinking with his two lonely brain cells connected by a fishing line.

"Well, Stony's been known to hike up to the back range northwest of Crystal Lake. Some tough country over there, though. If you go out, you need to get a good guide, though nobody here can help just now. You might could find a hunting guide, say at Chalmer's next door."

Roman's lips parted. Finally, useful information.

"The weather's supposed to turn bad, isn't it? Maybe they'll turn back. Is it snowing up there yet?"

"Oh, that front is supposed to blow right through. No big deal. But there's another one brewing. Might be more of a problem. Stony's a tough old coot, though. Prob'ly stay just to spite the weather."

Roman breathed out slowly, thanked the owner for his time, and hung up.

Another challenge: iking. Then again, maybe he could find a guide who used horses. Quicker and less work.

A few phone calls to hunting friends netted names and numbers. But when he called the guides, they were all closed for the night.

No big deal. He knew where Jake was now. Tomorrow he would find a guide. He went home, packed for hiking, and had a bourbon and water. After he watched the weather forecast, he went to bed and was asleep in minutes.

Planning a murder never kept him up.

CHAPTER 5

They had walked another five hours, ten miles by Stony's estimate. Jake hiked like a mountain goat, making Stony grin. Finally, someone who could boogie like Sonja. The exercise had lifted a curtain in Stony. *Time for fun, Mr. Grumpy Guide.* Even the blister on his toe had stopped whining.

The weather had cooperated except for the occasional dark cloud and burst of sleet that blew through too fast to make them get out their raincoats. The path leveled out at an elevation of near ten thousand feet. The clouds disappeared, leaving a sunny, warm afternoon. A scree of boulders was on the right side, a grassy slope with berry bushes in their autumn reds and orange leaves on the left. The trail disappeared around a bend above and to the right. Before the bend, the grassy slope on the left met the path at a copse of pines and aspens.

Stony slowed and stopped at the aspens. Yep. This was the place. He took a deep breath, stretched, listened and scanned the area—no one around but them. Good.

"Can I carry something else?" Jake said.

"Now that's the third time you've asked and the answer is still no. Thanks for asking, though. Just enjoy the hike. Don't worry. I'm breathing hard 'cause I'm getting a workout and I like it."

Jake had proven himself to be just that way, always wanting to help and easy to please. He was a guy Stony could easily enjoy for a week, or longer. Five days would be fine.

Stony looked up and down the trail again, verified they were alone. No one. Through the aspens on the left and over a slight rise, and they would be there. He motioned Jake to hurry.

Then he heard something and held out his hand, stopping Jake.

Caleb and a girl rounded the bend above them, walking down the trail. No way Caleb could see his place. No fucking way.

"Take off your pack and rest a bit, Jake."

"I thought—" Then Jake saw the pair. "Doesn't he work at your shop?"

Stony nodded. How did Jake know that?

"I don't want him to know about this place."

"Right." Jake took off his pack. So did Stony.

Caleb had on a day pack, tan shorts and tee shirt, no fishing gear, and a wide grin. The girl wore a pink tee shirt, no bra, and about the shortest white shorts Stony had ever seen. Her thighs were sunburned and long, and her greasy brown hair was pulled back in a severe ponytail. She stumbled and Caleb caught her. She looked at him with stoned, dreamy eyes. A bedroom smile.

Stony wanted to sit the guy down, hard, and talk to him, loud.

"How ya doin', Stoner?" Caleb chuckled.

"Been to Crack Rock, huh?" Stony traded digs. Crag Rock was another few miles up the path. Lots of kids made it there—sex and drugs.

"This is Yolanda."

She giggled, rubbed a breast with her wrist, and said, "Caleb, I'm hungry."

Stony wanted to roll his eyes. Of course Yolanda was hungry. At least she didn't have on a halter top. She'd probably had to put on the tee shirt to keep warm. The smell of hemp rolled off them like cheap cologne off a redneck in Natchez.

"Hi, Yolanda. This is Jake." Stony nodded. Jake bowed his head.

"Havin' a rest, huh? Surprised you made it this far." Caleb was such a card.

"See you at the shop." Stony was done with him.

Caleb's head wag and smile was pure melted sarcasm, no butter.

Yolanda gave Stony her dreamy smile, and Caleb led her down the path.

Before he was out of sight, Caleb twisted his head around and eyed Stony. "Dave was asking questions about you yesterday." He put his pinched forefinger and thumb to his kissing lips, like he was sucking in a roach. Then he laughed, went behind pine trees and was gone.

"Nice guy," Jake said.

"Right." Stony gritted his teeth. What the hell was Caleb trying to do? But he knew the answer to that.

He glanced at Jake. He deserved a great trip. Glanced back to where Caleb had disappeared. Might be Stony's last.

"Saddle up." Stony got his pack on, waited for Jake to strap on, made a last inspection up and down the hill, and strode quickly through the aspen, over a rise, and into thick willows. They bushwhacked their way through trees overhanging a narrow feeder stream. Fifteen minutes later they came to an open valley. Stony stopped and dropped his pack. "We'll be camping here."

The valley was cut by a glacier-fed river and surrounded by altitude-stunted pine trees and tundra. The rise and the thick willows protected this miniature Shangri-La from the sight of any hikers on the path. Stony breathed in deep, the air fresh and clean as the sky; it scrubbed out Caleb. The crystalline river full of cutthroats ached to be fished.

He planted Jake on a rock and organized the camp: a quick chore. He didn't carry much fishing gear. No need. A couple of rods, a two-weight and four-weight, reels and line to match, 5X leader and tippet, and one box of dry flies. Cutthroats up here were close to the dumbest fish around when it came to dry flies. That's what a guide lived for—dumb fish.

They walked to the river, though this late in the season it was little more than a creek.

"You don't need waders," Stony said. "Just rock-hop around. You can cross at narrow spots."

He let Jake practice casting in inches of water, where there were no fish. Jake caught on quickly, so they moved upstream where the stream rushed to the right of a VW-sized boulder, the backdrop to a deep pool that surely held larger fish.

"The idea is," Stony said, "to toss the dry fly into one of the little calm eddies or pools below the rocks and let it drift around like a bubble in the water. If it moves the wrong way, say the line gets downstream in the water and pulls it a little too fast, the fish will ignore it. Usually. Keep your rod high like this, so the line is off the water and—"

Bang.

Jake had a fish on and was yelling like he'd struck gold.

Stony netted the fish, a beautiful greenback cutthroat, not big but a jewel of the Rockies—dark-green back, fire-orange slash under the jaw, pumpkin belly, and black spots on a silvery side. The colors were accentuated by the afternoon sun and the lens of the water when they released it back into the river. Endangered species or not, Stony wasn't going to eat something so beautiful unless he was starving. He had plenty to eat back at the camp.

He helped Jake with several more casts while pointing out good water. Pretty soon Jake had it: how to catch 'em, play 'em, and release 'em. After that, all Stony did was take pictures, though he did want to use the extra rod he'd brought. The fishing was good.

They moved upstream a few hundred yards. Jake caught several fish, even a few over a foot, then stopped. He stood straight, stretched his back, took a deep breath, and smiled at Stony.

"Thanks, Stony. This is exactly how I wanted it to go."

"Hey, I'm glad you like it. I love helping people catch fish, especially ones who enjoy it as much as you."

Jake pulled out one, then another hundred-dollar bill out of his shirt pocket and held them out. "This is today's tip."

Stony wanted to snatch the bills, but he shook his head. "Thanks, man. But that's way too much. Why don't you see how things go the rest of the week?" Two hundred was more than Stony usually got for three days, much less four hours. He could use it, though, for the Sage four-weight. And maybe a little more steak than cubed leather.

Jake kept his hand out, holding the bills. They fluttered in the breeze. "I'm saying thanks. Don't insult me by turning it down. This is what I wanted, and you gave it to me."

Stony shrugged, took the bills and stuffed them in his shirt pocket. "Sorry. Not trying to insult you. Just—"

"Forget it." Jake interrupted and held out his hand, smiling. "Friends?"

Stony grinned and shook his hand. "Yeah." He quickly added, "Let me earn some of that. There's a pool up ahead that holds a few eighteen-inchers. And then—"

"Tell you what. I'd like you to fish with me, instead of watching."

Stony shook his head. "Can't do it, man. It's your trip."

"I know it is. And since it is, I want you to fish, too. I know you love it, and it would please me to see you catch a few."

Stony shrugged. "Okay. You move up to that pool, and when you're finished there, move upstream and fish that. I'll drop down and follow you. Sound good?"

Jake nodded and fished for another half hour. Stony caught one nice fish, but kept it in the water, hiding the fish from Jake, not wanting him to feel inferior.

Jake stood tall again and stretched. Stony walked up to him. "You okay? Ready for more?"

"I'm okay, but I'm done fishing. I'd like to take photos of the landscape while I'm up here. This is a beautiful spot. Would that be okay?"

The sight of Jake standing there, a contented grin on his face, the backdrop of snow-covered mountains and a rushing river behind him, burned into Stony's mind—but it didn't fit. Why would Jake want to rest? Didn't look tired, not even sweating.

Stony sighed, frustrated at quitting early and at the dangling question: *why*?

He handed over the camera. Jake took photos for another half hour, then handed the camera back. "Thanks. What a great place. But I'm hungry. How about dinner?"

"Okay. First, let me get a shot of you, right where you are. "

He took a few shots and then peered around the camera. Jake's eyes told a story the digital screen could never capture. A vision of a tiny boy stared back at Stony. Stony's fingers tightened around a machete that dripped with the blood of an entire Vietnamese village, the last being the boy's father. Stony had killed them all, singlehandedly. The boy's eyes penetrated Stony with thankfulness that he had been spared, but grief at the loss, and fear of the future.

Jake looked away, a parting glance revealing even more. Stony had that same feeling every day he stared at those two photos at home by the sink. He had run that day from Nguyen the boy, pitching the machete into the jungle, knowing he would never be the same.

This memory had seemed to bury itself after meeting Summer, a chance encounter at a charity function for Wounded Warriors. She was interested in the flies he'd tied and was giving away. He'd been with a few women after Sonja, but none like Summer. From the get-go he felt comfortable with her, even if he felt a little uncomfortable with what she wanted.

Jake walked up the stream bed, as calm as a green jungle without a breeze. Stony followed. He would not run this time.

CHAPTER 6

Despite all the thoughts circling in Jake's head, he couldn't help but enjoy the afternoon of fishing. The trip was going perfect. He had thought about his predicament for weeks before the answer had come to him. So damn simple. Yet timing was everything. Last week, all the planets, stars, weather, and—most of all—people had lined up. This was the week.

He knew Stony wanted to fish, too. Saw it in his eyes, heard it in his whoop every time Jake hooked one. When Stony tried to hide the big fish he'd caught, that spoke volumes. Stony was all Jake could ever hope for.

Then Jake began fading. Fast. Despite his fitness training for the last several weeks, he had to lay low. The leukemia had weakened him significantly, though since he'd stopped the chemo he'd felt better. But he knew. His blood counts had been so low. The cancer would kill him soon. All he wanted was to go back to the tent and sleep. But Stony would have become suspicious. And they weren't nearly far enough into the wilderness. Caleb and that girl had proved that.

So he said he wanted to take photos. It wasn't a lie. He wanted photos, just in case.

Just in case? Who was he kidding?

Stony's reaction to Jake stopping fishing was as transparent as a child's, looking down and curling his lips like he'd sucked on a lemon, disappointment obvious. Jake spent the next half-hour sitting behind boulders or lying supine to get "a good vantage point." It felt good to lie down. Too good. Almost nodded off. Shaking his head, he rolled onto his back to get up and stifled a scream. The bone pain was sometimes excruciating. He couldn't let Stony see that. Luckily, Stony was intently studying the stream. Jake recovered and stood, smiling when Stony looked.

In pain and dog tired, he still got great pictures. Although a child could have pointed the camera in any direction and shot the next cover for National Geographic. The crystal-clear stream meandered through a valley of rocks surrounded by green-leafed aspen laced with autumn's first gold. The vibrant colors played in the sunset over indigo, snow-capped peaks.

He finished and gave the camera back, and Stony took a couple of shots of him. Stony was a great guy. Too bad he was the one Jake had picked. But this was the only way.

Stony let the camera down and stared at Jake, his eyes vacant, as if he studied a distant problem.

On the way back to camp, a bull elk cruised in and drank from the stream, long enough for Stony to snap a shot. At the camera click, the big fellow popped his head up, glanced at Jake, and limped up the steep bank.

"That was unusual," Stony said.

"What?"

"They usually have a little harem this time of year. And with that harem, he would have been real territorial; should have at least given us a hard look and a head shake."

"Why didn't he have any ladies?"

"Gettin' too old. That's why he's up here so high. Probably sulking after losing his babes; trying to figure out how to get his youth back."

Stony had said it deadpan. Was he joking? Was he even talking about the elk?

That night Jake slept like the dead for three hours. Then the recurrent memory kept him from sleep.

December fifth, almost a year ago. The night of Summer's graduation, one of the few times Jake had covered all of Roman's patients. Usually Roman preferred to take care of patients he'd known for years, especially if they were in the hospital. But not this time.

That night, one patient started Jake on his treacherous journey— Charles Casper.

Casper was a long-time executive for MSI, Medical Solutions Incorporated, an HMO. He and Roman had been friends for a decade, went to church together, played tennis and golf together.

Imagine that—Roman going to church. But who would suspect a God-fearing man?

Then Casper's HMO wouldn't pay on Roman's patients. That led to a falling out of friendship, though Roman continued to be his doctor, and remained the consummate professional.

Several months later, Casper contracted a rare form of leukemia. Roman's dedication as his doctor became an obsession: learning all the latest treatments and taking care of Casper even when he was not on call. Jake had initially believed Roman blamed himself and would do everything in his power to save Casper.

The chemotherapy treatments took their toll on Casper. Once he'd been a striking, tanned, platinum-haired man with the confidence and broad smile of a movie star. But when Jake rounded the corner that fateful December night he saw a pasty-faced old crone with sunken eyes under a few wisps of yellow-white hair.

"Jake, isn't it?" Casper's voice still retained confidence and optimism. He wore creased, sky-blue pajamas with the initials C.C. embroidered in one-inch block letters on the pocket, red and shiny as silk.

"Yes, Mr. Casper. How are you?"

"Please, call me Charlie. I feel like I've known you for a long time, even if it is through Roman."

"Okay, Charlie. How are you doing today?"

Charlie wrinkled his eyebrows. "As you might imagine, not peachy."

Jake had reviewed Casper's chart before coming in the room and knew that the leukemia remission was over. His white count had climbed to twenty times normal, now three hundred thousand; his platelets were only one-fifth of normal, hardly any clotting ability left. If he didn't have a stroke or bleed into his bowels, his kidneys would shut down any day.

Casper had refused dialysis, preferring to die in the narcosis of renal failure rather than prolong the inevitable.

Jake was surprised the man was so chipper, though sometimes those on the cusp of death had a little spurt before the end.

Jake listened with his stethoscope and gently felt Casper's abdomen. Casper's lungs crackled and wheezed; they were filling up with fluid. His abdomen was bloated with a massive spleen. Bruises splotched his skin, and both legs were swollen right down to his sausage-like toes. All these signs indicated end-stage leukemia with kidney failure.

Death waited, close.

Why? Casper should be getting better. That type of leukemia usually responded well to chemotherapy. Jake had looked at Casper's medical chart. It had taken him half the night, but he'd finally understood. Roman had stopped the blend of chemo that was proven and started something else, stating in his notes that Casper was not responding. *Roman.*

Now Jake had the same leukemia.

Outside, the stream shushed at his mind, trying to quiet his thoughts. Stony breathed easy in the sleeping bag next to Jake. The tent ruffled and sighed with a slight breeze.

Exhaustion caught up with Jake. He finally slept.

The next morning he woke tired—more than tired—crapped out, as Stony would say.

Sitting up, it hit harder. He was burnt out, hollow, a husk of his former self. Yet somewhere inside, there was a kernel of energy, life, a will to live, still pulsing, deep, hard, like the nucleus of an atom. So much energy—all it needed was a little push. But too much and it might blow up. Or fizzle out. He had to use it slowly, a little at a time. It had helped him in the past get through dark days and darker nights.

"Fuck you, Roman!" It just came out. He quickly eyed the other sleeping bag. Stony didn't move. Damn. Jake had to keep a lid on it, take it easy. He had to have Stony, had to have his help getting deep in the wilderness, and his sympathetic sanction for what would come.

He wriggled slowly, beginning his move out of the sleeping bag while testing his joints. The hollow stiffness eased. No doubt about it, though: he was getting weaker. It would only get worse. He might have to use his emergency supply of insulin.

No. It was too early. That inner kernel would have to do. He had to get further into the wilderness. Besides, an OD of insulin would look like suicide. Summer and Carla would think it was because of them. They both already had such tragedy in their lives: Carla with that horrible accident and her screaming depression; Summer with her opposite reaction of eerie detachment and dating older men after she was in high school. The psychiatrist had told her she was stuck in a kind of Electra complex because the accident had hit her at a formative stage. She apparently blamed herself for not loving Jake enough to keep him with them after the soccer game, thinking that would have prevented the accident. Since she could not date Jake, she went after older guys. She kept getting hurt, but would not listen to reason and thought the psychiatrists were ridiculous. Carla couldn't work, and Summer was on an intern's meager pay, so they would both need his life insurance money. But the insurance wouldn't pay if his death was found to be suicide.

Sure, he was a coward for not confronting Roman. Jake even had a hard time confronting an employee who needed firing, much less a respected colleague whom he suspected of…murder. But if Jake did this right, no one would know what really happened, not even Roman.

Jake couldn't wait too long, though. Roman had to know he was dead so he would lay off Summer. A memory of her stared at him from the birth incubator, night-blue eyes keying in on his face…twenty-seven years ago. She was the first, the only. Jake's mother had doted on her. She had always wanted a daughter. Now at least she had a granddaughter.

Jake ached to see Summer now with her new doctor's coat, squeeze her tight, tell her how proud he was.

That would never happen.

He winced with the pain in his back as he slithered out of his bag. It took a minute and a few deep breaths to compose himself. He glanced again at Stony's sleeping bag. Empty. No wonder he hadn't moved. Jake pulled on a fleece top and blue jeans. He'd left his wool socks on last night, making his feet toasty and slipping on his cold boots less chilling.

He unzipped the tent flap and ducked out into the cold air: a shade more than nippy.

The aspen leaves fluttered. The stream burbled. No Stony.

He ducked back in, pulled on a wind-cutter fleece dome cap, then stepped completely out. The smell of coffee wafted up from a steaming cup sitting on a rock. Probably Stony's. Jake picked up his fly rod, and stood tall, trying to locate Stony.

Nothing. Maybe Stony was taking a dump.

He rummaged around Stony's pack for the coffee and found another cup. Surely Stony wouldn't go fishing without—

"How ya feeling this morning, Jake?" The low, gravelly voice with its soft Mississippi accent should have been calming, but it was so close Jake nearly flung the cup at Stony.

Stony ducked at Jake's throwing motion. "Whoa there, partner. Sorry to startle you. That cup of coffee on the rock is yours if you want it. Still pretty hot, too. This ain't McDonalds, so don't sue me if you spill it on your crotch. Well, you can sue me, but you won't get much more than those two bills you gave me."

Stony had materialized without a sound from the other side of the tent. He had twigs in one hand and dragged a deadfall log in the other. The loud rush of the creek must have drowned out the sound of the dragging log.

"Scared the shit out of me." Jake said. He started to put the cup back and paused. "You want a cup?"

"I'm part Indian. Sneaky's my nature." Stony dropped the log and squatted down by a stone circle. "'Preciate you're asking, but already had coffee an hour ago." He fiddled with a clump of pine needles and dried grass in the center of the stone circle, and then stacked a little teepee of twigs and larger branches on top.

"Planning a big fire?" Jake said.

Stony tossed the remaining branches on the growing pile beside the fireplace and squinted at Jake. "I won't use it unless we need it. Park rules. Only for emergencies. But," he pointed to the western sky, "see those clouds?"

Wispy peach curls high in the west reflected the rising sun. Gauzy clouds veiled the rest of the western sky in shades of purple and red.

"Pretty." Jake gazed upward, trying to appear innocent and amazed at the gauzy harbingers, but wanting to jump up and down and celebrate their true significance. All part of the plan.

"Yeah, pretty cold, pretty quick." Stony stood up and took his hat off, scratched his head, and eased the hat on again, eyeballing Jake. "You sure you don't want to trek outta here and try a different week?"

Jake shook his head and held up the fly rod. "Nope. It's this week or die for me. I feel great this morning. How about we get to fishing?"

"How about coffee and granola first?"

Jake sniffed in a deep breath of pine, coffee, and cold mountain air. He shrugged. "Okay, you talked me into it. That coffee smells good." The granola would raise his sugar way too high. Exactly what he needed.

They sat cross-legged on a small tarp to avoid the wetness of melting frost. The sun's warmth eased the ache in Jake's back.

Stony handed Jake a half-full tin of granola, poured white powder on top, added hot water and then stirred. "Better than home, and healthy, too." He beamed as if he'd served the best breakfast this side of the Mississippi.

"I thought a guided breakfast included pancakes, eggs, and cappuccino?"

"That's Hollywood Orvis in Montana with Brad Pitt and a movie crew. This here's the real thing. Not some dude ranch crap."

Jake munched a few mouthfuls and raised his eyebrows. "This stuff's great. What'd you put in it? Tastes like cream."

One side of Stony's mouth lifted in a crooked grin. "Trade secret."

Jake chewed on his granola. The hint of sage wafted over the morning-lit tundra. Shadows of trees on rocks danced in the breeze to the music of the mountains. The river percolated with rushes and burbles accompanied by wind *whooshing* through the gnarly, white-barked pine trees and the occasional *tink* of spoons on tin.

A truly grand last sonata.

CHAPTER 7

By seven a.m. Wednesday, Roman was on his way to Estes Park. He drove up the snaking Highway 34 beside the rushing Big Thompson River, comfortable in an olive L.L. Bean fleece vest over a forest-green, long-sleeved shirt, Calvin Klein stone-washed jeans, and a pair of Columbia hiking shoes he'd last used three years ago with The Bitch. His thoughts turned back to that glorious day in April, eighteen months ago, when he'd decided to kill his patients.

That day, lunch hour was spent trying to convince an HMO to pay his fees. After that, the afternoon began a slow swirl into a cesspool with three workman's compensation patients, patients he would never have seen before the insurance crunch. One could ruin a whole day. But three in one afternoon! Nothing wrong with them but a desire for more disability payments. Roman hated people who wanted something for nothing. He'd spent the last hour of the clinic from The Twilight Zone with a patient threatening to sue him if he didn't prescribe a medication the patient had seen on a TV commercial.

Finished seeing patients, he went into his office and closed the door. *God fucking damn it!* Medicine had gone to hell. He flopped into his chair, smoothed the sleeves and chest of his creased white lab coat, took a mechanical pencil from his breast pocket, and stabbed it into the armrest, grinding it round and round and round.

It hadn't been only that day, either. The previous year had been day after day of "modern medicine" drilling him in the ass. He'd tried to decrease his load of HMO patients, but then his patient base dried up. If he cut out workman's comp, a sweet piece of monthly income tanked. And with the new pharmaceutical splurge in commercials, every patient became the great and powerful Oz: they knew all.

The entire system of medicine was stumbling in a dark room full of knives. What modern medicine really needed was a visionary who could light the room and remove the sharp objects.

He was about to start dictating when an idea hit him. He could fix medicine. It would merely require a few adjustments to deserving patients. That was the key. Not just any patient, either. Only those who deserved it.

He had done it before. First to that bully in high school—he should have been more careful crossing the street in the rain, especially since his shoes had a large smear of KY jelly on the bottoms. And Mommy and Auntie. They got a special deal; they certainly deserved every bit of pain.

Roman had never let others run him or get in his way, though there was always someone who tried. No one ever suspected him, either. He usually waited at least a year between. His last masterpiece had been The Bitch. How sweet that had been.

After that he'd laid low, enjoying the souvenirs he had of each: the busted-out tooth from the accident scene of the bully, Auntie's underwear, Mommy's middle fingernail that he'd yanked out at the open-casket funeral, the lock of hair from The Bitch, and the others—he kept them in a special place. But after so long, looking at them didn't quite do it. The hiatus had lasted almost two years—well, not really, not even close. The itch needed scratching, especially with all those who needed his justice.

But then he had found the ultimate challenge: cure medicine. He had the perfect cover, the access, and a population rife with candidates. Why hadn't he thought of it before? Too busy chasing his tail around insurance trees, that's why. Before, curing disease had been a challenge, a puzzle.

Money had accompanied each solved puzzle. Patients had gratitude. Then patients had changed; money had dried up.

It was a good option.

It was the perfect option.

He knew he would do more good than aspirin or penicillin or any damn prescription he had ever written, or anyone else had written for that matter. Nobel Peace Prize material.

Yeah, right. That committee was too focused on all those sappy humanity lovers to realize how important a few deaths could be to the good of mankind. Hadn't they heard of Hiroshima?

Who could he start with? Maybe George Farnsworth or Charles Casper. Well, hell! He'd do two at once. He loved challenges.

He bit his thumbnail and felt his grin growing.

Someone knocked on his door. He pulled at the corners of his mouth with one hand, smoothing the ridiculous grin. "Come in."

Amy poked her lovely head into his office. The pink V-necked sweater highlighted her alabaster skin.

"Dr. Johnson, we're about all done out here. Do you want us to set the alarm, or are you going to be here for a while?"

"Uh." He composed himself, forcing dedicated concentration on his face. "I am definitely going to be here a while. A lot of dictation. Why don't you lock the door? But don't set the alarm."

Amy smiled. Those cute little dimples sprouted below big, brown eyes, sad but with—yes, he was sure of it—a touch of desire. *One day, Amy, one day.*

"Okay, Dr. Johnson. Don't stay too late now. You have a full day tomorrow, you know."

Wanting him and worrying about him. *Mmmm.*

"Thank you, Amy. You're so kind. I'll be out of here as soon as the work will allow." Dedication to his work should make her worship him even more.

She started to close the door, and he added, "Also, please thank all the girls for their help today, and for the card. That was very nice."

That brought her back in. Hadn't that been what he really wanted? A bit longer to look at her smooth skin, blond hair, full lips.

"Oh, Dr. J." She'd said it with true sadness clouding those chocolate brown, yummy eyes. What flawless skin. Never had he seen her wear one iota of makeup. And with her helping him out with female patients, he had been close to her. So close.

"You know," she continued, "all of us in the office loved her. She was a wonderful lady."

He cooled to her instantly, all business. "Thank you, Amy. You and the others run along now. I'll set the alarm." She had to bring up The Bitch. But it was as much his fault as hers. Why had he even mentioned the card?

Amy's eyes met his. His penis hardened. *Come closer, Amy.* He would have to think of another way. He would never bring up that woman again.

She smiled. "Okay. See you tomorrow." She waved with long, slender fingers, caressing the air before the door closed.

He sighed and rolled his head, feeling each neck muscle loosen. Having Amy could wait. The future of medicine, however, required immediate attention. He pawed through the patient files on his desk and found the one he wanted. Quietly, in his dictation voice, he spoke to it, as if dictating, but left the tape recorder off. "Mr. George Farnsworth. Workman's comp case. Always wanting extra doses of Oxycontin. This will require intense surveillance before the final judgment."

The memory of that day, that hour, that moment still made his pulse bound. Now the river raged over boulders to his left in its sometimes dangerous but always inevitable path to the sea. Those many months ago he had started his journey to fix medicine. He was still amazed at the care he'd taken and the wonderful beauty of the plan. The surveillance of George Farnsworth had been well worth it.

CHAPTER 8

Stony eyeballed Jake munching cereal. He looked almost recovered from yesterday. Even though he'd seemed plumb wore out, he never complained. And the threat of weather hadn't scared him. Had a sense of humor, too.

The morning sky reflected peach-colored horse-tail clouds. What'd they call 'em? Cirrus? Something like that. He frowned. That's what he needed to do: get serious and start headin' back.

Jake pointed his spoon at Stony. "I've been thinking. How about we hike in a little further today?"

Stony stopped chewing. Was Jake for real? Although it would be fun to show him a little more than the average adventure.

"I dunno. We might be getting into some weather, and I'd kinda like to stay within a day's hike outta here."

"I'll pay you three days extra, on top of the five."

Stony tried to avoid shaking his head. Damn. Money every time. But yeah, money was always good. Besides, one day of guiding would be more than he could get tying flies or waiting tables for a week in the winter. And three days? That would pay for the trip to Mexico. He usually shared the cost with two other guides. But with the extra money, maybe he would ask Summer to go instead. She would look great in a bikini.

He tried to swallow, but his Adam's apple stopped midway, the thought sticking. The money would be nice, but he should keep Jake safe. "I only brought enough food for six days, maybe seven. Eight's cuttin' it thin."

Jake chuckled. "Okay. I'll pay eight days for guiding me only seven. I really want to hike far into the wilderness for once in my life. Away from any people. I can still see the trail, and we're probably going to see some people if we stay here, right?"

Stony picked at his teeth, then slurped coffee. "Yeah, maybe a few." Eight days for seven. Hmmm. He eyed the clouds, remembering how poor the weatherman was at predicting mountain changes, and knowing he could take whatever was thrown at him. The ache in his knees and his back at the coming low pressure bugged him, but that was only pain. He'd done pain and survived. Many times.

"So what do you say, Stony?"

"Okay. Eat up. I'll pack." Stony tossed out his remaining coffee. *What the hell.* This was surely the last trip in the high country for the year, and he was in the mood for a challenge, a test of his skills. In twenty minutes he was ready, all traces of the camp completely obliterated. His idea of "leave no traces" meant exactly that. He made sure of it.

He shouldered his pack. "Let's get moving. I got a special lake in mind. Never told anyone about it. Probably four or five hours of hiking. Even if we get that cold weather, the lake's got another two weeks of good fishing before ice-in. And let me tell you, no one will be up there. Not even close. Those cutts will be hungry, storing up for winter. We're talking *F-U-N* fun."

They started fast, the high mountain air invigorating Stony, spurring him into a quick-time rhythm that allowed for no conversation. Behind him, Jake's breathing sounded labored, much more than it had yesterday. Against his desire, Stony eased his stride.

After another minute conversation crept in. "So, Stony, how did you get into guiding?"

Stony waited several steps before answering, trying to decide exactly how much to let out.

"Seemed like what I was meant for. Left home after high school. Headed for adventure. Didn't care exactly where. Made it to Alaska and rebounded back here, with a few stops in between."

Jake didn't answer, as if waiting for the gaps to be filled.

The rhythm of walking and talking gave Stony a feeling he could keep going forever and nothing could harm him: not weather and especially not someone as nice as Jake. A little more couldn't hurt. Besides, Jake was a good guy.

"Pa was a damn drunk, and Ma wasn't much better. Didn't figure they'd done much to help me up to then, so I did what the hell I wanted. Mostly I wanted to get outta Nachez, Mississippi. I could fish and hunt and knew how to take care of myself. Been doing it since I was two. So I figured I'd live life my way—"

Stony forced a cough, jerking the sentence to a halt. *Christ*. He was blabbing away like Jake was his best friend.

Those early days Stony had lived life his way, after he'd left home. From Natchez, he wanted Denver, needed it, a city in the West; out of Hicksville and into adventure. Bigger and better. Find work for the winter, then to Alaska. In Dallas he changed buses and hogged the back couch-seat, really two seats with a fold-up arm rest. He snoozed. At Wichita, last stop before the long run to Denver, he made a bathroom run, washed up, bought a snack, and got back on board. A guy occupied both his seats.

Carl Blackmon was tall, acne-pocked, twenty-going-on-twelve— a college guy from Colorado School of Mines on an engineering scholarship, coming back after a family funeral. He was amenable to sharing both the seats and two six-packs of Coors—something new— Dad had been a Schlitz and PBR man. Cruising across an unseasonably hot Kansas night, air-conditioning, cold beer, and talk of long-legged Cajun women and sucking heads off crawdads still made Stony sigh, wishing he could return.

Then again, life had a funny way of kicking you in the balls.

Their next pit stop was Limon, Colorado. Probably a nice town before the twister had rolled through, totally wiping out half the houses and the A&W across the road from the bus stop. It was fresh damage. The storm had taken out a corner of the bus stop—the bathroom. The pipes geysered water. Stony and Carl walked to the side of the bus stop and pissed out Coors behind an uprooted cottonwood. A dazed man stumbled around the A&W rubble, calling, "Annie, Annie!" The rescue squad pulled up. What a relief. Stony could have helped. Should have. He wasn't that way then.

When they reached Denver, Carl made Stony a deal. Come to his college rental in Golden, stay and help with the rent. Piddling rent, so Stony could build up funds before he took off in the spring for Alaska. It seemed perfect.

But it wasn't. Those engineer nerds must have needed lots of Coors after flexing their slide rules all day. Golden. Home of Coors and Mines. Mines was great; Mines did this; Mines did that. Did they say it because they felt the school belonged to them, believed it only catered to great minds, or—and this seemed the best reason—because it was a treasure the world must covet?

Stony left after a week. Mines was no treasure, only a rest stop for drunks. Maybe super-smart drunks, he'd give 'em that, but drunks like Daddy. The hell of it was, if Stony had stayed in school, he could have been an engineer. He'd barely studied yet made Bs in high school. But he had no intention of going to college. Knew what he wanted and did it; simple as that.

Simple. Right. If he had only known about the groin kick that was coming.

He gritted his teeth, put his head down, and hiked faster.

In a clear space, a few feet off the path, he noticed a pile of brown dung. An inexperienced eye might have thought a large dog had left it, maybe a German shepherd hiking with his master. Stony noticed the differences right away: four times larger than a dog's, with black and red berries pocking the large pile. He studied it another few seconds to make sure, and blew out a breath of relief. No fur. At least it wasn't eating meat. Yet.

He pointed at it. "Watch for bears. That's their scat and it looks fresh. Not that black bears will eat humans. They're pretty harmless, unless it's a mom with cubs and we surprise her. Even so, keep an eye out and keep talking. Loud."

He glanced back and saw Jake breathing hard. He slowed. They walked another minute and he glanced back again. Jake's eyes flicked from side to side, nervous as a squirrel caught in the open. The guy was losing it.

"Did you hear me? We need to keep talking." He twisted his head around. "You okay?"

Jake jerked his gaze up, a little wider than surprised, and wrinkled his nose. "Bear crap, huh? Does it always smell that bad?"

A puff of wind feathered Stony's other worry. Then a frigid gust slapped his face and staggered him. It took one full breath out of him, and lowered the temperature ten degrees.

He slowed and stopped to face Jake. *Forget fucking Mexico!* This was it.

"Yeah, the fresher the shit, the worse the smell. Just like us. Only bears can't flush a toilet. But forget about the crap. You feel that wind? It'll get colder than a dead coon's ass tonight. I think there's a pretty good storm coming in. We should probably turn back."

Jake face morphed instantly from scared shitless to cocksure, looking like he'd been fed the biggest line of the century. "Come on, Stony. The way I heard it you've been through the worst in Alaska. If the bears don't scare you, then I'm okay, too. Let's do it. It'll be a great fishing story for my grandkids. I promise to make it worth your while. Besides, I really need this." He paused and swept his hands out like a conductor of an orchestra. "What did they call it in the fly shop brochure? The adventure of a lifetime. That's what I'm after."

He let his hands flop to his sides.

"But if you think it might be too much for you, I guess we can turn back."

Stony wanted to laugh. Too much? Right. Adventure of a lifetime? Jake was absolutely right. This was nothing like Alaska in January with wolves howling all night.

Stony peeled off his pack and pulled out an insulated Gore Tex jacket. "Put it on."

He also tossed Jake pull-over waterproof pants. "Put these where you can get to them easy, in case it starts raining hard. Wet and cold are a bad combo."

Jake pulled on the jacket and stowed the pants. He was all grins.

Stony respected Jake for his determination, and felt a kindred spirit for his love of adventure. He donned his own jacket. He would go with Jake, despite the feeling that was beginning to well inside—a feeling of invincibility that had once dragged him to hell, where he'd seen friends die young and stupid in the endless rain that pelted their dead-blind eyes in a fucked-up jungle. He wiped his fingers on his pants to blot out the feel of closing the eyelids of his friends—and his enemies. They were all men who would never see another orange sunrise, feel a drop of rain, hear their children laugh.

Was adventure the true reason for Jake's push to continue, or any reason at all? *No one knows the big picture.* He was as sure of that today as he had been in Vietnam or Alaska, when he'd made a solemn promise to himself and Sonja and his dying daughter. *There are some promises you can never break.*

The trail beckoned and he walked forward.

CHAPTER 9

Roman slammed on the brakes and steered into the right-side bicycle lane to keep from hitting the SUV in front of him. Cars were stopped and backed up twenty deep on both lanes of the road. People were out of their cars clicking photos of bighorn sheep moseying up a sheer cliff to graze on a clump of grass. The sheep munched, then raised their curled horns and placidly gazed at the cars below.

Roman wondered if the sheep were thinking the same thing he was: *damn tourists.*

He tried the cell phone. No signal.

Fuck!

The stopped cars had multiplied. They now lined the road up the canyon around the next bend. Gahkablahkas, as they said in south Boston. He would be going nowhere for a while.

He took a deep breath and watched the sheep, almost hoping one would misstep and fall to the highway below. Even though it would take longer for traffic to clear, he would enjoy another verification of Americans' utter surprise at death. It would be a sure prod for more people to jump out of their cars and gawk. People were fascinated with death. It really wasn't anything special, seeing someone die. But planning someone's death by your own hand and watching them suffer and die slowly, like his carefully executed plan of Farnsworth's death? Truly exquisite.

Even today, Roman remembered Farnsworth's address—2110 West Vine Street—and the reason he had picked him. In his mind he replayed his mock dictation of that day, his voice professorial, as if addressing a room full of medical students eager to learn.

"Thirty-two-year-old white male, worked for Frito-Lay, hurt his back delivering vending machines. Poor man. On workman's compensation for two years. Ah, but he is due a large settlement. Likely he'll use that large sum to sequester himself in some Mexican hovel where no one can check on him and his fake disability.

"Don't think he malingers? You students are so trusting. Observe, as I have, the way he drops his limp when he thinks no one is watching. Note how he bends over and ties his shoes without even a wince of pain."

Then he'd dropped the professor's lecture and continued as if directly speaking to Farnsworth. "Perhaps your illness will soon become more real, Mr. Farnsworth. Maybe you will need that settlement more than you ever thought. You might actually need the money for what it was meant for: compensation. Injury compensation. Forget those margaritas in Mexico."

It had all been so right.

Right. Wrong. Did anyone really know the difference?

A horn honked to his left, and he blinked hard. A fat turd was out of her car snapping pictures, and the moronic driver in the car behind her was honking over and over. She was obstructing the man's view; it was hard to see around a Mack truck.

Suddenly he was back in his childhood South Boston basement, naked, his knees bruised on the cement floor, kneeling and licking Aunt Gladys, the holy tower of the Catholic grade school. She leered down at him above her white, elephant-like thighs, the leather belt held high, his bare ass already bleeding from her encouragements. His mother drank whisky and watched from the corner, her hand up her skirt, moaning.

He was so hard now he ached. Auntie knew what was right and what was wrong. She taught them in school every day. But she showed Roman her true belief of right and wrong, over and over, whenever she pleased.

Roman smirked. He would show everyone what was right and what was wrong. He'd already corrected several wrongs and there were no raging flames of hell licking at his heels, no Dante's devils sticking his ass with pitchforks. The first time he'd earned respect; the others along the way gained him money, though the dollars paled in comparison to the fun he'd had. His last stroke of genius had been his money-grubbing wife, two cancers and twelve hours—seven-hundred-and-twenty minutes—of exquisite torture. If only he could have been in her brain to feel her desire to scream, to run, to die. The pain must have been indescribable.

Her death held another bonus: lovely Amy's attention to him, the poor, lonely, grieving widower. Amy and her flawless skin. He shivered off the thought of her long legs wrapped around him. His hand started scratching the itch on his forearm. He gripped the hand into a fist. *No.* He would not scratch it. He shivered again and turned on the car heater.

The backup cleared, and soon he was through Estes Park, driving west on Fall River Road a few miles east of the northern entrance to Rocky Mountain National Park. Dark-brown letters were burned into a primitive, one-foot square sign made of blond pine: *J. J. Radner.* The sign was nearly hidden behind a pine tree. Roman turned onto the dirt road beside it. He followed it for a half-mile of rutted twists until he came to a run-down shack.

The location and condition of the sign and shack befitted the reputation Roman had gleaned from a phone call to a wealthy hunting friend. Radner shunned publicity and frills. An inner circle knew of his disdain for hunting legalities. As long as the proper amount of cash crossed his palms, state hunting regulations became mere guidelines. He knew how to keep his mouth shut, too. Despite ignoring laws, he stayed in business because he was smart. "But," Roman's contact had warned, "Radner can be difficult."

Roman sighed contentedly. He'd done difficult and ridden it into the ground. Greed trumped difficult. Every time.

He knocked on the door. A man opened it, and Roman gave him two crisp one-hundred-dollar bills. "There's more where that came from if you get me a trophy elk."

The hulking, dark man with an elongated face took the bills and snapped each note in his hands like he was testing a rope. Scars crisscrossed thick, black hair on the backs of his hands. He wore a brown Henley top that fell over frayed jeans. He squinted at Roman with inky eyes that were too small for his face, and rubbed at his stubbly chin with a thick index finger—sandpaper on callus. "Don't do powder or arrows."

Roman realized the man was referring to black powder and archery hunting.

"Neither do I."

Tiny rat eyes gleamed and glanced behind Roman. Then he inspected Roman and stuffed the bills in his pocket. "Hell are you? It ain't shootin' season yet. Or maybe you after some pretty pictures?"

The man's hick accent and word choice made Roman pause, but only briefly. After all, he'd grown up with Southies.

"Roman Johnson. Doctor Roman Johnson." Roman could not hide his name from this guide if he wanted his help. "I presume you're J.J. Radner, the guide I'm looking for. Here." He didn't bother offering his hand but gave Radner a slip of paper with a telephone number on it. "Call George Hartford. He'll tell you what I'm after. You remember George: scrawny guy, anesthesiologist, wanted a Rocky Mountain bighorn sheep last year. I believe you got him a nice ram."

"Oh, yeah—gas-passer. Crazy sumbitch. Almost fell off a ledge going after a shot. I don't know nothin' about killing no ram, though. He was just a crazy-assed shutterbug."

Roman shrugged. Radner was being careful. Good. "Call him."

Radner tweaked his head sideways, emphasizing his thrusting nose and upper jaw. He pursed his lips and motioned for Roman to sit on the dilapidated couch by the door.

Roman eyed the couch that must have all kinds of vermin crawling inside. He did not sit. Radner slunk out of the room as noiseless as a panther.

Roman perused the shop, studying photos of huge bear, elk, deer, and one giant wild boar, all with J.J. Radner holding the head or antlers. Several were with clients, but Radner seemed to have a thing for photos of himself.

When Radner came back, a grin opened up his face and revealed yellow fangs for canines and one missing front tooth—a mishmash of Wolfman and Barney Fife.

"Yeah, sure, Doc. No problem getting that trophy for you. Have to get back in the woods a ways. Nobody around. You get me? Can't be shooting elk in rutting season around these fucking tourists. They get pissed off. Think you're killing *na-ture*." The last word came out with long, high-pitched sarcasm.

The grin disappeared, and Radner's mouth collapsed into a scowl. "Poor baby nature." This time he emphasized "nature" like a bully poking fun at a geek. "Fucking bull would kill that tourist quicker than a fly fart. What'd he think of nature then? Dumbshit. Too many of them elk up here in the park anyhow. I'm only doing what nature intended: predators kill prey. Thin out the herd. Make 'em healthier."

He held out a beefy hand. "You can call me Rad. They used to call me J. J., but that was the old days. Nowadays, Rad is more cool. You know, like *radical, dude*." He laughed, a sound like a choked whisper.

Roman shook his hand. The man's piercing eyes and crouched stance felt far from the casualness that the nickname of Rad implied. He oozed power, assuredness, and the cunning of a wild beast. His grip was a tad too hard, probably to let Roman know who was who. Roman did not wince, but was glad when the handshake was over.

Careful. Roman had to be very careful of this…*Ratman*. That was it. That was exactly what he reminded Roman of: a rat. Only with the body of a small bear.

"Rad… Uh, there is one more thing. My partner is up in the Park fishing somewhere, and I would like to catch up to him. I have a surprise birthday present. He's fishing with a guide." Roman gave him the area the guide was supposed to be in.

"You know the guide's name?" Rad said.

"Stony."

Radner scratched his ear and squinted dark, rat eyes. "Yeah, I suppose. That's a good area for elk, too. Lot of space up there, though. Miles and miles of trees and tundra. Might be I can't find him." He tweaked his head and winked at Roman.

Roman took out his wallet and pulled out another two hundred dollars and held it out.

Radner puckered a frown, nodded, snatched the bills, and stuffed them in his pants.

"You're right, Doc. I *am* damn good at trackin.'"

Roman looked sideway at the man, clenching his jaw to avoid smiling. Rad was perfect. No questions. A little money and he would get the job done.

Rad disappeared for several minutes. When he returned, he strutted into the room, his ugly grin so wide it revealed every rotten tooth. "Okay, Doc. Think I found your guy. Let me get things loaded up. Give me until," his lips puckered and he squinted, "say, eleven o'clock."

CHAPTER 10

Jake had yanked on the dark blue jacket, trying to appear eager and not afraid, though the acrid smell of bear scat still flushed his adrenal glands. Sure, there were bear in the mountains. But here?

He frowned and then softened his gaze, seeing Stony observing him.

They walked faster, and Jake started warming from the core, the pain dulling, his muscles feeling strong—strong enough to put things off a little longer. Get to where he needed to be.

His breathing came faster, heart thumped, and that old feeling hit him. Running.

Christ. He hadn't run in two, make that three years. Swimming and biking were okay. But running owned him. He ached for it—the rhythmic runner's high had nurtured him for twenty years. Jesus, he missed it. What he wouldn't give for another—

Stony's gruff voice interrupted, "So you want to get back on the gab train here or what? That really was bear crap, and I wasn't kidding when I said we need to make noise." His words were machine-gunned, each word on top of the other. Was Stony nervous?

"Sorry, Stony. Guess I was thinking about running."

"Runner, huh? Well that explains why you're in good shape. That's good, 'cause we have several miles to go. You still up for it?"

"You bet. Can't wait."

Stony grunted and picked up the pace.

Soon they hiked past harbingers of high altitude—scraggly, bonsai-looking dwarfed pines with gnarly branches, thickened and bent against the near-constant wind that carried too little oxygen to give the trees much height. They'd reached the tree line.

Jake felt the altitude. Despite his running days, his new condition had him puffing. He thought of something else—he was saving Summer from Roman—and he walked faster, breathed easier. A memory flooded in. She was ten, had just lost a soccer game, and was crying. She was craning her neck, peering around, searching for him. He was supposed to be there, should have been. He wanted to jump out of the car and hug her with Carla, his wife. But he had to go. Not one, but two patients needed him in the ICU. She saw the car, but he was driving away.

The vision of her and Carla in the rearview mirror kept him awake nights, sometimes made him excuse himself in the middle of a patient visit. Carla had an arm around Summer, comforting her, standing firm on two legs. They were both waving. Carla had loved running and being a soccer coach. That day was their anniversary, and the last time her face was beautiful, the last time she would ever run. Carla had wrapped her body around Summer in the accident so physical injuries did not mar Summer. Yet, Summer did not escape unscathed.. Her entire personality had changed after that. Maybe she was right. If he would have stayed, there would have been no accident.

He stomped his feet a few steps, trying to force out the past and concentrate on the present, the beauty of the place. Summer would be safe now. If he thought about it too much, he would go back. Then Roman would kill her. The clouds were moving in, gray blankets covering the valleys, making the snow-covered peaks appear as massive ice bergs, stark against pieces of sky so blue and vast it filled up his mind.

He opened his eyes wide—wider still to absorb all of it, every visual molecule. If only Carla and Summer could be here with him. That would be absolutely perfect. But that was impossible.

He felt dizzy. From lack of oxygen, the mind-filling sights, or from happiness that it would soon be over? It didn't matter. The feeling was what he imagined an eagle would feel when soaring through the mountains.

The pain that had screwed up his sleep and his life for so many months seemed far away, though it lurked, waiting.

Damn it! He should have done this sooner.

That was the crux of his entire life—*should have*. Until now.

They crested the next hill, and the sight took away twenty steps of breathing. A hint of two dark shapes disappeared into the scrub brush. Further down the hill, the low berry bushes melded into slightly taller willows bent over a creek bed. The willows gradually gained height and thickness along the stream edge, until still further down the hill they gave way to tall pine trees, spotty at first, then clumped into a forest at the creek's end—an alpine lake. A herd of elk grazed and meandered in and out of the willows. Their heads rose at the sound of Stony and Jake approaching. The elk chewed and stared at them.

The small lake shimmered at the bottom of a bowl surrounded by snowy peaks. He could never fit it all in a photo or a painting. Even a movie wouldn't do it justice. The human eye and brain were able to capture it all, though: so vast, so many colors, the animals moving, the wind blowing, the backdrop.

It was so…he searched for the word.

Real.

He almost tripped over Stony. Stony knelt in the scrub brush and had slipped off his pack. He rummaged one hand inside the pack and fended off Jake with the other, all the while peering into the willows.

He glanced at Jake and whispered hoarsely, "Shit, Jake. Get down, would you?" He motioned his palm toward the ground.

Jake crouched, thinking Stony was getting his camera to take a picture. Then he saw the gun, a .45 auto load. He hadn't seen one of those for thirty years.

"I thought guns were illegal in the Park."

"We're not in the Park anymore."

Jake nodded. "You're not going to kill an elk, are you?"

Stony's look was complete disbelief. "Shh." He held up his hand like a stop sign and then, in a very quiet whisper, said, "This is for protection only."

Two of the bulls had huge racks. They trotted around with their noses jutted forward, tilted up, making the antlers lay back on their shoulders like long hair streaming in the wind. One slowed and stopped, punched his nose into the air, and blew out a squealing whistle that pierced the air for several seconds. The end of his call was punctuated by deep grunts, his hot breath condensing in the cold like a locomotive blowing steam. The haunting sound lingered as if the call was too much for the trees and mountains to absorb all at once.

Jake gawked, chilled by the sound.

Several of the strayed cows trotted back into the center of the bull's harem.

Bull elk could be dangerous during mating season. Maybe Stony's gun was for them. Jake should ask, but all he could say was, "So that's what a bugle sounds like, up close."

Stony nodded.

"You think those bulls are dangerous?"

Stony nodded again. He pulled out a clip and loaded the gun. "But that's not what the gun is for. It's for protection from that grizzly and the wolves."

"What?" Jake's entire body froze.

Stony pointed at the two dark shapes still in the bush between them and the elk.

One of the dark shapes poked its head up, studied the elk, and crawled forward on its belly.

Jake stared. Now *that* was a big dog. A really big dog. It must be…

He blinked.

A wolf?

He shook his head slowly but felt his eyes widen. *Son of a bitch.*

Stony tugged on Jake's sleeve, then had to repeat the maneuver several times until Jake snapped out of it and looked at him. Stony pointed to a wall of pine trees to the left of the elk.

Jake peered and squinted, but all he saw was a big brown bush.

"See that big brown bush?" Stony said.

"Yeah."

"It's no bush."

Jake studied the bush again. The trees around it swayed with the wind. It didn't. He followed a slight hump up to…eyes. Two dark eyes.

There was movement to the left.

Two more wolves, one light-colored and the other dark. They trotted toward the herd.

Another elk bugled.

All the elks' heads rose in unison, and their eyes got wide. Jake sensed that any minute the elk would spook and run right at them.

Shit! Elk-wolf-grizzly mayhem.

Jake's whole body tensed, ready to run, dig a hole. He'd read once he should hit the ground in a balled-up fetal position. Surely that would work.

Stony pulled on Jake's sleeve again, hard. "Easy, Jake," he whispered. "We'll be fine. Hunker down here and watch. Wolves and grizzlies aren't supposed to be in Colorado. But I'm not complaining. Like you said—a great story for the grandkids."

Using the wind to disguise the sound, Stony clicked pictures with each gust.

Each blast of wind felt stronger and colder.

Jake shuddered, not at the wind or the incredulity of the scene, but because the predators reminded him of Roman stalking Summer.

CHAPTER 11

Roman returned at eleven a.m. sharp. He folded his arms, pursed his lips, and glared at Rad as he walked one horse, then another, then a mule into the trailer. Eleven a.m. meant eleven a.m.—Rad should have been ready and waiting for him, not finishing up. Yet his relatively new appearing camouflaged shirt and pants, his movements slow and deliberate, all spoke of a well-prepared man. Roman supposed that was good.

Minutes later, they were in the truck, and after a half-hour drive always skirting but never entering the Park, Rad pulled into a clearing with a sign clearly labeled *Rocky Mountain National Park*. Rad unloaded animals and gear, and methodically, yet too slowly for Roman, packed their gear onto the animals, making sure each side was balanced. When the odd car or truck drove by, he glanced up, followed the vehicle for a beat, then went back to his work.

The sound of a truck approached, a distinctive knock percussing a rough idle. Rad stood. A rusty and dented Ford pickup motored in and parked by the horse trailer. A thin, wiry man got out, slammed the door with a rattling shudder, and strode right to Rad. He had grizzled auburn stubble and wore a New York Yankees cap that probably hadn't been washed since Babe Ruth played in the World Series. He peered at Rad with eyes the color of dirty dishwater, dropped a set of keys in his outstretched palm, then got in Rad's truck and drove the rig away, never a glance of acknowledgment toward Roman. Roman knew this because he had glared at the man until he drove off in a cloud of dust. What kind of hick would not even nod at you, especially if you were an important and wealthy client?

All that was left was the damn rusty truck—no horse trailer to give a clue about horses up the trail. Roman wondered if this was a ploy to avoid paying any license fees to the Park. This late in the season and with the national park cutbacks, they probably had too few rangers to monitor all the trails and would likely concentrate only on those with clues of use.

Dust blew across the road from the departure of the horse trailer; the junkyard truck ticked as the motor cooled; the horses shifted on their feet. Rad continued his incessant packing. Roman stewed.

They were on the trail by noon. Rad rode the lead horse; next, a mule carried supplies; Roman rode on the rear horse, relaxed and pampered, as the landscape of the Rocky Mountains unfolded. After little more than a mile, his butt reminded him why he usually avoided horseback riding.

To take his mind off the growing throb, he tried to enjoy the view. Vistas of mountains and valleys were everywhere. Not helpful. Thoughts of Jake— Ahh. Jake was probably tired. His muscles must ache. Was his nose bleeding on his shirt? *Excellent.* Shortness of breath? *How utterly wonderful.*

Roman relaxed so much he almost slid off the saddle.

He gripped the horse with his legs and leered at the hazy sun hidden behind a helmet of gray, cold clouds. Gusts of sleet stung his cheeks.

Jake could really make this much easier by just dying. Six weeks ago, his red cells were down, white cells up, and lots of blasts. Shit, his platelets were so low, he could have bled to death from a shaving cut.

Then Jake had "retired." Said he was done with tests and chemo. Sounded like an unhappy patient. Roman never liked unhappy patients.

Roman ducked to avoid a big branch, thankful that they were rounding the bend and for a respite from the wind and sleet.

Rad twisted around in his saddle, facing Roman. He'd donned a buckskin Carhart jacket, and it was zipped halfway up. "How ya doin', Doc? Enjoying our Rocky Mountain fall weather? You look a mite bit worried. Never you mind. I been in much worse crap than this up in Canada. This be a balmy summer's day compared to that."

"I'm fine." Roman wore a black ten-gallon hat with a white feather and a quilted down coat the color of the sky. He pulled the collar up higher. "I just hope you can find my friend soon. Do you know where his guide, Stony, took him?"

"Oh yeah, Stony. Fucking shithead. Catch and release. Be nice to the environment. Blah, blah, blah." He smirked. "You ain't exactly no tree-hugger yourself." He eyed Roman. "Am I right, Doc?"

"Well, I don't want to leave any traces while we're here."

"No traces?" Rad squinted at Roman and frowned. Then his face lit up like he'd seen Jesus at a revival. "Whoa, I get you now, Doc. This friend a yours is a *real* pal, huh?" He winked.

Roman winced inside. Somehow this Ratman understood Roman's trip had nothing to do with friendship, but the complete opposite. Even though Roman had been able to fool all his patients and even Jake. For a while.

Roman studied Rad's face and began to have serious doubts about whether to continue with him. "He is indeed a friend that I would like to surprise. What you imply is ugly. Please, get me to my friend, get me my elk, and then get me back to my car."

"Awh, don't worry, Doc. Your secret's good with me. Shit, you remind me of a client I had up in Ontario about five years ago. He wanted a polar bear in the worst way. And there ain't no way in hell you get caught with a dead polar bear, or you be going to prison. How you going to hide a bullet hole? You know what I mean? Anyway, he had hisself a *friend* too. Said he wanted to meet up with him at one of the cabins by the lake. Said he wanted to *surprise* him. You hearing me on this, Doc?"

Rad spit a sluice of tobacco over the side of the trail and thumbed the spittle from the corner of his mouth, snaking his brown tongue out to catch any residual. "Sure, I helped him out good. Got rid of the *evidence*, too. That was that. No traces. You gettin' my drift here, Doc?"

His rat eyes sparkled. "As long as the money's good, I'm your man." He paused. "You can keep somebody's mouth shut forever if—"

A gust of wind obliterated his last words. But it didn't hide the wink he gave Roman before turning back around.

Roman glared at the back of Rad's head: close-cropped black hair so thick it almost seemed part of the wool watch cap; a tiny, eight-ball head that sat directly atop a boulder. But surely Rad must have a neck to turn his head around. Not only was Rad physically imposing, the man was like a bear with a cat's instincts and a criminal mind.

Roman chuckled to himself. This would be interesting: a mental *and* physical test.

He clamped his legs firmer around the horse, sighing in comfort at the idea of soon besting Rad. He screwed his hat on tighter and gently heeled the horse's flanks to catch up to the mule.

The blowing sleet quieted Rad so Roman could think. How much did Jake know? He couldn't have proof. Had he told anyone of his suspicions? Probably not. Jake was a coward. He avoided confrontation. That's why he'd never held a job where he was the boss. The man had no backbone, which was part of the reason Roman had taken him as a partner. If Jake had squealed, something would have happened by now. No regulatory agencies had contacted Roman's office. No subtle questions from colleagues. And the best sign: no word from any blood-sucking lawyers.

It was simple: Jake was running.

Roman puckered his lips into a kiss. By running, Jake had signed the fast track to smooch the God he so adored. Roman was doing him two favors: putting him out of his misery and getting him to heaven. What a deal. Roman should probably thank God that Jake had gone on this wilderness trip. Sure. Thank God. Roman wished there was a God so he could show him how stupid he was. Accidents happened in the wilderness all the time. Roman glanced up at the sheet-metal clouds. If it snowed? Even better. It would cover tracks and hinder searches.

What do you think about that, God?

They rounded a hairpin curve, and Rad's black head bobbed and swayed. Roman frowned. He'd have to dispose of Jake's body in front of two experienced guides. He squinted at the horse's mane. Unless.

He grinned broadly and patted the horse's neck.

Unless Roman killed them all.

He wanted to shout that wonderful, beautiful, exhilarating thought to the gray day, slam his fist between the horse's ears, and sneer at God. That eight-ball swaying atop the massive shoulders was so rhythmic Roman wanted to break into song. After killing three people, he would definitely need to move away—to that European cottage in Switzerland he'd bought under another name several years ago. He'd always wanted plastic surgery.

CHAPTER 12

Stony wondered if the griz would take down the bugling bull. The griz would be fast enough, but a bull elk? Usually the wolves did the work and the bear took the prize. Yet this griz had survived in an unusual location, not the open, roomy mountains of Montana or Alaska. He'd been smart enough to survive hemmed in on all sides by civilization—not only survive but thrive, judging from his beefy haunches and glossy coat. So he must have killed before, without the benefit of wolves helping him. And now he was parked in the perfect place: downwind from the elk and the pack, and well hidden.

Very smart.

Something nagged Stony, though. What in the hell was a grizzly doing up here? Trapper friends of Stony's had seen wolves north of here, and there had been wolf sign spotted in the park every few years. So the wolves didn't really surprise Stony. Not like the bear.

The wolves trotted toward the elk. How would they take an elk, and would they get it before the griz? A wildlife photographer friend had shown Stony a video of a she-wolf in Yellowstone taking down a full-grown cow elk running at full tilt on dry land. She'd loped beside the cow until, matched pace for pace, she pounced sideways, biting and hanging onto the cow's throat until the cow slowed and died. But that was a cow, not a massive, fully antlered bull like the one they seemed to be after. Maybe in deep snow, crusted on top from melting and thawing, the wolves able to scamper across the top while the bull's legs mired to his shoulders. But here? Now?

The bull lifted and twisted his head, revealing the other side of his rack—or rather the broken-off stubble. He moved forward and limped heavily on one forepaw. Each step took him away from the rest of the herd.

Now Stony got it. Only a matter of time. Half his antlers gone and crippled: easy prey.

The clouds blotted out the sun, and the wind changed from cold to biting. The scene reminded him of Sonja and watching wolves in Alaska, after she recuperated from the hunters and the abortion. He felt exhilarated and nauseous. She had loved the wolves so much, but the hunters had been ugly to the wolves and to her. If only he could have helped her more. He flipped his hood over his head and glanced at Jake. If not for Jake, Stony would hunker down and watch this unfold, endure whatever.

Then again, perhaps they should move off and head for shelter.

He studied Jake. He seemed okay this morning. But what if the same thing that hit him last night hit him this afternoon? Damn sure wasn't about taking pictures.

Stony peered at the elk. He had lived most of his life in wilderness and never been as close to something like this. Maybe they could—

The wolves made their move. The two blacks headed toward the herd—casual—two dogs trotting down a back alley. What were they up to?

Where were the other wolves? Gone. Vanished like ghosts.

The two blacks eased closer, in no hurry, and the herd spooked, quickly accelerating across the tundra, away from the trees, away from the blacks—and away from the griz.

Had the wolves spotted the grizzly? Were they purposefully herding the elk away from it so they could attack them at leisure and avoid the grizzly taking their food? A wolf pack could easily make fifty miles in a day. The griz could follow, but if the wolves moved far enough, they could make the kill and gorge themselves before the griz arrived.

The two blacks slowed and stopped, their tongues lolling. They watched the herd move over a rise beyond the lake. They turned around and eyed the old bull. He grazed on tundra grass as if nothing concerned him, grazed methodically between the wolves and the trees, which held the griz.

Damn! The big stone with eyes was gone. Where was he? Had he smelled Stony and Jake?

Two old timers in a bar in Lyons once told Stony the grizzlies down in the San Juans got so smart no one ever saw them, so everybody figured they'd gone. Except—every year someone saw sign: scat or fur or prints, mostly in the high tundra country, but sometimes right close to a ranch. The theory was that those grizzlies had learned about man, realized how to stay away and keep alive. He'd also heard of a huge grizzly shot in Montana, twice the size of the usual Glacier Park bear. Turned out to be a carnival bear let loose. That bear had been very wary and mean, too, because of a sadistic trainer.

So what type of grizzly could this one be?

Either way—a smart wild one or a screwed-up circus bear—Stony had no desire for up-close and personal. The bear was obviously smart enough to stay hidden, surviving this close to ranches and all the hikers.

A smart griz could easily sneak around and hit them from the rear. Move through bush as quiet as night. He twisted his head around. Nothing behind them.

The wind picked up and snowflakes stung Stony's face. He blinked hard and squinted. Musty elk-smell was strong. A grove of aspen about fifty yards up the hill shimmered golden leaves with apple-green undersides. Horizontal waves of snow hazed any clear view. The aspen leaves would peak in another week if the wind didn't claim the best pictures soon. Snow already covered some of the downed yellow leaves.

Something moved.

"What's going on?" Jake whispered. "I can't see anything."

Stony ignored him, concentrating on the area of movement in the white on white. Not the griz. It was the gray, only a hint of ears—eyes—form, but enough.

I see you.

Not too many could spot that. If Stony hadn't spent many an Alaskan winter watching wolves in their element, he would have missed it too. The camouflage was perfect. The label "gray" was used by wolf watchers everywhere. In the distance it looked grayish as opposed to white or black wolves. But gray wolves were really black and gray and white, the best camouflaged wolf of any color. This one blended perfectly with the trees and shadows and the snow already coating the ground in white. If the gray hadn't moved it would have been impossible to spot. But he had, and Stony didn't take his eyes off him.

The wolf looked right at Stony—hungry, yellow eyes.

Shit! The wolves were not after the elk.

The gray vanished.

Had the gray actually seen Stony and Jake? Wolves keyed on movement, too. Had Stony moved? Had Jake? They were dressed in bland gray and tan and dark olive clothes to avoid spooking the fish, but in this snow they stood out like a chocolate smear on a wedding dress.

CHAPTER 13

"We may be in trouble here." Stony said. "Don't move."

Immediately he regretted his words. Jake wouldn't be able to resist. Give him thirty seconds and he'd pop his head up like an ostrich.

Stony quietly flicked off the safety on the .45, gripped the gun firmly with two hands, curled his index finger around the trigger, and started to raise the gun. It would slow down the griz and stop a wolf in its tracks. At least one. He prayed he wouldn't have to shoot the others.

The skin ant-crawled on the back of his neck. They were probably right behind him.

If he took his eyes off of where the gray had gone—

Jake craned his neck and scanned forward, where the gray had been.

Okay, Jake had the front covered. Stony would take a quick peek behind.

The two blacks were still there, herding the big bull right toward them. The old fella was hurt bad, the limp so pronounced that he almost buckled with each step. No running for him.

Stony squinted into the woods. Where was that damn griz?

Stony turned around. A blur of gray and black streaked toward the woods. He raised the gun, then lowered it, but kept the safety off.

The wolves were not stalking Stony and Jake after all.

"Did you see that?" Jake's hoarse whisper was like an excited kid seeing his first rattlesnake.

Stony nodded, smiled, and whispered, "Yeah."

The gray and black materialized on the tree side of the bull, closing. The old guy still believed he had it, lowering his remaining antlers at them. The wolves stopped and pranced just out of antler thrusting distance—a meager distance, for the old elk was weak. The other two blacks edged closer behind the bull, ready to strike.

A gold and brown blur rolled out of the trees like a huge boulder—the grizzly. The gray and black scattered in his wake as he smashed the bull on the side with a paw the size of a man's head, toppling the elk like it was cardboard. Before the rack hit the ground, the huge bear ripped into the bull's neck with jaws that could crush a man's skull.

A quicker death was hard to come by.

The other wolves flinched.

Stony and Jake jumped sideways.

"Jesus!" Jake croaked.

"Yeah."

Stony put one arm into a pack strap, the other holding the gun ready. "We gotta git. Those wolves will be pissed and the grizzly will rush anything even half this close to his fresh kill."

They backed up slowly and walked around the far shore of the lake. When they were out of sight, Stony clicked the safety on but kept the gun in his hand, glancing over his shoulder every few steps.

"Lucky devil," Jake murmured.

"Yep, that griz was in the right place at the right time."

"No, I meant the elk."

Stony frowned. Jake was probably right. That'd be the way to go if you were old and crippled and couldn't have women any more: a last show of bravado, then dead before you knew it.

He glanced at Jake. *Huh.*

But right now he could waste no thoughts on anything but the trail. In the high tundra, where few hiked on a regular basis, signs of a trail might only be a slight depression or a scar of dirt where the grass or lichen had been rubbed off. Landmarks like a clump of sage next to a certain brown rock were important, but those landmarks depended on contrast. White on white screwed that. If he hadn't hiked this area before, they would be in deep kimchi.

Deep, white kimchi.

Though dangerous, the snow was beautiful. It was white and clean and it smoothed the sharp angles, making the wilderness more gentle. Yet there was nothing gentle about this storm.

They'd been delayed by the predator-prey drama. Otherwise they would have been there by now, and Stony would have had the tent set up. They needed shelter as much as they needed to place distance between them and the predators.

How long had they watched? Seemed like only a few minutes.

But Stony's watch had ticked off forty-five minutes.

Shit! The way that storm was moving through it was probably laying down—Stony kicked the ground—an inch an hour. And the wind was already over fifteen knots. In another hour they'd better be inside the tent or they would be on their way to hypothermia and might stumble over a deep chasm.

CHAPTER 14

Killing Rad would be such a joy. Rad's jabber finally lagged after Roman began answering in grunts and monosyllabic nothings. Not much change in content. Snow started falling and the wind picked up, shutting Rad's mouth completely. Having such a good Catholic upbringing, Roman almost shouted *Hallelujah!* Instead, he sighed deep and long. Despite the pleasant thought of murder, Roman's thoughts had soured. He worried about the coming workman's comp hearing on Farnsworth. Perhaps he should review it in his head one more time, though he was sure he was safe. He had planned it down to the last detail: the glorious end of Farnsworth the Scammer. On the other hand, mulling it over brought back such fond memories.

Roman had begun his research seventeen months ago. Farnsworth's dilapidated house spoke for the entire neighborhood. Two empty houses nearby gave Roman a choice: one to the rear and one across the street. It had to be the rear house—no intervening road with unwanted traffic. Overgrown cedar bushes and trees grew close to that house. In the front and back yards, cottonwoods and elms shaded ragged patches of dead grass and dry dirt.

He carried a gun the first night, expecting meth heads or worse. Nothing but an old wino, easily driven off by threats of calling the cops. How disappointing, although another body to hide would have been problematic.

The next week of nights he watched—serene—what he imagined bird-watching through binoculars would be like. And what a bird. Farnsworth would limp and shuffle his garbage can out to the curb, wincing as if his back were killing him. Yet once inside he would walk quickly from room to room, sometimes bounding up the stairs. Usually he closed his drapes, but a few times Roman got a glimpse of the man working out in his basement, weightlifting for an entire hour, then running on the treadmill for another half hour. A bird, all right—a dodo.

Roman considered taking several short video clips and sending them to the workman's comp people. But someone might ask where the videos came from and need to investigate. *No.* What Roman had planned would be much more effective.

And just. The man deserved it for scamming all that money. There would be an element of fun in it, too.

Farnsworth was single, making it easy to catch him alone at night.

That April night eighteen months ago came back crystal clear.

Roman had finished in the office, set the alarm, locked the door, and stepped into a frigid night. It had been seventy the day before, thirty that day—typical for springtime in Colorado. Snowflakes, wet and big as silver dollars, fell from a windless gray twilight, hurrying him to start the Mercedes and turn on the heater.

His cell phone chimed and he flipped it open, reading the number on the screen—Jake.

"Hello." His words were clipped but not rude, not to Jake, his new, naïve partner.

"Hi, Roman. Carla and I were wondering if we could bring you something for supper. We thought, you know, after Leslie died, you might not feel like going out or cooking."

Everyone wanted to help because of The Bitch's death last month. He wanted to hang up.

He oozed politeness. "Thank you so much for the offer. But I already called in some take-out Chinese. I'll be picking it up on my way north of town to look at some property."

"Oh, are you planning on moving?"

Curiosity there, but also a touch of surprise. Good. Jake needed to be off balance.

"No, I invest in land, you know." He tried to sound nonchalant. After all, this was a natural part of his life—killing. "It helps me keep my mind off work and…other things."

"Yeah, I can see that might help." Jake sounded relieved. "Perhaps tomorrow night, then?"

"Okay. Sure. Why don't you bring it to the office tomorrow and put it in the fridge? I'll have it tomorrow night. Thanks."

"Oh, no. Thank *you* for taking me into your practice and allowing me to work more reasonable hours and take off a day like today. I went to a great movie with Carla."

"No problem. Hey, listen. I've got to run. Talk to you later."

Remembering that call, Roman gripped the reins of the horse and clenched his jaw and his fists over and over. After a minute he relaxed and rolled his head around slowly, loosening the muscles in his neck, and breathed out slowly, filtering out the last bit of politeness he'd ever felt toward Jake. He should thank Jake. After all, Jake was going to take the blame for Farnsworth, if it ever came to that. Jake had seen him a few times in the clinic. His name was there, his signature on the chart. Any investigation would eventually turn this up, as well as other, more scathing evidence Roman would plant.

Roman put out his tongue and caught a few of the snowflakes, and remembered more.

After hanging up from Jake, the snow had filtered down thicker, blowing sideways as he eased the Mercedes out of the parking lot. He drove to the Goodwill store and dropped off more of her clothes. A few more loads and he'd be done with her. How could one woman have so many shoes? At least Roman had got some of his money back from the diamond necklace. *Bitch.*

He shut the empty trunk.

A gust of wind stung his face with the wet snow and his olfactory nerves with the aroma of cow shit from Greeley. Up-slope lows always brought the southeasterly wind and the odor of stockyards from the stinking cowboy dump town of Greeley. He preferred the smell of hospitals, disinfectant, rubber gloves, plastic, and chemicals. *And* the small laboratory concealed in his basement, where he mixed his poisons.

He stopped at a local McDonald's to kill his appetite, then parked on a side street, waiting for the evening rush of people to dwindle and the coming of darkness.

Rad said something and brought him back to the present.

"What was that?"

"You hungry yet?"

"No." Conversation with this idiot wasn't really necessary, was it?

Rad glanced back, then forward again and shook his head.

The snow filtered between them, and Roman went back to Farnsworth, savoring that night, the memory of McDonald's french fries, and all the goodies after.

CHAPTER 15

That night, eighteen months ago, Roman had munched on the hot french fries, his favorite. Snow continued falling as his plan for Farnsworth crystallized. That was his forte, really—planning. He'd always been good at chess because he could think twenty steps ahead. That's why he loved oncology, all those different chemotherapeutic regimens with their timing and coordination and…planning. It dovetailed nicely with his study of industrial and rare herbal poisons.

He finished his meal and drove home. He slowed when he reached the end of his block. Perhaps he should switch off his headlights so no one would notice him driving up. Sleet intermixed with the snow, tapping and cracking on the roof. The wipers mesmerized, back and forth, erasing the dollops of snow and sleet, squeaking back and forth, back and forth. If he turned off his headlights, and someone happened to see his car, they would be even more suspicious. He casually drove into his garage as he did every night. Nothing unusual.

Next to him sat the gray Camry, waiting. Plain, not flashy, it would not attract attention.

Going inside the house, he located the storage box labeled "Halloween." He rummaged and found a brunette, long-haired wig he'd used for a party years ago, and pulled it on. Cotton stuffed in his cheeks and glasses without lenses completed his ensemble. A glance in the mirror revealed a stranger. No one would recognize him.

He stepped into the windowless garage and stopped to think. *License plates.*

But first things first. He switched off the overhead lights to the garage and sat inside the Camry. He twisted the ignition to *On*, but not to *Start*. Using the front wall and rearview to check the reflections off the garage door, he quickly verified the headlights, brake lights, and blinkers all worked. On both sides. No stupid stops from cops.

He turned off the ignition, hopped out, and turned on the garage light. He opened one cabinet, then grinned and opened the other. His prize was right where he'd left it.

Sometimes he marveled at his mind: how his subconscious could be planning ahead while he consciously tried to appear sad. At a funeral, for instance. His Freudian id had known he might someday need different license plates. Last year when he offered to tow away and junk Aunt Millie's rusted 1972 Plymouth Duster, no one had objected. All the hick relatives in Lamar were interested in was her silverware. How could they ever be related?

He grabbed the plates from behind a can of screws and nails and replaced the ones on the Camry. The inspection sticker in the lower right corner even had the number "12" on it. Scripto made excellent permanent markers that did not bleed in rain. He'd colored in an orange background and black numbers. Simple.

Almost ready.

The drain in the middle of the garage floor had been his idea. One of the joys of a custom-built house. He hated a dirty car. And it was hard to keep clean in the winter with all the snow and slush. So he washed it in the garage. A nice, big industrial-sized drain flowed directly into the storm ditch one block over.

He grabbed a bucket, snuck out the side door, and dipped it into a muddy puddle. Back inside, he poured the soupy mud all over the Camry's top, hood, and trunk. The mud dripped down the windows and sides.

He stepped back, frowning. Sure needs a wash.

Later.

He almost laughed. He went inside the house, grabbed a duffel bag and a foam-lined briefcase, and descended to the basement. He unlocked the room: his secret place. He'd built it himself years ago, after the house had been finished. All the tools were neatly organized in teak cabinets—wood was so pleasing to the eye. Into the duffel he placed a CO_2-compression dart tranquilizer pistol. Online shopping was so handy, quick, and anonymous. He opened the foam-lined briefcase and carefully placed syringes and needles, a small dark bottle of chloroform and another bottle of ketamine obtained from a dealer he'd found in Oregon, a custom mixture of Rohypnol, sufentanil, and other quick-acting herbal sedatives he'd concocted over many years. Finally he grabbed the sandwich baggies he had filled with vacuumed material and held them up, inspecting the contents—double-checking, something he always did. Yes, they were labeled: *Jake Roberts.*

He flicked off the light to the room, locked up, slid the wood panel over the entrance, and inspected it. Not even a hint that something lay behind the panel.

He went back out to the garage and unscrewed the bulb.

Darkness: his old friend.

He waited for his eyes to adjust and listened. The wind cooed under the garage door. He cracked the side door. No lights outside. The sleet had stopped, and large snowflakes fluttered and blew like the swarming white butterflies he'd seen in Manú National Park in Peru. Right next to plants that had supplied Roman with so many new poisons.

He closed and locked the side door, got in the Camry, and placed clean white tennis shoes atop the other items on the driver's-side floorboard. Covering everything with black garbage bags, he started the engine, hit the remote to open the garage, put it in reverse, and—

Their horses stopped, jerking him back to the present, interrupting his reverie. He stared at the back of Rad's head, that puny knob atop gargantuan shoulders, a thimbleful of brains controlling a T-Rex body.

Rad was silent.

Something was definitely wrong.

CHAPTER 16

The back of Rad's head bobbed as his horse ambled forward several steps. Still he remained quiet. They rounded a bend, and Roman's horse whinnied and jumped a step, enough to throw Roman forward onto the saddle horn.

Rad twisted around and enjoyed Roman's discomfort way too much. "Bear shit. Nelson must have got a whiff. Sometimes he'll bolt. Gettin' old, though. Slowing down."

"Lucky me."

Rad laughed. "I like you, Doc. You're funny." He leaned forward in his saddle, still chuckling.

Which was exactly what Farnsworth had said when Roman had told him to get off his butt and go back to work. The Ratman wouldn't laugh if he knew what Roman had done to Farnsworth that night last April.

Roman had been observing Farnsworth's house at night. The man usually watched movies until late, drank a six pack, and fell asleep on his easy chair.

That night was no different. After filling the dart syringes and getting everything prepared, Roman sipped coffee and peered through his binoculars. He waited. Twenty minutes ticked by. The poor man was so tired from his workout that he slept like a baby, eyes closed, breathing slow and even. Roman snuck to the covered back porch and listened.

Farnsworth snored loud enough to hear through the door. Roman slipped off his shoes and coat, piling them on the porch. He slipped the butt pack around to his front and removed the Tyvex coveralls and hair and foot covers. After he zipped the pack up, he remembered the key. He got it, rezipped the pack, and returned it to the rear. Then he suited up.

The key worked beautifully. Roman crept into position and fired the drug-filled dart into the exposed skin where the Scammer's tee-shirt had ridden up.

Farnsworth flinched and snorted twice, but never opened his eyes. His slumber resumed as peacefully as ever.

Roman was good. He'd even adjusted the dose to compensate for the man's state of inebriation. The Rohypnol cocktail would add to his slumber, yet not remove his ability to breathe. It would also eliminate any vague memories of the last half-hour…and what was about to happen. When Farnsworth regained his senses in a few hours, he would stumble to his bed in his usual state of mild inebriation, unaware of any untoward effects, and slumber peacefully. In the morning he would be refreshed, ready for his new adventure. And a great and glorious adventure it would be.

Roman waited another fifteen minutes, then walked and stood over the man, smiling at each deep snore.

So peaceful.

He lifted one eyelid and touched the cornea—no blink. The anesthetic had taken nicely. All Roman had to worry about was the man's airway. He grabbed the limp forearms and pulled him forward, easing him out of the chair and onto the floor.

Careful of the head. No bruises.

After positioning Farnsworth on his side in the fetal position and making sure his breathing was unlabored, Roman placed the pre-filled syringe within easy reach. Feeling for the spinous processes, he located the depression between vertebrae and inserted the larger introducer needle. It would keep the hair-thin epidural needle from bending and missing the epidural space. He grabbed the next syringe, which was filled with air and topped with the epidural needle. He inserted the thin wire of a needle slowly through the introducer needle, pushing ever so gently on the syringe.

Deeper. Deeper. There!

The air in the syringe gave a palpable pop as it flowed into the epidural space. He'd got it on the first try. Of course. He traded that syringe for the drug-filled one, injected the drug, and, in one quick stroke, pulled out all the needles. He pushed his thumb pad against the injection site. No hematomas tonight.

He sat Farnsworth up so the drug he'd injected into his spinal canal, a sclerosing agent similar to phenol, would gravitate down into all the lumbar and sacral nerve roots. It was heavier than water, so it needed a little help from gravity. He leaned the man's body sideways against the easy chair while continuing steady thumb pressure on the insertion site for two full minutes.

He inspected the site after releasing his thumb. If you knew what you were looking for, you could see the pinpoint puncture. But by the time Farnsworth started developing any symptoms, it would be weeks later and the needle track would be well-healed. Not even the best postmortem, aimed specifically at the lumbar spine, would catch it by then.

A car engine purred outside. It kept up a steady idle, loud but not moving, as if it had stopped outside Farnsworth's house. It was too late for visitors. Had someone seen Roman go in the back door?

He grabbed Farnsworth under his armpits and, with some strong tugging and jockeying, managed to get him back into his easy chair, tilting his head back so his airway was not occluded. He breathed easily, like a man with no worries.

Voices sounded outside.

The cleanup was the most important part. Roman needed time for that, though.

The voices got louder. A man and woman arguing. Not the police. But their racket might bring the police. On the other hand, it would also disguise the noise of the vacuum machine.

Roman collected all his tools and put everything in his briefcase. He found the vacuum, and, after a thorough cleaning, took out the vacuum bag and placed it in a black trash bag. He got a new vacuum bag from the kitchen, attached it, and vacuumed the hallway where he'd never been to make sure there was some used lint in the bag, but nothing incriminating. He inspected the room twice, sweeping the floor with the flashlight and even squatting to scrutinize the floor under the chair.

Satisfied, he pulled out the two sandwich baggies, opened them, and sprinkled little bits of the contents around the room. He walked over the area several times, making sure the particles got pushed into the carpet. Jake had probably never known his DNA could be so useful.

He chuckled at the snoozing Farnsworth, imagining him awakening from dreams of the Caribbean in an hour, possibly rubbing his aching back, thinking it was the damn chair, and going to bed.

Roman whispered, "Sweet dreams. Hope you like wheelchairs."

The arguing man and woman were now cooing at each other. Lovers at last.

Roman locked up, placed his Tyvex covers in a separate trash bag, put his shoes and coat on, and walked to his car, parked a couple of blocks away. The snow turned to rain; he was glad he had a waterproof winter coat with a hood.

Luck remained in his favor, his destiny always prevailing; the rain pounded harder, covering his tracks, and keeping any nosy neighbors tucked away. No one would ever know.

Roman's horse shook his head; the snow coating his mane misted cold onto Roman's face, a rude return to the present. He wiped his face and raised his hand to smack the stupid horse in the eye. Then he thought better of it. He didn't want to get bucked off. Arching his back, he sat straighter on his horse, stretching out the stiffness. He pushed on the saddle horn, easing the ache in his groin. A touch to one saddlebag reassured him that his supplies were with him, no dart gun or spinal tray, but adequate for what he had in mind.

"When the hell are we going to get there?" he said.

"Soon, Doc. Soon." Rad's words floated back. He did not even turn around when he spoke. And what the hell was that noise?

"Could you stop that infernal humming, please? The snow is bad enough."

"It relaxes me, Doc. You should try it. Humming in the snow is very relaxing." Rad's black fist of a head nodded back and forth to the rhythm of the horse.

Roman snorted in disgust. His mother had hummed, and poorly. Not relaxing at all.

The finale of Mr. Georg Farnsworth? *That* had been relaxing.

CHAPTER 17

Planning and preparation made luck. Roman was good at both.

After he'd left Farnsworth that night, he made it to his car parked in the next street and got in. Rain filtered down through cones of streetlights like dust in sunbeams. The late hour reminded him of all those on-call nights he'd spent with patients.

He started the car and murmured, "Now *that* was the best on-call night you ever spent."

He drove by a dumpster behind a drugstore. Perhaps luck did count: the top was open. He tossed the bundle of used needles and syringes into the dumpster and drove behind another store to dispose of the vacuum bag and the Tyvex.

The next weeks played out like a fine piano solo. Two days after Roman's injection, Farnsworth collected his settlement with workman's comp. A week after that, he was in Roman's office. His back pain was worse, now burning down both legs. The man obviously needed another MRI, which, of course, Roman recommended.

Farnsworth frowned. "How much is that?"

"Depends on where you get it, but usually around two thousand dollars."

"Two grand? I can't afford that."

"It's been over a year, and you could have another disc pinching the nerves, or, God forbid, a tumor."

"Cancer in my spine?"

"I've seen it before. Not pretty if you don't catch it quickly."

That had done it. Farnsworth shelled out part of his settlement for that MRI *and* a CT scan, because, as Roman had explained, they *were* complimentary tests. Quite necessary. The tests were normal. They didn't show any of the chemical burns on the nerves from the injection. It was too soon. But Roman had known that.

The pain worsened. Each time Farnsworth returned to the office more bent, more crippled. More testing, physical therapy, a second opinion, another second opinion, another MRI, Chinese acupuncturists, even Mexican hat dancers (What an imaginative name: ¡*Alternativo therapeutico!*). Farnsworth bled out his settlement in gushes of Benjamins.

Finally Farnsworth was wheelchair-bound and Roman began narcotics. Lots of narcotics. Then Roman consulted a pain management specialist. The diagnosis remained a mystery.

Farnsworth ran out of money. Roman visited him at home one moonless night, dressed in a black nylon running suit. He donned Tyvex shoe covers before entering. Farnsworth still had his house, but the inside was littered with paper. *What a fire hazard.* Farnsworth sat in his wheelchair, snoring, his cellphone and Marlboros on the table beside him, beer cans piled around him. The stink of urine and feces and sour beer hung in the air. Roman took the cellphone and put it on the floor, under the couch. He took Farnsworth's cigarette lighter, lit a cigarette, dropped it on the floor beside the man and waited until the papers caught fire. The flames licked higher, their orange and black dance as beautiful as anything Roman had seen.

He emptied the contents of a clear plastic baggie onto the carpet and mashed it down with his shoes. Then he left.

Roman's horse stopped and jolted him back to the present. Up ahead, Rad had halted and dismounted his horse. Heavier snow and darkness had arrived.

"All right, Doc. Time to get off the horse."

Roman ignored him, still caught in his memories. A few weeks after Farnsworth had tragically burned to death, an insurance investigator nosed around the office. Farnsworth's health record, of course, had Jake's tracks in it. If the investigator ever got samples of Jake's DNA, it would match the fire scene. And if the investigator had any merit, the trail would eventually link Jake to The Bitch's murder.

But then Roman remembered—tomorrow Jake would die. Jake would really *owe* Roman for all these favors. First relieving suffering, now keeping him out of a long, ugly legal battle—then getting him to heaven. What were partners for?

Rad made a clucking sound, and Roman's horse bucked.

He could not hold on. All the planning, and he would die of a broken neck before ever killing Jake.

CHAPTER 18

Stony trudged away from the wolves and bear, leaning into the teeth of the storm. The snow stung his eyes. The path began to disappear. He whipped his head around. Jake still followed, head down. Stony turned forward. The blanket of white now covered any signs of the path. He slowed, pulled out the handheld GPS unit, clicked it on, and waited for it to locate the satellites.

Cheater.

He had grown lazy and… Yep. Stupid. What kind of dumbass guide depended on a damn electronic wizard? It had rusted out the part of his brain that used to be his best way to survive—finding his position by compass and map. GPS was so stinking easy, though.

Deep inside him, he didn't trust the electronics. Like his friend, a navy submarine commander, had said, "One glance at a sonar screen tells what's ahead and where you were. But when things really count, when you're going to torpedo a ship, you make sure. Screw the electronic mumbo jumbo. Up periscope. See it with your own two."

He checked the GPS screen, then put it back in his pocket and modified his route south.

After another minute, he brought out the compass and a plastic-coated topographical map, folded precisely to allow quick visualization of their quadrangle.

Up periscope.

The map afforded a large view of the whole area despite the snow blowing across it. He stuffed the map and compass in his pocket and kept on the same track.

Who the hell was he kidding? It was all done with smoke and mirrors, when it came right down to it—little electronic circuits, gravity, magnetic north.

Not quite like Sonja. He remembered finding out about her homing pigeon skills almost by accident when he took her up to a secluded lake in Alaska. While walking around the shore, studying the water for fish, he missed seeing a log, stumbled, fell, and broke his compass.

He shook the compass, tapped it, tilted it.

"Fuck!" That would work—screaming at a compass.

It didn't.

That was a first, breaking the compass. It was also the last time he went without a backup plan. He had no GPS, no other compass. He was screwed.

"What's wrong?" Sonja said.

"I broke the damn compass."

"Don't worry about it. I'll find the way back."

He'd probably frowned at her too hard. Maybe he could remember the way back.

They started back; he led the way. She corrected him on two errant turns. He let her lead. She marched forward, never hesitating. He sulked for several minutes, then finally blurted, "You've been up here before. Right?"

She shrugged. "No, it's just something I can do. Once I've been somewhere, I can always get out and go back again."

After that, he never took a compass when she was with him, though he did make damn sure she didn't fall and crack her head.

Why is it some people got those interesting talents and others…didn't get shit?

The snow stung his face. That was all smoke and mirrors, too—genetics, DNA—way, way above his head. What Sonja had going through her brain was much more difficult to figure than an electronic circuit board. Why she ever loved Stony was even more mysterious.

"Hey, Stony?" Jake's high-pitched yell interrupted his thoughts.

"Yeah?"

"How much further?"

Snow covered Jake's watch cap and clung to his eyelashes and eyebrows, and his expression relayed an unusual message—not fatigue. Jake was nervous.

Must be the griz and the wolves. Stony had been around the wilderness his whole life and sometimes forgot that others never saw the wild like he did. They found it hard to get used to the sheer, in-your-face ugliness and power of nature.

"Maybe another twenty or thirty minutes and we'll be there. Oh, and don't worry about the wolves. They won't be tracking us. We'll be safe."

Jake's head quivered up and down, lips a tight line, eyes unreadable under the frown. His answer was curt. "Okay, no problem."

Nope, he wasn't worried about the wolves. There was something else.

"Are you okay, Jake?"

"Yeah. Fine."

"You want to rest a few minutes, we could. If we push on, we'll be inside the tent in a half-hour, drinking hot coffee and slurping soup. What do you think? Rest or move?"

The words "hot coffee" seemed to smooth Jake's face. "Let's get there."

Stony dug in. The words of his drill sergeant came back: quick-time, march.

After a minute of head-down striding, he squinted and clenched his jaw, a tiny panic creeping in. How long had it been since he'd set up a tent in snow? It wasn't something he'd planned on doing again after he'd done it once or twice. Just the opposite. He usually planned trips so he would never have to do it again.

Maybe he was losing it. He hadn't thought this trip out too well.

Come on, dude, he thought. *You've done it before. You can do it again. No big deal. Positive waves. Got to put out the positive waves, man.*

One more rise, and a dark lake sat at the bottom of a tundra bowl. A sand-colored cliff seamed with grass-green moss jutted high on the other side of the lake. A snowy glacier remnant snuggled into the base of the cliff and trickled its melt into the lake. The last lake with the wolves had been scenic, but that one had held few fish.

This one had cutthroats two feet long. Maybe longer.

The snow was already drifting about a foot high on the lip of the lake. Stony walked faster. He had to get the tent up right away or there would be no fishing. No living, either.

CHAPTER 19

I really wanted a little more time, Jake thought.

He'd eaten a huge breakfast, but he was hungry again. He drained a second bottle of water. They'd been hiking about ninety minutes but he was thirsty all the time.

He tapped Stony on the shoulder "Have you got another bottle of water? I seem to be out."

"Sure, man. Hey, this altitude will dehydrate you. Drink as much as you want."

He downed another half a bottle. But what he needed was that hot coffee and food Stony had promised. *Soon.*

The snow was really coming down now, which would make things easier. He wouldn't get in all the fishing he'd hoped for. But things never really worked out exactly like you wanted.

Summer had proved that. Initially, she'd done well in high school, even proved herself disciplined enough to get a black belt in karate. Then everything seemed to unravel. He remembered that argument nine years ago like it was today: "Dammit, Summer. Don't let this guy screw your life up. How can you just turn off school and leave? You're so close."

"I'm not like you, Daddy. I need to see what's out there now. I can't barrel on through school without experiencing life."

"Come on. He's a loser. You're better than him."

She'd had a crush on one of her teachers, an older single guy. Then she was gone like an autumn leaf in the wind. The address she left was a rundown rental where she'd lived for almost three months. He and Carla had driven out there once, but Summer wasn't there. Later she said she'd visited with Jake's mom in Pensacola. They did some sailing. She did love her grandmother and always gained strength from her visits. Spitting image, too.

Jake had been so sad that night when he and Carla drove away. He had really wanted to see her.

Then she came back. "Sorry, Daddy. I had to know." And that was it. She threw herself back into school, working so hard she finished with a bang and got into a six-year college/medical school. Other than that one fling, she'd always tried to be like him. He guessed that was all anyone really wanted to be—successful. Even if your dad was a shit sometimes, you ended up doing the same things he did: working too hard, too late, too long, and not being there at important times.

How could he have possibly missed her graduation from medical school? That had been inexcusable.

Or had it been fate?

Jake stopped for a pace and squeezed his eyes shut. Everything was fucking fate. *Right*?

Not this trip.

He sighed and sped up to catch Stony.

Maybe that evening last December *had* been fate. He'd planned to be at her graduation. Told her he'd be there. Then he'd had to cover for Roman. That's when he found out about Mr. Casper, and it had kept him there almost all night, away from her graduation.

Oh, Christ. He imagined how it must have been for her to inspect the crowd, one face after another, hoping, smiling in anticipation. But no Daddy.

Later she'd said she wasn't angry but had worried that he might have had a reaction to his insulin, and relieved when she found out it was only a problem patient.

She forgave him.

He hung his head. It had hurt her. He couldn't stand it that he'd hurt her once again. Tears dripped over his eyelids. He wobbled and almost fell, then caught himself.

Snow blew around the back of Stony's head in a vortex, leaving little shelves of snow on the outside pockets and the top of his pack. The wind died intermittently; the snow deadened any outside sounds, focusing his attention on the crunch and squeak of their steps through the new snow and the ruffles and rattles of the packs, and magnifying each breath as if they were the only two human beings in the world.

The lull disappeared, and the wind returned with vengeance. Jake felt encased and alone in a whirlwind of white. A herd of elk could be fifty feet away and he would never notice.

Or those wolves. He squinted into the stinging snow. Frozen tear tracks crinkled on his cheeks. Stony's back was a hazy outline only ten feet away. Except for the cold bite of the wind on his cheeks, he was warm, surprised at the cool sweat beneath his pack. His feet were cold, but they were always cold. Once he got some more water and food, he would be on top of the world.

Right.

He wiped his cheeks. Would exercise stimulate his white blood cells and immunoglobulins? Surely it would burn up some of that glucose collecting in his blood and muscles like the snow piling up around them. He chuckled to himself. Here he was, in the middle of the wilderness fighting a blizzard, and what did he think about? Cellular interactions. Someone should do a study on him.

He took a few more steps and halted. They wouldn't like what they discovered.

He turned around. Stony's steps crunched away, down the hill. The snow pelted the back of Jake's head. If he ran, Stony would never find him.

Jake started to walk away from Stony. *Good.*

CHAPTER 20

Jake took a couple of steps back the way they'd come. There was a curtain of snow. The faint outlines of their footsteps were rapidly disappearing. Jake hesitated. Were wolves behind that curtain?

He turned back around and hurried down the hill after Stony.

Stony slowed and stopped and started taking off his pack. The wind died and the snow flittered sparse, allowing Jake clear vision ahead. Stony had led them to another gorgeous place—a lake bordered by forest and tundra, with car-sized boulders and a cliff on the other side. Surely there were fish. The snow-coated ground around the lake outlined the dark water: a black inkwell surrounded by white velvet. The wind-ruffled surface devoured the falling snowflakes like it couldn't get enough.

Jake yearned for food and water. *Now.*

The storm's hiatus was short-lived. Stony tied up a lean-to tarp to block the wind and snow and directed Jake to sit beneath it. Jake leaned against a tree and watched the whirling snow over the black water and was either hypnotized by the sight, or he passed out from his condition, because he lost the next several minutes. When he shook his head to regain reality, he realized he was sitting cross-legged inside the tent with his coat off, and Stony was fussing over something in the back of the tent.

"I could really use some more water." Jake barely got it out. His tongue and lips moved in slow motion, as if glue had made them tacky.

"Sure, man. Tank it down. That's good." Stony's voice sounded chipper, but his face radiated pure suspicion. He handed Jake a bottle.

Jake guzzled the water. Stony crawled around him and unzipped the vestibule a crack. He lit the small, one-burner butane stove, poured water into a pot and put it on the burner. From his pack sitting inside the vestibule, he retrieved instant coffee and a packet of freeze-dried soup.

He nodded at Jake. "Leave this front zipper open a little. Don't want you to get sick from the burner. When the pot boils, turn off the stove here." He pointed to a metal wire ring. "Pour the water into the freeze-dried soup. It's a zip-lock bag. You close it after you add the water and squeeze it a few times to mix it. It'll take about five minutes to cook. I'll be back shortly. Got to do a few more things before the snow gets too bad. Make the soup and take it easy for a few."

Jake nodded and drank more water.

Stony eased the dry bag that contained the rest of the food out of his pack and zipped quickly out of the tent. He walked a few feet away and stood still, studying the lean-to. He nodded, satisfied the wind had not changed direction, though he decided to add more security. He dragged and placed two deadfall logs at the bottom of the lean-to as anchors.

He peered into the snow and wondered about the bear and wolves. Had they stayed with the elk? Human smell usually put them off, but not the smell of food. He tied one end of a parachute cord to the dry bag that contained the food, and the other end to a rock. He located a suitably stout and tall but skinny tree about a hundred feet away from the tent and threw the end tied to the rock over the highest sturdy branch he could find. After pulling the food bag up about fifteen feet, he tied off the cord, high on another branch.

He remained motionless for several minutes, listening and watching. The wind whipped the pine trees, whuffling and whooshing. The stream that drained from the lake gurgled. Jake rustled around in the tent.

Stony shuffled through the snow to the lake and filtered more water. On his return, he peered into the twilight for another long minute. Nothing there. Or so it appeared.

He zipped back into the vestibule and placed the water bottles within easy reach. The burner was off, the pot cooled beside it. He took off his boots and coat and zipped inside the tent. The warmth felt good, and his mouth watered at the soup's aroma. Another odd, sweet smell wrapped the edges. He'd smelled it before but couldn't place it. Something was not right about that smell.

"So, Stony. You must have done this quite a few times. I mean you had this tent up in no time, even with all the snow and wind."

"Yeah." His answer was almost a grunt, adding a quick, "No big deal."

Stony had almost forgotten to put down the footprint before putting up the tent; they'd have been wet all night. He must be getting old. Probably should do low-altitude, easy hikes in the summer from now on.

No fuckin' way, he thought. He would camp next week, and the week after that. By himself. Weather would never beat him.

"You get used to things like snow and altitude. Like anything else. The more you do it the better you get." He unzipped the vestibule and relit the butane, pouring water for coffee into the pot to boil.

Jake glanced at Stony, then stared into the blue flame. "Yes, I think you're right. But there are some things you do because they are a passion and they consume you. You do them so much that they take all your time."

Stony tweaked his head and puckered his lower lip. "Yeah, I'd agree with that. Like fly fishing. That's my passion. Can't ever get enough. Try to make the perfect cast, tie the perfect fly, do the perfect guided trip. Whatever."

Jake nodded and glanced up at Stony. "Sounds like you're doing what you love." He paused as Stony handed him a cup with a sprinkle of instant coffee in the bottom. Stony carefully poured steaming water into the cup, and the liquid swirled and foamed brown. The aroma swept into Jake's face.

He sniffed it deeply before taking a sip. "Oh yeah."

"Good shit, huh?"

"Yes, it is."

Stony breathed in and out with the wind, feeling the rhythm. The tent luffed, the coffee warmed his insides. He lived for this, to take people into the wilderness, have them stare nature in the face and learn fly fishing: a sport that would take them back into the wild again and again, each time arriving closer to becoming a real human being.

The rising steam from Jake's coffee was too close to smoke twisting above a burning jungle, a reminder of the unpredictable course of nature and life. Stony sensed Jake had a secret past, and wondered if he could help him overcome the darkness that swirled in him like the smoke in Stony's nightmares. The real question was: what exactly did Jake need?

Jake cleared his throat as if to speak, and Stony's sphincter tightened, not sure he wanted to hear what was coming.

CHAPTER 21

The wolf pack cruised in a slow trot through the falling snow. The snow allowed them cover but never kept them from their prey. A good meal had eluded them. The bear had tugged and ripped at the meat while hunger gnawed at them, deep. Some growled. One paced and shot in, hoping for a bite. The bear whacked as quick as a jaw snap, busting ribs and threatening more. The wolf limped off. The bear would sit on the carcass until he had eaten his fill: days and days. The rest of the elk herd moved on; the elk-smell diminished to nothing before the leader of the pack followed. Time to give up on this one.

Even as their easy lope carried them noiselessly through the twilight, they listened, sniffed and licked the air, grunting and whining their findings to each other. They had hunted together for two years and moved as one, a telepathic mind. The pack trotted through the trees, never touching the trunks, never slowing, always moving together, like a school of fish through a reef.

Had the bear not taken their kill, they would be sleeping: sated. But that was over, not even a memory. Hunger pushed them, heightened their senses. The hunt was on.

Occasionally they would lick or bite the snow, rarely slowing, always panting, watching and listening.

Though this was new terrain, they knew elk, and, just as surely, they knew they would find the elk and eat soon.

The leader slowed, breathing in through ultra-sensitive nostrils, twitching his nose slightly from side to side. The elk-smell was closer. But there was something else, another odor. Bad-smell. Two-legged beasts.

Rad caught Roman before he hit the ground.

How had Rad moved so fast? Roman stiffened and stood, despising the fact that Rad had gotten him thrown—then saved him.

Rad let him go. "Sorry, Doc. Nelson is a bit spooky. I was only trying to get him to come to me."

"Stupid animal." Roman wanted to kick the horse's leg and snap it in two.

Rad's black eyes got blacker. "Animals can sense bad vibes, Doc. Maybe you should ease up. He's just a horse. A good one, too."

Roman crossed his arms. "So what are we going to do about this snow? Do we have to go back?"

"Here. Hold the leads to the animals." Roman snatched the leads from Rad.

Rad drove three pieces of rebar into the ground about thirty feet apart. The rebar had two-inch flat metal washers crimped to the top to prevent ropes from slipping off. He clipped a rope to the top of each rebar and tied the other end to each animal's foreleg. Then he set up a chair and pointed to it. "Have a seat, Doc. I gots to put up the tent."

Soon, Roman was inside the large box tent; it was tall enough to stand in and cozy. He sat in a fold-out chair while Rad plopped something from a large baggie into a pot on the stove.

"First time you been on a trip like this, Doc?"

Roman had never been the outdoors type: a few hikes with The Bitch, but only to quiet her incessant nagging; a few hunting trips in cabins with patients in Alaska. Something about the question, though, made him consider his answer.

"Oh, sure. Living this close to the mountains is great for camping."

Rad chuckled, "Well, this here ain't nothing like camping. We got all the comforts of home. How about some red wine?"

Roman sighed. Total bliss. Perhaps he *had* picked the right guide.

Rad held out a glass, a corkscrew, and a wine bottle. The label was one Roman immediately recognized. A good year, too. He opened the bottle and let it breathe.

He nodded at Rad. "One for you?"

"No thanks. I got my JD." He slipped a metal flask out of his inner coat pocket and took a swig while stirring the food simmering in the pot. The aroma of onions, meat, and stew gravy made Roman's stomach growl.

He poured the wine and sipped, feeling warm inside and out, surprised at the comfort in this remote area. Rad ladled stew into his bowl. The hot meat tasted like steak and almost melted in his mouth, it was so tender. The carrots, onions, and stock warmed him. Rad was quite a chef. Cornbread, butter, and honey hit Roman's sweet spot. A few sips of wine, and he felt like he would melt into the chair.

"So, Rad, how do you find your way in all this wilderness?"

Rad had been sitting facing the small butane stove, eating stew and sipping hot tea. At Roman's question, his face lit up. He put his stew down, stood, and reached inside his chest pocket.

"This here unit is my baby. Goes with me everywhere. Makes traipsing through these woods like driving down Main Street. Course you gots to know how to work it."

"May I see it?"

Rad strutted over and, like a proud father showing off his first child, proceeded to review, in great detail, *all* the different functions. He beamed after he finished. "Quite a gadget, huh?"

Roman pulled out his own GPS. "I'm not sure, but I think this unit may have more functions than yours. I purchased it a couple of weeks ago thinking that I might, you know, go camping or something. We might need it as a backup, in case you got hurt or something. What do you think?"

Rad slipped his GPS back in his pocket and squinted sideways at Roman. "Right. Looks like the new Magellan. Heard good things about it. Never seen one. Think I could take a gander?"

"Sure." Roman handed his GPS unit to Rad. *Lesson time, cretin.* Roman was superior. *Face it.*

Rad gently took the unit and immediately turned around, shielding his actions from Roman. He sauntered back to his chair, all the while dunking the GPS unit into his hot tea and proclaiming in a loud voice, "Man, this sure is a cool unit, Doc. Wish I had one."

He pretended to stumble and let the unit drop, spilling his tea over it.

"I'm so sorry, Doc. Hope it's all right." He plucked it from the floor and blotted the unit dry with his shirttail, smiling and squinting and peering up, appearing to Roman as contrite as a patient who'd lost their most important medicine. "Should be okay. It's water resistant, right?"

Roman recalled that the salesman had said it was resistant to spills of water, though he had then proceeded to tell a boring story about how his unit had died an hour after he fell in a stream catching a huge fish and yada yada yada. *Please.*

Roman turned it on and saw the screen light up, then turned it back off. He was tired of this show-and-tell game. He had bested this…guide at his own game. Roman's GPS was the best. Clearly.

"Well, at least you know we have a back-up."

"That's good, Doc. You gone make a good guide one day." Rad's voice was as flat as his eyes, and he only smiled with one side of his mouth.

Rad was only jealous, thought Roman.

For several moments a dissonant current ran through the quiet as they finished their meal.

A scraping sound like nails on a chalkboard broke the silence. Rad smirked at Roman's startle and finished tracing his spoon around the empty bowl, grating metal on metal. He upended the bowl, his lips bared to reveal those ugly teeth. "We should get some shuteye. No tellin' what tomorrow will bring."

Roman's pulse quickened. Rad's face showed no humor. It was more mischief, or perhaps even…? No. The man was too stupid. And tomorrow Rad would find out exactly how stupid he was.

CHAPTER 22

Jake wanted to tell Stony the whole truth. He wasn't used to deceit. Perhaps now.

"How'd you get started?" Jake asked. "I mean guiding up here. Your family probably misses you, all the time you put in."

"Sure."

Stony's whole demeanor changed. He'd been attentive and bright-eyed, his arms relaxed and open. Now he drew his arms in like a praying mantis; he held his cup so close it covered his face like a shield. He stared into his coffee but did not drink. His one word had sounded distant, reminding Jake of a patient's funeral when a man said goodbye to his lifelong friend being eased into the grave.

Jake had been there.

He remembered back when the first inkling of this type of trip had crossed his mind. It had been two…no, more like five years ago. Jesus, time went by.

He'd gone from having a good job with a bad boss in the Navy to what seemed initially like a great job in civilian practice. After a year with too many patients and no time for his family, he started thinking about retiring versus getting another job with more free time. That was when he found the greenest grass—Roman Johnson, MD: initially a partner from heaven, now the devil incarnate.

"I need to step out and go pee," he said.

Stony's head jerked up from his coffee-gazing, his eyes dull and his voice hollow, echoing from a faraway place. "Finally getting hydrated, huh?"

"Maybe so, though I'm still very thirsty. Be back for soup in a minute."

"It'll be ready. You'll need this. Getting dark out there." Stony handed Jake an LED headlamp, his movements disjointed and mechanical.

"Thanks."

Jake huddled into a cramped ball in the vestibule and pulled on boots and coat, then strapped on the headlamp and zipped out.

Icy wind slapped his face and snow covered his boots. He strode away from the tent.

For the first time he worried about Stony. Stony was human, after all, and he seemed to have other issues. Was Jake being fair to him?

All Jake had to do was keep walking, and it would be all over; Stony wouldn't have to go through everything. He walked faster, moving farther from the tent. He debated how far to go. Far enough so his sugar-filled urine would not attract animals. The least he could do was keep Stony from being the grizzly's next meal.

The snow blew from behind and pushed him along through the ever-deepening drifts. The cold decided for him. He stopped and hurriedly unzipped. His bladder was more than full: high blood sugar causing too much urine. A minute longer and the dam would have burst. It seemed to take forever to empty, but God did it feel good. It reminded him of Tom Hanks as the crusty coach in *A League of Our Own*—the long, tinny tinkle of pee on the metal urinal; then the stream paused, Hanks groaned, and he peed more.

Ahh. It was the little things in life.

He finished and shuddered all over. The fruity smell of his urine made him glad he'd walked this far away from the tent.

Could he really do this? If he died out here, that should do it, right? Stop Roman from going after Summer.

Was he protecting Summer, or was he just a chickenshit, afraid of dying of cancer and running from Roman?

This trip was something he'd wanted for years. Now it was his last simple pleasure before ending it all. He would end the slow death by cancer; he would save Summer from that monster. Roman would stop. No other way.

He remembered her kissing Roman on the lips. Why had she done that? She'd said she was just being nice to an old guy who'd lost his wife.

Roman could never know Jake had committed suicide. He'd think he'd broken Jake. That monster would never get the pleasure. Summer could never know either. She'd blame herself.

Jake shivered. He turned around, into the wind. The snow stung; the cold bit his lips.

Death by freezing?

No, thanks. He would stick to his plan. They were definitely far enough into the wilderness. Time to commit. Before he thought about it too long, he pulled the emergency vial of insulin from his pants pocket and flung it into the snow like John Elway throwing a long bomb in the Super Bowl.

By tomorrow evening it should all be over. Peaceful. Quiet. Finished. He would not die like Charles Casper. Hyperglycemia and ketosis were hypnotizing. You might vomit a few times, but in the end you went to sleep. Forever.

He started back. *Just follow the tracks.*

He frowned. Even in the light of the headlamp, there were no tracks.

Maybe he had enjoyed that piss too much.

Hard to even see the ground with the wind and snow beating his eyelids to a squint. He squatted to minimize the pounding of the wind. Where were the goddamn tracks?

Up ahead, in the direction he'd come: white on white.

Wait. There was something. A dark shape.

The tent or a tree, or—his heart skipped.

Jesus. Not the bear.

CHAPTER 23

Roman awoke. Wind screamed and the tent flapped. He eased his head out of the sleeping bag. Freezing air wrapped his ears.

All noises vanished. No wind, no breathing.

He blinked and shook his head. Utter darkness and silence. Was he awake? Could this be a dream and he was floating in a void? The wind caught the tent sides again and snapped the fabric in a loud *whup*.

A flicker of light played on the tent door. The tent zipped open and a light danced inside, flitting over to Rad's sleeping bag—Rad's wide-open bag. Empty.

Roman sat up. "Rad?"

The light flashed into Roman's eyes, blinding him. "Yeah, it's me. Had to do some things."

"Jesus Christ! What could be so important in the middle of the night?"

Roman scrunched down into the bag. Multicolored spots from the light roamed across his closed eyelids. He shivered, and not entirely from the cold. For a moment he'd felt like Mommy dearest had opened the closet door he'd been in as a child—come to feed him after two days.

Rad's large frame silhouetted against the tent wall as he bent down.

Two clicks. Another click and a soft *whoomp*. Rad jerked back quickly and grunted. "Trust me, Doc. It was necessary. You got heat now."

Roman glanced at the floor. An orange disk the size of a Frisbee glowed.

"What's that? I don't want to be asphyxiated."

"Just 'cause I talk funny don't mean I's stupid. That what you think?"

"No. I'm cautious because I'm a doctor. And I've not camped in the winter before, so I'm curious."

Rad shed some of his clothes, flicked off the headlamp, and slipped into his sleeping bag, delaying his answer way too long for Roman's taste. "It's a catalytic propane heater. No chance of gassin' you. Not in a tent. Go to sleep."

Roman frowned. First Rad had saved him from a head plant off the horse. Now he was concerned about his being cold. Perhaps a little honey for the bear. "Thank you for getting a heater for me. I'm sure you didn't need one."

"Didn't get up for the heater. Something spooked the animals."

"What was it?"

"Nothin', Doc. Go back to sleep."

Roman clenched his fists. Forget tomorrow. He would wait until Rad started snoring, then strangle the motherfucker. How could he have ever thought Rad courteous?

CHAPTER 24

Get a grip, Jake thought. The shape couldn't be that bear. He was still having elk steaks.

His heart pounded; his legs tensed to run the other way, not wanting to become the bear's next meal. But if he ran, he would only be more lost. He studied the dark shape, his eyes squinting to pierce the blowing snow. No movement. Animals moved, trees didn't. A tree could shelter him while he collected himself and located the tent. What if the tent was the other way?

He shivered. This silent brooding was stupid. He yelled, "Stony!"

Twenty feet to the right of the dark shape, a sound floated through the blowing snow. He squeezed his eyes shut and shook his head, not believing what he'd heard. It sounded like a blue whale calling through a megaphone wrapped in cotton. Were the ketones in his blood causing hallucinations?

Maybe it was a man yelling *what?*

Or the zip of a tent?

A flashlight beam wavered through the curtains of snow.

"Over here, Jake!" Stony yelled.

"Got it!"

He leaned forward and forced each leg up and forward. The flashlight disappeared. He shielded his eyes; the snow stung like ice needles. The light reappeared.

He slipped and went down, snow from a drift slamming into his mouth and freezing his outstretched hands. The light was gone. Where was it?

He pushed up and stood, coughed out the snow and blinked a few times. The light was dead ahead, weak, but there. He trudged forward.

Finally he reached the tent. Stony's steel-belted arms dragged him in and brushed off the snow.

"Jesus, Jake. It was just a piss. Why'd you walk so far away?" Stony spoke to the back of Jake's head, but the frown in his voice stung.

"I don't know. I thought the animals might…" He twisted his head and peered at Stony, feeling like a kid being scolded.

Stony's frown changed to a grin. "Animals? You mean the wolves and the bear." Stony started to shake his head, and even made it wag to one side before halting when Jake looked up, dejected and hurt.

Stony kept the grin, and continued in a gentler tone, "Pee marks your territory. Animals shy away from human smell."

They would not shy from Jake's urine. It was too sweet.

The warmth inside the tent was remarkable. The butane one-burner sat in the other vestibule, boiling water. Having two covered vestibules made camping in weather simpler. Jake shucked off his coat and left his boots in the other vestibule. Stony zipped up the inner liner, and Jake sat cross-legged on his sleeping bag, leaning to one side, allowing Stony to crawl around him to make the soup.

Jake accepted a cup of soup, his mouth watering at the aroma. He sighed after the first mouthful. "Stony, this soup is nothing short of divine. What's in it?"

"Run-of-the-mill, freeze-dried chicken and vegetable soup with a few of my own added ingredients. Tastes a little different every time, but usually pretty good. Glad you like it."

Jake sipped more and peered over his cup at Stony, thinking of a distant time in officer's training camp, warming up C-rats.

"Were you in the service?"

"Yeah. Did a little stint with the Marines."

Jake nodded. The Marines fit Stony.

"Got called up when I was in Alaska." Stony looked away.

"Oh yeah? Guess you served in Nam, then?"

"Yeah." A quick and faint answer. Stony pulled his arms in like a shield to fend off any further questions.

Jake swirled his soup, now curious. Why was Stony avoiding the subject? "Hey, I served with the Second FSSG up in Camp Lejeune."

Stony turned his head and studied his cup.

Jake shrugged and decided to change topics. "So what do you make of this storm?"

Silence hung in the air. One simple word, "Nam," had changed Stony. The grip of Vietnam must still squeeze tight.

The wind slapped at the tent. Snow filtered down the side and occasionally sputtered with gusts, like sand thrown at a window.

Stony's head nodded up and down with each breath.

Jake shivered involuntarily and inched away from Stony. The top of his head dragged against the sloping roof of the tent. Nowhere to go. Jake had seen guys like this on the psych ward. One word, one movement, one stupid commercial on TV, and PTSD could snap their minds back into the war. And when that happened, look out. They could tear a bar apart, rip doors off hinges, and outrun triathlete cops. Some of Jake's cop friends had told him they couldn't believe some old guy with a white beard could outrun them. First they thought it was PCP. But it turned out to be the war—war mixed with adrenaline, fired by fear that had festered, deep.

That fear could do things to a human that were not human, and definitely not humane.

Stony shook his head, as if trying to flip snow out of his hair or fear out of his mind.

The hairs on Jake's neck became prickly icicles.

"Yeah, it's a good storm." Stony's voice was hollow and unhinged, and crept into Jake's chest like asthma.

What the hell was he going to do if Stony went berserk?

CHAPTER 25

The storm reminded Stony of Alaska.

After he'd left the disaster of Mines, he decided to chance it and head straight to Alaska. He left Colorado in a Kenworth pulling an empty lumber flat-bed. Those were the days when truckers took hitchers. They needed the company on the Alcan, a lonely place then. And dangerous. Stony was glad for the truckers, too: hard-working, kind, and would back you up in a fight.

Alaska: home of monster salmon and rainbows. He got started that fall on the Kenai River. He was different from the others. They used conventional tackle, many times snagging salmon with treble hooks big enough to anchor a drift boat. Snaggers were a disgrace to the sport of fishing. Stony stuck to fly fishing, something good his dad taught him on trips to Tennessee. Soon he had a name for himself. Then he had to start snagging fish, too, or he would have starved.

By spring he looked like a stick insect, he was so thin. He signed on with an outfitter and started guiding. He got quite a reputation: the skinny kid who flung fly line a mile and caught fish like he had a net on the end. The money flowed in. Dream come true.

Surely being this far north and out of the lower forty-eight they would leave him alone—or at least not find him. But he'd made a mistake. Social security numbers and post office identities should be kept separate, at least if you wanted to stay hidden, particularly if it was the only post office for hundreds of miles. The other young guides had figured that out. Somehow he hadn't.

August 15, 1969, he got it. They even got his full name right on that damn draft letter: Robert Stonewall Jackson. By Thanksgiving he was in Saigon City.

Stony shuddered and shook his head, his eyes moist. He twisted toward Jake. Jake's wide eyes shifted to the floor, though his mouth remained half open, and his nostrils flared. Stony kicked himself. The last thing he needed was a scared client.

"Sorry about that, Jake. Got lost in thought. This storm'll be gone soon. Don't worry. Tomorrow, while everybody else is in their four-walled prisons, finger-punching a mouse, and getting eye strain watching electrons etch a flat-screen, we'll be getting sunburned, surrounded by snow-capped mountains, and catching two-foot cutthroats."

Jake looked up. Stony blinked the wetness from his eyes and met Jake's eyes with a gaze as solid as the set of his jaw.

Jake let out a long breath, and his face relaxed. "Thanks, Stony. I was a little worried." He licked his lips. "You've been up in storms like this a few times, I'll bet. A little daunting to me, though."

"It's kinda scary if you think about it too much. But after you go through it a few times, you realize if you got the right equipment, you can live through this shit and tell the story."

The butane flame stuttered blue to yellow, and Stony's mind clicked back to Nam.

November 1969, he stumbled out of the plane in Saigon City: scared, green, and sweating not so much from the heat as from fear. Three years of high-school French plus a Cajun grandmother helped him test out well enough to become an interpreter and receive the rank of Specialist Four, a slight step up from the typical grunt. They called him Spec Jackson. He didn't get as many of the shit jobs, but his rank planted him close to Colonel Biggs, a native North Carolinian who hated gooks as much as he loved to tie flies.

"Hey, Spec Jackson," the Colonel said one night, his drawl making Stony homesick but also reminding him of Daddy, "how about coming over to my tent tonight?" That began the "sessions." The Colonel tied up his favorite dry fly for the Tukaseegee River and watched Spec Jackson tie Alaska streamers.

"One day I'll get to Alaska. Maybe you can guide me?"

"Sure."

Tying flies was fun. But being singled out? Stony wanted to get back with the guys.

Soon he found out the real reason for his sessions: so the Colonel could pump Stony about how the men felt about him. Stony gave out as little information as he dared.

Then Stony started making excuses to avoid the sessions.

After two missed sessions, the Colonel called him in. "Tomorrow's a major battle. We'll need you at the front lines to interpret for any POWs. Dismissed."

Stony ran back to his unit, glad to be with the guys and getting into some action. Maybe it was punishment, but he didn't care.

The next day, so many men were killed Spec Jackson was needed in actual combat. That's when he got his nickname. A sergeant saw Spec Jackson wait in ambush, standing like a stone statue without moving for an hour, then kill five VC without wincing, without smiling, without frowning—no emotion at all.

"Face like stone," the sarge had said. Another man said, "Yep, always been that way. Can't tell what kinda poker hand Stony's got. He don't move. Don't twitch."

Stony didn't understand it, then. He only knew he could do it. Later, an Army shrink offered two explanations. One, bow hunting with Daddy required standing perfectly still for hours. Two, when Daddy beat him for not being perfect, Stony had showed no emotion, initially hoping that would stop the kicking and punching, but mostly wanting to piss the bastard off. It had worked; Daddy beat Stony harder. Finally one time, Daddy got so revved up he keeled over from a heart attack. He lived, but after that he'd lost interest in beating Stony. The shrink pointed out that this had been a powerful reinforcement. *Right. Shrinks.*

Stony's next Vietnam assignment was to a unit with a sneaky-assed motherfucker of a sergeant who was the spitting image of Daddy. The guy controlled all the supplies and stole half of them. His power over the unit was more than any colonel's. To make sure his superiors loved him, he lied about the number of VC the unit killed. And if he didn't like you, he gave you fucked-up weed. Stony knew *that* from personal experience.

One morning, Sarge sent Stony and another guy out on a patrol by themselves. Sarge personally gave them the radio before they left. Once out there, they were ambushed. His partner was killed. Stony called for help, but the radio didn't work. There were no batteries. That day he actually thanked Daddy. Stony used those hunting and stalking skills to kill every VC in the ambush and in the village nearby, with a machete. All except one small boy. Stony made it back by late afternoon. The sarge looked at Stony with fried-egg eyes, and almost choked on his C-rats when Stony walked out of the jungle with facial camouflage made from VC blood.

The next day they celebrated Stony's massacre. The sarge even shot the photo that Stony had kept, the one he still had on his kitchen counter.

A week later the sarge went to pee. It was dark. There was an explosion. All they found was Sarge's left arm and his hat. Had to watch for claymore mines. Lots of those around. Had to be careful, especially at night. The shrinks loved that story.

After that, the jungle waved purple-black leaves; the sky faded to brown; the gray, pasty faces of men stared at Stony with dark eyes; and his body moved like a robot he controlled from a cloud. Weed didn't help. Neither did the shrinks.

The next week he left Vietnam. Three hundred and thirty-two days: not a scratch.

Stony blinked hard, turned the butane off, and got out some zip-lock baggies.

"Yeah, it's a good storm. But you know the old mountain men: they didn't have butane burners, no freeze-dried food. They still survived. Slept on the ground, rode horses through blizzards. And hell, those were Montana and Alaska winters. This Colorado stuff is a little dink compared to a Montana snowstorm."

"It won't really be sunny tomorrow, will it? We're probably done fishing."

"This storm might blow through quick. If not, you can still have fantastic fishing days in snow, especially if the wind goes away. The snow filters down, everything is quiet, and the fish rise like there's no tomorrow, trying to eat everything they can before the lake freezes."

Stony paused, his eyes focusing on distant waters. "And this lake? Hell, there's cutthroats as long as your arm. We'll find them tomorrow. I kid you not."

Jake did not look convinced. He started to say something, then stopped.

"What?"

"Nothing. I didn't think cutthroats got that big up here."

Stony wasn't buying it. Something else was eating Jake.

Maybe Jake could be opened up sideways. "So, Jake, what do you do for a living?"

Jake's eyes glazed over like a window in a steamed shower stall. "I'm retired, now." His voice was weak and he stopped eating.

The sound of his voice and his face... *Not tonight*, Stony thought. If Jake did what he did yesterday afternoon, that was it. They were going home tomorrow morning, snow or no snow.

CHAPTER 26

But Jake didn't turn over and go to sleep, or cover his head with a pillow, or vomit or wheeze or anything else that would indicate he was sick. He only sat there, not speaking. Something was eating at Jake but he wasn't telling.

Stony grunted. "Huh." Though surprised, Stony understood the need for secrecy. He put more optimism in his voice, "Hey, you know, retired is good. It allows you to do stuff like this. Hell, you can travel and...lots of stuff."

Jake nodded and spooned in the soup, slowly, deliberately, one bite after another, no space for words, no time for elaboration.

Stony kneaded the back of his neck with one hand. He was going to be with this guy for a few days. If this snowstorm lasted, they would need each other. Jake seemed all right, but there was something askew, a feeling that kept nagging Stony.

Nope. Stony would not pry. *Leave it alone.*

Yet he remembered the time he'd ignored a feeling in a hot jungle— and a VC had slit a friend's throat. His lips thinned and he squinted one eye. *Shit!* Not only would he have to pry, he'd have to be the Chatterbox Guide.

"You know, I had an uncle who retired early. Didn't look old enough to retire. Like you. Anyhow, he chauffeured commodity traders in New

York City; listened to their advice and made a bundle. Went to New Zealand to fly fish with the rich and famous. When he came back, he said, 'Nicest folks you'd ever want to meet. But shit, Stony, there's more sheep than people. And the fish? They're like teats on a sow grizzly—you know they're supposed to be there and sometimes you glimpse a few from a distance, but no way in hell you're ever getting close enough to touch one.' He went back to New York City to drive cabs. Loves it.

"I couldn't do that. All those people. Can't even imagine. I'd rather be here, miles from anyone. How about you?"

Jake shrugged.

Stony moaned inside. What the hell was bugging Jake?

Stony's conversation muscles hurt, but he would give it another try.

"Once, in Wyoming, I guided a guy and his wife from back East. She walked out of that airplane, and the more she looked, the wider her eyes got, like somebody injected Open Spaces right into her brain and it had peeled back her eyelids. On the ride to their cabin she kept mumbling, 'There's no trees. No trees.' Like she was talking to a ghost. Funniest damn thing."

Jake's lips widened a tad. But no joy there. He kept his eyes on his soup.

"Next day she caught a twenty-six inch brown on the pond by the cabin and whooped like a college girl at a football game. She smiled for the photo—but then her happy left. Her eyes jerked back and forth like a caged animal. *No Trees* flashed on her face like a psychotic road sign. That night at dinner she blurted out, 'Don't you get lonely out here? The people are so far away from each other.'

"I told her, 'We like our space out here. That don't mean we're not close to each other.'

"She didn't say much else. Next morning her husband looked like a whipped puppy and told me she had to leave. They flew out that afternoon."

Jake frowned at Stony, not quite avoiding eye contact.

"The point is some people can't handle it out here. Open space makes them clam up. They don't say shit unless they're in the middle of people and trees and cars and buildings. Like that lady and my uncle and…you."

Jake made eye contact. "That's not it. I probably should tell you something."

CHAPTER 27

Stony waited. He was ready. This was it.

"I, uh—"

The wind popped the tent, like a sniper firing in a quiet jungle.

Jake flinched and looked down. He said nothing else.

Stony wanted to yell obscenities at God for creating wind. But instead he crawled on hands and knees to the corners of the tent and pulled at each one to see if the stakes outside were loosening. On his way back he noticed Jake was again fiddling with his spoon, scraping at the bottom of his cup.

Stony sat cross-legged and tried again. "You planning on doing any traveling?"

"Oh, I'm taking it one day at a time." Jake's voice trailed off.

Stony craned his neck, twisting his head down, trying to catch Jake's eyes.

"You all right, Jake? Thought you would enjoy that dog and bear show back there. Didn't think it would scare you so much. Probably screwed up the whole trip, huh?" He said it gently, as if he were helping a two-year-old find his lost toy.

Jake straightened and looked at Stony. "No, I'm fine. I'm a little in awe, that's all. This wilderness is pretty raw. Must be a pretty cool life you have."

The wind increased, whopping and ruffling so loud they had to almost yell.

"Yep. Sure has been. Wouldn't give it up for all the vodka in Russia."

Jake actually chuckled, "Maybe there *is* more vodka in Russia than tea in China."

"Every Russian I ever knew had to have a lot of vodka. And there's a lot of Russians."

The wind and snow tattered and sputtered like a percussion band.

A sound pierced the din. Jake tensed.

A mournful howl started high and ended low. Though it sounded far away, it penetrated the night and the flapping of the tent like it was right outside.

Several others joined in.

Stony felt his molars showing with his grin. "What a beautiful sound, huh?"

Jake's eyes ratcheted from side to side in white-rimmed terror. "Jesus, that's those wolves. Are they after us?"

"Nah, they're only talking. You know, like you might read a book before you go to bed? They talk to each other instead of read."

He looked at Jake's wide eyes and added, "Definitely not after us. Too many elk."

"You think they'll sleep through this snowstorm?"

"They'll probably all huddle together. Usually they'd be up all night huntin'. But it'll be tough for them tonight."

As the chorus of howls continued, Jake tilted his head, eyes still wide. "I didn't think wolves were up here. That's pretty unusual, isn't it? And that grizzly bear? That's odd, too. Right?"

"More than that—at least, if you believe the rangers. They don't want to scare anyone, though. Ranchers and tourists would get crazy if they even thought a griz or wolves were up here. I've seen some signs of griz every now and then—paw prints and scat too big for black bear. And the wolves? Well, some of the old-timers tell me they see lone wolves here and there. Probably strayed from Yellowstone. Needed new territory, you know. But to see a whole pack?"

He rubbed his ear and closed an eye. "Maybe they're only traveling through, feeling out new territory before they go back to Wyoming. But I can't imagine they'd want to travel back through that moonscape in the middle of Wyoming. Lot prettier down here."

He uncrossed his legs and pulled his knees up, encircling them with his arms, then sighed. "Hard to say what they'll do. One thing's for sure. Don't figure either one of us will ever see that again. That's why I stayed—this morning, I mean. You understand?"

Jake nodded. "At the time I was scared to death, though. And you were as calm as… Well, I'm glad I picked you as my guide, that's all. Looking back on it, I will definitely cherish it for th—"

The wind blotted out his words, huffing and humming through the trees. A large batch of snow plopped on the tent and scrabbled and slid down the side.

No more howls.

Jake blinked his eyes, and he almost didn't get them open again. Stony thought that any moment Jake would nod off—then Jake opened his eyes wide, as if to wake himself up. "Maybe you could send me some of the photos?"

"Yeah." Stony paused. "Pictures." He studied his fingernails, and then the backpack. He rotated his fist in one palm, around and around.

"I know what I saw. You know what you saw. I've told bigger lies about fish. It was as real as the snow outside."

He crawled over to the backpack, took out his digital camera, crawled back, and sat. He turned it on and studied the screen. He pressed the *Delete* button, over and over.

"Wha… What are you doing?" Jake was obviously trying very hard to take it in and to stay awake. But he was almost gone.

Stony tilted his head and kept his eyes on the screen. The camera beeped each time his thumb tapped *Delete*. "It'll be a good story. But be careful who you tell it to. Get my drift?"

Jake nodded. "I know someone like that. Poison to beauty."

"Who would that be?"

Jake didn't answer, only stared at a dark corner of the tent.

CHAPTER 28

When the leader of the pack sniffed the bad-smell, he reflexively did what he had not done since he was a puppy: he halted and lowered his head and cowered.

The others stopped and milled about him, whining and crying. Why was their leader cowering? Why were they not moving? They were hungry. The food was out there. The elk-smell was driving them crazy. They respected him, though, and would allow him this slight faltering. But not for long.

The snow gusted into his face and he lost the smell. Standing tall again, he peered around for his alpha female. Comfort came with her nuzzling his shoulder and licking his nose.

He sniffed again. The elk-smell was close, but so was the other, the bad-smell.

In his loner days, he'd broken off from his first pack and found his first she-wolf, brave but too daring. Or maybe that winter night they had both been too hungry, pushing through deep snow for days. Amber lights appeared, as did the acrid odor of large, loud, two-legged beasts who rode even larger beasts, which were nervous, sensing being stalked. She could not resist those large beasts, a meal not running away—meat waiting to be eaten. The yellow flickering heat and the bad-smell of the two-legged beasts should have warned them off. But she would soon have pups to feed and was famished. She'd gotten mean, too. Even taken a bite from his ear. Hunger did that. He knew.

She slashed into one of the large beast's haunches, tearing out a piece. The beast fell and wailed, and he knew he must finish it. He ran for the neck.

A loud sound cracked the air, as if a tree had burst in a forest fire.

She fell, whined, and her dead eyes stared. The two-legged beasts yelped and crashed through the woods toward him, waving long sticks in the air. He sniffed her and trotted away. Had the cracking sound and the two-legged beasts brought death?

Their yelping stopped. He turned and gazed at the upright animals that pursued him. One pointed a stick at him. A flash of light. Searing pain bit his shoulder. The crack reverberated, closer. It came from the stick that flashed. He ran that night for a long time before he stopped and licked his wounds. The two-legged beasts brought pain and death. He remembered their smell, and hated and feared it.

He had survived to create his own pack, find a new mate. The bad-smell was back. He did not want to lose her. The pack was hungry, but they must avoid this.

Jake wanted to tell Stony about Roman. But he was afraid Stony would think he was a fool for thinking it, like he probably thought about Jake's fear of the wolves.

Had he been a fool those many months ago, over Charles Casper?

After Jake had felt that huge, leukemic spleen in Mr. Casper's abdomen, suspicion slipped in. Casper had denied claims for cancer treatments on Roman's patients. Roman had worked very hard on industrial toxin patients, becoming a local expert on toxins that caused cancer, particularly leukemia. Like the kind Casper had.

Jesus. He'd lost track of time—and his daughter's graduation. Yes. He was a fool.

Remembering what he'd found in Charles Casper's medical record brought back the panic. What could he do? Roman was respected. Jake had no hard evidence. But it was clear to him that Roman was killing Casper as some sort of sick vendetta for denying claims.

How could Roman, a doctor, someone who had dedicated his life to helping people, have done that to Casper? Was it because Casper denied claims for Roman's patients? Ridiculous. Jake wondered if the high ketones and sugar in his blood were making him hallucinate.

"Hey, Jake, you okay?" Stony gripped him and shook his shoulders.

Jake rocked back and spilled now lukewarm soup in his lap. "Yeah. Guess I was thinking about work. Boy, this altitude makes me tired."

He snuck his fingers below his ribs and felt for his spleen. It had to be swollen, chock full of leukemia cells. Was it as big as Casper's?

Not yet.

Stony grabbed the cup and spoon, stowed them along with his own in a zip-lock baggie, then zipped that one in another. He dabbed the spill on Jake's lap with some water and a chamois, put the camera back, and pulled out something from the backpack.

"Thought you wanted to forget about that shit for a while."

It wasn't a question. Stony gave Jake a pair of forceps with a fish hook in it.

Jake shook his head and blinked hard. "What's this?"

"You'll see."

He put the forceps in Jake's hands and had him hold it out from his body, steadying his elbows on his knees. "Hold it like so."

Jake understood. Stony had made Jake into a human fly-tying vice.

Stony fitted headlamps onto both of their heads. He directed Jake to keep his light focused on the hook, then proceeded to tie a fly.

Jake had tied a few flies before, so this was actually interesting and kept him awake.

"The secret and simplicity of this fly is the soft hackle," Stony said. "A little thread for the body, two wraps of starling feather, a couple of whip finishes and you're done."

Jake held the forceps steady, only opening and closing them to replace a finished fly with a bare hook. Stony tied up a dozen flies with quick, nimble hands, as dexterous as any surgeon Jake had seen. Halfway through,

Stony's left hand cramped and he shook it, and Jake got a glimpse of a raised gray scar in the web space between his thumb and index finger, about the size of a pencil eraser. Or maybe a cigarette burn.

"What happened?" He pointed.

Stony scratched his nose. "Nothing."

In thirty minutes, they were finished, and Stony started stowing everything.

Jake didn't wait for Stony to finish. He quickly huddled down into the warmth of his sleeping bag, shivering, wondering whether from the cold or his body trying to keep from going into diabetic shock.

CHAPTER 29

Roman was warm in his sleeping bag, now utterly convinced he had missed nothing with Farnsworth. Yet he could not return to slumber after Rad had turned on the heater. His thoughts raced. Which GPS unit was better? How would he dispose of Jake in the wilderness? Jake could never be allowed to leave. And that thought brought him to Mr. Charles Casper and Jake's meddling in his case.

Eighteen months ago, after Roman had needled Farnsworth's spine, he was so revved up he couldn't sleep. He had to get started on his next project changing wrong to right. He entered the office at six a.m., locked the doors behind him, and strode into his dictation room, locking that door as well.

He sat down and repeated the word that had been tripping off his tongue all night: *HMO.* Now there was a major wrong. And correcting Charles Casper was exactly the way to end that wrong.

But it had to be a work of art, and fitting. No simple bullet or quick nudge in front of a barreling semi.

He pulled out Casper's health record: Charles Casper was a local administrator for the HMO MSI—not to be confused with CSI, though they did work in dark and mysterious ways, and had beautiful plastic actors as their main characters. But unlike CSI, MSI could never be construed to be the good guys. Except their CEO and top administrators.

They weren't just good, they were outstanding at funneling cash into their yearly bonuses and away from doctors and patients.

Roman studied the record, murmuring, "Mr. Casper. Denying so many of my patients' claims. How the hell am I supposed to get my money? Hmmm. What can we do for you? Oh, look at that. You get your testosterone shots from us once a month."

That would be an easy one to fix.

Roman got up and strode to the medication cabinet, unlocked it, and found the vial of testosterone labeled "Charles Casper." Casper always called Roman by his first name. No "Doctor Johnson" for him. It was "Roman," like they were friends, good buddies, on the same team, had gone to the same medical school. But Casper only had a master's in business.

Charles had no idea what it was like to be a doctor.

However, he always wanted the latest and greatest drugs, even though he denied them to his "clients." Whatever happened to the word *patient*? Forget about thousands of years of calling them patients. Now they were "clients."

Roman remembered the wink and grin from Casper when he suggested that Roman could get the testosterone from one of the drug reps, or pharmaceutical representatives, as they titled themselves now. Drug pushers, more like it. If Casper got free drug samples from Roman, he would not have to pay those pesky pharmacy co-pays that his own HMO enforced on all the other patients.

"Well, *Chahlie*," Roman spoke quietly to the chart, but with a distinctively upper-crust Bostonian accent, his diction crisp and deliberate, "why don't we give you the latest and greatest office sample of depo-testosterone. Nothing too good for you, old buddy, old pal: Mr. Charles Casper, the rising administrator for MSI.

"And," he paused, "you're so special, you deserve a little kicker. That way, you can try out your own HMO policy concerning cancer." One of the many herbal poisons Roman had collected from Peru mixed with a benzene product would do quite nicely.

Months later, Charlie was struck down with leukemia. A rare form, too. Poor man.

Luckily for him, Roman had studied that type of leukemia extensively, so Charlie got the latest and greatest chemotherapy with VIP treatment, right in Roman's comfortable office. Roman understood how important people hated being in a hospital surrounded by inferior worker bees. Roman administered the chemo himself: such a caring doctor. And he added the same Manú cocktail as in his wife's chemo. Why not? Charlie was his buddy. It would take a year for him to die. No connection at all with The Bitch's death.

Sleep enveloped Roman quickly after these soothing thoughts.

He never noticed Rad slipping out of his sleeping bag, dressing, and leaving.

CHAPTER 30

The cold and snow were outside. Inside, Jake was warm, his thirst abated. He dreamed…

He is nine years old, back in his boyhood home. It's very early in the morning but still dark. The wind is blowing snow outside the picture window. The air is thick with the flakes, white locusts that lay down peaceful and smooth, twinkling in the streetlight. Wind whistles in the cracks of the windows—crescendo, decrescendo.

He shivers and starts at the other sound: raspy, wheezing coughs that echo throughout the house.

Dad is sick.

Yesterday Mom said, "Just a bad cold, Jake."

"But it's been so long."

"Only a week. He's getting better."

A week. Dad was never sick.

Last night, he'd opened the door to say goodnight to Dad after another coughing fit and saw it before Dad shoved it under the blanket—crimson on the white handkerchief.

"Oh, hi, Jake." Dad wheezed and choked back another cough. "Kind of a bad one. You should get outta here. Don't want you to catch it."

Like a baseball? Did you catch it in your hand? In your lungs? You'd need the right mitt and a good pitcher who could hit the target.

The wind dies and outside the snow flutters down easily—white ash from the fire in Dad's lungs. The cough starts again.

Hands over ears. Can't blot it out—Dad's strangling on…blood.

He runs to the front door.

Opens it. Steps out into the cold night.

Closes the door, quick.

Finally the cough is gone.

Quiet. Peaceful. White. Beautiful. He wants to fall backward into it and flap his arms up and down. Make an angel. The angel will bring Dad out of it. They can throw snowballs together.

Tires crunch squeakily on the new snow. The snow-deadened slap of the morning paper on the driveway announces the new day.

He sighs. The cold air hurts when he breathes too deep. Maybe Dad just got too cold?

But he knows better. The whispers from yesterday afternoon about the chest x-ray—tumors.

The blood.

The closed door beckons. *It's up to you. Save Dad. You can do it. That way you can play catch with him in the spring, go fishing this summer.*

He opens the door, goes upstairs to his room, takes out paper and pen and writes it down. That's what Dad had said. If it's important write it down. So he does.

I want to be the best doctor in the world.

Jake woke. Even now, with the tent flapping in the snowstorm, he could see it, like a neon sign flashing:

I want to be the best doctor in the world.

It had sustained him, driven him through his toughest times in medical school and residency.

He coughed. The tent ruffled; the snow crystals spluttered on the sides like sand thrown against a window; Stony rustled about. Every sound was too loud, too crisp.

Jake's heart pounded.

If he could have known as a nine-year-old what it took to become the best doctor in the world, would he have still written that down and believed in it all those years? Striving for that goal, he'd been helping two dying patients in ICU and left his wife alone on their anniversary. She'd driven Summer home from her soccer game and had a car accident and lost her leg, burned her face so badly that the subsequent plastic surgery had been worthless. But she had saved Summer by curling her body over her. She was a brave woman.

She loved to run and coach Summer's soccer team. Everyone always thought Jake had married the most beautiful nurse in the hospital. If he would have known all those things, would he have still believed in that goal all those years? The blind eye of youth—without it, progress would flounder in the wisdom of age.

There was nothing wise about Roman. What in the name of God motivated him?

Didn't matter. Soon Roman could never get at him again. The stranglehold, not unlike that of cancer on his father, would be over.

He sighed deeply. As he breathed out, it juked him again: a lonely song played the guilt of leaving his wife and daughter and gnawed at his insides. But he had reached the end. He could not fight the good fight anymore.

But what if Roman didn't leave Summer alone? The gnawing in his stomach erupted into an acidic burn in the back of his throat, and it was hard for him to breathe.

Stony worked by the vestibule, his back to Jake.

Roman might go after her, and what was to prevent him from continuing to kill patients? Yet Jake felt like an atom nearing absolute zero Kelvin, all energy about to stop.

Stony moved back and forth, busy, his broad back sturdy.

Perhaps there was another way. Stony could help. Jake sighed and asthma-tight fingers relaxed their hold on his chest. Everything would work out. No one would ever know. Except Stony. But he wouldn't tell. Not Stony.

He pulled the drawstring, cinched the sleeping bag around his shoulders, and turned over onto his side, away from Stony.

Summer's laughing face lit his mind and eased his breathing even more. He swallowed. The burn in his throat and the pain in his gut had disappeared. He twisted side to side, took a deep breath and let it out. The pain from the cancer was gone, too. He rolled onto his side and fell asleep.

On the other side of the tent, Stony's nerves twitched. There it was again, the tickle at the back of his neck. Something or someone was outside.

CHAPTER 31

The storm raged outside, and Stony shrugged off the feeling of being watched. He kneaded the scar on his left hand, an old stab wound from a pencil caused by nightmares. He was done with that. Wasn't he?

He rubbed his hands and looked behind him. Nothing but the tent flapping. He stowed all the utensils, checked the tent corners one more time, then crawled into the vestibule. He put on his coat and shoes, grabbed the used utensils and leftover food in baggies, and zipped out into the storm.

He stood and waited. The snow pelted his face and obscured anything but a few dark shapes. Trees. The prickle accosted his neck, this time stronger. He jerked his head around and glared into the storm. After a minute, he shook his head. Fear in a storm was what killed you.

He quickly found the rope, let down the food pack, and placed the food and utensils inside. He stopped and listened. Wind whistled, trees groaned, snow skittered on the tent like a mouse on paper. He pulled the pack up again, tied off the rope, and walked back to the tent.

Before he went in, he stood stock still. A wave of snow slapped him in the chest. All he could see was dark on dark: hopefully just trees and rocks.

He brushed the snow off and zipped into the tent. In the vestibule he took off his shoes and coat, then crawled next to his bag. Stripping to his long underwear, he slid quietly inside the sleeping bag. Jake breathed easy, as quiet as a sleeping child.

—

One of the yearling wolves growled and ran at the alpha. The leader nipped the challenger. But it was not enough. The youngster kept coming with gnashing teeth. At the next attack, the leader grabbed him by the scruff of the neck and shook him and threw him down on his back and stood over him, baring teeth and growling low. This was a lesson for all to see. Do not challenge the leader and stay away from the bad-smell. Always.

His mate reinforced his lesson by nipping at the rear haunches of the youngster after he was allowed to get up and trot away.

The leader and his mate nuzzled and groaned, reviewing previous times with this difficult and different yearling. That youngster had always gone his separate way and was growing more distant every day. He was always the first to challenge any decisions by the leader. And he seemed to always be hungry.

They were not surprised when the yearling loped off into the woods and disappeared into the white, his nose pointed in the direction of the bad-smell.

The yearling left. He was tired of putting up with the alpha, who supposedly knew everything. He could best the alpha at any time. He was bigger and stronger. Why the others put up with a leader who was not even the same black color was beyond him. No more. He could have challenged him. But the female and others of the pack would not have it. It was time for him to break off.

The elk-smell was so near it drove him crazy. Why the old leader did not come for food was another puzzle. Maybe he wasn't hungry enough. But the yearling was.

He came upon the two-legged beasts' den and stood, yellow eyes studying every move. They were slow, easy prey. When they went into the tent he sniffed around it, but could not find an entrance. He trotted off and paced. He paced some more and finally lay down and waited.

The sounds inside the den grew quiet. The light went out. The yearling's stomach rumbled and he stood and walked forward.

CHAPTER 32

Occasionally Jake moaned in his sleep, and Stony wondered about his dreams. Probably troubled. Everyone had secrets that ate at them. Stony had his share. He wondered if the cure for Jake's problems would be as drastic as Stony's.

Right after Nam, Stony went back to the Defense Language Institute Support Command at Biggs Air Force Base, near Fort Bliss, Texas. He taught French and Vietnamese gook-talk to new draftees. Never killed anyone else. But he knew it lurked: that rage, the ultimate, godlike power over life and death. They promoted him to staff sergeant and asked him to stay, but he got out and ran back to Alaska. He had to escape that urge, that hunger.

Things were going great. Then the Colonel called. Wanted Stony as his guide. *Shit!* At the last minute, Stony tried to cancel the trip, but his boss said *no*. The Colonel had paid his money. Stony was going.

They fished the Alagnak River, camping and tossing the same flies they had tied in Nam. The Colonel turned out to be a great guy. At the end of the trip they were waiting for the pick-up, and Stony started teaching him how to Spey cast and how easy and artful it was to mend line, using the long rod to slide a snake of line upstream so it would not drag his fly. Usually the pilot cruised in on a Murphy Moose he'd built himself, the whirring sound of the descending bush plane a pleasant signal for the end of the trip. But this time a helo flew in to pick them up, and the *whop whop* sound—

Stony's eyes glazed over, and his head jerked up at the approaching chopper. Suddenly the Mekong Delta surrounded him. He dropped his rod and ran for cover. He had to get out of the open, away from the rice paddies.

He fought the fucking gook who hauled him out from under the bushes. Later, the pilot who had dragged him out from the tangle of overhanging evergreen roots by the river said Stony gave him a split lip and a black eye. He was damn lucky that was all Stony did to him.

The doctor prescribed pills for shell shock or combat fatigue, or whatever they called it. Load of crap was what it was. After a few pills, Stony felt like he'd taken a bad cocktail of moonshine and weed. Why do that shit when you could get fucked up right? He got some real Tequila and real weed. Didn't see light of day for…*Christ*…must have been the whole summer. Somehow he'd functioned well enough to get more weed and booze—but not much food, because he dropped thirty pounds. They had told him at Walter Reed he needed to lay off the MJ and alcohol; since his dad was an alkie, he had a good chance of becoming one, too. But they were doctors. What did they know about guiding in Alaska? No way was he ending up like his dad. *Uh-huh.*

Lucky for him that the Colonel decided to check up on him again. He found Stony, or at least a bag of bones with Stony's face. He threw away the booze and weed and nursed Stony through the shakes and nightmares and got him into a VA hospital in Montana.

After six weeks Stony was sane again, though he still kicked himself every day for turning out like his dad. Good old Daddy: the alcoholic Korean War vet. Stupid young Stony: the alcoholic Nam vet. He did have one thing going for him, though. He never did work for the railroad, like Daddy. That boring eight-to-five, retirement-the-prize job would've killed him.

Fly fishing saved him. He tied flies at night, fished most of the day, and, once he was confident, started guiding again. Off-season, he waited tables and stayed away from the booze. Gradually, like a fire-scarred forest, he came back.

Only two and a half years had passed since he'd stepped off that plane in Saigon City, but it felt like ten years had been sucked out. He managed to stay sane, and felt lucky for it. He knew other vets who'd escaped to Alaska. Sure, they walked and talked, only there was nothing left inside. Shucks of their sanity and souls crawled to the bars and flapped in the Alaskan wind. The odor of a grilled hot dog, the sight of smoke or trees swaying a certain way in the breeze, or *Jesus no* a helicopter flying by, and they were back in-country; those shucks of sanity became burnt ash, floating away in a wind that could make them completely disappear. Some kept on going to war, joining motorcycle gangs for camaraderie, booze, general mayhem, and sometimes the ultimate rush—killing.

Stony loved the sound and vibration of his own Harley massaging his groin, cruising so fast that concentrating on staying on the road kept all other thoughts at bay—losing time, that immortal torturer. Just do it—nothing but wind-sound, countryside, and a machine vibrating your core, shifting up or down depending on your mood and the road.

One night he was cruising on his hog down a particularly deserted and dangerously curvy mountain road when he felt it coming, knew it was there, waiting—that big curve with no guard rail. If he missed it there was nothing but thin mountain air for three thousand feet— vast emptiness and the total freedom of never having to worry about anything again, not booze, not weed, not friends, not life. Just gone. How would that be? Deliciously peaceful? Painfully empty? Would there be a hell with fire and pain, or maybe a never-ending frustration at not catching the biggest fish? At the last moment he turned.

Something had happened when he came back from the depths this time. He began to like people again. He enjoyed hearing their stories, listening to their joys and helping them get back to loving life, away from the cities, smoke, smog, sidewalks, computers, deadlines, and bosses: all the things that squeezed the human spirit into plastic.

The plastic people appeared to be real, maybe bent a little—but they melted down and broke too easy. It wasn't the real thing. Close, but really just shit.

The real thing needed open spaces, fresh air, cold mornings, hot days, and freedom.

Fly fishing did that to clients. They could take a deep breath…pause as long as they wanted, and actually take the time for several more breaths, take the time to soak up a vastness that dwarfed their problems, see the beauty of a real world maybe they'd never seen except through the eye of a camera. The only thing they had to worry about was the fly and the fish, or not even that. The freedom changed people, maybe for only a few minutes or weeks, but sometimes for a lifetime—like him. Who would have thought a piece of feather and fur wrapped on a hook, tossed through the air in order to capture an eight-inch, cold-blooded wiggly thing would be so therapeutic. Or was it only another addiction? Well, maybe that, too.

He'd learned to survive in the woods by himself—got a reputation and gave some survival classes. But that only touched the surface. His brain held volumes.

So he knew how to do this: absolutely. He knew he could get through this storm and the next, with or without Jake. His instincts had served him well in the past.

Jake breathed easy. Stony's hand ached. He closed his eyes and saw blood dripping from his machete onto a headless body. Something bad was coming.

CHAPTER 33

Jake could not catch his breath. His heart galloped and his mind panicked until he sat up. A pounding headache slammed him behind the eyes, forcing him back down.

What the hell was this?

Was it the altitude?

Why hadn't it happened the night before?

Probably a combination of the altitude and impending coma from lack of insulin. It would be over soon.

He forced himself to breathe slower. After a minute the panic and headache subsided enough for him to relax even further. He almost nodded off, but had to concentrate every third or fourth breath, forcing himself to breathe deep.

Just like Dad. Jake wanted to get up and run, throw himself off a cliff, stab his eye with a knife. Anything but this.

But the memory trapped him…

Mom's holding Dad's hand close to her chest and squeezing Jake's hard against her thigh. Dad is sitting up with pillows behind him, trying to catch his breath, eyes closed, frowning with effort. His face is gray, his cheeks hollow, and his arms like scarecrows, sticks inside pajamas. His breaths come closer and closer together until his eyes open in panic and he grips the sheets. Mom squeezes Jake's hand harder and says, "It's all right, dear. It's all right."

The doctor comes by for his second visit. No hospice care back then, only a doctor who gives an injection of morphine that calms Dad down for two or three hours. Six hours of peace in twenty-four. He no longer eats because he choked after his last meal and coughed for twenty minutes. That was days ago. Besides, he's breathing so fast, how could he fit in a bite? Breathing is all he has.

The doctor has to leave. Mom gives the next injection. She is always so strong, much stronger than Dad. She leaves for a break.

Jake's turn. He holds Dad's hand. It's only Jake and Dad now. Dad's breathing settles, the medication doing its job. The frown disappears, his hand relaxes, and his head lolls back onto the pillow. His chest remembers though: it starts rising slowly, gradually speeds up, then pauses and starts up again. Usually Dad's grip gets tighter and tighter as the breathing speeds. But this time he stays relaxed. The pause doesn't end. Dad doesn't flinch, doesn't move.

Jake wants to scream *Hooray, it's over!* At the same time: *God damn it, stupid doctors! Save him! Somebody, please save him!*

Instead, he sits still, holds Dad's hand: the hand that had held Jake's face, kissing him good night; the hand that had thrown baseballs, Frisbees, footballs; the hand that had pulled Jake out of the lake when he slipped on the mud; the hand that is gradually getting colder and will no longer do anything.

Jake smiles at Dad's peaceful face. "It's okay, Dad. It's okay."

Gently, ever so carefully, Jake unhooks his hand from Dad's and places Dad's hand on the sheet. Don't wake him from the peace. Get Mom.

She comes. Jake cries. She does not. He wonders why. She calls the doctor, who says he'll come soon, but for now, cover him up, pull the sheet over his face, and close the door.

That's what they must do: close out the smell of alcohol, feces, and death; leave the room, a room aching from months of pain and near asphyxiation, a room whose walls echoed Mom's and Jake's soothing voices, punctuated by Dad's torturous, hacking cough; a room now quiet.

But wait.

Take a good look before closing the door. Will his soul rise and go to heaven? There it is. A light, a glow on the ceiling. That's it. It must be. There is a heaven. God really did help Dad go peacefully.

Every time someone asked Jake why he wanted to be a doctor, every time Jake wondered what specialty he would go into, the answer was as easy and natural as the wind outside and the grizzly killing the elk: his calling was oncology.

He fought as long as he could to save patients from the disease that had taken his father. He saved many. But some he could not save.

In the end, when his cancer toxins and potions failed, he never felt like a failure, because he did not abandon them, like so many others of his specialty. He was there to experience the calm peaceful movement of their soul. He was there to comfort the family.

Sometimes he was the only one, the only one to hold their hand in the night. He was there.

He remembered his mother again, her giving the injection before Dad died, her never crying afterward. She was very strong. Summer was like her in many ways. She never cried after the accident. Not weak, like Jake.

Yes, she was strong. She would be okay when he was gone.

His breathing evened out, the headache left, and he went to sleep.

CHAPTER 34

Roman lifted his head. Was that a howl? The winded snapped the tent, and snow scrabbled on the sides. Roman strained his ears to hear beyond the darkness. Was Rad breathing or was that the wind? He pulled the pillow around his ears and turned over. He needed at least a little sleep. Tomorrow would be a big day.

He hadn't used violence in a long time. Subtle poisoning was more his style, like he'd done with his wife. But he would have to resort to violence to kill Jake—though it should be easy to make it look like an accident. After all, the wilderness killed a few people every year from falls while hiking.

He *could* have smothered his wife. But that would have left too many clues.

The Bitch. She had been his prize project. She'd become a little too nosey about his finances and the death of a patient. And of course the necklace. All she loved was his money, not him. With her murder he had been extra careful. Ask any detective—the husband is always the first suspect.

It had been a great challenge. Very delicate. Blame had to be deflected, insure others were made more suspect. As a doctor he could get DNA samples. Easy

He had initially focused on her tennis coach, Ken. She had said the teaching sessions lasted so long because she was so bad that Ken had to keep repeating things. Three hours for one lesson, and at a motel. She had had a lot more stamina with Ken than with him.

Ken had been a very viable suspect—until he stopped seeing her. Then Roman had planned a much better option. He'd thought about it for months before he actually went through with it. An abhorrent idea— taking on a partner—finally became the perfect plan.

Jake.

Poor Jake. He'd had such a terrible, terrible time in his previous practice.

A well of intense pleasure bubbled in Roman's chest, thinking of their first conversation. Jake was one of those *idealistic* doctors—loved the patient care, hated the business. Roman had said, "I assure you that I will handle all the business aspects of our practice. You can practice medicine. I think you'll find me fair."

Two sentences and he had him hooked. What a sucker.

Roman enjoyed the concepts more than the patients. Life and death always fascinated him. And the power to decide who lived and who died... Well, who wouldn't love to be God and make a lot of money, too?

Oncology was perfect: to wield the power of chemotherapy over life and death. What more could a man want? Give just enough poison—the patient would live longer. A tad too much or not quite enough—suffer and bye-bye.

Farmers and ranchers and most Europeans accepted death as a part of life. Citified Americans were never exposed to death, or so rarely they ignored it. Then, when it reared its head in their face... *Not in the US of A.* Americans thought they should live forever. Cancer? Hell, that was a little bump to overcome.

Roman was precisely the man to help them.

And they paid. Oh, how they paid. At least until the insurance crisis.

He had a hard time empathizing with patients, though. They brought on their own cancerous problems, like smoking and drinking and having inferior genetics.

Another reason to hire Jake: empathy. Jake could spend hours with one patient on their deathbed, and he actually seemed to like it.

So how could Roman make anyone believe Jake would kill Roman's wife? Well, he *had* spent a lot of time with her as her doctor. He *had* prescribed the chemotherapy that had killed her. And once they investigated Farnsworth's crime scene, it would only be a matter of time. Maybe.

Then again, if Jake spilled the beans about Casper…

No. That was not going to happen.

Tomorrow Roman would make sure of it.

CHAPTER 35

Something was different.

For a breathless minute, Stony's ears were on full alert, sleep instantly dissolved. He waited, then relaxed. It was not sound, but the lack of it. The tent sides hung as motionless as drapes in a house; no snow scratched down the sides. It was much colder, though. He turtled his cold head down into the sleeping bag so that only his fleece cap was exposed. After a minute he peeked out. Ice crystals coated the tent above his head, and his breath smoked into the dry air.

With the snow had come the cold front. Hopefully the cold would leave as quickly as it had arrived, like last year, leaving them a wonderful Indian summer. On the other hand, it could just as easily stay winter, snowy and cold until April, like after that crazy Labor Day ten years ago. Stony hoped the Farmer's Almanac was right this year: unseasonably warm fall, then lots of snow in December. Usually he didn't care. Weather came, he dealt with it. But now he had to deal with Jake, too.

The only sign of Jake's regular breathing was his steamy exhalations.

Stony reached out and grabbed fleece pants and top, pulling them into the sleeping bag for a few minutes to warm them, then inching them over his long johns. Quietly unzipping the bag, he wriggled out, careful not to nudge Jake. He rolled and stowed the bag in the corner, then crawled like a stealthy dog through the low tent into the vestibule, slowly, quietly unzipping a small crack in the door. He lit the butane burner and heated water.

If the weather cleared, maybe they would sit tight. If there were more clouds on the horizon, Jake would have to buck up for a forced hike back the way they'd come.

He pulled on another pair of socks and his boots while he waited for the water to boil. He turned off the burner and sluiced the steaming water into his waiting cup, swirling it into the instant coffee granules—not as good as pressed, but adequate. Maybe the smell would wake Jake. The odor was almost like a skunk, but even this whiff got Stony's mind revved.

He waited, expecting Jake's eyelids to flutter open. But now Jake's breathing sawed in and out, an audible accompaniment to the steam, like a tiny locomotive in the tent.

Stony finished the coffee, wiped out the cup, and re-stowed everything. Pulling on gloves and another top layer, he gently slapped the inside of the vestibule door to flip off snow outside before stealthily zipping out of the tent.

He rezipped the tent, blinked at the brightness and put on his sunglasses. The open vault of blue against all that white almost blinded him, even with the shades. No clouds. He stepped into the wet whiteness—about eight inches deep. He sighed at the black lake and the contrasting white snow that surrounded and gentled all the sharp edges of the lake. The white was an ocean flowing up to the craggy peaks, interspersed with patches of black-and-white aspens and groves of the greenest pines he could remember. Damn. How could people live in the city?

The lake drew him and he walked—so predictable, the fish like a magnet.

The wind-blown snow had lipped a drift over the northern edge, and the sun had already warmed it enough that staccato drips sparkled like rain.

Being on the west shore, he got the glare bad, but he tried to see anyway, shading the sun with his hands, peering into the depths. No good, too much glare. He plodded to the southern shore. A window to the deep opened and he saw them. They cruised about twenty feet out like small sharks searching for breakfast. He knew the cutthroats would pounce on any fly cast within ten feet of their forward vision, so great was their desire to store up before winter.

The clear skies and hungry fish were a good omen. Might as well stay a few days and let Jake fish and work out whatever it was that nagged him.

Stony quickly skirted the south shore and was on his way around the far shore when something moved on the hill, the same hill they'd come down last night. It had been in the corner of his eye, so he stopped and studied the hill.

Nothing.

He waited.

Cold dripped onto one ankle and leaked down to his foot. In his snow-shuffling rush around the lake, snow must have snuck in between his pants bottom and the top of one boot.

He didn't move.

Snow fell off a tree bough, *shiffing* onto the ground.

Warm, dry feet were important, so he started back to the tent, trying to keep one eye peeled on the hill while avoiding falling over hidden rocks. The velvet-white brightness made him squint behind the shades. After several steps he had to stop again, this time not for caution, but for beauty. He scanned the panorama: white suede, dark lake, layered pines, blue sky. Damn. Winter's contrasts were as different and beautiful as spring. He could understand a snowboarder's worship of powder waiting to be cut through. He started back to the tent, feeling warm inside despite his cold feet, knowing no snowboarder would ruin this view.

Before unzipping the tent, he inspected the hill again.

Nothing.

It had only been in the edge of his vision, but he had learned a long time ago to trust all his vision. He might see only a small movement while he was walking the shore of a river, but he'd learned to stop and cast to that movement. Invariably there was a fish.

Something was there, but what?

CHAPTER 36

Jake hurt everywhere.

He opened his eyes, and his thoughts came to him like a bubble popping through thick mud. *What is this place?*

The cold jolted his memory. His face felt frozen, a rigid mask that mirrored his insides.

He nuzzled his icy cheeks deep into the sleeping bag. All his muscles ached, and he could barely lift his head. After his face warmed, he unzipped the sleeping bag and tried desperately to sit up.

He flopped back down. Too weak. But the headache was gone.

He propped his head up on one hand, his elbow resting on the floor, his eyes scouting the tent, feeling like a boy again, looking for his dad in the gray light of dawn.

No Stony.

The effort of supporting his head caused his neck to cramp. He let his head down and zipped up the bag over the top of his head, only one eye and his lips and nose exposed.

What the hell was he going to do? His muscles were already fading. How was he going to continue the masquerade of fishing today? Stony was already suspicious.

He would have to do the best he could.

Right.

Sometimes that was not enough. Yet that was all he could ever do.

Sometimes you had to prioritize. Some things were more right than others.

Were his priorities mixed up?

No. Not today. He was doing the right thing. It had to be. Stony would see that.

And surely *she* would.

He'd finally got it right. Love. That magical word that ruled lives, created kingdoms, and destroyed civilizations.

He had loved. Oh, yes, he had loved.

He loved people, the sounds of their voices, their concepts, their differences, the nuances of their characters. And he loved taking care of them, supporting them in times of need.

Medicine had been a jealous mistress. But in the beginning he never found her jealous, only demanding. Anytime he needed her she was there. And even though she demanded of him, he could demand of her, with endless rewards. Patients were a reward in themselves, but they also heaped on praise and gifts. The harder he tried, the better it got.

It was a never-ending love. The only limiting factor was his ability to open his heart and care. Carla knew that, even way back then as a nurse in the ICU. She told him she felt it when he was with patients.

A sound outside brought him back to the present. The tent hung motionless. He listened—it was as silent as his call room that night, so many years ago. Yet the lesson learned that night was as fresh as yesterday.

An old black woman had come to the ER in full arrest. He'd saved her, brought her back from the clutches of death. How stupid he'd been—a naïve, stupid resident. She was transferred to ICU on a ventilator, pupils fixed and dilated. That's when he remembered who she was. In the excitement of the Code Blue, he had not really looked at her or registered her name. He was too busy remembering what drugs to give after each defibrillator shock. Then it hit him, she had been his patient once: Georgia Johnson, a vibrant woman, with children and grandchildren who thought she walked on water. She had great stories about Fourth of July family celebrations: spitting watermelon seeds, cleaning turnip greens, hugging a daughter, kissing a grandson. She loved food and people and life. Cooking was her way of giving love to her family, and the more scrumptious she made the food, the more love she felt she gave. Her food got raves, but she ate it, too, and she had developed diabetes. The food she shared in love had stopped her heart.

Jake had "saved" her. But her brain was gone. She would never love again.

In the glare of the ICU lights he sat across from Georgia's bed: her glazed eyes were taped shut; her mouth was skewed in a snarl from the endotracheal tube taped to her head; IV tubes ran into her arms, supplying the necessary nutrients; a urine bag hung from the bed coming from the Foley catheter in her bladder. A clean white sheet neatly shrouded her shell of a body. Karen Ann Quinlan had been in this position, and decisions about her life and death were made by committee. He did not want this for Georgia. But rules required an EEG to prove her brain was dead, unless…

Carla, his wife and head ICU nurse, knocked on the door frame. "Jake, Mrs. Johnson's daughter is here."

He jerked his head up. "Thanks. I'll be right there. Did you call the nanny? Is Summer okay?" Summer had been sick with chickenpox for a week.

"Yes, she's fine. A little itchy, but no fever and she ate a good supper. She's sleeping."

This was hard for both Carla and him, but he seemed to worry about Summer more than Carla did. Carla said Summer was his blind spot. He leaned in and gave Carla a kiss on the lips.

She pointed outside the door. "Her name is Susan." Then Carla left.

He reviewed Georgia's chart and sighed; this was going to be rough.

Susan entered with bold steps, a decisive woman in her late thirties. "Momma would *not* want this. She told me she never wanted any machines if there was no hope."

He felt her displeasure, yet he smiled at her, silently agreeing, realizing how much he hated seeing Georgia as a brain-dead, organ-prep. "I know. She was my patient. She told me the same thing."

"If you knew that, how could you do this? She wants to die, not live on some machine. She wants to go to heaven, to be with our Lord."

"Even though I'm her doctor, I cannot just unplug everything, not unless the family agrees to it."

"I'm her family. She lives with me. I take care of her. I know what she wants."

Her eyes pleaded. She didn't have to beg, though. He was already on her side.

"So you want me to turn off the ventilator? You understand she will likely die?"

Her eyes sparked hope and her face relaxed in relief at the possibility of someone actually understanding.

"Yes, sir. I understand that."

He took her by the arm, led her to her mother's side, and after she said goodbye, he turned off the machine.

While Carla watched, he held Susan's hand and felt smart again. He wondered what his staff attending physician would say in the morning. Feeling the love of Georgia's daughter when Georgia's heart stopped, Jake realized he didn't care what his attending thought. It was the right thing. He was sure of it.

There was a time to die, and technology did not have the soul or the heart to know when.

The next morning he was not so sure. Maybe he had been too quick to pull the plug. Those doubts faded in daylight but still returned on nights he was alone and feeling unsure of his future. But eventually he would recall that moment with Georgia, her daughter, and Carla close by, and calm would return, like it did this morning.

Jake fell asleep again so fast he did not hear the steps outside the tent.

CHAPTER 37

The delicious smell of coffee woke Jake. Adding to that good feeling, he also noticed his face was warm. Things were looking up.

But his bladder—ouch. And he was so thirsty and nauseated. But he had to pee. Quick.

Stony's gravelly voice said, "How ya doin' there, pard? Sleeping pretty hard. Hell, I been up a while. Checked you a few times and you never moved. I was beginning to wonder if you were okay."

"Yeah. I…I'm okay. It's just… It was so cold that I wanted to stay in the warm sleeping bag and must have fallen asleep again."

Jake wriggled out of the bag to his waist, careful not to strain. Didn't want to wet the sleeping bag. "Smells like you've got some coffee."

"Oh, yeah. And a little oatmeal over here if you're interested." Stony nodded to the boiling water.

"Sounds great. First, though, I need to take a whiz."

"Yeah, when you're at this altitude the first few days you have to pee a lot." Stony's words were right, but the tone was suspicious: how could anyone pee so damn much?

Jake twisted and scooted out of the bag, the pain of last night gone. He put on pants, shoes, and a coat and zipped out of the tent into blinding brightness. The cold air made him suppress a cough. He walked five feet and made yellow snow, the steam rising from the small craters created by his urine. The fruity aroma was barely perceptible. Surely there were no animals around now.

He sighed and gazed at the lake, a smooth black mirror reflecting the brightest sun he could ever remember seeing. An elk bugled over the hill, an eerie sound in the pure, quiet white. He shivered and zipped up, then stretched his arms to the blue zenith. He wanted to shout thanks. He felt good. There was barely any pain, and his energy was back, though he knew it would be short-lived. He started to walk back.

That's when he saw something, or at least thought he saw the glimpse of something brown, or maybe black, disappear over the top of the hill behind some pine trees.

He sidled back into the tent and zipped it closed, hoping the cloth would be a good enough barrier against…whatever was out there.

"No problem finding your way back this time, I'll bet. Huh? Nice and clear out there this morning."

"Yes it is. So beautiful." Jake felt it was truly beautiful, but his words sounded flat, even to his ears. So, when he sat down across from Stony, he could sense Stony's suspicions had grown another notch.

"Don't let this weather get you down," Stony said. "The cold and snow will be gone soon. By tomorrow or the next day we should be back to our normal fall beauty. Might be a little muddy and wet, though. In the meantime, the fishing today should be spectacular. A little cool, maybe. Are you up for it?" He handed Jake a cup of coffee.

"Yeah, that's what I'm here for." This time he managed a little more enthusiasm.

He had almost decided to tell Stony the full story this morning. But the timing wasn't quite right.

He drank some of the coffee, and his thirst hit him full bore. "Hey, Stony, is there any plain old water? I could use some—as well as the coffee, I mean."

"Sure, buddy. Here, take three or four bottles. I filled up some extra. You seemed to have a mighty big thirst yesterday."

"Thanks, Stony." Jake downed the whole bottle and took another right after.

Stony eyed Jake chug down bottle after bottle.

Jake wiped his mouth with the back of his hand. "Hey, I thought I saw something out there. Do you think…?"

Stony smiled and shook his head. "No. I don't think so. Those wolves are long gone. I think it was probably an elk or—"

A shot cracked and they both flinched.

Definitely a rifle, and not far.

Stony's eyelids squinted partially closed, the muscles in his jaw rippled, and he pursed his lips.

Jake frowned. "What the hell would someone shoot out here? Aren't we too close to the Park?"

"We're close to the border. Bull elk are in full rut with racks as big as they get. It's early in the season, too, so they haven't been at it so long that they've lost a lot of weight. That spells T-R-O-P-H-Y. Especially for those that don't mind bending the law a little and coming over to the Park."

"You mean poachers?"

"Yeah, I guess you would call them that—if you were in England. Over here? I call them assholes."

"Should we notify somebody, I mean, like a Park Ranger?"

"Well, if I knew exactly what happened and if there was a Ranger close by, then possibly."

Jake nodded and sipped coffee. "It sounded pretty close."

"Hard to say. With the altitude, fresh snow, and no wind, sounds travel a long way. Could be two or three miles."

"So…what now?"

Stony scraped the last of his oatmeal out of the cup, stuck the spoon in his mouth, then licked it carefully while he studied the cup. "Tell you what. I'll get you started fishing for these cutthroats on this lake, and then I'll mosey up that hill and take a gander."

Jake drank more coffee and sat the cup down. Stony handed him a cup of oatmeal.

"Thanks, Stony."

"You're welcome, partner."

He forced the oatmeal down, despite the nausea. Stony seemed so casual. "It's really cold out there. You think the fish are really going to bite?"

Stony's eyes crinkled and he laid his head back and laughed, a laugh that made Jake smile, a laugh that Jake imagined made the grizzly bear that was almost certainly following them giggle. Then he remembered the poacher. What if he'd heard that laugh?

When Stony finished, he continued to grin at Jake, and he wiped a tear from one cheek. "Goddamn, Jake. I thought you came up here to fish, buddy. Let me tell you something. Those fish are going to smash that fly as soon as it hits the water. They're getting ready for a long winter and they need food. In fact. Damn! I wish I didn't have to go over that hill. It's going to be one of those days: a once-in-a-lifetime day. Hell, there's some fish in there…shit…probably two feet long or longer, with shoulders that could pull a small child into the depths. They don't come out except for days like this. And if we get a little cloud cover later on, which I think will happen, *whooeee*! You talk about fun?"

"Sounds perfect," Jake said. Stony was indeed just the man Jake needed. It might be Jake's last day, and going out in style was exactly what he had in mind.

CHAPTER 38

Gunshots cracked and Roman's eyes snapped open. He sat up, glanced at Rad's open and empty sleeping bag, threw on a fleece jacket, and rushed to push the tent flap open.

He blinked at the bright sun and snow. Once his vision recovered he saw Rad dragging a limp dog—possibly a large husky—by its tail into the camp. The head flopped from side to side, revealing huge canine teeth. Rad grinned at him and started skinning the animal, an action which quickly put Roman back inside the tent.

The aroma of French toast, sausage, and coffee wafted in, so he got dressed. Once outside, Rad offered him orange juice and fresh-brewed coffee. Roman could have gotten used to this if it wasn't for the man's incessant questioning.

"Mornin', Doc. Sleep well?"

Roman glared at him. "How the hell can you sleep with the wind screaming in your ears and the tent flapping, not to mention dogs howling?"

"Those were wolves howling, and I got me one. This here's a great day. I got me a beautiful wolf pelt, and we're going to meet your *friend*."

Rad poured Roman a cup of coffee. "This guy must be some kind of friend. He a doctor, too?"

"No, just a friend." Then Roman tried to change the subject. "How did a wolf get here, and what are you doing killing one? That's illegal."

"Oh, the wolves have been here for a while. And lots a things is illegal, Doc. Like getting' a trophy elk in ruttin' season. Or killing your friend. Why you want to get rid of him?"

"I told you. I only want to give him a present."

"Oh. Right. Only I ain't seen no present."

"I have it tucked away." Roman sipped his coffee. "You get caught killing a wolf, and you'll go to jail."

"Who'll tell them?" Rad gave him a sideways glance.

"Never mind. How about this: how do you know where Stony is, and how soon do you expect to find him?"

Rad sneered. "There you go, doubting Thomas. You do read the Bible, right, Doc? Let me put it this way: how'd you like a patient asking you how you knew they got cancer and when they be cured?"

"You are not my doctor. You are a guide. My contract with you is to find someone and get an elk. I am not asking you to save my life. You came highly recommended, and I was told you knew how to use discretion. I believe I've more than honored your fee, and I have lived up to other, shall we say, necessary bonuses."

Rad's eyes became flat, dark stones.

Roman averted his gaze to the pelt and could not help but stare. There was nothing beautiful about the wolf pelt, grizzled and bloody in the morning sun. Flies buzzed. They would probably be here another day to dry the damn skin. Another wasted day, and Jake was getting away.

He looked up at Rad. "Do you really have any idea where we are going, other than to get more wolves for you?"

Rad's eyes glinted with humor. He grinned and held his palms up and out, like he was being robbed. "After all we been through. Can't *believe* you don't trust me." His tone dripped with mockery.

Roman wanted to rub Rad's nose in the bloody pelt, but he caught himself. Was Rad baiting him? A cunning criminal in a bear's body. "I never meant to imply that I did not trust you. I didn't sleep well, and I would really like to deliver my present to my friend as quickly as possible and get home."

Rad adjusted his black baseball cap, pulling down on the bill with his right hand and snugging the rear of the cap with his left, as if his appearance really mattered. He faced the stretched-out wolf skin and reached out and ran his flat palm from top to bottom over the fur.

Roman wanted to shout, *You dumb hillbilly, petting the dead skin of a waste of time!*

Rad turned his black, hard eyes on Roman and said in a low, quiet voice, "While you been getting your beauty sleep this morning, I been out scouting. The tracks is not hard to find, if you know what you're doing. They go right over that there hill."

He paused and squinted at Roman, his eyes slits. "You know, I think I deserve something for that latest insult."

For the first time in a very, very long time, Roman felt a small tingle of fear. It was the man's full presence, not merely the fearless tone in his voice or the predatory, can't-wait-to-eat-you look, but his stance, his movements, and the general feeling there wasn't a damn thing Roman could do except—

He pulled out two crisp one-hundred-dollar bills and held them out, avoiding the man's eyes. "I understand perfectly. I do apologize for any offense, and I have the utmost trust in your abilities."

Small upward twists at the edges of Rad's mouth revealed his eye teeth. He stretched out a gorilla hand that snatched the bills from Roman and pocketed them in an instant. "Hey, don't worry, Doc. I don't hold no grudges. Long as we continue to understand each other."

He turned back around and said, matter-of-factly, as if what Roman had given him was expected and part of the bargain. "Get your stuff together. I be packing up, and we be outta here in a couple hours."

Roman didn't hesitate. He ducked back into the tent. He was done with this conversation. Fear made some men avoid danger. It made Roman destroy it: like Mom and like Auntie. Rad's days were numbered. Only the method remained.

CHAPTER 39

Jake and Stony geared up and walked to the lake. A musty, humus smell wafted up from the dark-brown gap between water and grassy edge. The hot summer had left the five-foot gap in most places, and only a dollop of white-gray glacier remained on the far side. Last night's quenching snow had engorged the moss on the exposed rocks, and they appeared freshly wetted with a dark-green glisten, as if a giant had slurped off the top layer of lake a few hours ago. A fine surface mist whirled and hung ghostlike over the surface. Where the warmer lake water lapped the edge, the snow had disappeared.

A gentle breeze blew and cleared the fog. The lake was so transparent you could see every rock, every wrinkle forty feet from shore. Beyond, the water became a dark, mysterious void.

Stony positioned Jake and they watched—patient—quiet—the water and the bottom.

"It's about two feet deep before that drop off." Stony said. "The deeper water is where the big boys hang out."

Where they stood sloped gently to the water, a wide beach of fine rocks that crunched firmly underfoot. Stony would have Jake practice his casts in the shallow water, a continuance of the gentle beach, and likely chilled more overnight, so no fish would cruise there. They'd gone to deeper warmth.

Stony pointed. "See that?"

Small rings puckered the mirror surface and proclaimed the edge of the deep-water dropoff. Jake squinted. Fish noses barely broached the surface of each dimple. Tiny insects buzzed about two feet off the surface.

"We got ourselves a midge hatch. But first you need to practice in the shallows. The rig's got a hopper with a little midge pupa as a two-foot dropper. These fish will still be keying in on hoppers, 'cause it was only a couple of days ago they were flying and flopping all over this lake. And that's a big meal."

Jake had noticed dead grasshoppers on the side of the lake when they'd walked down.

Stony patted Jake on the back. "You know what big meals mean, don't ya?"

Jake chuckled. "Yeah. Big fish."

"That's right. But bright sun makes them a little shy. They may still get attracted to that big splat of hopper, but then, out of caution, back away and see that little bitty midge and say, 'Okay, I'll just get a little snack and go on.'" Stony rubbed his hands. "Either way, you got 'em."

Jake felt tentative, even though he nodded and proceeded to cast. He wasn't used to casting so far on this flat lake after the short casts he'd done the last few days on a stream. He hung up several times on the grass and bushes behind him and slapped the water in front too hard.

"That's all right, Jake. Takes a while to get the rhythm of lake fishing. Take your time."

Jake relaxed and started to feel the rhythm of the cast. The hopper landed further and further out, and calm washed over him.

The snow was already melting, dribbling off the mini ski-jump drifts on the windward side of the lake. The sun warmed the back of his neck. How could he have doubted Stony's weather forecast? It was turning out to be beautiful, though a faint haze of gray-white clouds lingered over the western sky: not the wispy cirrus clouds of two days ago, but a thin veil of cotton pulled straight along the blue horizon. He caught Stony glancing at those clouds between Jake's casting attempts. Each look hung a bit longer, though Stony always returned to Jake's hopper. He glanced back at Jake and nodded at the hopper, a subtle reminder that Jake should pay more attention to their business at hand.

Jake wanted to say, *Yeah, I want to catch fish. But my time is short. Have to take it all in. Every minute.*

He cast again and watched Stony out of the corner of his eye. He could not have asked for a better guide. Stony knew how to fish and how to survive.

Hopefully he would also know how to leave well enough alone.

They moved to another area of the lake. On the next cast, a long shadow cruised up slowly from the depths. It slammed Jake's hopper fly. The excitement of watching the huge fish in the crystalline water was almost too much for Jake, and he almost missed the set. But that huge cutthroat held onto the fly like its last supper, and even though Jake raised the rod late, the hook set well. Stony hooted at the take, which awakened Jake's fishing muscles. After the fish was securely hooked with the rod bent nearly double, the two men's eyes met and they both broke out laughing.

Jake would normally fight the fish hard to get it in quickly so as not to tire the fish and increase its chance of survival after release. But today he played the fish and reveled in every pull, every tug, and every rush of the big cutthroat, allowing the fish to rule the battle for a little while, allowing a moment of sun and snow and flash of water and direct connection to something wild and beautiful and free.

The moment passed when Jake realized the fish only had an illusion of freedom. Jake really had control. The line slackened and the fish was gone. *So much for control.*

Yet Jake felt more wonder and joy that the fish had escaped than if he had netted it for the trophy picture to take home.

Wild and free rocks! He pushed his arms up to the sky. "Yes!"

Stony beamed. "That was a nice fish, Jake. But you know what? You just made my whole season, dude. You get it. It's the battle, the journey, the connection to this world we have forsaken for the asphalt and electrons. You're there, bud. That was truly a nice fish. And that's how big fish get bigger: escaping danger. There will be another one, maybe even bigger. But if not…who cares? You know. I know." Stony slapped Jake on the back and grabbed him around the neck with the crook of his elbow and hugged him to his chest. "Damn, that was fun."

He let go, and Jake nodded and chuckled, feeling like his father had congratulated him for getting straight As in grade school.

He wasn't sure what was more fun: fighting the fish or losing control and having it escape. Maybe he should go with the flow instead of controlling it. Like Stony.

Yeah, right.

Stony stayed for a few more casts, until Jake landed a sixteen-inch cutthroat that had such vivid gold and orange and green that it appeared to be computer-enhanced. Jake almost laughed. They had developed computer enhancement to make things look more *real*.

But this? You couldn't get more real—the writhing, firm muscle of wildness. He could barely hold it as it slithered in his hand, the gills flaring in a gasp for air, the slime coat enhancing its struggle, the ice-cold water numbing his hands when he released it into the depths.

Stony took photos of Jake holding the fish against a background of snow and mountains, and then held the waterproof camera underwater for some shots of the fish swimming through the clear lake. He winced once and almost dropped the camera, shaking his left hand and swearing at the painful cramp. When Jake asked if he could help, Stony smiled and took a few more shots.

Then Stony sniffed the air and squinted toward the top of the hill on the other side of the lake. He gave the camera to Jake. "Okay. You've got it. I'm going to check out that gunshot over that hill. Be back in an hour or so."

Stony plodded away through the snow toward the long hill on the other side of the lake.

For an instant Jake wanted to call Stony back. But he couldn't. This was it. He would leave a note with the camera: *Please send the pictures to Summer and Carla.* Then he realized Stony did not know who Summer or Carla were.

Pity.

CHAPTER 40

A scant breeze floated a rippling nightgown of fog over the dark lake, making the fish more brazen in their attacks on the fly. Fish after fish Jake released. God, what a morning. Never had he dreamed fly fishing could deliver so much in so little time.

He stood tall and stretched his back. Sage and birch poked through the melting snow, the sun halfway to noon. The morning had flown by. The early fatigue had left him for a while. Now... He stumbled and caught himself. His legs and back ached.

He admired the last fish, hooked the fly on the rod, and sat on a rock that seemed meant for sitting—flat and dry and perched as high as a chair off the ground. He sipped water. The sun glared down the distant hill where Stony had disappeared. How long had he been gone?

A campfire odor wafted down the hill. Could that be Roman? He feared it, but then wished for it. *Come on, Roman. Come get me. Forget Summer.*

He would love to see Roman's face when he found Jake's dead body. Maybe Jake would be one of those people who hovered above their dead bodies, and he could enjoy Roman screaming at the sky and tearing at his hair. How he wished.

But Roman would probably just say "Good riddance" and walk away.

The lake beckoned. He didn't want to give in just yet. The fish continued their frenzied feeding. He took a deep breath in and let it out slowly, trying to taste every molecule while pondering fly fishing and all the fish he'd caught.

He slowly shook his head. It was a strange sport, really: waving a stick in the air with a line and a piece of feather and fur tied to a hook to catch a fish—then let it go. Why did he and Stony enjoy it so?

The fog lifted; the lake reflected blue sky and dark mountains; a cool breeze brushed his face; and he wondered why *more* people did not enjoy it. Perhaps they had tried, but hooked more trees and bushes than fish. Jake realized he'd learned more from Stony in three days than he had on his own in five years. If he had only got a guide years ago, he could have been enjoying this while he was healthy.

A wave of nausea hit him, and he pushed himself to stand.

He wanted to fish more, but his body was telling him otherwise.

He stumbled back toward the tent, feeling sad at the approaching end. He'd escaped the asphalt and electrons, as Stony put it. After years of fighting traffic, busy clinics, and deadlines, he'd lost himself in a mountain stream and lake. For a while his only thought had been perfecting the next cast. He'd played one game but now must move on to the other: the main event.

His vision started to gray. He blinked hard and vomited. Wiping coffee and oatmeal from his mouth, he struggled toward the tent.

CHAPTER 41

Stony trudged up the hill, and, while thinking about Jake, slipped once, immediately bringing back the old familiar twinge in his lower back. He concentrated on his steps and decided to take his time. No need to add problems. He would pay for that slip with back pain for the next few days. But no pain meds. Not for fifteen years. He wasn't going back there. What would his life have been like had he not paused for eight years after that accident? What if that accident would have come in Vietnam instead? Maybe he could have received treatment before he'd left. Maybe he would have got his shit together and not wasted those years.

Yeah, maybe.

But life never came to him that way. It usually waited until he was cruising along, happy as a lark, like he had been for a year after treatment in Alaska.

He'd been making good money. He left treatment feeling pretty good, not wanting to go back to counseling but to get back into the fly fishing and guiding. He had pretty good friends he could talk to, keep him sane.

The backpacking trip was with a client and his family: a guy not much younger than Jake, pretty wife, teenaged kid. Then another guy in an off-road four-wheeler came cruising down the path toward them and surprised Stony. When Stony saw his camouflage and the rifle, he thought it was Charlie.

He ran. Didn't say anything, didn't holler. Just ran: right off a twenty-foot cliff with a fifty-pound pack on his back.

It wasn't a real bad injury: couple of broken lumbar vertebrae. It took months, but they healed up okay. In the meantime he had to have something for pain. Back then there were no designer pain meds, only morphine and Demerol.

This time there was no Colonel to rescue him.

He went from city to city, finding doctors who would feel sorry for his broken-back story and prescribe narcs until they figured out he was addicted. Since most of the towns only had one or two doctors, he ended up moving a lot. He slept in his truck camper. Luckily he had that, though he rarely had money for propane. He gave blood, plasma, platelets—whatever they were taking for money so he could get his drugs.

But he never went back to alcohol.

He didn't keep much other than a fly rod and reel, though he never moved it from the back corner of the camper.

He lost a few teeth, twenty pounds—thinking about it now, closer to thirty-five.

Finally, a young woman, half-Canadian and half-Russian, took an interest in him.

Why?

Jesus. He'd been a wreck. Couldn't imagine anyone taking an interest in him.

Had it been pity?

Whatever it was, she helped him. The best thing she did was get him back out of the cities and into the wilderness where he belonged.

He'd seen her before, the first time at the restaurant where he waited tables. She would come in some nights during the long winter and have a few beers, a big steak. One time he asked what she did in the middle of the winter in Alaska.

"I study wolves."

Sure she did. A tiny little lady like her would get blown away by the Alaskan winter.

"Seems like a pretty difficult life out here in the winter. Do you go out by yourself?"

"Yeah. It gets a little lonely sometimes. But the wolves keep me company."

Dear Sonja. Her Canadian father had had a flare for a Russian woman, and Sonja was the result. Her father also had some Inuit in him, and her mother some Japanese, so she had definite Asian features: a small woman, with high cheekbones, black hair, and lush lips. But her eyes were not dark. They were the glowing light-blue of an iceberg where the sea lapped before the ice disappeared into the depths. Those eyes drew him into a world of mystery and discipline and, most of all, love.

She was shy, likely due to a scar that ran down one side of her face. It made her seem weak at first blush. But nothing could be further from the truth. One of the wolf hunters had given her that scar during the rape. They thought it would break her. It had made her strong.

Stony stopped and leaned over, breathing hard and thinking about Sonja and the rape. Maybe that's why she wanted to help Stony. She was Yang, the sun, and he Yin, the dark. He came across as tough, but underneath he was weak. She had a great grandfather from the French side of her Canadian who had served with the French resistance during WWII, so perhaps she understood Stony's wartime demons. Maybe she just loved to help lone wolves.

Whatever it was, Stony owed her his life.

Summer may not have saved his life, but she was helping him get it back together.

He stood, stretched his back and moved up the hill. Jake needed him now. Soon, his pace slowed and, despite the nag in his lower back as he neared the top of the ridge, he ducked low. He wanted to see whoever was on the other side without them seeing him.

CHAPTER 42

The smell of a campfire made Stony crouch even lower, *swishing* through the snow on hands and knees to the top of the hill, fearing who might be on the other side more than he feared wet pants. He glanced back toward the lake, but pine trees obscured most of the view. He figured it was about a mile—forty minutes up, less back down. But no need to hurry. Let Jake enjoy himself.

He peered around a snow-covered bush, down into the depression and the distant camp. Poachers did not like oversight. They had been known to dispose of witnesses. And with winter coming, it would be a long time before any search parties would be able to get up here.

He flipped his sunglasses on top of his head and pulled out the small field glasses from his inner coat pocket and surveyed the scene: two horses, a mule, a large tent, two high-powered rifles leaning against a tree, and—

The large, dark man: Rad. What the hell was he doing?

At first it appeared as if he were skinning a strange-looking deer.

That was no deer. It was one of the wolves.

Stony put the binoculars back in his pocket and dropped his head, rubbing his forehead with his hand. He whispered, "Jesus Christ."

He grabbed a handful of snow and rubbed his face with it. The ground moved and his head spun. He steadied himself and spat to get rid of the bitter taste fouling his throat. Two deep breaths cleared his head. He wiped his face clean with the crook of his elbow.

What the hell was he going to do?

Rad could shoot the eyes off a fly at five hundred yards.

And there was Jake. Something wasn't right with Jake.

He spat again. He had taken down poachers before, though Rad was in a different class. Still, he was just a man.

He pulled out the binoculars and glassed the tent. Another man came out of it. Obviously a client. Guy must have stepped off the plane from some city: designer cardigan sweater and a big ten-gallon black cowboy hat with a white feather sticking out of the band. Goddamn Texican, probably. Needed to try on a Rocky Mountain adventure for a quick trophy, then wash his hands of it with a lot of cash and go back to his ranch or high-rise office in Dallas or Houston.

He felt a tiny smile begin. *The Grumpy Guide returns.* He thought of Loren and her wanting to be a guide. He hoped she never saw a guide like Rad.

So…Rad had a client, too. That evened the odds a bit.

Stony ducked lower. Had Rad seen him? Stony put the binoculars back in his pocket, flipped down his sunglasses and started to edge away from the summit. Then he noticed the tracks in the snow. The tracks, a man's footprints, came up the hill from Rad's camp, then down the hill Stony had come up. Stony crawled down the hill following the tracks. When he judged it safe, he stood, brushed off the snow, and continued tracking. The footprints led to a tree where the snow and grass was matted down into a messy blot. No footprints went any lower than the tree. Stony stood in the messy blot. From here, his tent was clearly visible. Rad had been watching them.

He jogged and slipped as fast as he could down the hill toward his tent, wincing at his back but not caring. He hoped Jake had caught a lot of fish. Rad knew they were here and would not want witnesses to his poaching. It was time to leave, and in a hurry. They couldn't go back, though. Rad would see them.

Something puzzled Stony. Rad had watched them yesterday, but shot the wolf today. Why had he been scoping them out?

He stopped and called Jake on the walkie-talkie—no answer.

With the melting snow, the way back was even more slippery, and he had to concentrate to keep from falling. Every now and then he glanced at the lake. No Jake. Maybe he was behind one of those big boulders catching cuts. Hopefully he hadn't started walking up the stream.

Thirty minutes later, he reached a point where he could take in every part of the lake and survey behind each rock.

Where was Jake?

Stony marched to the tent. Probably getting some more water. What was it with the guy and water? Stony had known people to get thirsty before at altitude, but not like Jake.

"Jake, you in there?" Stony yelled at the tent. He was in a hurry now, thinking about the poacher. Needed to put some distance between them.

No answer from the tent.

If Jake had wandered up the hill to fish that stream… No telling what Rad would do.

He decided to check inside the tent first before venturing up the stream. He reached to unzip the front flaps of the tent, but a gust of north wind slapped the unzipped flaps back and forth.

What the…? Stony knew he had left it zipped closed.

He leaned over and poked his head into the tent. Jake was lying on his side, his shoes still on, motionless.

"Jake! Come on, Jake, wake up!"

Nothing. Not even a twitch.

A sweet-sour odor drifted up from the motionless man. *Damn!* Jake must have snuck in a flask and had a little too much last night. Stony'd had clients like that before. Now he understood why Jake had crashed so soon the first day.

"Jake! Wake your drunk ass up, you motherfucker. There's a damn poacher skinning a wolf only half a mile away. We got to get out of here."

Jake did not move. Stony kicked Jake's thigh. Nothing.

Stony caught himself before kicking again. He would have smelled alcohol on Jake last night or this morning when he was coaching him in casting. Hell, with Stony's addictive past, he would have known from Jake's actions even without smelling it. But maybe he had been so preoccupied with worrying about that gunshot that he'd missed the signs.

Then it came back to him: there *had* been a whiff of something when Jake hooked the fish. But not alcohol.

He shrugged into the tent and shook Jake's entire body until he got movement. "Come on, Jake. What's going on?"

A moan.

He shook harder.

Another moan. No motion.

Stony had to get Jake moving. Now!

CHAPTER 43

Stony slipped his shoes and coat off, did the same to Jake, and zipped the tent back up. Rad was coming. They didn't have long.

Jake made a few grunts, and his eyes fluttered open. He squinted at Stony like he was trying to remember something. He opened his mouth and croaked, "Water."

"Got some right here."

Stony unscrewed the cap off a bottle and poured water into Jake's open mouth, not caring much that Jake choked on the first mouthful. A few swallows, and Jake pushed up on his hands, trying to sit, then flopped back down, then pushed up again, the gagging odor of rotten fruit puffing out from his movements like dust from an old feather bed.

Stony waited, sitting cross-legged, impatiently seething. This was the final straw. Any second he would slap Jake. As soon as he had given what had to be a stupid explanation for this...this bullshit.

Jake finally worked his way up into a cross-legged sit and held out a shaky hand for the bottle of water. Stony handed it over and glared as Jake drained it as fast as anyone could drink. Stony snatched the empty. He wanted to throw the next bottle at Jake, but restrained his anger and calmly handed it to him. The tent flapped in the wind. Jake gulped.

Halfway through the bottle Jake paused, then cradled it in his lap. He looked at Stony and said meekly, "Thirsty."

"No shit." *I'm about to kick your ass.*

The tent flapped and fluttered. Jake cleared his throat. He stared at the bottle and took a few deep breaths.

"Okay, Jake. You want to fill me in?" *You dirtball.*

Jake jerked his face up at the sound of Stony's voice, as if he were surprised that Stony was still there. "Yeah. Guess it's time."

Stony held up a hand, suddenly remembering. "Before you get started, we need to break camp and move. There's a poacher coming soon, and he's a mean one. I think he knows I saw him skin a wolf, a protected animal."

Jake frowned. "I don't know if I can go very far, Stony. I'm pretty sick."

Stony held back a smile. *Maybe a walk will clear out the alcohol or whatever, you shitbird.* He was still the guide, and maybe Jake had a good explanation. "Well, all you'll have to do is walk a little ways. But trust me, if we don't get outta here soon you'll be a lot more than sick, and I ain't about to lose my first client."

"But—"

"No buts. Get your shoes and warm stuff back on, and get out of the tent. I'll pack your shit. Drink another couple of bottles of water. But stay out of my way. I'll be moving fast."

When Jake was dressed, Stony got him out of the tent. Jake leaned against a tree, and in twenty minutes, Stony had everything packed up.

Jake appeared brighter. A slight breeze riffled the lake. A gray line of clouds covered most of the southwestern sky.

The breeze died. In silence, Stony finished tying the damp, rolled-up tent to his pack.

"Why would that poacher come after us?" Jake said.

Stony slipped the pack straps over his arms, shrugged into the heavy pack, buckled and tightened all the straps, and started walking down the hill before he said flatly, "You ain't listenin' well." The Mississippi accent was thick when Stony was mad. And his voice was pure Mississippi mud. "Get your ass movin.'"

Jake followed.

"Stony, who is this poacher? Come on. Tell me what's going on."

Stony kept walking, turning his head to the side so Jake could hear the reply he spat like spent tobacco. "I'll tell you once we get safe. Now move!"

CHAPTER 44

Stony walked for several minutes before his head cooled enough to think straight. His anger faded to the feeling that whatever was wrong with Jake—drunk, stoned, whatever—it just about had him down for the count. They needed to get to a new camp quickly, or Jake might not make it. But he was still pissed. So he pushed it: to get there, and to punish Jake. Each time he glanced back, Jake was there. He kept up.

The breeze at their back helped their momentum, but those gray cotton-wool clouds meant another front was moving in, and this one might last several days. The way back now meant a roundabout trip. Not the way they had come: too close to Rad. Instead, they would have to go through terrain that Stony was beginning to think Jake might not make. Unless...

They walked hard for three hours, Stony pushing as fast as he thought Jake could go. He stopped only briefly to unpack more water for Jake, doling out one at a time, until finally he reached the fourth and last bottle. He was damn thirsty, but Jake seemed to need it more. There would be a stream soon. Stony would filter water for himself then.

At the last stop, Jake sat and looked haggard and his voice sounded worse. "How much further?"

Stony tilted his head: there it was—the faintest burble echoing through the trees. He said, "Not far. Maybe another half hour. Can you make it?"

"Do I have a choice?" Jake propped his chin on his hand and peered meekly at Stony.

Stony shook his head and glared. "I ain't carrying you."

Jake stood up, determination creasing his face. "Let's do it."

The snow was melting quickly, though in many places it had evaporated off the warm ground, leaving no puddles. Occasionally snow piles slipped off overhead branches and caught Stony on a shoulder. In the last hour, the terrain had changed from barren tundra to groves of pine, and Stony had glanced at the GPS more than once.

And then they were there—a clearing with pale green grass and willows hiding the creek that made its presence known only by the occasional gurgle and the visual slash of water winking through distant pines up the hill.

What had started as a glorious, sunny morning was now a haze-filtered, gray afternoon.

Stony made camp quickly, putting the tent up while Jake sagged, his back against a tree, then slowly sat down, unfocused and dull. Stony glanced at Jake on and off as he worked, satisfied he had been right, at least about Jake being at the end of his rope, yet unhappy at Jake's appearance. He didn't relish carrying Jake on his back. But he would. He worked faster, trotting to the stream, quickly filtering a few bottles and drinking them down, then finishing the job with a gallon of filtered water for Jake. Jake was dehydrated, and Stony believed more with each minute that it was not alcohol or drugs. Jake was too polite and… Hell, he just didn't seem like the type.

When he returned, Jake was flat on his back. Stony pulled him up into a sitting position and made him swallow some water. And, like before, the water seemed to perk Jake up. Once he got a few swallows, he started gulping and took down a quart. After a minute he took a deep breath and let it out slow. "Sorry. Must have dozed off." His voice, though more cheery, sounded tired, and his eyes, though more animated, still held a vacant stare.

The walk and work had cooled Stony's anger, and Jake's appearance spoke of suffering. He left the water with Jake and heated more, making instant soup. Jake took the soup, sipped it, then drank it down while Stony sat and waited, occasionally meeting Jake's eyes.

After Jake finished the soup, he gazed at Stony steadily, his eyes clear, his jaw set. "Okay. This is it. I've got leukemia." His words hit the air like mud on a flat rock.

Stony puckered his lips and studied the nearby pine tree. He wanted to slap himself for even suspecting Jake of drunkenness. It wasn't the first time a client had hidden an illness from him. They figured this might be their last fling before dying, so they hid it for fear the guide would call off the trip. Jake was probably going in for chemotherapy next week and wanted to do this trip before—

"But it's not just that."

CHAPTER 45

The pine trees whispered and creaked as a gust of wind peppered the tent with pine needles and chilled the sweat tracks left by Stony's backpack. He frowned at the gray clouds, now thickened to an ominous, dark curtain. "You can tell me about it later, Jake. First, get inside the tent, get on dry clothes and socks, and get into the sleeping bag. Rest up and get warm while I get ready for this next storm. It'll dump a lot more snow. We may be here a while, and I don't have much time to prepare."

After he got Jake tucked in, he went outside and erected the lean-to and tied up the food as before. The snow came down much thicker than the prior storm. This was going to be a doozer. It was hard to see even twenty feet. He filtered more water and gathered plenty of wood and placed it about ten feet directly in front of the tent. Thinking about Jake almost getting lost the other night, he sliced tinfoil into long, thin strips, tied their centers with string, and secured them to the top front of the tent.

After he was finished, he stood back and surveyed his work. He sniffed the air, taking his time. Long ago, it had been a poacher, no less, who'd taught him that man's sense of smell, if properly trained, could rival any animal's. If one poacher knew that, Rad did too.

Luckily the wind was blowing from the direction they'd come, from where Rad would follow. The wind was gathering force, but, judging from the swaying trees, was still only averaging around ten to fifteen knots. Soon that would increase, and the blowing snow would make any travel impossible, and would make smelling things almost as tough. But for now he could still catch the faintest whiff of Rad's campfire.

He couldn't smell the grizzly and wolves, but they were still out there. He had bear bells in his pack. If he tied them to a stick, the wind would jangle them and keep the predators away. But Rad would hear them too. Like blood to a shark. Anyway, Rad's campfire would likely scare the predators off. And maybe, just maybe, now that Rad had a wolf skin, he would turn back. One wolf skin would bring a very sizeable sum on the black market, definitely more money than Rad's client was paying. And with the storm coming in, why would he stay?

A few hard pellets of sleet rattled on the lean-to above the tent and stung his cheeks. Nothing more he could do now. The storm would come. They would wait.

Once in the tent, Stony was surprised at Jake sitting and sipping steaming liquid. The small butane burner was off and to the side, next to a pot of steaming water and a couple of empty water bottles.

Stony gripped his hands into fists and gritted his teeth. He felt like punishing Jake for lying to him, and pushing Stony to trek so far out into the wilderness. "Let me show you how to use that filter." He paused. "Don't really want to be getting up in the middle of the night to filter more water."

Jake's sunken eyes stared back through a face that seemed to have aged ten years, his skin the color of clay with deep wrinkles in all the wrong places.

Stony relaxed, and his anger deflated. He would make as many trips to the stream for Jake as was needed. Jake needed all the help he could get.

Jake motioned for Stony to sit down, and then started speaking in a voice barely above a whisper, "There's some things I haven't told you."

Stony sat and eyed Jake.

"Yeah, I've got leukemia, but I've had insulin dependent diabetes most of my adult life."

Stony nodded. *Yeah.* Now he remembered that fruity smell—ketosis. A friend of his in Alaska had a wife with diabetes who'd been real sick a few years ago when Stony was there. That smell had permeated the cabin. His friend had explained it was her body eating up her muscle and making ketones that came out in her breath.

Jake continued, "I figured this trip would be my answer. You see, the prognosis on my leukemia is pretty grim. I've got maybe four to five months. And I'm an oncologist, so I pretty much know what's in the future for me—chemotherapy and radiation. The type of leukemia I have is not easily cured, or even slowed down. And there can be a lot of pain. That's already started."

Jake paused to drink his tea. Stony poured hot water in a cup and dipped in a tea bag. This sounded like it might take a while. Tea always helped him concentrate.

Jake's voice gained a little volume, emphasizing each word. "I need insulin. Without it I'll get pretty sick. Eventually—hopefully pretty quickly—I'll go into coma and die." Then he paused and stared at Stony. "It'll be a peaceful death."

Stony squeezed out the tea bag, put it in a baggie, and slurped his tea. He nodded. "Dr. Kevorkian, huh?"

Jake's stare became a glazed window to a confused mind. Then, slowly, subtle recognition played over a slight smile. He blinked, the mere act of opening his eyes an obvious effort. He said quietly, "Yes, something like that."

Anger welled up in Stony and he spat out clipped words. "So you came on this trip to commit hari-kari and lay it on me!"

Jake shook his head and frowned; his voice soft and sorry and came in waves. "No-o-o. Stony, I don't want to lay anything on anybody. I was just… It wasn't supposed to… I was supposed to die without you knowing any of this. You know, that lake and the sun and the great fishing. Thanks for that. You gave me something there that… Anyway, it would have been perfect. I was getting pretty sick—thought I would lie down this morning and it would be over. But then you came back and we had to leave, and I was still okay, and…"

Jake hung his head, holding the steaming cup with both hands. The lean-to ruffled in a slight breeze above their heads with the gentle crackle of sleet punctuating each puff. Jake's head bowed even deeper, and the cup started to tilt.

Stony reached to grab the cup. Was Jake going to sleep—or into a coma?

CHAPTER 46

After waiting more than an hour for Roman to "get his things together," Rad wanted to toss him into the fire. He finally ordered Roman to get on his horse while he finished packing the mule.

Roman sat on his horse, smirking down at Rad. If Roman moved off that horse, Rad would break the condescending prick's neck. Well, maybe not. He needed to get the prick's money first.

Rad finished tying the wolf skin on top of the load, and the mule shook its head and bucked, its rear leg muscles quivering like flies crawled on them. Rad controlled the reigns and clicked his tongue on the roof of his mouth. "Whoah, mule." He said it soft and gentle and rubbed the mule's muzzle.

He squinted at the sun. The zenith was past, though it was still warm. He stood up and wiped his face. A trickle of sweat traveled into the small of his back. Loading and balancing the tent and all the supplies onto the horses and the mule took a few more minutes. He settled the mule. The wet snow was already melting; brown and green earth showed in many places. Gray and black rocks poked through, reminding him of an old TV show with hippopotamus heads surfacing on the Amazon river. He tilted his head—maybe that had been the Nile or some river in South Africa. Who gave a fuck?

He mounted his horse, signaled Roman to move out, and started humming. He was in a mood—a contented, money-in-the-bank mood.

A wolf skin, the high country, snow, riding a horse he loved, and having a client whose deceit and wealth would allow Rad to be happy for a very long time: what more could a man want?

The tune he hummed was his mother's favorite song—"Clair de Lune." She'd played it to him in the early morning on that old piano in the bar when he was waking up. Even though she was tired from working all night, she'd made him breakfast and played him the tune.

Digging into his inner chest pocket, he pulled out a plug of tobacco and his pocket knife. He flicked open the thin, sharp blade and cut off a piece, put it in his cheek, and replaced the knife and plug.

He chewed and spat out brown sluice and hummed some more, wiping his mouth while joggling back and forth in his saddle, easily settling into the rhythm of the horse and the sun and the sky and the mountains. This was where he belonged. He'd argued with others about how best to manage this wild country. They would've hated him for killing that wolf. On the other hand, he knew something they didn't. There were lots more wolves. He had seen them. They were coming back with a vengeance. More dead elk every year. Soon the ranchers would be getting pissed about dead livestock. It would only be a matter of time before the federal government would take wolves off of the Protected Species List. So he was, once again, ahead of his time.

Never had he killed any wolves until yesterday. He'd observed them, watched their numbers grow. He'd even made sure they remained timid by shooting at them, though he'd never hit any.

But that one—the dead one the mule still shied at—that one had been different. It had been a loner sitting on the hill, watching Rad. That one had unnerved him. No man and no damn wolf backed Rad into a corner. He struck first. It always worked. He glanced back at the pelt, spat again and chuckled. The dominant species had won again.

He shot a quick sideways glance at Roman the god-doctor with the black hat and the white feather: master and commander. Other clients had believed the same, but they had learned. Roman would, too. In the end they all paid and never squawked, because they wanted even less to do with the authorities than he did. Roman seemed different, though—more ruthless. Perhaps this would be Rad's last poaching trip. He would retire after this to Canada somewhere not even Roman could find, come out every now and then to get another payment, and disappear back into the wilderness.

He glanced again at Roman. Maybe Roman had money, but there was something he didn't have. Rad took in the vastness surrounding him, breathing in deeply, as though he could take it all into his heart and bottle it up and keep it there. He breathed out and breathed in again, wanting more.

The path ahead had treacherous spots. Better keep his mind on that. The money would come later.

CHAPTER 47

Roman wondered if Rad had lost it. He'd been so gentle to the mule—and now he was humming like a little child in a reverie, completely lost to everything and everybody. Good. The stupid turd would be humming when Roman stuck a knife in his mouth. *That* would shut him up. First, though, they had to find Jake.

But maybe Jake was already dead. Maybe he had taken a bottle of insulin from the clinic fridge, one of the special, spiked ones Roman had been poisoning for months.

Had Jake found out?

It would have been difficult for him, because Roman had only done a few bottles here and there. But enough. After a while, Jake had lost color, didn't act like such a happy guy in the clinic. *Of course*, Roman had been very concerned for his wonderful partner. Only natural to be concerned and check a friend's blood count. *Of course*, it had come as a shock to find out Jake had been anemic with a high white count. "Maybe," Roman had said, "you have Rocky Mountain tick fever. Probably picked up one of those little bloodsuckers fishing or hiking." Roman even talked the trusting moron into a month of antibiotics while he upped the dose of toxin in the NPH insulin bottle.

Roman had looked so sad when he'd brought the news. "Oh, Jake. I am so sorry. You've got acute myelogenous leukemia." Roman would usually use "AML" when talking with another doctor. But the words had a ring to them, a seriousness that deserved full enunciation for any client, though most especially to see the effect on Jake.

"Jesus." Jake gave Roman more than Roman had hoped for: slack-jawed terror.

"I could treat you…but maybe you want someone else."

The nearest oncologist as good as Roman was in Denver, an hour's drive. In good weather.

"You would do that for me?"

Now *that* was trust. Jake must have completely forgotten Mr. Casper.

"Sure. Be happy to. Let's get started today."

So they had. Roman had started Jake on his special chemotherapy laced with marrow toxins.

Yet, even with Jake's insulin-dependent diabetes, with its defective immune system properties, goddamn if Jake hadn't hung on. So Roman had used something else.

Their horses crested the rise and made their way slowly down the slippery, melting slope. When Rad stopped, Roman's horse stopped, too. No command, no pulling of the reigns. It just stopped. So did the mule. The animals knew the routine without commands. That could benefit Roman once Rad was gone. They would likely know the way back at least as well as Rad did. Of course, Roman had his GPS; no need to worry. Even if the animals balked, he could master the wilderness as well as this gorilla guide could.

Rad dismounted and walked toward the trees, all the while studying the ground and some round spots in the snow. Roman put the signs together quickly—no real secret here. Stony and Jake had camped here last night, and their steps went down the mountain. Duh. Who needed a guide?

Roman fingered the gun he'd been carrying in his coat pocket. *Do it right now.* Get rid of Rad, follow the footsteps, finish off Jake and the other stupid guide, and dispose of the bodies. Up here in the wilderness, disposing of the bodies should be easy, what with the wolves and bears and all sorts of scavengers. After a few weeks of gnawing and chewing, the only thing left would be bones.

Human bones.

Hmmm. He would have to think this through a little more.

As if Rad had heard his thoughts, his head lifted, and those steely, pebble eyes bored right into Roman. "I believe this is where your *friend* camped, and his guide—good old Stony. They've been gone…I'd say… several hours."

He peered down at the remnants of the snow, then up at the sun, squinting into the afternoon light. "Most of the snow'll be gone soon. Getting sloppy already. Be tricky to track. I'm thinking Stony knows we're on to them. Otherwise, why would he leave? Great lake to fish in. Perfect for your friend."

He rubbed his chin. "Maybe he heard that shot this morning. And if he knows we're after him, he'll probably lead us the wrong way to begin with."

Roman took his finger off the trigger. Conditions would make it harder to track them, and if Stony had a ruse…

Tricky devils, these guides.

"You're the guide. I trust you, and I'll wait for your decision."

Of course he didn't trust Rad. He only needed his expertise. Once Roman saw Jake, though, Rad was done.

Rad's black orbs seemed to swallow the sun, and…? Was that disbelief in his eyes? Rad licked his lips. Whatever Roman had seen was gone. Yet he had seen it. Rad didn't believe Roman trusted his decision. Nothing new there. But the other look in his eye was mutiny. Rad was thinking about going against Roman, despite the money. Not good. An inkling of fear touched Roman behind his neck and he despised it. He ran his fingers over the cold gun in his pocket but resisted the urge to take it out and shoot Rad over and over until there were no more bullets.

Rad mounted his horse again and heeled the side of the animal while reining its head around toward the original direction it appeared the footsteps were headed.

Roman blinked. "I thought you said they were going in a different direction."

Rad sat crossways and eyeballed Roman. "Well, I ain't no mind-reader. I don't exactly know where he's going, so I got to follow the trail 'til the trail peters out. Then I'll do some figurin'. In the meantime, why don't you sit back and relax and enjoy this beautiful fall weather. The snow's melting, sun's out, it ain't too cold no more, and we're going after your *friend* to give him a present. Isn't life bold?"

Rad winked at Roman. It was an ugly wink, something Roman imagined a troll might do.

Roman gave Rad his best grin without showing the fear that he felt, and loathed. "I understand."

He did. Feeling fear could not be tolerated. The best way to combat fear was to get rid of it.

Rad's small black hat atop his massive shoulders rolled with the rhythm of the horse.

Roman really didn't need Rad. Following these footprints was child's play. He tightened his grip on the gun in his pocket.

CHAPTER 48

Stony's touch on Jake's hand to lift the cup wasn't hard, merely a slight tap, but Jake's head snapped up like it was on a string, his eyes wide. He jerked and spilled hot tea on the sleeping bag. Neither of them moved to clean it up.

After blinking a few times, Jake said, "I'm sorry, Stony. I heard you'd been through…a lot, and I thought you'd understand when someone was ready to go."

Stony felt like his face had been slapped with a wide belt. The thought took him back instantly to Alaska and Sonja.

Sonja's Russian-accented English echoed down the hallway of the cabin. "Stony! You vill get out of de bed. Now!"

He'd pushed away the nightmare of multicolored snakes latching onto his throat like leaches from *The African Queen*. He had spent a fitful night in dry heaves, and the sheets were soaked in the sweat of opiate withdrawal. He scratched at scraggly hair but could not get at the worms crawling into his brain. All he wanted was sleep.

She slapped him hard on the cheek. Her ice-blue eyes glared at him, only inches from his face.

"Did you not hear me? You must get up! It is time. Come now, you think a few sweats and nightmares means you cannot get up and work?"

"Work?" He sneered, almost wishing for the snakes to return. "How can I work? I haven't eaten anything, and I'm so weak."

"What is that? You think this is free lunch? Getting your ass out of bed now or I will be throwing it into that corner with your vomit."

It was useless to argue with her. He peeled off the wet sheets, sat up, and grabbed his jeans. He stood and fell on the floor.

She watched him fall and turned around and walked down the hallway. "Soon as you're fooling around is done, I'll be in kitchen."

Goosebumps speckled his arms and stomach. He shivered, pulled on a fleece top, and stood. He retched air. His vision got grainy. He gritted his teeth and breathed in and out. After a minute he put on his jeans.

This was it. He could never go through this again. His legs were steady enough to reach the hall closet, pull out the gun and…

One pull of the trigger and the snakes would be gone.

Yet he could never do that to her. She had tried too hard for him, pushed him when he needed it, cuddled him when he could go no further. He would never get as lucky again to find someone like her. She made him realize there was something else he could do with his life, there was someone who appreciated him, who loved him, who would carry him through to the time when the real end might come.

Now…he stared at Jake. Was Stony all Jake had? A lonely cancer doctor dying of cancer. That was messed up. "This is it, huh? You're all alone. Got nobody. Just want to fade into the sunset in the Colorado Rockies."

Jake looked right, then left, as if confused. "Fading into the sunset, yeah, but I'm not all alone."

"What do you mean, you're not all alone? Why would you want to kill yourself if you have someone?"

"Well, I don't want them to go through a long drawn-out ordeal of pain or me getting chemotherapy, becoming sicker and sicker. I've seen my dad and enough patients do the same. I can't do that to my wife and daughter."

Stony gripped his cup, wanting to fling it at the man. "You have a wife and kid? Are you fuckin' kiddin' me, man?"

Jake nodded, his chin so low it tapped his chest. His voice was even softer, fading fast. "Yeah. A couple of days ago I was feeling so good, I nearly stopped my plan. It felt like a remission from the leukemia. It was great. Then the bottom fell out. I didn't know if it was the ketosis from no insulin or the leukemia. I thought if I drank lots of water the ketosis would go away. But…I don't know. It didn't work. I'm ready to go, anyhow. My partner tried to kill me and he's the reason I got this fucking disease." He paused and shook his head. "It's a mess."

Stony kept pondering the idea of Jake having a family that he was willing to abandon. Stony would never have that child he wanted. He had Kim Lyn, but that wasn't the same as blood. Sonja had been pregnant with his daughter when she died in that cabin in the woods. The doc said it was from the abortion she'd given herself after the hunters had gang-raped her. Her anatomy had got screwed up, and she'd hemorrhaged. She had been lucky to even get pregnant. She had saved wolves and had saved him. He could never save her, but he had promised her he would help others: every day, every breath he took would be to help, not kill.

The wind picked up, billowing in the west side of the tent. The crackling of sleet was replaced by a softer sound: snow.

Jake's thinking was as screwed up as Stony's had been as an addict in that cabin in the woods.

But Stony would help him.

He had promised Sonja.

Hell, Stony was about the only one who *could* help this fucked-up doctor, especially with that blood-thirsty poacher after them.

CHAPTER 49

Roman took his hand off the gun. What if Stony used some woodsman's trick to disguise a change in direction? Rad was Roman's only hope right now to find Jake. Roman could find his way out with his GPS, but that would not lead him to Jake. He had to find Jake.

He leaned to one side in the saddle and grimaced. Riding all day yesterday had been painful. More of the same today would be torture. How did cowboys ride for weeks and weeks, day after day? No wonder it had taken so long for civilized sanity to come to the West: It had to be imported. Cowboys ejaculated crushed, deformed sperm that bore only morons—bowlegged, hemorrhoidal morons.

For the first hour he felt bruised, the second injured, and every minute after, serrated. He had decided the saddle must have a drill boring into his scrotum when Rad halted at a dry stream bed, dismounted, and mumbled, "Wait here."

"Right." He forced himself not to whimper. He sat for a minute, thankful for the lack of movement, wondering if he would be able to dismount. Then the horse pulled down on the reins and began grazing on the grass, shifting from side to side. The pain stayed. No question. *Off. Now.*

He reined the horse in and gingerly lifted his right foot out of the stirrup, flipped it over, and…nearly fell off the horse. He clung to the saddle horn until his feet found earth. His inner thighs quivered but he stood.

What a relief.

He let the horse wander while he massaged his legs and took some careful steps on the round-rocked streambed, long dry of water. The muscles loosened. He let out a breath. Finally he could think about something besides his butt and crotch. This had to end soon.

He had to rid himself of this Ratman. His incessant humming and cheerful chit-chat were driving Roman crazy, not to mention his threats of blackmail. Shooting him would be quick and easy. The shot might be heard, though—possibly by the other fucking guide, Stony. Rad's skull would eventually be found with a bullet hole in it. Roman would be the first suspect.

How about falling off a cliff? An accident. Roman had read about that happening to an experienced Park Ranger a couple of years ago in the Mummy Range, not far from here. Precedence was important.

He squatted, stretched his inner thighs, and decided he needed to take some Motrin to allay his pain, allowing him more speed of movement. He was too handicapped right now to surprise a sleeping sloth, much less a panther in bear's clothing.

Snow began to fall.

Another reason to get this over and done. Without Rad, Roman would have to hurry to get out of this mud pit, before it turned into endless white curves with no visible landmarks and a treacherous, frozen undercoat.

The sound of scrabbling footsteps from down the empty streambed turned his attention to Rad, picking his way slowly back up.

Roman found the Motrin and swallowed several with a few swigs of water.

They would be traveling back to civilization soon. If the way down was anything like the way up, there would be cliffs, nice tall ones. There should be one just right for Mr. Ratman.

Rad arrived. "I found your friend."

Roman's insides jumped.

"Really. How far away?"

"They're camped about a mile on the other side of that grove of trees. If we hurry we can be there before dark. Then we wait."

"Wait? Why wait? We can surprise them. I can deliver my present, you can teach Stony a lesson, and we'll be off. I still need that trophy elk, you know."

Rad clasped his hands on his slight paunch, a belly almost exactly like a bear's. His face transformed into the troll Roman imagined lived inside.

"Still you pretend."

He unhooked his hands, scratched his broad chest, and stared with inky orbs that made Roman want to take out his gun and shoot him. "You want to do this right?"

Roman frowned.

"If you really want to kill your friend, then we have to get rid of Stony first. He's no chickenshit, and if I know him, he'll be packin'."

Rad actually had some brains in that tiny head. "So what do you propose?"

Rad yawned and crossed his arms on his massive chest. "We wait and make sure they're asleep. I go in and get rid of Stony and then you can have your fun with your *friend*."

He dropped his chin and raised his eyebrows. "You realize this will cost you, Doc."

The full measure of Rad's blackmail hit Roman. *It would never end.* But Rad would never get one cent. Stony wasn't the only one packin'.

Roman tried to keep the anger out of his voice. "Money's no problem. But we don't want to leave any evidence. How do you propose to get rid of the bodies?"

"Can't be giving all my secrets away, now can I, Doc?" Rad scratched his chest, turned and walked to the horses, humming.

Roman reached deep in his pocket and grasped the gun. *You motherfucker.*

CHAPTER 50

Stony took a deep breath and loosened his grip on the cup. Jake needed kid gloves, not a sound thumping. He poured hot water in the cup and looked at Jake. "What'd you say? Something about your partner?"

Jake's head lolled then dropped, pinning his chin to his chest. His trunk began to wobble.

Stony gently steadied him with one hand, and Jake's head came up slowly, only to ease back down. Stony put his cup down. He took Jake's cup and shook his shoulder. "Jake, come on. Wake up. What'd you say about your partner?"

Stony had to lean in close; Jake's voice was slow and barely audible. "Yeah, he gave me benzene or some poison, I think, in my...chemo. Didn't want me around because...I saw what he did to Casper."

Jake's head flopped like a rag doll's and his body sagged. Stony tried unsuccessfully to support him, and the effort caused him to spill the remaining teaspoonful of Jake's tea onto the sleeping bag. Jake started to roll onto the side of the tent. Stony grabbed him and laid him down, then inched the sleeping bag around him.

Jake was breathing, but very irregularly. Stony took out his first aid kit. Mistakes with past clients filled that kit: epinephrine and inhalers for asthmatics, nitroglycerin and aspirin for heart attacks, and, yes, insulin for diabetics who forgot theirs. After one near disaster, he always kept a couple of bottles of the stuff with some needles and syringes.

He'd learned a bit about diabetes since that client had almost bought it. There was long and short-acting insulin; the long peaked in six to eight hours, the short one in an hour. Jake likely needed both. But how much?

Stony remembered what his friend had said about his wife in Alaska: high blood sugar makes you sick and kills slow; low blood sugar kills fast.

He frowned. Why hadn't Jake just given himself a large dose of insulin? That would have been a lot quicker. Did Jake want the extra suffering to atone for some kind of sins?

Jesus. Jake was really fucked up.

Stony pursed his lips, but could not hold back the smirk. Words of wisdom from Mr. Straight Arrow, Stony the Grumpy Guide.

The smirk flattened. This was serious. More than that. Jake's life depended on Stony's next decision. How much insulin?

He drew up a third of a cc of each of the short and long-acting insulins, rolled up Jake's sleeve, and injected him in his deltoid muscle. He wasn't sure, but he had to do something.

Jake flinched and opened his eyes. "What are you doing?" His words were slurred.

"Helping you out, partner. Just helping you out. Say, how much insulin should I give you?"

But Jake was already unconscious.

The snow fell heavier, fluttering on the tent like a moth inside a lamp shade. Stony pulled on a microfleece top, made soup, sat cross-legged, and waited.

He checked Jake's pulse. Seemed regular, but fast. Breathing was less ragged, too, though it was very shallow. Maybe that was a sign of sugar being too low. He shook Jake again, but no response.

Over the next fifteen minutes, Stone joggled, shoved, and shook Jake. The only response: Jake's breathing seemed more labored.

Stony pinched Jake's face hard. Jake moaned. If his sugars were too low, he wouldn't do that, would he?

"Jake!" Stony yelled and slapped his face.

Jake woke.

"You gave me insulin?" His voice was brighter, though angry.

"Yep." Stony sighed and sat back. Then he sighed again. That had been close.

Jake glared at the roof of the tent. "Fuck. Can't even do what I want to out here in the middle of nowhere."

Stony sipped on soup, then crunched on a granola bar.

Jake muttered, "I thought you'd understand. I thought you'd let a man do what a man has to do." He sat up, haltingly, with the sleeping bag still around him. He slipped one arm out and grabbed a bottle of water. He gulped it down, then wiped his mouth. "I thought you'd understand."

"Yeah, you said that already. But I think I'm missing something here. Why don't you explain it to me, Jake? Because it sounds like a man with a wife and a daughter wants to kill himself just because he got cancer."

Jake squeezed his eyes tight. His whole face contorted and he cried. "You don't understand."

Stony waited.

Jake turned his head, but Stony could see he was wiping away his tears. "When I was a boy, my dad died of cancer, lung cancer."

"Sorry to hear that."

Jake sat and turned looked at Stony. "Yeah, well, it was before the days of Hospice. I was in the same house when he was suffocating on his own blood and phlegm. I was holding his hand when he died. In the middle of it all I made a promise to myself to be the best doctor in the world."

Jake squeezed his eyes shut again. A tear beaded at the corner of one eye.

"I thought that was what I wanted. Growing up, it was always science, science, science. I was inside studying while everyone else was outside playing, enjoying themselves. That continued right on through medical school. Do you understand what I'm saying?"

"Yeah."

"I'd always wanted to be a cancer specialist because my dad died of cancer. Maybe I could save someone else's dad so they could enjoy time I didn't have with my own dad."

"Honorable."

"Yeah, yeah. As it turns out, I had a knack for it. I understood the medications, juggled all the numbers, the new studies, everything. And I helped a lot of patients live a little longer. Then, with the ones who didn't respond, the ones that died, I found out what I was really good at. And it wasn't curing their disease."

CHAPTER 51

Stony raised his eyebrows. What the hell was Jake talking about?

"This is going to sound stupid."

Stony waited.

Jake took a deep breath and let it out slowly. "I felt like I could help their souls go to heaven."

Jake peered at Stony, like he was expecting a laugh. Stony only nodded.

"It was like when Dad died. I knew. I could see, and I felt… There was this light and he…he went to heaven. I just knew it. And with patients, it was the same, and it was… Well, I hate to say it, but it was like a high. When I was present at their deaths, I could see and feel things."

He paused and sighed. "Anyway, I loved my job, but in the end it screwed up my family."

Stony's eyes hardened as he said matter-of-factly, with an edge of sarcasm, "Oh yeah. Tell me about your screwed-up family."

Jake leaned forward and glared at Stony.

"Yeah, you think you've got a corner on a screwed-up family, right? Try this out. While I was trying to be the best doctor in the world, I left my wife alone on our anniversary. I should have been driving, but she drove, had an accident, and lost her leg and most of her face. I was in the ICU with two other patients, striving to be that goddamn best doctor in the world. I arrived two hours after she was in recovery."

He shook his head and sighed again, then continued without waiting for Stony to respond. "I jumped out of that practice into this one, thinking I'd have more time for my wife and daughter. Then I do a good thing and cover for my new partner, Roman, and I miss my daughter's medical school graduation. And here's the kicker: I missed her graduation because I found out Roman is a murderer, and now he wants to kill her. Summer is my only kid, Stony. He's going to kill her unless I'm out of the picture. So you tell me. Why the hell should I live?"

Stony sat back on his haunches and gaped. His thoughts raced. Summer. *Jesus. I'm screwing his daughter?* Maybe not. An uncommon but not rare name. There were a lot of retired hippies in this area, a few Indians. He'd seen names like Sky, Spring Venus, Running Angel. He had to find out, but gentle. Careful. Jake was on the edge. He did not need to know about him and Summer.

"Your partner, this guy, Roman, a doctor. You think he's a murderer. Pretty strong accusation."

"Yeah, he's a cancer doctor, too. I joined his practice about three years ago. He had a great practice, making good money. Everyone in town said he was the best. I only wanted to concentrate on the patients. He wanted to concentrate on the business. Seemed like the right fit. Then, about a year ago I found out...more like, got suspicious that he was killing a patient. He gave the patient leukemia. Same thing he did to me."

Stony held up his hand, "Wait a minute. Gave him leukemia? I'm not a doctor, but give me a break. You can't give someone leukemia. That's just stupid. It's not infectious, right?"

"Actually, there is a form of feline leukemia we believe is started by a virus. But, in man, probably not infectious. Have you heard of polyvinyl chlorides?"

"Yeah, don't want to work in those factories."

"Exactly. Chemicals used in the manufacture of PVC, especially benzenes, can cause leukemia. Now, this doesn't happen in everyone exposed to benzenes, but a much higher proportion. So Roman—he's some kind of twisted guy—I found out he was giving a patient, a Mr. Casper, something like benzene in his IV. Casper was in the hospital for sepsis, a blood infection, which I believe Roman also gave him. Casper's immune system was weakened by the infection, and then he got leukemia. After that he got worse and worse. Everyone, including me, believed it was inevitable, due to the leukemia. But we were all wrong."

Jake took another swig of water. "Last December I was on call in the hospital, taking care of Mr. Casper the same night Summer graduated. I was only supposed to be there an hour, then go to her graduation. But something about the chemo Roman was using and the timing of everything didn't seem right. I got the guy's health record. It took me a while to read it all. I was in his room and his IV infiltrated. I decided to take it out, and some of the fluid ran onto the floor. I got a whiff of hydrocarbons, a little like a gasoline smell. Why would there be an aromatic hydrocarbon in chemotherapy?"

Stony sighed inside. Summer was older than a high school grad. Not the same girl. "So you had this IV fluid analyzed."

"Not exactly."

CHAPTER 52

Stony was sure about how to handle the weather outside. The wind would blow, snow would fall, maybe even accumulate a foot. No big deal. They could hunker down and survive it. But how to handle Jake? He had no idea.

"What do you mean, 'not exactly'?" Stony said.

"What little was left in the bag had all leaked out. The nurse came in, and I was embarrassed. I thought maybe there was some cleaning fluid on the floor that I'd smelled. The nurse cleaned everything up before I could get a drop. I read back over Casper's record. No real evidence. Roman was my partner, for God's sake, and well respected. He'd saved so many patients; they loved him. Hell, everyone thinks he's this great guy. I'm the new guy on the block. I guess I didn't want any confrontation. Never have liked that. So, I dropped it and forgot about it."

Stony rubbed his jaw with his knuckles: sandpaper on rock. "So you just *think* he was killing this patient. What the hell are you—"

Jake put up a hand. "After I got leukemia and started chemo, I got to thinking about it. Seemed like a weird coincidence that I got the same kind of leukemia that the patient had. I tested some of the fluid in one of my chemo bags. A benzene compound came up, along with some other bio-molecules, plant-like. "

"Wait a minute. You let this guy give you chemotherapy after you thought he was poisoning a patient?"

Jake hung his head. "I didn't know for sure. And come on—he's a doctor. Not only that, he's my partner and one of the best in the business. I believed if anyone could help me, he could."

"Right."

Jake didn't answer.

"Okay. So he was poisoning your chemo with something like benzene. I still don't get it. Doesn't it take years for that to take effect? And you already said it didn't cause leukemia in everyone."

"That's if the benzene is in drinking water, say ten parts per million. But he was injecting it directly into my blood. Much more toxic."

"You had the bag of chemo analyzed, right?"

Jake closed his eyes and shook his head. "I had the bag hidden, but he must have found it. He is too goddamn smart, that's all."

"So you're just screwed if you get exposed to benzene once, huh? I mean, does the effect last forever?"

"If the exposure stops, the bone marrow can rebound."

Stony waited.

"It's been almost two months since I stopped Roman's poison chemo, but my blood count as of two weeks ago hadn't changed."

Jake frowned at the water bottle as if it were impure. "When I got sick…" Confusion and sadness broke in his voice. "Roman seemed to know so much about my type of leukemia. When I came into his practice, he did a lot for me, showing me the ropes, giving me choice patients. When he lost his wife I felt sorry for him. I understood his pain. I'd almost lost Carla. Oh, she's my wife. Sorry, I forgot to tell you."

Jake shrugged.

"Summer's my daughter. I told you that, right?"

"Yeah, she just graduated from high school."

"No, medical school. She's a doctor."

Stony squinted. Old enough. But Summer had never said she was a doctor.

Jake slapped his thigh. "You know, you might know her. She said she picked up your card at a Wounded Warriors charity event. That's partly why I'm here. She said you seemed nice, so I asked around about you."

Stony didn't move, didn't change his face, not a muscle. If he did, he was sure it would give him away. His stomach felt like the bottom had fallen out. His heart raced. He wanted to run away, get out of there, leave. This could not be happening.

He swallowed. "Yeah. Summer. I remember her. Nice girl. You should be proud, doctor and all."

"I am. Thanks. Anyway, she's like that, wanting to help people out. She felt sorry for Roman, too. She went to the movies with him once, nothing serious, more like she wanted to comfort him. When they came back from the movies he hugged her at my doorstep and then he kissed her cheek. She gave him a peck, and then he gave me this weird look. It was definitely a threat. But it was more than that. It was obscene." His voice trailed off.

Then he shook his head again and gritted his teeth, determination back in his tone. "It took me a while to realize how stupid I was. He's a fucking lunatic. Who knows what other patients he's murdered? I think he hated Casper because he was an HMO executive and denied claims for Roman's chemo. Now he's after my daughter. If I die, he'll leave her alone. He has to."

Stony couldn't help but think that getting rid of an HMO executive might be good.

But Roman molesting or even killing Summer? Snakes coiled in his chest.

"Did you report Roman to the police?" A dark haze of jungle smoke began to filter over Stony's mind. If he could only get the police to take care of this.

"I didn't have any real proof. Summer said he never made any advances. And she would know. But that look, like he was some kind of sexual deviant. After I suspected him and stopped the chemo, he became cold. I saw him outside my house a few times, like he was stalking me."

Jake sighed. "By the way, how much insulin did you give me?"

"I think about three tenths of a cc each: the long acting 'N' stuff and the short acting 'R' stuff."

"Why do you have insulin? Are you diabetic?"

215

"No, I had a diabetic client once who forgot her insulin, so I decided to carry it with me. Easy to do. I replace it once a month during the warm months, and it lasts even longer when it's cold, like now." Yes, it was cold. But Stony's hands felt wet with the heat and sweat of the jungle. He looked at his palms, expecting to see blood and sweat dripping onto the ground.

Jake frowned, "How did you get insulin?"

Stony shook off the jungle. He had to concentrate. "Come on, Jake. Ever hear of Canada and the 'Internet Pharmacy'? Simple. I figured I might need it if someone forgot their insulin."

"Like me."

"You must be joking."

"Okay. You gave me about thirty three units of each, which is a good start, but not nearly enough for ketoacidosis. I probably need some base. You don't have any sodium bicarbonate, do you?"

Stony wanted to think, plan a way to get out of there as fast as possible. Get to Summer, help her. But then there was Jake, who'd just tried to kill himself to save her. He had to think.

"Stony?" Jake said.

Stony couldn't remember the question. Besides, he didn't want to talk. He raised one eyebrow at Jake.

"Bicarbonate?"

Stony shook his head.

"How about some potassium? Or something for nausea?"

Stony breathed in slow through his nose and out again. "No potassium, but I have some chopped dried dates. I use 'em for cramps. The Internet says they have a lot of potassium. For nausea, I have Dramamine."

Jake scratched his cheek. "Yeah, dates are a great source of potassium. But they also have a fair amount of sugar."

Stony waited.

Jake breathed a heavy sigh. "Okay, it'll have to do. I feel a little better already. Don't want to drop my blood sugar too fast, so dates it is, and give me a Dramamine."

Stony gave him a handful of dates and the pill.

Jake swallowed them down and gulped water. "I need to pee."

He left. Stony held his head in his hands. This was serious shit. They had to return, but that asshole, Rad, was coming for them. How the hell was Stony going to get back fast enough to save Summer? No way this asshole, Roman, was going to stop with Jake. He might already have her.

Jake returned and immediately climbed into his sleeping bag. "Oh, uh, thanks, by the way. Sorry about all this. It seems now like it was a pretty stupid idea. Though there was a lot of shit that led up to it."

Jake's eyes shut, then opened, then fluttered a few times and slowly closed. He sighed and mumbled. "I gotta sleep."

Stony sat Indian-style, looking at Jake. He thought about his feelings for Summer. He thought about Jake and his stupid idea. He thought about that crazy Rad and his wolf. Then he shoved Jake. "Let me get this straight. You're thinking that committing hari-kari will get this guy Roman off your back and save your daughter and end all your worries? Does that say it?"

Jake snored. Stony wanted to shake the shit out of him, but he was bone-tired, too. He got into his sleeping bag.

Death had called Stony once. Death: sweet release from the tedium, the struggle, the sheer boring ineptitudes of life. He'd been there. Stony's return had been hard. Likely, Jake's would be, too.

If what Jake said was true, Roman did not deserve to live.

Stony shook his head. Sonja's soft voice as she bled to death came back to him "Don't even think about killing anyone. Never again. Do you promise?"

"Yes."

Every day he remembered that promise. Every day it kept him alive.

The soft *lupp-lupp* of the wind on the lean-to was deadened by the snow. The flakes fluttered against the fabric: Snow moths—a new fly to try on the cutthroats.

What the hell was he going to do?

Jake's breathing sawed away. He could retrace their steps, but then he would have to kill Rad. Once he got back he might have to kill this Roman guy.

Snakes squirmed in his chest.

CHAPTER 53

Jake dreamed of a saffron afternoon, the sun playing its shadowy fingers through the fluorescent yellow-green aspen onto a grassy meadow in the Rocky Mountains. He was…

A rabbit?

A rabbit surrounded by long, succulent autumn grass, golden-edged green. Content but nervous—good grass, nice warm sun—yet abject fear simmered inside him. He was ready to sprint, flinching at each sound that was not the leaves fluttering in the breeze.

Jake knew, deep in his subconscious, that this was a dream spawned by his recent rereading of *Watership Down*. But it was cool being a rabbit. So why not?

Several young rabbits crowded around him. Though he felt nervous, the kits played, bumping, hopping, and running, as if there could never be hawks or bobcats. He occasionally glanced at the sky and at the nearby woods. If only he could be a little taller, or up on a hill, he could see a bit further.

Then he recognized one of his friends—no, not a friend, his daughter. Summer was a rabbit, too? He wasn't sure how he could tell the difference. They all had the same little noses and eyes. But no, Summer's face was distinctive: upturned nose, pink cheeks, and those azure eyes that pierced him with cool assuredness. And then she spoke.

"Hey, Daddy, I'm going to go up on this rock for a little better view."

Why hadn't he thought of that?

She scampered onto the rock and lay on her side, soaking up the sun and keeping an eye on the distant treeline.

A dark shape ran by Jake. It was another rabbit: big, black, and nasty, one white ear. Its huge back legs kicked out and flipped Jake's daughter off the rock. She landed on her back in the grass. The black rabbit was on her immediately, fangs bared.

A vampire rabbit?

The black rabbit stared at Jake.

Roman.

It was the same venomous look Roman had given to Jake when he'd come to the door with his arm around Summer. That was when Jake knew he had to leave. He had to keep her out of this. If he stayed, Roman would find a way to kill her as well.

The black rabbit sucked on Summer's neck. Her blood dripped a bright crimson against the golden-green grass. Then Summer bared fangs and attacked Roman's neck. They both moaned in pleasure.

Jake quivered and looked up. He needed a hawk. A dark outline drifted over the grass and rocks, heading right toward—

He awoke.

The tent was not completely dark: a faint glow on the roof implied a full moon. The sounds reminded him of the Gulf of Mexico, the luffing sails of his boat catching the wind in small *pops* and *whuffs*. He and Summer had loved to sail with his mom. Mom always insisted on taking the helm. Like that night with Dad when she had—

What had she done exactly? What injection had she given Dad?

The dark shape in the sleeping bag across from him moved. He relaxed. Perhaps Stony could help him combat Roman.

He gripped his fists into tight balls. Why had he involved Stony?

Jake started to unzip the sleeping bag. He would walk away into the snowy night. End it all. He would surely be frozen to death by the time anyone found him. Ketoacidosis would seal his fate. Maybe he'd rifle through Stony's backpack and take the insulin and throw it into the snowy forest. If he died, Summer would live. Roman would not touch her once Jake was gone. Or would he? Would that end it?

Then he remembered her kissing Roman. No peck like he had told Stony but full bore on the lips. In his dream she'd enjoyed their mutual blood-sucking. Did she like Roman? The look in her eye had been like Mom's after she had given Dad that final injection: a woman who knew exactly what she was doing.

He must be hallucinating from the ketosis. He shivered. Stony's sleeping bag was nothing but a dark hulk. Jake could not hear him breathing for the wind, but imagined peaceful breathing, a man without worries, sure of himself—even with all the shit Jake had just piled on his plate. Still, it was unfair to put Stony through this.

Stony's remarks about the senselessness of Jake's plan to euthanize himself had pried a crack into his previously rock-hard resolve. Was there another way? Yet he could not put Carla and Summer through a death like his father's: slow, tortured, agonizing. Even in Jake's patients, a few of their family members, after witnessing the agony of drawn-out cancer death, had been so depressed they attempted suicide. Then again, other families used the last months to solidify weak bonds into memories that healed them spiritually before their loved ones died. And then there were the others, the exceptions to all the rules, the ones who gave him hope with every treatment: the patients who beat the cancer completely.

He sighed and relaxed. The wind died and he dozed.

The high-pitched whir of the tent unzipping started, then stopped.

He opened his eyes and his heart raced.

Someone was coming into their tent.

CHAPTER 54

It took hours, but Roman and Rad had finally arrived. They'd walked the horses and mule down a dry stream bed, a valley between slopes thick with pines. Each step was slippery on the snow-covered rocks. On one slope, there was a clear space between the pines. They stopped there. Roman shivered and kept an eye on Rad, who worked in the snow and cold in shirtsleeves, as if it were a balmy summer's eve. He unloaded a few things, hobbled the animals, and climbed up the slope through the clear space. He took out binoculars and began glassing something on the other side of the hill. It reminded Roman of the nights he had watched Farnsworth. His shiver became relentless. He pulled on a down coat, cinched down the hood, and edged his way up the hill. Rad needed watching a bit closer. Roman wanted to know exactly what they were getting into.

Rad twisted his head at the sound of Roman's approach. "What are you doing up here, Doc? You should be relaxing, having some wine."

"I believe I have a sizable investment in this operation. Get used to me being close."

Rad snickered. "No problem, Doc. Why don't you take a look?"

Roman took the binoculars and peered at a small tent at the base of the hill, in a meadow beside a clump of pines and about a quarter-mile away. There was no movement. The wind ruffled the tent sides. Occasionally, thick waves of snow clouded his view. If Stony and Jake were inside, they must be asleep.

"Have you seen them?"

"No. But who else would be out here? I followed the track. It's them. We wait until dark, and it'll be easy to sneak down to the tent and surprise them. Didn't you say your friend was sick? So they're probably resting up after the long hike. Seven miles in this sloshy stuff would wear anyone out—anyone not riding a horse, that is."

Roman raised his eyebrows. It had worn his ass out, even riding a horse.

Twilight was on them. Another hour. Not long.

A scraping sound made him lower the binoculars. Rad was sharpening a ten-inch bowie knife. He caught Roman's glance with another ugly wink. "A good sharp knife comes in handy out here. Know what I mean, Doc?"

Roman stared at the man. Bullets beat knives.

He went back to watching the tent. "I bet you dulled it this morning on that stupid wolf." He paused and focused on the tent, now only a shadow in the failing light. "You sure you don't want to go down there now? It will be difficult when the sun goes down."

Rad snickered and Roman heard the leathery slip of the knife being sheathed. "No problem tonight, Doc. Full moon."

Roman pulled the binoculars away and looked up. Nothing but gray and blowing snow. "What about the storm?"

He peered at Rad's face. Any minute Rad would apologize and look embarrassed. Rad had made a mistake. The next one would be fatal.

"We'll just have to see about that, won't we?" Rad smiled, showing his gapped teeth.

He was so sure. Yet the snow was coming down like it would last for days.

Rad held out his hand. "How about those binocs, Doc? You leave the guiding to the guide. Grab a chair off the mule and relax. I'd make you some coffee but the smell would travel and…" He winked again.

Roman gave him the binoculars, gritting his teeth. He stuffed his hands in his pockets and grasped the gun in his right. The report would be muffled by the jacket pocket.

But there were still too many loose ends: the weather, and Stony, and, most of all, the secretive, stealthy Rad. Roman turned away and scooted back down the rise. He could not kill Rad, not yet. Another hour.

He drug out a chair and a bottle of water, wishing for a tent. Time passed. Darkness and snow surrounded him in a cold void. Pretty much like the dark side of Pluto.

Time crept. He rose and stomped the feeling back into his feet for the third time. Snow scattered from his hat. The wind died. Snowfall lightened. Silent darkness engulfed him.

He twisted around quickly, envisioning Rad behind him with the long bowie knife poised to slice his carotid artery and spray a pool of warm blood under his dying body. But no Rad materialized.

The full moon assaulted the darkness, at first a twilight glow, then stuttering brightness as blowing wisps of clouds floated over the white orb. Finally the sky cleared and the unobstructed lunar face smiled benevolently on the snowy mountain reverie. There were those who thought the moon's "face" a rabbit, ready to hop away. *How jolly*, thought Roman. The temperature had plummeted with the clearer sky.

Rad motioned for Roman to come up the hill. He probably wanted to gloat. The storm was gone. The full moon shone.

An excellent guide. Roman chuckled. Too bad this was his last trip. At least the walk up the hill would get him warm. He trudged up.

"Got a bit cooler, huh, Doc?" Rad had donned a parka. He gave Roman the binoculars. "You've been waiting for this. Watch."

Rad moved down the snowy embankment as easily as if he were walking on a noonday trail. Roman had to marvel at the man. He was in his element, and Roman was not. He shivered. Perhaps he would wait a bit longer to kill Rad, at least until daylight.

Roman focused the binoculars. Rad stalked slowly. He was at the tent. He reached down and, with a flourish, unzipped it.

He dropped from sight, and the tent collapsed.

CHAPTER 55

Jake's heart stopped at the sound of the zipper.

"Get your shit together. We're movin' out." Stony's low voice came a racing heartbeat after the zipping sound.

"Jesus, Stony! What the hell is going on? I thought you were asleep." Jake sat up, rubbing his eyes, his heart galloping. Stony was rolling up his sleeping bag, his headlamp flashing back and forth across the tent like a firefly on speed.

"The storm let up about an hour ago, and something woke me. I investigated. That damn poacher is following us. I thought his dude client would slow him down. Seemed like a real dandy, with that black ten-gallon strutting a white feather."

Jake grabbed Stony's hand. "Did you say a black hat with a white feather?"

"Yeah. So?"

Jake scooted quickly out of his sleeping bag. "That's my partner, Roman." He put on his fleece top and pants and felt around for his headlamp.

"Your partner? The murderer? What the hell is he doing up here?"

Jake found the headlamp, slipped it on his head, and turned it on.

Stony put out his palm to block the bright light.

"Sorry." Jake turned his head.

Stony continued packing things. "So why would your partner be out here, and how are you so sure it's him?"

Jake put on his boots and began rolling up his sleeping bag. "It must be him. I've seen him wear that hat to a barbeque: white feather, big ten-gallon black hat. Probably wants to get rid of me personally. Make absolutely sure."

Stony secured his sleeping bag to the snow-covered backpack he'd already retrieved. "You think he's here to kill you?"

Jake wished he could see Stony's eyes. He needed to feel Stony's casual assuredness, know that Stony could get him away from Roman. But the blinding headlamps prevented eye contact.

He stuffed his bag in his backpack. "Yeah."

"Why would he come all the way out here, in this storm no less? How the hell does he expect to kill you? I'm here."

"You don't know him. Not sure I do either, really, but I get the impression he'll do anything to get what he wants."

Stony grunted. "That explains Rad. Okay. Turn off your light and stand back. We might need this tent. I had to use the backup, so I'll need to secure this quickly."

Stony rolled and tied the tent while Jake pulled on his jacket and pack.

"Who's Rad?" Jake said.

"His guide. The poacher."

Stony finished, and made one last inspection, the light from the headlamp doing a pixie dance on the snow. He shouldered his pack. "Cinch up your boots around the ankles. It'll help prevent ankle sprains. We'll be moving pretty fast in this snow. If you get tired, holler, but not too loud. We don't want them to hear."

Jake tightened his boots quickly, and they were off, Stony only a vague moonlit shape winding his way through the shadows and trees like he had radar. With only the occasional slip, they were through the trees and out into an open meadow within minutes.

The full moon was a bright disk that made the new snow a glistening iridescence. Stars seemed close enough to grab. The valley was gentle and the view seemed to go forever. Jake paused and took it in. You didn't see that every day.

Stony was moving away, faster. Puffs of steam rose from his head. Jake pushed forward, each step an effort though there was only about eight inches of snow, and it was light as air. The insulin and fluids had helped, but he still felt exhausted. After a few minutes, the faint shadow of game trails were visible where the snow had blown thin. Stony followed the trails, moving even faster.

The full moon's kind face begged conversation. Jake thanked the orb for its benevolence, then did a double-take. The face looked like a rabbit. Summer sucking Roman's blood flashed into his head.

He tripped and almost allowed himself to fall, stay down, forget all this.

Instead, he moved faster. Footprints led over the hill. Stony was gone.

Jake crested the ridge. Stony stood halfway down the other side. He motioned with his hand for Jake to halt. Jake wanted to flop onto the ground and rest, but propped his hands on his knees and panted. Stony listened. He peered left into some distant trees. Stony motioned to Jake to keep moving, but changed directions ninety degrees to the right, following the ridge to the other trees. Once they reached the trees, Stony slowed, allowing Jake to get right on his tail. Stony stopped and whispered, "We'll be going slower now. You okay?"

Jake breathed hard. Without the insulin and fluids, he would have stopped long ago. "Yeah. Slower is good, though."

"Okay. No words, now. We have to be ultra-quiet." He gave Jake a piece of nylon cord and tied the other end to his coat zipper. "If you need something, pull, don't talk."

They walked slower, but for at least half the night, it seemed to Jake. Stony picked every step to avoid any noise. Jake tried to follow his actions, feeling like a hunter instead of prey. At one point, Stony stopped and held both palms out at Jake. His look was clear: Not a sound.

A howl split the silence. Jake's heart thumped. Was that a horse trotting? He strained his ears. Nothing. A deer bounded out of a nearby thicket.

Stony waited for several minutes, then pointed forward and started walking.

The howl broke through again. In all the excitement Jake had forgotten the wolves. Where were they?

Stony slowed and motioned for Jake to get close. The sight ahead made Jake's heart pound faster. A tent was trampled to the snowy ground with black stains on top of the entrance. It was too cold for the stains to be mud.

Stony flipped on his headlamp and the black turned to red. Blood.

CHAPTER 56

Rad couldn't believe his luck. Finally Stony and his client were in his rifle sights, bending over the tent, inspecting Stony's handiwork, no doubt. *You're dead, motherfuckers.*

An hour before, when Rad had unzipped the tent, something had hit him hard in his right buttock. He fell into the tent and cursed at the pain. The tent pitched in on him, and he instinctively whipped the knife backwards, hoping to gash whoever or whatever had struck him. The knife hit something firm. It sounded like wood. What the hell?

He changed the knife to his left hand and felt his butt with his other hand. A wooden stake was stuck firmly into his butt muscles. The stake was attached by what felt like rope to a branch. He pulled hard at the stake and slid it out. Warm blood oozed over his glove and onto his wrist. The branch was still under tension, pushing at his hand. He rolled over and let it go. It swung over his head and crashed into the nearest bush.

He grunted and pulled a handkerchief out of his pocket and stuck it into the hole in his butt cheek.

Stony. Underestimated him. He'd heard the guy had been in Nam. *Fucker'll pay.*

He stood gingerly. Roman was starting down the hill. Rad waved him off and limped slowly up the hill while pressing the wound with one hand.

—

Roman watched Mr. Mountain Man limp up the hill, almost wanting to cheer at the injury, yet concerned that he hadn't found Jake or Stony.

"Hey, Doc. Looks like getting your friend will be a little tougher than we originally planned."

"What happened?"

"Nothing a little bourbon and my first aid kit won't fix. I'll need your help to clean out this wound."

"Wound?" Roman crossed his arms. He was no damned surgeon.

Rad pulled out a silvery flask from his saddle bag, unscrewed the top and took a pull, wiping his mouth with his glove, leaving a black smear on his cheek. "Yeah. Got me a pretty good puncture wound on my butt from a Punji stick surprise set by good old Stony. Motherfucker. It won't kill me. Just need you to clean it out before it gets infected. Then we'll be moving out. They won't be far."

"Punji stick? What's that?"

Rad held out a headlamp and the first aid kit. "You know, in Vietnam. Sharpened sticks in a pit. When you fell in… You get the drift."

"You fell into a pit of sharpened sticks?"

"Never mind, Doc. Put this light on and clean out the wound as best you can. Pour a little whiskey in it and fix it up. You know what to do. Right?"

Roman revised his first opinion: this wound might be his chance to get rid of Rad without getting any blame.

"Sure." He grabbed the light and first aid kit from Rad. "Bend over. You might want some more of that bourbon. This is going to hurt."

Rad took another pull from the flask, gave it to Roman, and pulled his pants down as he bent over. Roman turned on the light and almost gagged at Rad's fur-covered butt. The thumb-sized hole oozed dark blood. Roman dabbed away the blood with a gauze pad and pushed the first aid kit's meager forceps almost two inches into the ragged puncture. He pulled out a piece of shredded, blood-soaked fabric, then poured the liquor inside the cavity.

"Shit." Rad hissed through his teeth. The wound oozed dark red, and Rad put his hand back for the flask. While Rad was preoccupied with drinking, Roman took a piece of clean gauze, quickly wiped it on his muddy boot, and stuck it into the puncture. A little tetanus and pseudomonas would give Rad a new perspective on life. And death.

He placed another piece of clean gauze on top and taped it down, knowing the puncture should be left open to drain, hoping Rad was in too much pain to notice.

"There you go. Sitting on the saddle should put a bit of pressure and keep it from bleeding. Might help the pain, too."

Somehow the pain seemed to strengthen Rad. He pulled up his pants and stood as easily and solidly as ever. "You think that's pain? *Sheeat*, Doc. Try living with my pa for fourteen years."

He rummaged in the first aid kit, retrieving a bottle of pills. He unscrewed the top and poured four white tablets onto his gloved palm and popped them into his mouth, chasing them with bourbon. He screwed the top on the pills and the bourbon and packed both in the first aid kit in the saddlebag.

"Mount up. Stony and your *friend* are getting away. I'll do Stony for free, now."

Rad un-hobbled the animals, and the two men mounted. A mournful howl broke the silence. Rad tipped his head back and howled, too. Then he yelled, "You want a piece of me? Come and get it. I could use some more skins."

A relatively warm breeze feathered Roman's face. The wind pushed at their backs, and Rad led them down the hill. They rode past the collapsed tent, following the path of Stony—the guide who had tricked the panther-in-a-bear suit. Roman felt more confident by the moment that he could do the same with Rad.

But he began to wonder more about Stony.

CHAPTER 57

They rode for fifteen minutes and were deep in a pocket of woods when Rad halted. He got off his horse and hobbled it. "Whatchu waiting for, Doc? Get down offa there and hobble your horse. You seen me do it, so get at it. I got some walking to do. Can't do everything."

The moonlight and tree shadows played over Rad like an eerie dream. Roman observed every detail, hoping to find the soft underbelly in Rad's bear-like toughness. Rad patted his shirt pocket, took out the bottle of pills, and popped a few in his mouth. From the saddlebag, he retrieved the flask and a water bottle. He slid the flask in his inside chest pocket, sloshed the pills down with the water, then squinted at Roman as if wondering why he was being inspected. Roman slid his gaze sideways but still saw Rad stick the pill bottle and water into his coat pockets with one hand and unsnap his scoped rifle with the other.

Roman dismounted, groaning with exaggerated relief, hoping to disguise his study of Rad. The groan had some truth to it; he was glad to get off the horse. "What are you doing?"

"For a doctor, you're a bit dense. I'm doubling back. Stony thinks I'm some stupid bull coming at him full tilt. Well, just because he's been to Nam don't give him no market on sneakiness. I been hunting and trapping a long time, and he ain't the only bobcat I've chased. Hobble the horse. Now!"

No one talked to Roman like that. He turned aside as if to hobble the horse and put one hand in his pocket for the gun.

A sharp prick under his chin was accompanied by Rad's foul breath. Roman froze.

Rad held a long blade under Roman's chin, his whispers tickling Roman's ear. "Whatchu got in the pocket, Doc? Take your hand outta there."

Roman gripped the gun. He could do it now, put a bullet in that black, rat heart.

A sharp pain under his chin changed his mind, and he jerked his hand out of his pocket. "Jesus, Rad." He tried to sound afraid. Blood trickled down his neck. He wiped it with his hand.

Rad reached around Roman and retrieved the gun out of his pocket.

He backed off from Roman, chuckling. "Think you could kill me with this little pee-shooter?" He held out the .22 pistol in his palm like it was a baby's toy.

He glared at Roman. "Next time I'll gut you."

"I was merely checking the safety so it wouldn't go off when I hobbled the horse. It's for protection, for Christ's sake. You're going to leave me here and go ambush Stony, right? So I have to have something. You heard the wolves. You've got one of them on the mule and your blood is all over that tent back there. They're probably following us. I need protection." Roman had to make it sound pleading, though he wanted to stick the barrel of the gun in Rad's mouth and pull the trigger—click, click, click—pea shooter right to the brain.

Rad's dark-orbed stare was like an executioner weighing which punishment to mete out. He grabbed his rifle, which was leaning on a tree. "I'm doing Stony and your friend for free. But this?" He held the .22 in the air. "This'll cost you." He smiled. "Over and over." With a flick of his wrist he tossed the handgun into the darkness.

Then Rad melted into the forest and was gone. Not a sound.

Roman waited until he was sure Rad was gone, then rummaged through the mule's load. Rad had a .45 pistol somewhere; Roman was sure he hadn't carried it with him.

He found the collapsible shovel and unfolded it, screwing down the lock bolt. He swung it through the air. A good alternative for now. Cut off Rad's tiny head.

Rad moved away, quickly and quietly, studying his options. Stony had probably doubled back, though likely he had come in a circle, so if Rad hurried, he would be at the tent before Stony. There he would wait. His father had taught him many things about hunting, but patience was the most important. He could be invisible and wait for hours, if necessary.

After five minutes of trudging through the snow, his wound throbbed like a bad tooth. He stopped, yanked his pants down, ripped the tape off his ass, and pulled the gauze out, sucking air through his teeth in pain. He threw the gauze into the darkness, took out the flask and poured whiskey into the wound. It burned the wound but cooled his leg as it ran into his pants. After gritting his teeth for another minute, he pulled up his pants and walked on. The golf ball of pain still bored into his butt, but less than it had. He touched the pill bottle in his pocket but held off taking more. Those antibiotics had nauseated him once when he took too many.

It had taken him almost an hour of backtracking, walking through clumps of trees and running through clearings, to get back to the tent. About two hundred yards away, he spotted his prey. Two men were stooped over the tent.

He sighted in on them with his rifle scope. *You're dead motherfuckers.*

To steady his aim, he dropped to one knee. Pain seared his ass cheek. He stifled a scream and jammed the rifle butt into the ground to keep from falling on his face. It was going to be no good, trying to shoot like that. A sturdy branch on a tree a few yards to his left presented another option.

Quickly he stood and walked to the tree, uncovered the scope, steadied the rifle on the branch, and sighted in on the man walking away with the large backpack. Probably Stony. The man turned around and a light shown on his face. Definitely Stony. *Thanks for the light, motherfucker.*

Rad aimed at the nose, took a deep breath, let it out slow. He squeezed the trigger.

CHAPTER 58

Stony peered into the tent, clicked off his headlight, grunted, and began walking away. "That ought to slow you down, Rad."

"What do you mean?" Jake said. "Whose tent is this? Are you sure there's no one hurt inside?"

"No one's there. It's my tent. A decoy. And it worked."

Jake turned on his headlamp and surveyed the scene again. Blood. The wolves would smell it and come.

He strode after Stony, his headlight illuminating Stony's backpack. Stony turned around. The light lit Stony's face.

Then he was gone.

A rifle shot cracked the silence.

Jake ran for Stony, already blaming himself.

His headlight danced in front of him.

"Shit!" He turned off the light and stumbled forward in sudden darkness. He put his hands out, as if he were a blind man. Outlines came into view as his night vision came back. He got to where Stony should have been.

Nothing. Only a body-sized imprint in the snow.

"Jake." Stony's voice hissed from about twenty feet to his right. "Over here. Get down."

Even though it was a whisper, Jake heard it loud and clear and was on his hands and knees crawling as fast as he could through the snow.

Stony hid behind a small clump of bushes, his pack off. He held his hand to his temple. There was a black smear on his forehead. Jake moved closer.

Stony whispered, "Hold pressure here while I get out some tape."

"What the… That's blood. You're shot in the head—Jesus—Must be Roman, or maybe his guide, what's his name—Rad?" Jake's hoarse whisper piled frantic words together. He stared at Stony but didn't move.

Stony took a wad of fresh snow and put it on his forehead wound. He grabbed Jake's wet, gloved hand and put it on top of the snow bandage. "Pressure. Here. Now, or we're dead."

Jake pushed on the spot. Stony reached into an outer pocket of his backpack and pulled out a wide roll of dark tape.

"Okay, when I say let go, do it." He taped the first bit to the back of his head, then came around. As he was about to go over Jake's hand, he said, "Let go."

Jake pulled his hand away, and Stony wound the tape around his head like a turban, getting a piece of watch cap and forehead in each wrap. The soft ratcheting sound of the tape being stripped was unmistakable.

"You're duct-taping your head?"

Stony tore off the tape, stowed it, and pulled on his pack. "It works. Let's go"

They scrambled up the hill, expecting another shot. On the other side of the hill, down in a stream bed, Stony paused and looked behind them.

Jake grabbed a bottle of water and sucked down half of it.

Stony seemed to be straining to hear. The gurgle of the stream was loud. Stony shook his head, turned, and strode into the trees. Jake followed. It didn't take long for him to finish the water.

They walked further. After a half-hour of struggling to keep up, Jake croaked, "Stony!"

Stony slowed and turned around.

"I need food and insulin, and a couple bottles of water."

Stony peeled off his backpack, then retrieved and handed over a granola bar and two bottles of water to Jake. "How much of the 'R' and 'N'?"

Jake clumsily tried to open the granola bar, but after two attempts took off his gloves and tore it open. "Twenty units—that's two big marks on each needle."

Stony had the insulin ready in the minute it took Jake to eat half a granola bar and drain most of the bottle.

Jake lifted his jacket and shirt and injected the insulin under the skin of his abdomen. Stony disposed of the used needle and syringe in an empty water bottle, gingerly placed the bottle into an outer pocket of his backpack and shouldered the pack. "You'll have to eat and drink while we walk."

"What about your head? We should probably dress it up right. You've got a first-aid kit, right?"

Stony walked away.

Jake finished the granola bar and stuffed the empty package in his pocket. He drained the rest of the first bottle, stuck it in the top of his shirt, and jogged after Stony's disappearing form, up and down and through more trees. Soon they were on a steady downhill slip and stumble with a quick hand out on a tree or rock to keep from falling.

After what seemed like hours of stumbling and trudging through no visible path and two episodes of prolonged slipping ending in Jake falling against Stony, they stopped. Stony steadied Jake and slipped off his pack again, taking out a bottle of water and the GPS. He studied the small, lighted screen between swigs.

Jake let his pack fall to the ground. He took out and drank the entire second bottle. "You got any more water?"

"One more. But it's another hour until we get to a stream, so take it easy." He took the empty bottles, put them in his pack, and handed Jake the last bottle of water.

They put their packs on and walked down the hill.

Jake hoped Stony was right about the hour.

This was not exactly the way he'd planned it, and he could feel that inner kernel going fast.

CHAPTER 59

Rad started squeezing the trigger. His foot slipped on a patch of ice and the rifle fired. He caught himself with the bad leg, and his ass wound screamed. So did he. "Shit!" Though it hurt like a bitch, he mostly swore at his luck. He sighted in where Stony had been.

Nothing.

A puff of cloth *had* come off the side of Stony's cap, hadn't it? Yet there was no body on the ground. That meant Stony was wounded, not dead.

Stony was not someone to play with. Like hunting a mountain lion, if you didn't see the carcass, you needed to make sure you had all your dogs and help before you chased it. A wounded cat was dangerous. Stony was worse. And there was his client, Roman's friend. He might have a gun, too. Like fucking Roman.

Rad walked back toward Roman. It felt right to kill the good doctor and walk away. But then there were all those future earnings. The primitive cabin in the Yukon wilderness was cheap. Hunting and fishing were wonderful. But a man had to eat something besides game and fish, had to have certain *accoutrements*, had to travel occasionally, enjoy life. Inuit women were not cheap. But all his new lifestyle would require was collecting payments from special clients. Like Roman.

Another day and he would have Stony. The question was: should they chase him through the night?

He paused in a clump of pine trees, leaned up against one, and gently probed his wound with a finger. It was a more painful than it should be. Had Stony coated the stake with poison?

He pulled his pants down again and washed out the wound with water before finishing with the whiskey. A gust blew through the trees, chilling him as he pulled up his partly wetted pants, though the breeze seemed warm on his face.

A gauzy haze of clouds would soon darken the moonlight. Pulling out the GPS, he turned it on and waited for the lighted screen to finish acquiring the satellites. He had an idea where Stony was going, but he wanted to make sure.

After confirming the direction, he switched it off and took two more antibiotics. Hopefully they would do for whatever Stony had placed on the Punji stick.

He walked slower, needing extra time to figure a plan before he got to Roman.

An elk's bugle pierced the quiet night, probably two miles away. Too bad they couldn't get that trophy elk…

What was he thinking? Roman had no desire to hunt anything but humans.

In a while he smelled the mule. He crept closer and observed Roman.

Roman sat on one of the chairs he'd unpacked. He sipped water and chewed on jerky. One hand gripped the shovel, held low and out of sight. There had been only one shot. Rad must have failed again. The imbecile.

Rad walked in. The animals stayed quiet.

"You didn't get them, did you?" Roman kept his words level and calm. He tightened his grip on the shovel.

Rad glared at Roman. "I hit Stony, but a wounded cat is nothing to play with. There's only a few hours until daylight. We can move faster then and avoid any further surprises from Stony. I know where they're going. We'll rest a few hours, then catch 'em."

"Probably missed because of the whiskey and those pain pills." Roman relaxed his grip on the shovel. He could not kill Rad now. He needed him for tracking.

Rad's laugh was low and gave Roman chills. "I drink more bourbon before noon most days. It was just…bad luck."

Rad walked to the mule and said out of the corner of his mouth, not looking at Roman, "And, I don't take no pain pills. These are antibiotics."

Roman eased the shovel onto the ground and scowled. Antibiotics. Damn. Plan A was fading. Plan B, where he shot Rad or chopped off his head with a shovel—not going to happen. Plan C—a rock to the head—more promising. But when?

"Okay," he said. "I could do with sleep. Do you want me to change the dressing on that nasty wound?"

Rad eyed him suspiciously, "No. It feels better without the dressing." He smiled at Roman, a false note in his words. "But thanks for your concern, Doc. I'll put up the small tent, and we can get us a few hours' sleep."

Roman watched as the bear in a man suit quickly set up a three-man tent. They took the sleeping bags inside. Rad heated water and poured it in a bag with freeze-dried stew. After it had sat for the allotted seven minutes, they stood outside the tent and ate quietly.

As Rad finished, two howls broke the night, one at first, the other joining halfway through.

Roman frowned. "Aren't you afraid the wolves will come after us, from the smell of the stew?"

Rad winced when he leaned on the bad side to slip out his knife and .45.

Roman eyed the gun, trying to be nonchalant but watching it closely.

"No," Rad said. "They won't come around the smell of dead wolf."

"Oh. I thought…" But he let it die when Rad started to smirk. "Never mind."

They undressed and slid into the sleeping bags. Rad put the .45 and knife on the other side of his sleeping bag. He was snoring in minutes.

Roman began unzipping his bag to get out and crush Rad's puny skull. Rad snorted and turned over, facing Roman. Were his eyes gleaming? Roman stopped pulling on the zipper. They were so close to getting Jake. Maybe he should wait. He planned the next day like a fast-forward chess match, over and over. Rad could easily best Roman tonight. But tomorrow? Not a chance.

Roman dozed.

A gunshot woke him.

Rad was out of his sleeping bag and had his gun and knife. "Fucking Stony. I'll get you for this hip."

CHAPTER 60

Jake's legs felt like rubber; his knees burned with each step. He'd been following Stony down a steep trail for at least an hour. A warm breeze blew across the back of his neck. He snuck sips of water, pausing at each switchback, then hustling on, following Stony's dark outline as quickly as he could without slipping.

Jake was falling further behind at each step. The next time they stopped, he'd ask Stony to get more water. When Stony left, Jake would do it. To live, he had to.

He would find Stony's gun and go back for Roman.

A screech to rival any ghoul echoed on the wind. Jake jerked his head around, peered into the moonlit haze, and stumbled against a tree. He stopped. The screech repeated, now recognizable as an elk's bugle. Jake put his hands on his knees, breathed in hard a few times, and trudged on, squinting at Stony's shadowy form while concentrating on each step.

Two owls hooted, one low-pitched, one high.

Jake murmured, "Damn menagerie out here."

Stony stopped and looked back. His face was half-lit by the moon; a vertical shadow from a pine tree hid the other half. The lighted half was so calm that Jake immediately felt better, yet he wondered about the other half. Could this be the drama and comedy of real life? They would escape assassins only to be eaten by wolves. He imagined the dark side of Stony's face in a huge grin.

Stony shrugged off his backpack, pulled out the gun, then put the pack back on. He motioned for Jake to get behind him. What the hell was going on now? The breeze did not seem so warm any more, the sweat on his neck icy.

Once behind Stony, he peeked over his shoulder. A veil of clouds dimmed the moonlight. The foggy gloom reminded him of the English moor from *An American Werewolf in London*. Statue-still, neither man breathed, but Jake's heartbeat reverberated in his chest so loud and fast he could hear nothing else. His heart was pounding a drum message to the wolves: *come and get it*.

He realized he'd been holding his breath, and let it out.

Up the hill, a shadow flicked across the path.

Stony raised the gun.

Jake's foot slipped, and he caught himself. "Sorry."

The shadow floated across the path again, and the ghostly outline of a bull elk bounded up the hill, his hooves clattering against rocks.

Stony lowered his gun, and Jake relaxed.

Stony put a hand on Jake's shoulder and whispered, "Kinda spooky, huh? Maybe I'll change that dressing on my head, now. It's starting to throb."

Up the hill but to the right of the elk, branches snapped. It seemed deeper in the woods, further away than the elk; Jake wasn't sure. The wind made it hard to judge.

Stony froze and peered into the darkness.

A huffing sound and a cry like a creaking swing in a playground floated down to them. A dark mound crawled up a distant pine tree, the sound of claws ripping and pulling at the bark.

A larger hulk emerged from the shadows by the tree.

"Run." Stony said. "It's a momma and her cub."

Jake was already moving, the outline of a bear spurring an immediate response.

They ran, slipped, slid and crashed down the path. Jake prayed he would not fall, but he did; a sharp stump stabbed him just above his knee, and he cried out.

The bear bellowed from what seemed like mere yards behind them.

Stony grabbed Jake's arm and pulled him up, glancing behind them quickly. He pushed Jake forward and ran right beside him, holding his arm firmly as Jake limped quickly down the path.

Jake was tired, so tired. And the pain in his knee? *Must stop.* Let it be over. He would be dead and Stony could go on without him. That would be okay. He slowed.

Huffs and crashes came closer. The jaws would be first, probably take a bite out of his back or thigh. Or head. A branch slapped his face. He limped faster.

The sound of rushing water filtered from below.

They came to a chasm, a deep drop-off to a stream. There was no escaping the bear. It was inevitable—death by mauling.

Stony pulled his arm and they clambered down onto a narrow path beside the drop-off, then almost ran.

Jake craned his head around to locate the bear, fully expecting a huge paw to slap his cheek, tear out half his face. Darkness and noisy crashes filled the shadows.

He stumbled against Stony, and they fell and rolled down the path.

The bear was coming and they were flat on their backs. *Shit!*

Stony stood, yanked Jake to his feet, and they stumbled down the path again. The air felt warmer. Jake sweated rivulets under his wool cap. He pulled off the cap and stuffed it in his coat pocket.

The crashing came closer. Jake glanced up. The looming shadow rumbled down at them.

Stony pointed and pushed Jake toward a narrow, suspended footbridge that hung across the canyon, the closest part visible in the moonlight, the rest disappearing into a void.

Jake resisted for an instant, until he heard the heavy plodding behind him.

Even in broad daylight, Jake would have tested each plank going across the bridge. Now he wanted to ease forward slowly, pulling on the rope and smacking each board with his foot. But Stony pushed him forward, reaffirming that the bear would be worse than the fall. So Jake ran and limped forward, hoping that none of the planks were rotten.

Stony prodded him from behind until they were halfway across—then Jake could feel the distance between them growing. He wanted to stop and see what was happening behind him, but he moved his feet forward, gripping the thick rope railing like a stroke victim starting to walk again, sure each step might dance into thin air. If the boards gave out, he prayed he had the strength to hold on with his hands.

The mother bear huffed and growled from behind. The bridge began swaying from side to side. Was she on the bridge? He wanted to go back and help Stony, but instead Jake moved his feet faster.

A gunshot sounded close behind him and he lurched ahead, almost reaching the other side.

Then he tripped and fell forward, blindly flailing with his hands out into blackness.

CHAPTER 61

Despite limping and hobbling and struggling to get into his clothes while holding his gun, Rad was out of the tent in minutes.

Roman slid out of his bag and sat on the cot.

Rad poked his scowling face into the tent and growled an order, "Get your ass movin.'"

"Why do you think it's Stony? Probably another stupid hunter."

Rad lurched into the tent so fast Roman flinched. "That's not a rifle, you idiot. Stony has a .45, and that's what it sounded like."

Roman brought his quickened pulse down. That was the last time Rad would ever call him an idiot. He stood and put his hands up, palms out. "Okay, okay. I'll be ready in a minute. Any chance of getting coffee?"

Rad clenched his fists, shook his head, and left.

Roman got dressed. Once outside, he stayed out of Rad's way. Rad peered at the GPS several times between packing items, then finally pocketed it and was a blur of motion, grunting and growling every time he bent down.

The eastern sky glowed, though stars still twinkled in the west. Roman's watch read 6:08. A scant, warm breeze rustled the trees.

He grabbed a food bar from his saddle pack and mounted the horse, thinking about how he would end his association with Rad—permanently.

Rad limped over to Roman and held out a bottle of water. "No coffee, but here's some water. It'll be a few hours before we catch up to them. We're fifteen miles from the nearest decent road. I'd say Stony and your *friend* will meet their maker long before they'll see the dust of that road."

Roman took the water. "Thank you, Rad. Oh, by the way, there will be a nice bonus in this for you if we get it done today." He hoped his voice was not too syrupy.

Rad's face brightened. "Oh, it'll be done today. Count on it." He squinted at the sky. "Besides, there's another storm coming, and this one's a doozy." He adjusted his holstered gun and mounted his horse.

Twenty minutes later, they stopped. Rad leaned forward in the saddle and uttered a contented, "*Mmmm.*"

"Find something?"

"Oh yeah. I *did* wing him." Rad pointed at the ground. "He's bleedin'."

The horses ambled forward, and Roman peered at the inky, red blots in the melting snow. Stony was hit. *How wonderful.* But Rad had been lucky. "If Stony wouldn't have fired his gun when he did, you'd still be sleeping. The trail would be cold and muddy and—"

"You know quite a bit about trackin', do you, Doc?" Rad's gaze had entered the *Twilight Zone.*

"Not really. But it doesn't take a wizard to know that everything here would be a sloppy mess in another hour."

"That's true, Doc. But it's also true that I can track a mountain lion three days after a rain. Course, you wouldn't know that, 'cause you've never seen a mountain lion track, like those over there right next to the deer prints. Mountain lion love deer, but humans are a close second, once they get a taste." Rad watched Roman like a cat watching a mouse trying to get out of a maze. The previous hatred was gone. Now his gaze was more curious and satisfied, like he wondered how long it would take for the mouse to wear out or freeze in fear. No matter what, he didn't need to do anything but wait, and he would eventually have a meal.

Roman pursed his lips. He flung his arms out and turned from side to side, like a conductor of an orchestra. "Okay. I'm sorry. But I still don't get it. Why the hell would Stony fire a shot? Surely he would know we'd hear it."

"Dunno. Maybe he thinks we gave up. Maybe he had a good reason. Maybe we're not the only ones tracking his blood. I don't see no dead deer, and that sure as shit was a big mountain lion."

Roman grimaced at the back of Rad's head. He was definitely done with this wilderness experience. He yearned for the sterile walls of the ICU.

Rad hipped around on his saddle and smiled. Roman calmed his face. "Don't worry, Doc." He grabbed his gun in the holster. "I got you covered."

Roman glared at him.

Rad shrugged and turned around. The horses moseyed; their hoof sounds muffled to a squishing in the melting snow.

Rad pointed up at a mound in a pine tree. "Here's a tracking lesson for you, Doc. What do you think that is?"

Roman squinted through the shadows. Near the top of one pine tree was a dark, shaggy tumor ballooning out part of the trunk. "Some kind of fungus or mushroom."

"Porcupine. No one ever thinks to look up there. But they are all over the place."

As Roman watched, a small black face peered out from the ball of quills.

Rad twisted around again and eyed Roman. "Just doing my guide thing, Doc." He chuckled and faced forward, humming and swaying lazily from side to side, occasionally bending far forward, inspecting the ground and grunting recognition at some sign.

Roman sneered at the black thimble of brains. A rock to the side of the head would do nicely. Not too big. It would have to appear like an accident. He shivered and pulled his collar up around his neck.

Soon he was leaning back in the saddle, the path having taken a steep downhill slope. His crotch ached from rubbing against the saddle horn, but the sun warmed his back, a pleasant feeling that balanced out the pain. Almost. They were moving faster now that Rad had found the trail. He said that Stony and Jake had been running when they had gone down the hill.

Rad stopped his horse, slipped off it, and knelt on the ground, all in one quick movement. He frowned and stood up quickly, wincing and grabbing his hip. His gaze ratcheted slowly around in a complete three-sixty.

"Did you lose them?" Roman said.

"No." He continued scanning the area.

Roman wanted to slap him to get an answer.

Rad squinted into the gray morning.

The sweat on Roman's back trickled cold over prickling hairs. Something told him to not make noise. He whispered, "What is it?"

"Bear."

CHAPTER 62

Jake landed on sodden, flat ground and twisted around to see his fate. *What the hell?*

Stony held his gun in one hand, the elbow crooked around the rope railing. In the other hand, he held a lit flare high in the air, its orange sparks flying toward the bear. The bear was big. She bounced on her front paws but remained on the edge of the bridge, shaking her head and glaring at Stony. Stony swayed the bridge back and forth.

The bear huffed and bawled. Stony sprayed sparks in an arc. The bridge swayed. The bear studied Stony with inky orbs, the orange reflection of the flare like two pupils from hell, nightmare eyes Jake never wanted to see again. Then she huffed once, turned around, and trundled back up the hill, her rear haunches swaying easily, as if she had all the time in the world.

Stony pointed the flare at the spot where the bear had disappeared. The ropes and planks creaked. The bear was gone, but still Stony swung the bridge. The sparks died. Stony threw the flare at the spot where the bear had been. He waited and watched. The swaying dampened. He tucked the gun in his pants and turned toward Jake. His hands gripped the side ropes and he walked forward.

Jake slipped his pack off and fell backward onto the wet earth. He gazed through the trees at the zenith and sighed. Suicide would have been so much easier.

The dark shadows of trees swayed, almost like they had taken on the rhythm of the bridge. Back and forth, back and forth. Mesmerizing. It reminded him of rocking Summer when she was small, and how her crying had always abated when she gazed into his eyes.

One edge of the sky brightened. The trees became more visible. Even without the sun, he was warmed in a blanket of relief, though he ached for daylight and sunshine. He might never walk in the dark again.

Tomorrow had come and he was still alive. It felt good.

"Not bad for a couple of old guys, huh?" Stony's low voice comforted him.

Jake opened his eyes and lifted his head up, chin on chest, frowning at Stony. "You shot the bear?"

Stony smiled broadly. "Nah, just tried to scare her. Didn't make her budge. Then I remembered the flare. Usually black bears aren't so aggressive. She was protecting her cub so it took a little extra. Don't think she'll be back."

He held out his hand to help Jake sit up. "How's the leg?"

The pain had lessened, though when Stony pulled him, he winced at a sharp stab in his lower thigh. "Still there. Maybe we should take a look, now that we're not running for our lives."

The injury was merely a bad thigh bruise, but it stabbed him when he walked. Stony fashioned a walking stick out of a pine limb. Jake peed again, a never-ending problem as long as his sugar stayed high. He sucked down water and chomped on a Granola bar, getting ready for the insulin. He couldn't afford a low blood sugar; something pleasurably in between would be nice. He yearned for the glucometer he had purposefully left in his car.

"How much 'R' and 'N' this time?" Stony pulled the insulin bottles out.

"Probably ten of each."

After Jake injected the insulin, he peered at Stony. "I'm feeling better. What do you think about going back and taking care of Roman instead of running?"

Stony eyed Jake and puckered in one side of his mouth, like a lemon was stuck there.

"I know. Guess I'm desperate. I'm afraid once we get back he'll keep coming."

"You sure you don't have any evidence against him?"

"Nothing."

Stony shook his head. "No way we're going after him. You're about as strong as a newborn puppy. Besides, Rad's pissed. He won't miss next time."

He pulled a bottle out of his pack. "I know your leg hurts, but we have to move. Take some ibuprofen. Maybe the walking will loosen your leg. We've got several hours ahead of us."

"I'll be okay. It's only a bruise. Let me change that head dressing."

Stony gave him no argument. Jake carefully cleaned the long bullet graze and taped down clean gauze. Then they walked.

Soon the pain lessened, and Jake only used the stick at slippery spots.

Dim light and a glow from the eastern sky illuminated the path down the mountain. A few remaining songbirds chirped and sang and flitted in the trees. They gave Jake hope that life still existed. But it didn't take long until his legs and feet began to ache. Two indigo birds with peaked heads, what Stony said were mountain jays, followed them down the mountain, hunting for any remnants of food, their raucous caw a warning. Jake wondered if the warning was about Jake and Stony or something else.

Time was suspended in concentration: plod here, step there, slip and pain; plod here, step there, slip and pain. How long? Two, three, four hours—maybe more. It didn't matter. He couldn't focus any more.

"Stony." His voice cracked, so quiet he barely heard it himself.

Stony kept walking.

Jake stumbled forward. He forced a deep breath in and pushed it out, "Stony!" A croak barely louder than the bubbling stream.

Stony did not stop. He plodded like a robot: step, step, step, step. Oblivious. Moving ever further away.

Jake shouted again. A louder croak. And again.

Stony slowed and turned slightly. "Yeah."

Jake's voice sounded like he was gargling pebbles from the stream. "Need to stop. Need water."

"Okay." Stony waited for Jake to get closer. "Grab it out of my pack."

Jake slapped Stony's backpack like a drunk slapping the shoulder of an old friend. "All done. No more."

Stony's answer was matter of fact. "Okay." He un-shouldered his pack, grabbed the filter and disappeared into the forest.

A tiny voice in Jake's head said, *Don't let him go.*

CHAPTER 63

Jake brushed the thought aside. They were safe here and Stony would be back in a few minutes. Though he had that inkling of danger, there was a snow-covered flat rock waiting beside him, a great place to lie down. *Oh, yeah.* A short nap would be great. No. If he slept now he would not get up. . He sat on the rock, more like plopped onto it, his legs were so weak. Who cared if the layer of snow on top made him wet?

He blinked hard and shook his head quickly, trying to jolt himself awake. What if Stony didn't come back? Right. Stony not come back. The real question was: could he stand up again? Maybe after some water and a snack. He probably needed more insulin. The weight of his small backpack pulled. He let it fall off his shoulders onto the rock. *Oh, Jesus, that felt good.* How the hell could Stony carry that fifty-pound pack? It was probably only forty pounds now, but still.

Some weights were heavier than others. The day after Summer's medical-school graduation, she'd locked her arm in his and taken him for a long walk. Her words echoed as fresh as the snow. "Daddy, don't worry. I understand. You were trying to help someone. Important things must be done by those who can do them."

"I should have been there for your graduation. Instead I was with some stranger who was going to die anyhow."

He'd almost told her about the real reason he had missed her graduation: Mr. Casper and how Roman could be poisoning him. Would she have believed him, helped him?

Instead he said, "I want you to know how proud we are of you. You stayed the course despite hard times and disagreements with me and your mom and our plan for your life and—"

"Daddy," she interrupted, "hear me out on this. I have to experience life. I have to. That's the way I am. I'm not someone who can read about it or be told a story and be happy. I have to stare it in the face, pinch its cheeks, and, if necessary, smell its ugly breath to decide for myself if it's something I can deal with or not, and then move on."

Of course. That described her perfectly. Though tragedy had seemed to follow her, with friends committing suicide and teachers disappearing, she'd held her head high and moved on. Even after she left home in high school and fallen into a rabbit hole for months, she'd eventually found herself. Her grandmother helped, that was true. How great was that? Summer's and Jake's mom, both steel magnolias. Samurai steel. The end result: Summer a brilliant doctor.

His eyes watered. Though it was not something he had consciously hoped for, he realized now—at this unlikely moment, in the freezing cold, parched with thirst, after nearly killing himself—that his daughter, his joy of life, had given him something more than herself. She had emulated him enough to follow in his footsteps. Granted, she had at first wanted to be an ophthalmologist and now seemed settled on radiology, specialties a bit more detached from patients than an internist or oncologist would be. Not that he was so great. God, after tonight he would see patients in a whole new light. He would see *everything* in a whole new light. He would stop the pushing, the constant clawing to be the best, relax enough to watch her grow.

He thought for a minute about the times he'd missed. A tear dripped down his cheek, and he brushed it off. He would convince her, *must* convince her to stop pushing, though he doubted he could teach her much in that regard. She seemed to already know.

Perhaps soon she would find someone and have her own family. The word struck him—family. That's what he had. His wife, his daughter, his wife's family, his patients, his employees—they all cared about him, and he cared about them, too. And he realized that, for the first time in months, he wanted to live. He had mouthed those words to Stony hours ago. But it had felt more like something he should say, not something he really believed. Right now, though, it overflowed and brought a fresh kernel of energy. Life was his for the living, and by God he would live it to the fullest. What he had left.

The fatigue was gone. The eastern light spilled brightness. He breathed like a newborn gasping its first breath. He was *alive*. He could love, cry, laugh, giggle, spit, curse, and be there for her. Roman would *not* take this from him. Even if he only had a few months, he would live them. Truly live.

Stony returned with a canvas satchel full of water bottles.

"Here you go, Jake. Drink a couple of these and have a granola bar. Let's take a break. We've been walking pretty hard and put enough distance between us and Rad."

"Thank you, Stony, for everything."

Stony's eyes faded west.

"Stony, please look at me."

He glanced back. "Yeah."

"I know you think this is all in a day's work. But what you did was extraordinary. You took me from the brink of depression and suicide to once again believing in myself and wanting to love and live again. I'll never forget it. You saved my life. If you ever need anything, anything at all, you let me know. Okay?"

"Sure." The tenor of his voice, the sideways glance of his eyes, and the clenching of his jaw told Jake that Stony would never ask. It was not in his makeup. He did not live in a tit for tat world. That's just the way it was. But one day Jake would help him, as sure as he was alive today. That was just the way it would be.

"Drink up," Stony said. "We don't want to rest too long. As it is, we probably won't make the road until after dark."

After strapping his pack on, Jake walked forward, his legs lighter. Soon it felt like he was in a forced tap dance through mud down the mountain, constantly catching his balance and slapping his feet. But after an hour, he actually felt better. After another, even pretty good.

The sun warmed them and lit up the brown, beetle-killed trees they walked beneath. The mud dried and they made better time. Stony even revised his prediction—they would get to the road before dark.

CHAPTER 64

Roman squinted at the ground from up on his horse, trying to discern prints. A bear? What else could go wrong? He wanted to grab Rad's .45, kill Rad, kill the damn bear, kill the fucking horses and mule, and call in a helicopter to pick him up. It would feel good, but not as good as shooting Jake in the head. No, he wouldn't shoot Jake. Too kind. But he would kill him. Today. Right after Rad took care of this bear.

Would Rad's rifle kill a bear? Goddamn it, he loathed depending on this Ratman. But bears he hadn't counted on. He'd heard of grizzlies being shot multiple times and still mauling people to death. *Shit.* "What do we do now? Should we turn back?"

Rad kept squinting behind them.

Roman glanced over his shoulder. Again. He squirmed in his saddle.

"No," Rad said. "It's behind us. Must have been spooked by Stony's gun. The prints lead up the trail."

Roman hipped around in his saddle, his head jerking side to side, eyes wide. "A grizzly bear is behind us?" His voice was high pitched, but he didn't care how he sounded. At this point he only wanted to get back to civilization.

"No, Doc. You're dumber than I thought. There ain't no griz up here. It's a black bear. Won't hurt us."

Roman gritted his teeth and eased back around, glaring at Rad.

Rad's grin was wide and mocking. "Not exactly your turf, is it, Doc?"

Roman pursed his lips, gripped the reigns tightly, and tensed his legs. If he heeled the horse now, would it run over Ratman? Probably not. The damn animals loved him.

Rad squinted at Roman and mounted his horse. Had Roman's horse given Rad some sort of sign?

Roman breathed in and out, slow and easy, relaxed his legs and smiled. Rad was a good guide, excellent in the outdoors. Good at making his clients respect that. But Dr. Doolittle he was not. He was only getting on the horse to move on. To his death. He should have played into the grizzly bear fear more. Would have kept him alive longer. "Okay." Roman said. "You've made your point. What do we do now?"

"Follow me, Doc. We'll be there soon." Rad turned his back, heeled his horse, and started humming.

Roman followed Rad for several minutes, seething, then realized they were coming to a switchback with a long drop on one side. Rad hummed and seemed oblivious.

"Rad," Roman called. Nothing. He tested again, his voice louder. "Rad!" But Rad kept humming and swaying back and forth like he was in a groove of some idiotic *Home on the Range* soundtrack.

Roman dismounted quickly. This was the perfect opportunity. Roman would scramble up the hill, which would hide his mount from Rad's view. Once Rad turned the corner of the switchback, he would be directly below Roman. Using a rock could work. Had to work.

Roman clambered up the rise, slipping and struggling to reach the top of the switchback overlook. He was almost there…then slipped back ten feet. *Shit!* He wasn't going to make it.

But then he was at the top. Ready. He quickly surveyed his position— fifteen feet above where his target would soon be; a nice bunch of trees to hide behind. Now to find a rock. He surveyed the ground. Not a big rock in sight. What about a large tree limb? He pulled on the trees surrounding him. Nothing moved. Nothing dead.

It had been only thirty seconds since Roman had reached the top. Rad had kept up his incessant and loud humming and was slowly rounding the switchback. Roman's chance would be over in ten seconds.

Scanning the ground down the hill a few feet, he found the rock. It was about half the diameter of a soccer ball: big enough to do damage, but not so big he couldn't throw it accurately. At least he hoped.

He hid behind the clump of trees and hefted the stone over his head. His arms almost buckled. He had to do this quickly. He sprinted from behind the trees and, as if he had played soccer with the rock his entire life, made an Olympic overhead throw-in with both hands, aimed right at Rad's head.

Rad had finally decided this would be the last trip he would guide. He was in a rhythmic trance, humming loudly, swaying back and forth in the saddle, and everything clicked. That wolf skin would bring him good money. He'd changed his mind about Canada. He would go to Mexico, buy himself a small beach cabana, retire with a good Mexican woman— Cuervo Gold and warm sunshine on his back the rest of his days. He was tired of working so hard and—

What the hell! Out of the corner of his eye, a shadow rushed at him. Then pain and darkness.

Roman was ecstatic. He'd hoped to topple the man off his horse, hitting him on the chest or shoulders. But it had been a direct head shot.

Rad's head jerked backward.

Yet he held onto the reins of the horse as he slid sideways off the saddle to the ground. He was dragged a few feet, pulling the horse's head around. Roman frowned. Would he take the horse with him? Something gave way, and Rad released the reins and toppled over the side of the switchback. It was not a terribly long fall, but far enough to be convincing.

Roman slid on his butt and legs down the side of the hill until his feet reached the path in front of the horse. He grabbed the reins and peered over the side. The Ratman's dark form lay motionless in the shadows.

He had to make sure.

He secured Rad's horse to a tree, grabbed another rock just in case, and carefully crabbed sideways down the hill toward Rad, who lay on a ledge. After Roman made it to the ledge he walked toward Rad, slowly, and with each step raised the rock higher, staring at the dark hulk. Had Rad moved? Was he feigning unconsciousness?

Finally he stood over the motionless body, holding the rock at shoulder height, watching. Rad's head lay on a pillow of snow in the shadows of a lone pine. His face was gray against the white snow. It appeared as if black oil splattered his left temple, slicking his hair. A blade of sunlight lit Rad's cheek, and the black oil became blood red. A jay cawed. The horses spluttered and shuffled their feet. Water trickled close by.

Roman huffed a soft chuckle through his nose. It had been a temple blow. Perfect. Should have an epidural bleed going by now. He felt for his pen light to check the pupils, but stopped the motion and shook his head. *You're not in ICU anymore, Toto.*

He prodded Rad with the toe of his boot. No movement. He raised the rock over his head and heaved it down point blank, smashing the man's skull.

He bent and pulled the gun out of Rad's holster and shoved it in his coat pocket.

Climbing back up the hill, he grabbed the reins of the lead horse and muttered, "There. That wasn't so hard, now was it?" The horse twisted his head around as if to answer.

Roman chuckled and went back to his own horse, found his GPS, switched it on, and waited for the unit to gather satellite signals.

Nothing happened.

CHAPTER 65

Using his time-honored method of fixing anything electronic, Roman shook his GPS unit. When the screen didn't change he shook it harder.

Nada.

He went to the fail-safe method and pounded it against his palm.

Nada. Zip. Zilch. *Shit.*

Maybe he had put the batteries in wrong?

He reached into the saddlebag for extra batteries. He thoroughly inspected the unit, took out the batteries and replaced them, twisted them from side to side to get a little more contact, returned the cover, switched it on and waited.

The screen remained grey.

What had happened? What had that fucking Ratman done?

Then Roman remembered the salesman in the sporting goods store and his warning that while this particular model was outstanding in the number of bells and whistles it had and was the latest and greatest edition made by a respected company, it had one problem: it was not waterproof.

The tea Rad had spilled on it. Had he done it on purpose? Rad's vague, dark form seemed to chuckle at Roman from down the hill. He threw his GPS at the corpse.

"Fuck!"

He angrily slipped and stumbled down the slope toward the corpse. Rad's GPS was probably in his pocket. But what if it had broken in the fall? How would Roman get off this mountain? Did Rad have maps and a compass?

He searched Rad's pockets. Granola bar. Pill bottle. Then, something metallic: a large pocket knife.

No GPS.

Where was it? Maybe it had fallen out when Rad tumbled down the hill.

He inspected the ground, paced back and forth, here and there brushing the snow aside with one foot.

Nothing.

Then he saw it. Rad's unit glinted in sunlight, having landed in an area with no snow, several feet to the side of the body. Roman's heart sank. The unit was in a puddle of water and mud. He ran and snatched it out of the water, drying it on his coat. An experienced guide like Rad would have a waterproof unit, right?

He hit the *On* button. A wave of sweet relief soothed him with the illuminated word on the digital screen: *Searching…*

The screen display was different from his. Not made by the same company. Roman almost screamed. He hated electronic gadgets. He would have to learn to use a different gadget, and without an owner's manual.

How could someone as dense and animal-like as Rad learn how to use and even rely on it in the wilderness? He'd shown Roman some of the little tricks and intricacies of the unit only yesterday, how it could track-back onto areas that he had been before.

Perhaps Rad had been on this trail before. He'd probably used the track-back function to follow Stony down this trail. That son of a bitch had never seen any tracks on the ground at all.

He spat on the man's body.

All Roman had to do was find the track-back screen, and he would be in business.

The display was blank. He hit the function button and then *track-back*. A map popped up. Simple. It even showed the switchback they were on.

He studied Rad's body, the distance to the trail and the horses, and back to the body. The body was too close, too obvious. He rolled Rad and the rock he'd used over the ledge. Rad's body flailed like a limp rag doll thrown down the stairs. It disappeared between two large rocks, the crunch of its stop a faint echo up the cliff. Nothing was visible in the shadows where it had disappeared. Maybe the noonday sun would reveal the body for an hour or so. But the rest of the day it would be in shadows. Good enough. Roman peeled off a branch from the lone pine and swept and pushed the remnants of blood-splattered mud and snow over the side, then tossed the branch after it.

He scrambled back up the slope and tied his horse's reins to the mule's pack. He walked up to Rad's horse, untied the wolf pelt, and tossed it over the edge. It rotated through the air, bounced once on a rock, then rolled under some pines, totally invisible.

Roman patted the horse's neck. A foot in the stirrup, and he was in the saddle. What was it Rad had been humming? He began humming "Clair de Lune" as he rode down the mountain.

The mule and the other horse followed. The sun was out, and he was going to find his friend. *Isn't life bold?* The horse snorted and a raven flew from a tree.

CHAPTER 66

They walked with the morning light at their backs, Stony surefooted and quiet, Jake plodding behind. The overgrown game trail weaved close to the rushing river. Jake stopped once at the sight of a magnificent waterfall that sprayed mist over the trail and rainbows of color into the sunlight. The roiling water mesmerized him and the crashing sounds blotted out his aching knees. The powerful water disappeared into a plunge pool and flowed downstream, seeming to take with it Jake's adrenaline surge from the bear ordeal. If he could only sit for a few minutes.

He jumped at the tap on his shoulder. "We need to keep moving. Rad probably heard the gunshots." Stony's bright face gave him comfort, but he realized the truth in the words: Roman and his ruthless guide were coming. He nodded and followed.

Soon, all he could think of was putting one foot in front of the other. Stony picked up the pace, striding forward with a bounce that amazed Jake. It was as if the river had energized him.

Stony began to talk in excited tones as they walked. Jake missed the first part of the sentence, "…not that we have to worry about that black bear any more. If it would have been a grizzly, I'd still have the gun out. Some of my buddies in upstate New York say that in the springtime you don't fool around with black bears. They attack and maim. But not here. Probably too many people in New York."

A gust of wind rattled the trees. Jake slowed and looked up. Rows and rows of pine trees, parallel vertical lines, straight and evenly spaced, caught the morning sun against the blue sky—a dream photo shoot. All he had to do was look. Beauty was everywhere. He trudged forward.

Loose rock slid underneath his foot, and he nearly tumbled into Stony, who had stopped, attentive eyes peering around.

"You hear that?" Stony said.

"Yeah, the wind is picking up." Even as Jake said it he knew there was something else, a noise he had registered but not grasped. He could feel his face sag as he peered up. At this point he really didn't care: he was beyond tired, almost done.

"We need to get through these trees. I know you're tired, buddy, but those are beetle-kill trees. That's why they sound like hollow gourds bumping in the wind."

Jake frowned, but nothing registered.

"Can you move it faster?"

Jake nodded, and Stony immediately strode down the path.

Jake moved as fast as he could, but his legs felt like a zombie's, moving at the hips with little strength or speed.

Stony slowed and glanced back, yelling over his shoulder. "Jake, whatever you need to do—" But before he could finish the sentence, another gust rattled the trees. This time Jake heard it, the sound of the trees was like bamboo wind chimes, a crescendo of drums that grew closer from their left, the wind driving the bouncing rattle until it was directly overhead.

A loud *crack* finally got his attention. He jerked his head around. What he saw revived his adrenaline glands.

He ran. What he'd seen were trees falling like dominos. The crashing behind him got louder. He ran faster and tripped and fell forward. Stony braced his fall, but his momentum pushed Stony into a backward stumble. Jake fell on top of him, Stony's backpack cushioning their landing, though their foreheads smacked together, cracking like two coconuts.

Jake drifted. A voice came to him as if in a tunnel, echoing and far away. "Jake, come on. Wake up."

A hand slapped his cheek, and he blinked and shook his head. Stony had pulled Jake into a clearing, away from the trees and taken off their packs. Jake was sitting with his back against a pack. He raised a hand in protest to Stony's raised hand. "I'm awake already."

"Let's go." Stony grabbed his hands and pulled him to his feet, and immediately started walking down the path.

Jake stumbled forward and twisted his head around. "What about the packs?"

"Leave them. We don't need that shit now."

What if it snowed or rained again? They might need—then he remembered Stony had said they were not far from help.

A crack sounded to the side, and a tree crashed onto the path yards in front of them, hopefully the last of the wind casualties for a while. A deer bounded through the trees from the left and, in two beats, had jumped over the fallen tree and into the river. They bush-whacked and high-stepped around the tree, only to be confronted with huge rocks that hid the trail, now little more than a trace through the bush. Surely the trail would open up if they were going the right way. Instead the bush got thicker with the brilliant reds and yellows of fall. For one instant the colors seemed beautiful in the morning light, and then in the next, when Jake struggled to push through, the bushes lashed his face and arms, now an ugly barrier to freedom.

Dead pine trees surrounded them, even in this island of dense undergrowth. A falling tree might still catch them, and this fear kept him moving. Stony led the way, and Jake was following so close he kept a hand out to avoid being slapped in the face with a branch's backlash. So when they came around a corner, his hand kept him from immediately seeing why Stony had jerked to a stop.

They'd breached the edge of the undergrowth; an immense, vertical rock cliff confronted them. They would have to scale it or go back the way they had come and detour into the pine trees, or ford the river.

Jake lowered the hand that had been protecting his face and saw the biggest obstacle. A full-grown mountain lion lounged atop a ledge on the rock cliff, stretched out like a house cat sunning itself, waiting for something interesting. It watched them, and its black-tipped tail twitched.

Stony flung his arms out wide and screamed. The cat stood and snarled and fidgeted back and forth on the ledge. Jake was sure it would pounce on them at any moment.

But it disappeared around the bend, the dark tip of its tail flicking away like a snake.

Stony eased into the river. "I hate to do this to you, but we've got to try and cross the river. It's bound to be better than getting eaten by that cat, or getting smacked on the head by a dead pine tree."

Jake gasped when the water hit his legs. It felt like ice, but luckily it was only knee deep, and the cold felt good on his bad knee. He could not see the bottom, though. Melting snow had turned the previously clear water the color of coffee with too much cream added. Stony instructed him to wrap his arm around Stony's neck while Stony grabbed the back of Jake's belt. They walked across the river like a three-legged racer in slow motion, plod after plod.

Jake watched the water. It made him dizzy. Another crash on the bank and he remembered the mountain lion and craned his neck around, searching.

The river grabbed him, and his feet lost their grip on the bottom.

CHAPTER 67

Roman patted the horse's neck. This was easy. With a GPS and a good horse, he could have bested Buffalo Bill. Who needed a guide? He'd handled the horses and the mule down the hill with only one tense moment when the mule had balked at a particularly steep and slick stretch of snow.

If he could only locate Jake. How far ahead could he be? Roman started scratching his forearm, over and over. It felt good but hurt. Then he stopped and grinned. If Jake was too far away to find today, it was no real problem. Jake would eventually end up in a hospital. *Home sweet home.*

Roman readjusted his aching butt in the saddle. After all the pain Jake had caused, Roman really wanted to finish it here—and do Stony, too. Getting rid of two guides in one day? Roman would have to write a memoir.

Footprints meandered in and out of the snow and half-dried mud. This tracking stuff was not so hard. Perhaps Rad had been following a trail. Poor Rad. He'd been *such* a good guy. Roman took a swig of water.

Roman's cough startled the horses and echoed off the trees. He coughed again, then cleared his throat several times. Must have swallowed down the wrong pipe.

The footprints broke west. Roman dismounted. This did not match the track-back on the GPS. What were they doing? The GPS screen gave the time as two p.m. Through the trees in the direction of their tracks, he saw something weird: a suspension bridge. Then he realized there was a dilapidated cabin next to him on his right, only a few rotten logs outlining the prior structure. Why had the hillbilly built here? He looked up. The snow-painted crags of the Rockies were on two sides. Not worth the effort. The bumpkin should have lived on the other side of the river. Better yet, he should have lived in the city.

How would Roman get the animals over a suspension bridge?

Movement in the distance caught his eye, too far away to make out.

He rummaged through the saddlebag, found the binoculars, and, after adjusting them to his eyes, glassed the area where he'd seen movement.

What was it? He let the binoculars drop, but still saw nothing.

He glassed the area again. Two men exited a clump of trees and walked across a meadow. They entered a forest on the other side. One was limping and following the other. Jake and Stony.

He let the binoculars hang on his neck and reviewed his options. The bridge seemed rickety, but downstream the canyon only deepened: probably no way to cross for miles.

He took out the GPS and panned out the viewscreen. *There.* He put a finger on the screen. Stony and Jake were headed for a bend of road about eight miles due west.

Would he have time to catch them? Unless they started running, he could overtake them in an hour, maybe ninety minutes. But he would have to use the bridge.

He dropped the GPS in his pocket and observed them again with the binoculars. If he started across the bridge while on the horse they could easily see him. Without the horse? *No.* He must have the horse; he could never catch them on foot.

He eyed the bridge and then the cabin. Surely that hillbilly had built the bridge to withstand the weight of a horse.

Roman would wait another fifteen minutes for them to get well into the woods. Then he would start across.

He stretched and took a deep breath of the cool air, and let it out slow. Okay. This was a pleasant place. The view was impressive. Even though he was cool, he wasn't cold. The day was warmer than yesterday, much warmer, and the snow had almost disappeared completely. A rising mist coated the ground, playing in and out of the trees like cotton poking out of a stuffed animal. The river had picked up force, now alive, rushing to the sea with more of the mountain-mud color and less of the sky in its gurgled opaque reflections.

He tethered the animals to a tree and sat on a dry flat rock, listening to the river. He was like the river that had molded the mountains into their beauty, taking away dirt and leaving majesty. He molded people's lives, taking away good people's cancer and taking away the people that had become a cancer to those good people. He rid the earth of insurance agents, workman's comp fakers, blood-sucking wives, and other prying meddlers, like Jake. Jake would never understand. To have a beautiful world, one needed to be ruthless. A favorite mentor of Roman's had said, "In order to make your patients better, there are times you must cause them pain." Well, in order to make his profession better, Roman could inflict the necessary pain, and no one would stop him from purging the weak. He would weed out those who didn't understand how to…improve medicine.

He removed his hat, held it at arm's length. The white feather against the black hat. He loved it. Sometimes you had to kill the eagle to display its beauty for all to see. He fit it on his head. One day they would thank him. They would look back on his accomplishments and realize that he had saved medicine and the world from becoming a network of fools. Doctors rule medicine. Not insurance companies. Not patients. Doctors.

The small wolf pack had not found a single elk, and the alpha male had fended off another hungry yearling, but this time he had suffered a wound to his hindquarter. Fatigue, hunger, and pain got the better of his instincts. He gave in and followed the smell of their dead brother through the night, revenge not an issue, only survival. He nearly bolted at the occasional strong whiff of man. But the wolves' padded feet quickened through the forest at the odor of the large, slow-moving, four-legged meals that accompanied the man. And when the pack actually saw the horses and rider on the ridge, hunger revved them to a frenzied pacing.

They circled once, still obeying the caution of the alpha male: *be careful with that one*—the two-legged hunter. Though hunger gnawed at their empty stomachs, their instinct for caution and stealth allowed patience. So they followed at a distance, waiting for an opportunity, sniffing and watching, always watching, always tasting the air.

A foul smell made them stop and circle. It was another of the two-legged creatures. The leader did not pause long. They would not feed on this foul one, just as they would not feed on a dead grizzly. Was it fear, or the taste? More the taste. Not quite right. He led them on to follow the other four-legged beasts that moved slowly. But one of the pack, the other challenger, could not resist. He was too hungry, and it was fresh meat. He jumped in and grabbed a bite of Rad's cheek and swallowed it down. The alpha male pounced and force him on his back. The alpha snapped and snarled, curled his lips and put his full weight chest to chest. It was over in an instant. This time the cur slunk away, the alpha supreme again, despite his waning strength. If they did not eat soon, though, he sensed an end to his leadership. The others' hungry eyes reflected less and less respect.

He ran to follow the two-legged rider and the meaty meals. The pack followed.

A low growling sound rippled the hairs on Roman's neck.

The wolves. What else? They had been on his mind all night, and now they were here. The horses shuffled and whinnied, yet Roman didn't panic. The wolves wanted revenge for what Rad had done. They had the wrong man. They should thank Roman. But no. They wanted to kill him.

You're merely dumb dogs. He slowly, carefully reached in his pocket and grabbed Rad's .45.

CHAPTER 68

Jake lost his footing in the river. Stony kept his and kept Jake from taking a swim, but it became obvious they were never going to make it across the river. Each time they got to the middle, the current was too strong. So they waded around a big rock, down a hundred yards, then back onto the bank.

Jake sat and rested while Stony stood and kept an eye out for the mountain lion.

"He's probably gone, but they can be tricky," Stony said. He shrugged. "Actually, it's a good thing we didn't get to the other side. We'd have to wade back across. The river heads more east now and there are no roads on that side."

"How far?" Jake felt like the kid in the backseat on a long drive, but he had to ask.

"Not long. Maybe another hour or so."

Jake put up a hand, and Stony helped him stand. They walked.

It was more than an hour. Much more to Jake. The squishy sounds from Jake's wet socks were gone. The ball of one foot burned with a blister. Dusk would be on them soon.

Stony slowed. "I've got something I want to ask you."

"What's that?" Jake slowed, too. That was better. He wanted to sit. *No.* Summer and Carla were waiting.

"You wanted to die. Probably alone. Is that right?"

"Yeah. But that's over."

Stony eyed him. "Right."

Jake started to say something, but Stony put up a hand. "Hear me out. One time I wanted to be all by myself, too. Just go off, get me a cabin. Ever seen those cabins—well, you might call them shacks—out there in the middle of the prairie, east of Cheyenne? You know, east of nowhere, south of dipshit. All you got is some rolling hills, antelope, maybe a few head of cow, a horse, and at least three rusted old trucks shading long grass coming up through the seats. That was me, only the cabin was in Alaska, with elk, bears, and wolves instead of antelope, cows, and horses. I even had two snowmobiles, though they were rusted and had ferns growing up through the steering wheels."

Stony stopped and gazed into the distance.

Jake didn't want to stop walking. He felt the need to keep his inertia going, but he couldn't get around Stony, so he halted and waited, standing beside of Stony.

Stony's glazed eyes pondered some distant puzzle and closed gently as he slowly lowered his chin to his chest. Rhythmic slow breaths moved his chest and chin in unison. The creek trickled and the wind softly rattled the few remaining yellow-green aspen leaves in the trees that overhung the path and glowed in the late afternoon light. The wind and the snow had accomplished their duty: robbing the aspens of their former beauty, now only thin, tattered relics of golden glory.

Jake's legs and feet ached, and when he tried to stand straight he faltered, almost falling, his muscles nearly too weak to balance. Yet mentally he felt stronger. Something had been lifted from his heart. The joy and energy resembled the feeling when he'd got his first car.

A new smell crept into the air—not the clean odor of pine trees, but diesel fumes. They must be getting close to the road. A part of him wanted to go back, go back to the wilderness and stay there, away from everyone, hold onto that energy that he was sure would melt away like sand castles at high tide once he returned to civilization. He wondered if that was why Stony had stopped walking. Maybe he wasn't ready to return, either. Jake understood Stony's love of solitude, being out here with only wolves and bears. What a life.

Now Jake would have to go back to his own turf: the hospital and… people. Was he ready?

Stony shook his head and his eyes fluttered. "I'd pretty much had it with people telling me what was the right thing to do and what was the wrong thing to do, those people who got me into Vietnam, those people who talked me into drinking and carrying on. At least that's what I thought. I didn't realize it wasn't those other people. It was me. I was the one who wanted to leave and be by myself. Forget about everything except for the animals and nature: a bit like that movie *Jeremiah Johnson*, where the guy goes off and says to hell with it. But, if you noticed, he couldn't get away from people. They were there—the Indians, the crazy lady, the little boy who survived the Indians and her craziness.

"That's what I tried. Went off by myself, rustic cabin in Alaska. It was great for a while. I mean, I didn't have to answer to anybody but me. I could hunt, fish, pretty much live off the land. And drugs and whiskey. Who needs veggies or fruits. Every now and then I had to make a run into town for rice and beans. And more drugs and whiskey. In the middle of the winter I stopped making runs for a long time. I didn't care. Then someone knocked on my door. It was like a dream. Not even sure I got up to open the door. She walked in and…took care of me. Got me back to the land of the living. Others helped, and here I am, instead of my rotting carcass fertilizing salmon runs."

He paused and studied Jake. "Anyway, I guess what I'm trying to say is: People saved me. People need people."

Jake raised his head and an eyebrow at Stony.

"Yeah, I know. Me and Barbara Streisand. Hokey but true. I think if we don't have people we dry up. We get sucked inside ourselves and our demons eat away at our sensibilities, our sanity, our very souls. Then, we die."

"I understand."

Stony put a hand on Jake's shoulder. "I'm not so sure."

Stony squinted and frowned at the meadow they'd crossed a half hour ago. Jake turned quickly to see, but only caught vague movement. Had it been an elk?

"What's wrong?" Jake stared at the meadow.

Nothing moved. Probably the wind or a tree bough losing snow.

Stony kept inspecting the meadow. "Where was I? Oh, yeah. Death. You and Dr. Kevorkian. We shoot horses when they get old; we put dogs down when they have cancer. Why do we let human beings suffer? Dr. Death 'helped' people die who didn't have anything to live for. You felt you were suffering, you weren't any good for anybody, you had two bad diseases; might as well bump yourself off and get rid of a dead weight."

"Okay, that was part of it, but—"

Stony put up a hand. "Let me finish. Maybe animals suffer because they haven't got the capacity to think about something else—to distract themselves, put pain out of their minds. Humans? We can do that. And the thing that helps us most is other people, their company, their love. What if those patients of Dr. Death got involved in a group of people that did things they enjoyed, with people who loved them? It runs both ways. You need other people, but they need you. I mean, Jesus Christ, you're a doctor. People need you. You could do a lot of good before you die. A lot of good. There's something to be said for that, you know. Something more than a little bit to be said for that."

"You're right. I was only thinking about myself. But I've changed my mind."

"Have you? What about Summer? If you live won't Roman kill her? What's to keep him away from her?"

Jake glanced at the meadow, then Stony, then back. Jake hadn't really asked Stony to protect them from Roman? And maybe he shouldn't.

"Me. I'll do it. I have friends. I know an old patient who's a retired cop."

Jake gripped his hands into fists. "If I have to, I'll kill Roman. I have a gun."

"Kill him, huh?" Now Stony's eyes stared into a meadow much further away, one Jake knew he could never see.

276

"Can you help me?" Jake said.

Stony closed his eyes. "Yeah. I could help."

Then he opened his eyes and stared into Jake's. "But I won't kill him. Had enough of that a long time ago. "

Snow started falling: big wet flakes. Jake felt as if he were floating on the surface of a mountain lake without a breeze. He wanted to hike back in and stay forever.

"I can't kill him either. But I have no real evidence to convict him." Jake wondered if there was another way.

Stony studied the distant meadow, the falling snow, and rolled his neck and shoulders.

"Let's go. We'll talk about this later. You need a doctor."

CHAPTER 69

Jake awoke, slightly panicked. He wasn't home, but everything was familiar—white sheets, IV, antiseptic smell. He was in a hospital bed in ICU, IV in his left hand, pulse oximeter clamped onto his right index finger, monitor above his head showing heart rate, pulse, blood pressure, oxygen saturation. The wall to his right had a large window, curtains pulled halfway. Outside it was dark with a faint outline of a spruce tree, snow on the branches. On the wall in front of him was a clock, the hands reading ten 'til four. There was a white board with *Welcome to Larimer Valley Hospital* and *your nurse is Samantha* written in red letters. To his left, Carla was in the easy chair, legs up, blanket over her, sleeping.

His panic eased a bit. A vague memory of last night—Carla crying and hugging him in the ER, bright lights, a doctor—what was her name—Dr. Cynthia Leon.

Stony sat in a chair behind Carla, one side of his head with a fresh bandage. He nodded at Jake. Jake nodded back. The panic left completely. He closed his eyes and slept.

Stony watched Jake go back to sleep, thought about getting back into the sleeping bag he'd rolled up in the corner, then decided six hours would have to do. He stood quietly and left, softly closing the door behind him.

A park ranger Stony knew, Randy, was at the nurse's station. Rangers were the police of the Park. He'd already questioned Stony earlier in the

ER. He caught Stony's eye and motioned for him to come over. They shook hands.

"How's he doing, Stony?"

"Okay."

Randy smiled then glanced at the clipboard on the counter. "You know a Dr. Roman Johnson?"

"Not really." Stony got a look at the clipboard. He didn't know where this was going but was sure Randy would never believe what Jake had told him.

"Guess he was up in the wilderness, too. He's in the ER. Said he was attacked by wolves. Said he's Dr. Roberts's partner." Randy's look was expectant.

Stony raised his eyebrows. "Huh."

Randy waited, picked up the clipboard, studied it. "He said he came out of the Park about the same place you and Dr. Roberts did. You see him up there, talk to him at all?"

Stony shook his head. Never did talk to him.

"How 'bout wolves?"

"Nope, just what I told you before."

Randy flipped the page on the clipboard to the second page and read off what Stony had told him in the ER. "'German Shepherds and huskies. Fed 'em some fish and they took off.' That it?"

Stony nodded. "Guy's a doctor, right? Probably inexperienced and mistook the dogs for wolves. I'm sure he had a guide. Ask him?"

"That's the problem." Randy let the top paper flip back and tapped it with his pen. "He did have a guide, a guy named Radner, but Dr. Johnson said the wolves attacked Radner, who fell off his horse into a ravine. Then Dr. Johnson shot one of the wolves or dogs or whatever, his horse bolted, and he never saw them again."

"Quite a story." Stony tried to keep the rage out of his voice at the thought of Roman shooting a wolf.

The Ranger now looked more resigned. "Yeah. Wild dogs makes more sense. Couple of local ranchers said they had been missing dogs. Dr. Johnson was probably pretty hyped out."

"So how is Dr. Johnson?" Stony hoped his emphasis on "doctor" was not too obvious.

"Had a few cuts. ER doc sewed him up. Got a tetanus shot and left the ER a few minutes ago."

Shit! Stony thought. He still had the keys to Carla's car from earlier, when he'd put his .45 in the glove box before going back to the ER. But there was no time to retrieve the .45. The weight of the pocket knife in his pants pocket was a comfort, though.

"He coming up here to visit Dr. Roberts?"

"Nah. Called a cab. Guess he wants to go home."

Stony hoped the nervous gripping of his hands had gone unnoticed. "You going after Radner?"

Randy's phone chirped. "Excuse me." He answered it.

Stony wanted to run down the stairs and follow Roman, make sure he was not coming up here. But if he just took off, Randy would wonder why. If he asked Randy to watch over Jake, there would also be more questions. Answers would be tough and unbelievable.

Randy talked. And talked. Then ended it.

"That was my wife. I forgot. We're going to breakfast with friends. I gotta get home, shower, and get ready." He grabbed his clipboard and started off, then turned back.

"Oh, about Radner: this storm's a bad one. We'll have to wait a few days to look for his body."

Stony nodded. "Have a good breakfast."

Randy nodded and left.

As soon as the elevator door closed, Stony hurried to the stairwell. He could probably ask Carla where Roman lived, but it was better if she didn't know what Stony was about to do. He took the stairs two at a time and came out next to the ER. He made it to the exit in time to see a man with a white hat and black feather get into a Yellow Cab.

The elevator dinged behind Stony. Randy was coming.

Stony sprinted to Carla's car, a Volvo, praying Randy wouldn't see him.

The Volvo chirped when he touched the unlock button on the fob. He clawed the snow-laden door open and jumped in, immediately turning off the courtesy light and watching the exit through the very edge of the windshield, where no snow had stuck. Randy came out and started toward the parking lot.

The cab was disappearing out of the parking lot onto Doctors Lane. He twisted the key. The starter turned over but did not catch. He turned it off, pushed the accelerator down all the way once and tried again.

The engine started. He moved the defrost to max, twisted the wipers on, and started forward, barely able to see through the ice cobbled on the windshield, but enough to drive. Just enough. Randy walked past him on the right but was focused on something in the distance.

Stony drove slow at first, then, when he got to Doctors Lane, turned west and sped up. The cab was nowhere to be found. He mashed the accelerator, and the front wheels spun on the snowy road. Too early for plows at a hospital? He took his foot off and slid to a stop at the light at South Lemay Avenue. Which way, north or south? He racked his brain. Had Jake ever mentioned where Roman lived? Stony tried to recall the front paper on Randy's clipboard. Had to be Roman's address. 113 Silver Cloud Way, or had it been Silver City Way? For sure he'd seen the town: Loveland.

To get there he could take I-25, only ten minutes east, but probably plowed and pretty fast, though it was pretty far east of Loveland. Where would a rich doctor live in Loveland? Four possibilities. Two were on an acreage either southeast or west of town. He thought about what Jake had said about Roman and his tailored suits, about Roman's greenhorn hat and clothes. No acreage. Have to get dirty. Too much work. The third possibility would be around Lake Loveland. Noisy boats didn't fit Roman. That left Marianna Buttes. Too far west to take the highway.

He turned south onto Lemay, then west on Prospect until he hit Taft Hill, the furthest west southern route to Loveland. He turned south. There were tail lights in the distance. Too dark to tell if they belonged to the cab. He sped up, risking a slide, but felt the heavy Volvo take hold of the road. A snowplow must have recently been through and sprinkled sandy gravel in its wake.

His stomached gnawed, and though he was wide awake now, he knew if he didn't get coffee and food soon, he would be punchy. Six hours of sleep didn't cut it after the last two days.

The car ahead went under a street light. It was a Yellow Cab. Stony eased off the accelerator and followed at a distance.

After forty minutes, the cab stopped, and Roman got out of the cab and went inside the house. 113 Silver Cloud Way. The irony made Stony smile. Lights came on. He sat in the Volvo for thirty minutes, engine off. All lights inside winked out. No one exited. It was five-thirty.

Stony called Nguyen and arranged for him to watch Roman for the day while Stony went back to the hospital. He had to protect Jake and locate Summer. Roman could easily contact someone else to finish the job. He'd hired Radner—so what was to keep him from getting others to help?

Nguyen arrived about six, the sky beginning to lighten in the east. He had an old tan Datsun, took care of his cars well. Stony left him parked a block further away with good binoculars.

It was six-thirty when Stony walked down the hall to Jake's ICU room. Dr. Leon was at the nurse's station and gave him a nod. He nodded back and slipped in the room. Carla and Jake still slept. He woke them, wanting everyone wide awake for Dr. Leon.

Jake was slow to rouse and spoke in slow, deliberate sentences, as if his thoughts were taking an extra second to connect to his lips. "Gotta get more rest."

"Yeah, I know. But Dr. Leon is coming. Thought you might want to be awake for her."

Carla sat up, moved her prosthetic leg over to the side, and stood. "I want to make a trip to the ladies' room before she gets here." She walked into Jake's bathroom and closed the door.

Stony waited until she closed the door and leaned in to Jake, lowering his voice. "Bad news, partner. Roman is back. Probably killed Rad."

Jake sat up straight, eyes wide. "Damn!"

The door pushed open and Summer walked in. She eyed Stony, then pushed through and hugged Jake.

This was going to be awkward.

CHAPTER 70

Jake fought back his horror at the news of Roman and smiled at Summer. The toilet flushed in the closed bathroom, and water ran in the sink. He blinked his eyes, ran his tongue around his tacky mouth. Summer hugged him. He tried to embrace her with the IV and pulse ox, but only managed one arm. He closed his eyes and smiled. She was safe.

Carla came out of the bathroom. "Morning, Sweetie. This is a surprise."

"Hi, Mom."

Carla scooted behind her and regained her seat in the easy chair.

"Daddy, Mom and I were so worried. Why'd you go for so long? What happened to 'a day or two'?"

He was still worried about Roman. Could he be coming here? "Well, it was so beautiful out there." No way was he telling her the truth. "I thought maybe a few more days, and I could get my head straight. I always wanted to go out camping like that. You know, deep in the woods, no one around."

She peered at him, azure eyes suspicious. Ever since she'd been six, any time he told her a half-truth, she stared at him. She might only stare for a few moments, then go on about her business, not calling him out. But he would invariably spill the rest of the story.

This time? She was already hurt. Yet his stomach rolled at not telling her the whole story. That, coupled with the worry about Roman, made him want to throw up.

He willed a sincere gaze. She *must* believe him. "Even though we had a rough time, I'm glad we did it. It was probably the best experience in my life."

"At least you're alive. Mom and I were frantic. I can't believe you did this." Then she paused and tilted her head and smiled. "Actually, I can believe it. I'm glad you had a good time. Maybe one of these days you and I can do some camping or fishing. What do you think?"

"I'd like nothing better." One day he might tell her.

She hugged him again, a long hug, like if she let go he might disappear again. He relaxed into her and managed a two-arm squeeze. God, it felt good. A memory to be tucked away forever.

Stony eyeballed them and smiled. Dr. Death be damned.

Summer gave her mom a hug, then looked at Stony. Carla was facing away from Stony, and Summer's body was between him and Jake. Stony frowned and shook his head, trying to send her the thought: *You don't know me.*

Jake made it easy. "Honey, this is Stony, the guide who saved my life."

"You saved his life? Oh, my God. Thank you so much." She dodged her mom's easy chair and pressed her body to his, firm breasts against his chest, warm breath in his ear, a whisper. "We have to talk."

He made sure his embrace appeared clumsy and scant. "Couldn't have done it without his help. Glad it worked out."

She gave him a peck on the cheek, squeezed his ass, then brushed her tongue across his lips as she released him.

Stony felt his neck and face warm. He looked at the floor. This could not be happening.

"Without him," Jake said, "I would be a frozen meatsicle for bears and mountain lions."

The door opened again, and Dr. Leon walked in.

Jake introduced Summer and added, "She's also a doctor, soon to be in a radiology residency."

"Very nice," Dr. Leon said. "Good luck." She was all business, in a hurry on her morning rounds. She told them all the labs were looking great, CO_2 and BUN down, sugars better controlled—then listened to Jake's heart and lungs, felt his belly, and said, "You'll be going to the floor today."

She turned and was almost out the door when Jake said, "What about the CBC?"

"Fine. Everything normal."

"Normal?"

She faced him. "Yes. Something I missed?"

"You don't know, do you?"

"Know what?"

He rubbed his forehead with the knuckles of his right hand. "I guess you didn't get my records. I've got leukemia. I was on my last downward spiral before I went camping. Kind of a 'last good time' fling."

"Huh. Well, we've done several CBCs, and they're all normal. I'll be happy to show them to you. I could call Roman; maybe he could get the old records."

At the possibility of contact with Roman, Jake gripped the sheet in one fist under the blanket, but said calmly, "No, don't bother Roman. He needs his rest. But I'd like to see the blood counts, if you don't mind." It was training from internship onward: make sure you see each test result yourself; don't trust an intern or nurse to tell you the result. Not like Dr. Leon would lie; he just wanted reassurance, with his own eyes.

She immediately brought in the lab printouts of his cell counts. He scrutinized each page three separate times. They were normal. Absolutely normal. *Jesus.*

Summer was jubilant; Carla laughed.

Stony swatted him on the back. "Guess that good old fresh air did you a world of good."

Dr. Leon smiled. "Glad to be the bearer of more good news. If all continues well, you'll probably go home tomorrow."

"Thanks," Jake said.

Stony didn't like that. Not one bit. He had to arrange help to guard Jake at discharge, to watch Jake and Summer afterwards. This was too fast.

When Dr. Leon left, Stony said to Jake, "Excuse me for a few minutes. I'll be right back."

He followed Dr. Leon to the nurse's station. "Can I speak to you for a minute, Doc, about Jake?"

He wanted to tell her Jake was in danger, that Roman would kill Jake and Summer if she let him go too soon. But that would not be the thing to do.

A nurse had already handed her another patient's chart and was speaking about last night's progress. Dr. Leon turned to him, lips tight. "I can't really tell you anything about him without his permission."

"It's not that. It's just… Well, Jake has a lot going on right now, and I was hoping you could maybe keep him, you know, not let him go home tomorrow."

"This is a hospital, Mr.…uh…"

"Stony. Just plain Stony. And I know—"

"If he has a medical reason to stay, we'll keep him. Otherwise, he'll go home. We don't want him to get a resistant infection. Besides, patients always do better at home."

She smiled, tight lips, steady gaze. He wasn't going to win this one.

He shrugged. "Okay. I understand." He supposed she was right. The hospital was Roman's home turf, and could be the worst place for Jake. He turned and started for Jake's room, but stopped outside and pulled out his cellphone. If ever there was a time to call in favors, now was it.

After talking with Nguyen and two others, he went into the room. Summer had traded places in the easy chair with Carla, who was standing and had her customary scarf around her scarred face and was pulling on her coat.

"Mom's going home," Summer said, "to get things ready for tomorrow."

Stony nodded. They said their goodbyes, Carla left, and Summer turned halfway in the chair so she could see both Stony and Jake.

"Okay. You wanna tell me what really happened out there?"

She was smart, Stony gave her that.

"We fished, there was a snowstorm, we fished, we camped, we fished some more, we camped some more, we told a few stories, your dad got sick, we came out." Stony smiled at her. "End of story." She knew this was total bullshit. And maybe she would realize there was a reason for it and drop it. He had to discuss with Jake how to handle Roman and whether to tell her everything or just have someone with her at all times. *Yeah, right.*

He could hear her: *Why do I need guardians? Just because I'm a woman? I can handle myself, you know.* Maybe that was true. But against Roman?

She opened her mouth, and Jake interjected. "Well, it was a little more than that. Stony is pretty sparse on words. We ran into a bear and her cub. That was exciting. There was a mountain lion and we had to ford the river. I fell in and—"

"I suppose that's where Stony got the injury to his head?" She pointed at Stony's bandage. Her lips were tight and her eyes glared at Stony.

"No. That was from a tree branch when we were running from the bear," Stony lowered one eyebrow and motioned with his hand so Jake couldn't see it—palm cupped, fingers toward his chest, back and forth, the universal sign for *Cut it. No more questions.* He would tell her later.

Her eyes gradually relaxed. She sighed and shook her head. "I gotta go to the bathroom."

Before she closed the door, Jake facing the other way, she glanced at Stony, a look that said she knew this was total bullshit.

The door to the bathroom closed, and Stony got close to Jake and whispered, "Roman told the ranger that wolves attacked him. The ranger asked me, and I told him they were wild dogs, a Husky and a German Shepherd. I think he believes me. I also think Roman killed Rad. Roman's home now, but I worry about you and Summer. You need protection. What are we going to tell Summer about Roman?"

"Not a thing. I'm not telling her anything else. And you don't have to worry about me or her. I have patients who can help me, a retired cop and a Korean couple who offered their help anytime. I'll call them today."

"Can they get here today?"

"I don't know."

The toilet flushed.

"I'll have someone come today. Have your friends cover tomorrow. They'll need to cover the car when you leave, all the way to your house, and then watch your house. Okay?"

The sink water burred then stopped.

Jake nodded.

Stony stood back in his corner. The bathroom door opened and Summer came out. She glanced first at Stony, then at Jake, and shook her head.

"So…how's the residency going?" Jake asked.

It was a good diversion, though Stony knew he would soon have to tell her more, not just because she would demand it, but to help protect her. She needed to watch her back.

Father and daughter fell into a comfortable conversation about medicine. Stony excused himself, stating he had to take care of some business. He would have to leave the hospital, leave Jake and Summer without a guard for a few hours. Couldn't be helped. Nguyen would let him know if Roman left, anyhow. There was the possibility of Roman sending someone else, but Stony felt sure Roman was sleeping. He had a few hours.

CHAPTER 71

Nguyen reported that Roman had come and gone, never looking over his shoulder. Either Roman didn't believe someone was watching him, or he knew and didn't care. Stony figured the latter. Roman was so sure of himself that he believed no one could stop him.

Stony would have to do it tonight. He told Nguyen, went to the hardware store, then home to collect more supplies. The drive up the Big Thompson canyon took precious time, and he was out of touch by cellphone for forty-five minutes, but he needed the supplies at his home.

While he was in Estes, he went by the fly shop to check in, though he was sure there were no other trips going up with all the snow in the high country. Also there was a pair of needle-nose pliers he'd left in his locker. He would need those. Bob saw him come in and quickly excused himself from a customer and came over.

"Where have you been?"

"I was on a trip. You knew that."

"I thought you said five days."

"'Five or so' were my words, I believe."

Bob rubbed his chin with his cupped hand and glanced nervously at the front door. It wasn't like Bob to pin Stony down.

"What is it, Bob?"

"Caleb says you're smoking pot and drinking in the shop. He told Dave, and Dave wants to speak to you."

"Wait a minute. You know I'm clean." Stony's voice had gotten loud, and the customer at the register glanced over. He lowered his voice. "It's Caleb and his stoner friends." Stony should have spoken to Bob about this before he left. *Damn.*

"Not what Caleb told Dave. Said you're losing it. That's why you didn't report back in after your trip was over."

"If you know I've been back, you know I've been helping my client, who got sick on the trip and required hospitalization."

Bob sighed and turned to go back to the customer. Stony couldn't see Bob's face to tell if the sigh was relief at knowing Stony had been helping a client or frustration that Stony could be doing drugs again.

He glanced over his shoulder. "Let me take care of this customer first. Then we can talk. Go in the back room. Don't leave."

Stony could easily prove he was clean. But why should he have to? Bob should have taken his word. He walked to the back room, keyed open the locker and found the pliers. Why did Bob want him back here? The more he thought about it the angrier he got. Bob should trust him more.

The front door jingled. Maybe Bob had called Dave.

Stony didn't have time to convince Bob or Dave, and knew his anger might make him look guilty. He walked out the back door.

On I-34 back to Loveland, the Big Thompson River splashed beside the highway. Usually, the river captivated Stony: thoughts about a big fish in this hole, a great day at that one. But today his thoughts were elsewhere. What was he going to do about Dave? How he could manage to protect both Jake and Summer? How he could get rid of Roman forever? The one thought that kept coming back was that there was no cellphone coverage in the canyon from Estes to Loveland. He mashed on the accelerator.

Around the next bend he saw the cop on the right side, pulled over. *Shit!*

He braked, knew he would pass the cop going ten miles over the speed limit, knew he would be pulled over, and it would take him fifteen minutes longer to get back.

But the cop had another car in front of him and was standing outside the driver's window, already occupied. Stony let off the brake so the cop wouldn't see his brake lights and coasted by. Around the next bend, out of sight of the cop, he poured on the speed again. His tires squealed, he got a finger from one lady he passed on a curve, but he made it down to Loveland in record time, about thirty-five minutes.

He parked his car in back of Nguyen's, who waved a hand in the rearview and motored off.

Stony waited and watched, occasionally drinking from a bottle of water, wondering what to do about Dave, then dismissing his concern as stupid. As soon as he had a chance, he would tell Dave everything. Everything about Caleb. Dave could never know what Stony was about to do.

The sun went down and lights stayed on in several rooms of Roman's house. Stony was sure Roman could not resist waiting to take care of Jake. And when he found out Summer was with Jake, it would be too tempting. He would go to the hospital. Nguyen would be there, though.

Nguyen's outer appearance belied his power. At five foot two and a scant hundred-twenty pounds, he didn't look like much. But his father had taught him well before he died, or rather, before Stony had killed him. All Stony remembered, in his post-killing haze, was seeing a boy kneeling beside his father, gripping his father's head tight to his chest. Stony raised the machete and peered into that boy's eyes— It had been like a switch. He saw, he knew, and he ran, throwing the machete into the jungle.

Later, his drugged-out buddies applauded Stony's slaughter and filled him in on details he either couldn't remember, or wouldn't. They told him that when his carbine had jammed, he'd grabbed a machete hanging in the hut and filleted the entire family. Somehow the boy had got away. But that was okay, they said. Stony was a hero. In a marijuana and heroin high, he remembered talking with such—such utter bravado. He remembered the feeling of power he had had with the machete as he scythed through bodies, necks, arms, legs: raw, jaw-gripping, mind-expanding power. Later, that feeling of Ultimate Power came back to him, in his dreams, only to be fouled by overwhelming guilt and grief, awakening him in a pool of sweat and gouging his stomach until he vomited. In these recurrent dreams, there was always the boy watching him with eyes so sad, always asking the ultimate question: *why?*

These dreams had haunted him for years, at first intermittently. Then, about fifteen years after he'd left Vietnam, they became steady—every night. Sleep became something of the past. He decided he could avoid the nightmares if he avoided sleep, or at least limited it to a few hours a night. He would spend the extra time doing something useful. Twenty hours each day needed filling. He worked two jobs and went to school full time. Eventually, after another two years and almost getting his degree, he succumbed to the law of nature: during a midday class, he stabbed his own hand with a pencil.

Stony rubbed the scar on the back of his left hand. It ached when the weather changed, and it cramped up on him at times: when releasing fish in cold water, or after tying one too many flies. He flexed his hand and remembered the hospitalization after the pencil stabbing.

The wound on his hand had healed much quicker than his psyche. He'd gone into a deep depression. After weeks of psychiatric treatment and repeated discussions with one young psychiatrist, he knew what he must do.

Once he got out of the hospital and saved enough money, he bought an airline ticket to Vietnam and searched for weeks. But Nguyen was the most popular surname in Vietnam. After many a discussion with bartenders and restaurant owners, he learned that Nguyen could be a first name, too, but *that* was not common. That's when he finally found him, that little boy who haunted his dreams. Nguyen Van Nguyen had a wife and one two-month-old girl he could barely feed. He owned a small restaurant but could not make ends meet. It took Stony several nights to explain who he was and why he was there. He wanted to take Nguyen back to the States and help him succeed.

Several times Stony had wondered if Nguyen had come back so he could more easily exact revenge and kill Stony. But soon he realized Nguyen, the man, had long ago forgiven what Stony the soldier had done to Nguyen, the boy.

Stony set up Nguyen into the restaurant business in Loveland with the help of other Vietnam vets. Within a year, Nguyen had a thriving business and no longer needed Stony's help, though Stony continued to babysit Nguyen's little girl every chance he got.

What years of therapy couldn't do, one act of kindness had. Stony's nightmares had stopped. He slept again.

So when Stony had asked Nguyen to watch over Jake, there was no hesitation. Stony and Nguyen understood each other, and like any buddies from war, they would die for one another now. They both knew they had been an integral part of War—the ultimate destroyer or redeemer. Stony had volunteered to be a hero and come away destroyed. Nguyen had been destroyed and come away a hero. He had saved Stony's sanity and, ultimately, his life. But he knew Stony had also saved his life, in a flash of clarity during a reign of blood-lust insanity.

Stony eyed the house, all the lights still on. What if Roman didn't leave? What if he called someone else to finish Jake off? Stony needed evidence to convict Roman, the sooner the better. Plan B would take longer, and maybe too long. Tonight was better. He looked at his watch. Seven p.m.

Finally, the lights blinked out, and Roman left. Stony waited. A half-hour passed. After ten more minutes, he shouldered the satchel and walked around the block. A poorly lit alley ran behind Roman's backyard. He kept in shadows and went easily over the privacy fence. Several cedar trees lined the sides of the backyard, obstacles to prying neighbors. He brushed off his shoes before stepping onto the back porch, then donned shoe covers and pulled on Silastic gloves. In no time, he bypassed the security system, jimmied the lock on the French doors, and slipped in, closing and locking the door behind him.

Using a strong penlight, he searched methodically, starting with the master bedroom and bath. It took almost an hour to find hardly anything, only two syringes and needles in a special sharps container hung in the bathroom. Probably decoys. He tapped on walls and floors. Nothing. No hidden caches.

His watch glared at him: five more minutes. The garage was next.

The penlight beam seemed to reach forever into the huge garage. This was going to take too long. But the neat organization gave him hope. He rushed from cabinet to floor, systematically covering every square inch in three minutes.

Still nothing.

Only two more minutes and he had to be out of here.

CHAPTER 72

Stony sighed and started up the stairs to the kitchen…one of his shoes tapped against the back of the stairs.

Hollow as a wood box.

He got on his hands and knees and studied the stairs. They appeared normal. But as he moved the flashlight beam, he noticed a hairline seam running down the drywall on one side of the staircase. He pulled on the stairs, and they opened like a secret door, hinged on one side along with the cut piece of drywall.

Behind the door sat a key-locked cabinet.

A car engine sounded from outside. He froze.

The car drove by. From his inside coat pocket, Stony retrieved a thin box with lock-picking tools. Within a minute the cabinet was open. Inside he found the jackpot: poisons, illegal drugs, syringes full of various medications and a litany of articles on poisonous herbs—all items that could be used to get Roman convicted.

He stuffed a few items into a small backpack for possible use later even as he realized three things. First, this was only circumstantial evidence at best. Second, courts took forever; Roman had lots of money to make bail and he'd be out. He might kill somebody else, and that might be Jake. Or Summer.

And then there was the last thing. Roman had to pay for his past murders.

Just kill him and be done with it. The thought had been barging in more regularly the last few days. He could make Roman's death completely untraceable. He could make Roman disappear, and no one would ever know where to find him.

His head swam and he stumbled, catching himself with one hand against the wall. He blinked hard: once, twice, three times. Each time he blinked, Nguyen's young, boyish face flashed like a frame of a movie clip, each frame showing more details of the bloody massacre, and the boy's eyes went from sad to accusing. Stony bent at the waist, hands on his knees, and breathed deeply. Every fiber in him begged to be released from his vow to Sonja, his love and savior. *Never kill another man.* Roman was more evil than anyone he had ever encountered. But a promise was a promise. Sonja deserved that. And Stony knew he could not go through that again—the nightmares, the drugs. He'd already seen hell three times. It wasn't anything like fire and brimstone. It was cold and empty, and the only feeling was total dullness: no hunger, no thirst, no joy. Just time. Immeasurable, incessant time.

There had to be another way, something that would end Roman and his reign of terror over Jake and anyone else. It must end.

Stony knew others that would kill Roman. All he had to do was give them the word.

But he would still be responsible, even if he didn't pull the trigger.

He wondered about Roman's heart—his soul. Surely, as a physician, even with all the evil he had done, he had something good inside. Jake had said Roman had saved a lot of people.

Maybe Stony could turn Roman away from his killing addiction, just as Stony had turned away from his own addictions. Perhaps Roman could do something beautiful and contribute as a physician. *Now you're thinking like Jake.* Roman was too far into his killing addiction. The evil was embedded—too evil to change. Wasn't it?

He needed to leave, but he couldn't move. Could Roman be too far gone? People had been known to change.

He'd seen men come back from Vietnam addicted to killing—the rush, the power, the realization that they were not only allowed, but given *carte blanche* to murder at will. Hell, he'd been there himself. With help, those men and Stony had all moved away from the dark side and were now contributing members of society. It had taken time and good people to help, but it was possible. Maybe there was a way.

He replaced the materials, moved the stairs back, started into the kitchen, then paused. He lifted a foot up and inspected the bottom of the shoe cover with the penlight. As he suspected, the black grease and brown dirt from the garage door coated the cover. He clucked his tongue and pulled two fresh covers from the satchel and placed them on before hurrying back in the house, closing doors and inspecting where he'd been with the light to make sure everything was the same as when he had arrived.

He exited the house, reset the alarm, and stepped onto the back yard before he took off the gloves and shoe covers and stowed them in the satchel. He glanced around and listened for a minute, then shouldered through the cedars, flipped over the fence, and was in his car in minutes.

He sighed and wanted to beat on the steering wheel, feeling frustrated at the night and backed into a corner. He couldn't use the law against Roman. He couldn't get a friend to kill him. But there was no way in hell he could let Roman get Jake or Summer. Or anyone else.

He started the car and drove away.

Down the alley, Roman sat in his car and watched Stony's car move off. There was a wry grin on his face.

CHAPTER 73

Supper had come and gone, and like all hospital food, it had been bland and unappetizing. Neither Jake nor Summer had eaten it. Summer had said she would go out for food but needed a nap first. She'd been asleep for a half-hour. Jake's eyes were heavy. Maybe he would take a snooze, too. Outside it was dark again, seven forty-five by the clock on the far wall. Summer slept in the chair, her face smooth and unfettered, her breathing regular and relaxed.

He didn't really want to sleep. What if Roman came in now? They were helpless. This wasn't the wilderness; this was Roman's turf. He could get in and out without a problem. Stony had said someone would be here, but no one had shown up yet.

He gripped his hands. For the first time in days, they were slick. Summer shifted in her seat, snuffled once, and settled back down.

Fatigue from the events of the last few days and his sickness dragged at him. He took a deep breath, let it out slow, and moved his shoulders around to feel the soreness, a reminder that he had done something important this last week: he had decided to live. Roman had gone home after the ER visit. Nothing would happen at the hospital.

Jake wondered how the hell his blood count could be normal. There were case reports about people with cancer, leukemia and other types, that had gone into remission after stressful events. He'd pretty much filed those away with other case reports in his mental file of *So Rare It Will Never Happen Again*. After all, that's what case reports usually were. He had stopped the chemo weeks ago. Maybe his body had rebounded.

How many times had he used that word "remission" with patients?

A cold, black fog rolled over his heart, and he wanted to pull the covers over his head and hide from the world. It was the feeling he'd had when Roman had first told him he had leukemia. It was hopelessness, draining all energy and life, taking all love and pushing it over a cliff, graying any light and color, deadening all sounds—

Stop. He was not going there again. Somehow he had been given a new life. He was done with those thoughts forever. In his mind he took a bright, multi-colored quilt and wrapped it around that black fog, then folded it, folded it, and folded it again, until it was so small it disappeared with a flash.

Roman's haughty face kept resurfacing. He was gone. Home. *Stop worrying.*

Dr. Leon had said Jake would likely go home tomorrow. She had kept his IV in overnight as a precaution. His diabetic ketoacidosis had cleared, and other than mild aftereffects of dehydration and exposure, he felt great. Well, okay, maybe he could use a little more sleep.

Jake smiled and started to doze.

The squeak and thump of the door opening to his room awakened him.

He opened his eyes. Summer had turned on her side, but no one else was there. He closed his eyes and soon was dreaming of mountains and pristine meadows.

Nguyen arrived at the hospital room after dark carrying a large brown paper sack. He opened the door. Jake and Summer slept peacefully, though at the squeak of the door Jake stirred. Nguyen let the door swing shut. Getting a chair from one of the nurses, he put the bag down and parked himself outside the room. Patience he knew. He read a *National Geographic* until the two inside began to stir. Then he grabbed the brown sack and walked in. He introduced himself, explained his relationship with Stony and the reason he was there.

"I told Stony," Jake said, "that I could handle things. He doesn't need to do this. You don't need to stay." Jake almost felt sorry that Stony would have to resort to this diminutive man to protect him.

"I stay. Stony get mad if I go. Beside," Nguyen's black eyes twinkled as he bowed his head at Summer, "you only have one little lady to help you. I strong; know karate."

Summer smiled at the tiny man; the top of his neatly-cut black hair might touch her shoulder if he stood straight. "You'd be surprised what I know, and how strong I am."

"Good. Then we both strong, and together we help Dr. Jake. Stony be very happy." He bowed his head again, not a strand of gray to reveal his forty-four years, and lowered the grocery sack to the floor. He took out a *National Geographic* magazine and sat on the chair Stony had occupied.

Summer smiled at Nguyen. "I want Stony to be happy, too. He's a good man."

Before Jake could think of a response, a mouth-watering aroma filled the room.

Summer nodded at the open grocery sack. "That smells wonderful. What is it?"

He beamed at them. "Oh, I bring food for everyone. My daughter help make fresh today. She is very smart. Stony love her, help her go to college. You hungry?"

After filling up on pork-noodle soup, sticky-rice cakes, and stir-fried duck and pork, Jake let Summer go home. Nguyen stayed.

Jake wasted no time in snoring.

Early the next morning, when Roman came through the door with his syringe full of poison, there sat Nguyen, reading the same *National Geographic*. He was a slow reader, but thorough. He watched Roman with eyes that saw everything.

CHAPTER 74

Roman's sixth sense warned him someone had been watching him. Tonight he decided to find out who.

Before he'd left, he'd turned on a hidden security camera attached to his privacy fence in a location between the cedar trees that allowed a good view of most of his back yard and the back door. He left and drove three blocks down the road, turned the car around and returned one block east. The dark alley that ran behind his house would be perfect. He turned west into it and switched off his headlights, drove slowly in the dark and parked and switched off the engine. His back fence was visible, but not the back yard. He toggled on the remote video viewer. The back yard fluttered onto the screen; the eerie greenish tint of the night-view camera reminded him of *The Blair Witch Project*. Now that had been a stupid movie.

He waited.

Nothing.

He tapped his fingers on the steering wheel. Perhaps he should go to the front of the house, though he couldn't imagine anyone breaking in there due to the bright streetlights.

After another half hour, he reached for the key to turn on the car.

At that moment, a shadowy figure slunk into the other end of the alley and climbed over his privacy fence in a half a beat.

Roman watched the video screen and gritted his teeth at the quick view of the man's head and face when he bent over to put on shoe covers. The black watch cap hid his hair. But the face? Roman had never actually seen Stony. He tried to remember the views he'd had of him through binoculars. All he'd seen was a man with a shock of cinder-black hair carrying a pack.

Roman relaxed his jaw and took a deep breath, letting it out slowly. Who else could it be? The workman's comp idiots would never do something so blatant. Rad had said Stony had been in Vietnam. And Stony had set a trap for Rad that had worked. It *had* to be him.

Roman grinned. Challenges were what he lived for. And this man had turned out to be almost as resourceful as Roman. Almost.

He watched Stony enter his house, hoping he would find the evidence planted under the stairs and present it to the police. When the police ran a DNA and fingerprint analysis, they would only find Jake's. And when they asked Roman about it, he would say, "I found them in his locker at work after he retired. I guess he forgot about them. I wasn't sure what to do, so I hid them. Jake is such a nice guy. I could never believe he would kill my wife."

He replayed the tape of Stony and froze the frame of Stony's face. The image burned into his brain. He let the tape play. When Stony opened the back door, a cold stillness crept from deep inside Roman, and a calming rage seeped into each nerve ending. *You violated my house?*

He murmured to the screen, "Rad was resourceful, too. Look what happened to him. And he was a *badass* guide. You're going to pay for this, Stony."

Not far away, Summer peered through unusual binoculars, so expensive that only a very few people in the world even knew about them. The Zeiss lenses had been specially ground, and a non-reflective coating prevented the flash from the lens revealing her location, even in daylight. A digitally-enhanced zoom gave crystal-clear images up to two thousand meters. The high pixel digital zoom allowed her to blow up images from five times that distance. The CIA would be jealous.

She watched Stony come out of the house, took a sip of green tea, and continued her surveillance. She liked the way his back hair flowed with only a hint of silver catching the moonlight. He moved like a man half his age. Was there something wrong with her to like him so much?

Roman returned thirty minutes later. She continued watching all through the night, long after Roman left, in the wee hours of the morning.

CHAPTER 75

The next day, Stony left flyers for Nguyen's restaurant at Roman's office. Then he went to visit Jake. When he walked into the hospital room, Nguyen bowed his head, and they hugged. Jake sat up. Stony smiled. A warmth spread through Jake he hadn't felt in a long time.

"How you doin', Doc?"

"Not bad at all. Much better than yesterday. I'm going home."

"Are you sure you're ready? Summer and Carla want you home, but they also don't want you bouncing back in here. By the way, where are they?"

"Summer had to get back to residency. Carla went home to get things ready. She'll be here soon to pick me up. We had a heart-to-heart. I decided to take a break from practicing for five or six months. You know, reevaluate things. Carla agreed. We need some time with each other. Summer is busy in her residency and we have no major expenses, so it's the perfect time. And boy, am I ready to leave this hospital."

"What about Roman?"

"There's nothing I can do about Roman. I have no proof. The best I can do with this is leave it alone, forget it."

Stony felt his jaw go slack, and a long sliver of ice slid into his chest. "You sure that's what you want? Seems to me Roman is a man that won't give up easily. He'll keep coming after you."

Jake clasped his hands and seemed to inspect one thumb, rubbing the other one over it several times. "I didn't want to tell you. Thought you might think I've lost faith in your abilities. It's not that. You've already done way too much. Besides, this is not your job, watching after me and my family. You're a guide. So I hired some people to watch Roman."

"Hope they're good. From what you told me, Roman's pretty slippery."

"I've made contacts over the years—patients. One Korean couple had experience in Vietnam and Laos, their equivalent to our CIA. The husband is in remission from Hodgkin's disease, so they're very grateful. There's also a retired cop from New York who I treated. A bone marrow transplant saved him from multiple myeloma. Whenever I see him in the store he always tells me about his son, a basketball player who got a scholarship to CU. Thanks to his remission, he'll see that son play collegiate ball. They'll be out there, watching. I trust them."

"That's great. Maybe you could introduce them to Nguyen?"

"They'd probably get along well with him."

Stony pursed his lips and eyed the floor. "So I guess I'll be getting back to the restaurant this afternoon. I wait tables in the off season. Need to make money for this trip I've planned. Going out to Wyoming for a bit of fishing in the next two or three weeks, so you may not see me for little while."

A knock on the door interrupted them. A man in a gray suit with chipmunk cheeks and an acne-pocked face stepped in. "Excuse me. Dr. Jake Roberts?"

"Yes."

The man's quick, hazel eyes seemed to evaluate everything in the room with one furtive glance. They lingered on Stony. He flipped out an ID card and badge. "I'm Jason Silverman, an investigator for a workman's compensation firm that represented a patient of yours. I need a moment of your time." He stared at Stony. "Alone."

"If this is about that guy Farnsworth, I already gave a deposition on him. Maybe I should get my lawyer."

"That's up to you, sir. You have that right. We've had a hard time tracking you down. I just wanted to clear up a few things in light of some new information. You see, Mr. Farnsworth died about two weeks ago. Were you aware of that?"

"No, I wasn't. Perhaps you can arrange a discussion later, with my lawyer present."

The man's eyes seemed to shine, as if he'd got the desired effect. "That's fine, Doctor. Sorry to catch you like this. Hope you're not too ill."

"Actually, I'm doing quite well. Thank you."

"Glad to hear it. You'll need your energy." The man's face beamed. This guy was really enjoying himself. "Bye. See you soon." He smiled at Jake, but only with his mouth, his hazel eyes a flat, thousand-yard stare through Jake. He glanced sideways at Stony and was gone, the door thudding shut behind him.

Jake frowned at Stony. "Sorry about that. Roman took care of several workmen's compensation patients, and I had to see one several times because Roman wasn't there."

"If he was Roman's patient, why did that guy say he was yours?"

"I don't know. I *do* know lawyers include every doctor in lawsuits, even if I saw the patient only once; the more deep pockets are involved, the better the payment. And if the guy died, they're like flies to honey."

"Want me to look into it?"

"No. This is trivial. I saw the guy maybe three or four times, gave him pain meds, and that was that. Roman was his primary doctor. My lawyer can take care of it. Like I said, you've already done more than enough."

Jake paused and eyed Stony. "You know if there's anything I can ever do for you, all you have to do is ask. If you ever need money, a place to stay, medical care, anything at all, you name it."

"Doc, you don't have to worry about any of that stuff. We're even-steven. Drop by the restaurant one of these days. And if you ever want to go fishing, give me a holler."

They shook hands and were about to let go when Jake pulled Stony in and hugged him. Stony returned the embrace. Neither moved.

Stony eased away and walked out the door.

CHAPTER 76

Roman watched the hospital for a long time after failing at his attempt to poison Jake. Damn that gook midget! Undoubtedly Stony's Vietnamese restaurateur friend. Wasn't he special? Well, Stony would be buried with that gook. Right along with Jake. Whatever it took to please his partner and his guide. His very nosy guide.

Silverman walked out of the hospital, grinning widely.

Roman wanted to send the man a thank-you note. The chances of convicting Jake of Farnsworth's demise were slim, but DNA and circumstantial evidence had convicted others of lesser crimes. Silverman's workman's comp bosses would be frothing at the mouth over a lawsuit to get some of their money back.

Three more hours of watching the front door of the hospital were fruitless. Neither Jake nor Stony left. Jake's medical record was very revealing; Jake was definitely going home today. He also was not going to die of leukemia. His death would come much sooner.

Since Jake had not appeared at the front door, maybe Stony had arranged for a back-door exit. Stony was smarter than the average fishing guide. But Roman was even smarter—internal medicine *and* oncology, for Christ's sake. Smarter and more practiced at what he did. Death was his living room, his library, his work. And murder? That was his playground. He was damn sure not going to take his ball and go home.

He envisioned ramming an arsenic-coated baseball down Stony's throat as he lay strapped to a gurney. That was how this game would end.

He started the car and shoved it into gear to check out the ER exit on the other side of the hospital. He turned the corner and was confronted by a cacophony of sirens from three ambulances and two cop cars. At least five cops and several attendants milled about the back entrance. In the dim morning light, the yellow and red lights of the emergency vehicles were like strobe lights against the tall windows of the ER. A cop directed traffic. He eyed Roman's car as if daring him to come closer. Roman backed up and turned around, sure no one had recognized his face.

He watched the lights and confusion in his rearview mirror as he drove away. A calm came over him. He was patient. Stony might have a lookout at Jake's home. But at some point they would not be watching—or Roman would divert their attention: soon. Right after he completed one important detail. He called a number on his cellphone.

Jake was glad to be going home with Carla. Summer would be there, too, though she would leave after three days; that's all the time her residency would allow off. After checking the morning labs, Jake's doctor had said, "Your bicarb is normal, sugar's down, and, as far as I can tell, you're in a complete remission from the leukemia."

Could he have been cured? If not, he would definitely make the best of the time he had left. Thanks to Stony, he was anxious to get back to medicine. Not with Roman, but another practice, perhaps with the government or a university. He did not want to worry about the business of medicine at all. Summer's excellent grades in medical school had allowed for grants to pick up most of that stupendous tab. He could finally stop worrying about expenses and concentrate on Carla. Their relationship had dwindled—not that it was bad, just a bit stale.

Carla drove him out of the hospital parking lot, unaware that several eyes watched.

In a tattered pickup truck in the alley across from the hospital, Stony sat, munching on a granola bar and sipping coffee.

Another block away behind the dark-tinted windows of a black Camry sat a blue-jeaned man with jaw and head shaved so closely they appeared waxed, at odds with thick black eyebrows that hovered over unblinking gray marksman's eyes. He raised large binoculars, then was as motionless as a stone until his cellphone vibrated in his chest pocket and he answered. "Yeah. No problem." He replaced the phone. His breathing became imperceptible; his heartbeat as slow as a marathon runner's. Beside him was a locked suitcase. He glanced at the suitcase on occasion and intermittently laid his palm on the top, gently fingering the leather. His hand itched for the contents; his index finger flexed in anticipation. He had waited for hours, arriving before dawn on a near-empty street that now hummed with traffic. He would wait as long as it took. The military had taught him all about waiting.

A block to the left and a block to the right were two other vehicles of Japanese make. Occupants in each trained binoculars on Jake, the excellent optics allowing observation of every detail—kissing and hugging his wife, their animated discussion while he cupped her cheek, his loving gaze into her eyes, and his tears of joy.

Some of the hearts behind all those watching eyes were moved, but most watched impassively.

The bald man chuckled and said, "What a sap."

When Jake's wife pulled out of the parking lot, Stony and one car followed. The two Asian occupants in the Nissan truck did not. They were parked next to a brick building and scanned the area with jungle-camouflaged Leupold tactical binoculars. They would have preferred a Korean model, but none came close to the quality they needed. The woman had her black hair back in a bun and wore a *Broncos* navy blue sweatshirt with orange script, pressed denim jeans, and a pair of white K-Swiss running shoes. The man had close-cropped black hair graying at the temples and wore gray sweats with *D.U. Law* stenciled in black on the front.

After several minutes, the woman in the driver's seat tapped the man on the shoulder and pointed. Their two pairs of telescoped eyes pointed in one direction. Neither moved for long minutes. A passerby peeking in the window would have sworn they were posed manikins. A lifetime of martial arts had taught patience, as had a prior career in which impatience meant sure death.

Half an hour went by. The man began scanning again, his binoculars moving slowly left to right, up and down, as rhythmic and methodical as a metronome. The woman didn't move except to breathe.

The man put his binoculars on the seat and said a few words to her, but she remained a statue. He moved to open the door. His side window exploded, and the man slumped back with a neat hole in his right temple, the left side missing a large piece, leaving a ragged crater. His brains covered the neat hole in the woman's right temple. The missing left side of her skull, along with the long-shaft .45 slugs had broken her side mirror and splattered against the brick wall. She lost consciousness so quickly that she slumped forward, still holding the binoculars to her eyes. The binocs hit the steering wheel in such a manner as to prop her head, making her appear as if she were glassing the dashboard.

Roman sighed at the scene. *So peaceful.* He gazed through binoculars out of the second-floor window of a deserted hospital waiting room, thinking how utterly alive he felt, every detail so vivid. The motionless man and woman were no longer troubled, no longer concerned or of concern. The brains and blood dripped off the wall and he imagined the soft plunks as they hit the road. The brick wall glowed, cinnamon and warm in the morning sun, small pieces of embedded, broken glass twinkling as if sugar had been sprinkled on top. A tiny, neon-yellow bird landed on the radio antenna of the truck and sang its tiny heart out. Roman whispered, "You'll not be keeping me from Jake anymore now, will you, Mister Viet?"

He folded the small Zeiss binoculars, placed them in a case in his shirt pocket, and sauntered to the elevator, pushing the down arrow. The incident should give Stony a feel for who he was dealing with. A doctor, not some dumb guide like Rad.

The elevator pinged and the doors opened and he sighed as he entered and pressed the one, a tiny full moon with a vertical slash of imperfection.

The gentle thump of the closing doors vibrated through him, as pure as any tuning fork. His frequency: murder.

"Stony, Stony, Stony," he murmured. "You're not the only one who can shoot well at long distances, though it helps that my man keeps in such good practice. Unlike you. You coward."

Roman would soon travel to that quaint town in Greece where a peaceful villa awaited him. It was his reward. After all his hard thinking and relieving the world of so many absolutely worthless beings, he deserved it. Colorado law might not agree, though the chickenshits had only executed one person in almost fifty years. Still, he might be the first. The tranquil warmth of Greece awaited. But not until after Jake.

A part of him wished his man had also taken out Jake. But Roman wanted to feel his own hands clench Jake's throat while his ugly wife watched, to see Jake's face turn purple, to stare into his unbelieving and bloodshot eyes. He shivered. Jake's death struggle in his hands was an exquisite thought. Then he breathed slowly. He must be more careful, use others to do his work for him. As long as the money held out. Greece wasn't cheap. Good thing Rad had got his money first. Not that he'd ever use that cash at his house. *Poor man.*

The bell dinged, and the elevator stopped with a gentle jolt. The elevator doors opened and he strolled out of the hospital into a bright, heavenly-blue Colorado morning.

He sighed. Life was beautiful.

CHAPTER 77

Two days later, Roman had everything ready. It was time. Two days ago when Amy had described the man who'd left the restaurant flyer, Roman had planned it for today. Payback.

He strolled into the restaurant, joy in his heart at the coming confrontation. The sign in the entrance said, "The receptionist will seat you." The corner table had a nice window. He might as well fully enjoy himself. He sat without waiting and placed the flyer on the table.

A man walked over with menus. He wore faded blue jeans, a white t-shirt, and cowboy boots. His face was definitely that of the man who'd violated Roman's home, the hair the same wavy gray-black that Roman had seen through binoculars, the same man who'd helped Jake hobble through a meadow. Roman raised an eyebrow, wondering why Stony was still here. He should have run the second he'd seen Roman.

"What kind of sandwich is good?" Roman never ate Vietnamese food, fearing some rat might get ground in. Now if they sacrificed a cat or dog? That would be fine.

"The Bánh Mì is good. Pork and vegetables and a crispy baguette." Stony's tone was friendly and matter of fact.

Could this be the wrong man? Stony should be cowering. "Okay. I'll take that. You're Stony the guide, right?"

"You almost got it right."

Roman frowned.

"My new title is 'The Grumpy Guide and Chatterbox.'" He paused. "It attracts the tourists." He chuckled.

"You don't know who I am, do you?"

"Sure, you're Dr. Johnson. A lot of your patients eat here. They say you're pretty good at what you do. Some say you're a wizard."

Roman shifted in his seat. He glanced back and forth at the table and his menu. Stony should be livid about the death of his Viet friend. What—

A small Vietnamese man rounded the corner from the kitchen and grinned. He walked to the table, and Stony put an arm around his shoulder. "I believe you met my friend, Nguyen Van Nguyen, at the hospital. He owns this establishment."

Roman felt his face drop, but instantly forced a polite smile. "Yes. How nice to see you." Roman remembered the morning he'd met Nguyen. All too well.

That morning, Roman had cracked the door to Jake's room. Jake had been snoozing. Roman opened the door and walked in. He had the syringe halfway out of his blazer pocket when the door bumped closed and he turned his head. He'd nearly flipped the syringe out. Nguyen had studied him over the top of a *National Geographic*, a large orangutan on the cover, a much larger ape than Nguyen. Roman dropped the syringe into his pocket. They had exchanged pleasantries. Nguyen said he was Stony's friend. Roman had excused himself, nodding at the snoring Jake. "I'll be back later. He looks like he could use the rest." He'd left the room and made a beeline for the stairwell. The door shut behind him. He ran down the stairs, wanting to scream. *Goddamn it!* Stony again. Had the fucking gook seen the syringe?

Gazing at Nguyen now, Roman wanted to leave, find the hired sniper, and give his bald head a much closer shave with a chainsaw. He covered his pursed lips with his hand. Good help was hard to find.

Nguyen reached out a hand, and Roman shook it. The man's large eyes, black hair, white shirt, black suit, and small hands gave Roman the image of a baby panda bear rather than an ape, offering a paw in welcome. Then the paw crunched hard and Roman winced.

"Oh, sorry," Nguyen said, withdrawing his hand. "Strong hands from work in kitchen. You can have extra dessert if like." His words were friendly, but his eyes were as emotionless and calm as a stuffed animal's.

Roman nodded. "That would be great. I love Vietnamese food. What do you suggest?" He gripped his aching hand under the table and crossed his legs. He would have to take on this chink himself, slowly. *Oh, yes.* Slow would be best.

"You like banana and cream?"

"Yes."

"I think Chè Chuôi is best."

"How's it—never mind. I'm sure it's wonderful. Thank you."

The panda baby raised a paw and left.

"Anything to drink?" Stony said.

"Water," Roman's voice was flat, his eyes on the table. He did not raise his eyes until Stony left. Stony was supposed to be quaking and furious. But this?

He closed his eyes and sighed. He had to remain calm. Stony had tricked Rad. Perhaps this was another ruse. He wanted to leave and rethink the whole business, but he must find out the identity of the Oriental woman and man who'd been killed. Who'd hired them? Or were they even involved? He remembered the tiny yellow bird perched and singing on the radio antenna. Had he paid for a hit on bird watchers?

Stony brought the sandwich and water. Roman eyed him but did not speak. When Stony walked toward the kitchen, Roman almost called him back to ask for the dessert to go, then thought better of it. He might learn more when Stony returned with the dessert.

The sandwich surprised his taste buds, and he decided to eat more Vietnamese food from now on—though this particular restaurant did not have much of a future. That thought made him chuckle. Then he choked on a piece of crispy baguette.

He coughed. Nothing. He tried again and it felt like something moved, but he barely crowed out any air. If he stood and threw himself onto the ground, that would work.

He stood. Strong arms wrapped around him and punched against his upper abdomen. The classic Heimlich maneuver.

He coughed out the baguette.

Stony let go of him. "Are you okay, Doc?"

Roman sat and glared at Stony. The way he said "Doc." It was like Rad, the stupid ape.

"I was fine. Why the hell did you do that?"

Stony squinted like he was watching an alien eat a cockroach. "Someone dies in our restaurant? Bad for business." Then he turned and walked away.

The dessert arrived, but Stony didn't bring it. Roman took a few deep breaths. He was fine. Never in danger. How could he die? He had too many people to kill.

"Where's Stony?" Roman asked the young Oriental woman who shoved the dessert bowl onto the table, spilling a line of cream over the edge of the bowl.

She glared at him. "He's gone. Other business, you know. You can pay me, unless you want to pay my father." She had no hint of a Vietnamese accent. Roman groaned inside. American-raised with an attitude.

"Right. I'll pay you. Any idea how to contact Stony?"

"Sorry, we don't give out that information. Besides, I don't think he wants to see you again. Enjoy the dessert. It's my favorite."

She spun around and strode off. Her ass punched side to side in tight jeans. He must sample more Oriental cuisine, soon.

Stony was upset. *Poor baby.* Roman spooned in some of the dessert: banana pieces floating in creamy tapioca. Delicious.

CHAPTER 78

Roman felt odd that evening. He sat down to watch the news and it only got worse. The images on the TV were doubled, and his breathing was...not...right. Maybe coffee would help. He had plans for the night and didn't want to fall asleep too early. He pushed out of the easy chair, but his legs were rubber bands that could not support him. He fell to the floor. Then his vision grayed.

What the hell? His mind was working overtime, but his body felt like it was in a tar pit, each movement an effort that took forever. His eyelids kept closing.

Stony must have drugged him.

There was a rattling at the front door, and he heard it open. He tried to see, but he could not even open his eyes, much less move his head. Footsteps echoed across the wooden-floored foyer, and then muffled from the living room carpet. They stopped by his head. He could feel someone staring down at him.

"Doctor Johnson. How nice to see you again. "

You fucker, Stony.

"I bet you're wondering what in the hell we did to you. Let's just say it's a taste of your own medicine. You really need the full-course meal, but I won't do that. I can't. I made a vow. Your friend, though—you know, Dr. Jake Roberts? He has something interesting in mind for you."

Roman wanted to lash out, take the knife out of his pocket and slash Stony's carotid and watch him bleed, staining the white carpet burgundy. But he could not even flinch. Breathing required concentration. He tried to think of Stony, but unless he concentrating on breathing…he stopped. *Shit!*

Concentrate. In. Out. In and out. The *out* came pretty easy. But if he didn't focus, the *in* never came. And his heart was trying to run away.

Rough hands turned him on his side and pulled his arms behind him. What felt like a plastic band encircled his wrists. A thin ratcheting sound accompanied the band tightening to the point of pain.

He wanted to scream *that hurts, you motherfucker!* But he couldn't say anything. He couldn't *do* anything. He could feel and hear; the smell of Stony's sweat nauseated him.

Rough hands reached under his armpits and pulled him up to sit with his back against the easy chair.

He tried to open his eyes. Only a tiny slit of light rimmed the bottom of his lids.

The sound of tape stripping off a roll, and then his lips were crushed against his teeth with wide tape, pulled tight and flattened against his cheek and jaw. He couldn't breathe through his mouth. A flicker of panic tripped his sprinting heartbeat into skips.

"Yeah, that's right, Doc. Now all I have to do is stick two fingers up your nose, and you can't breathe at all. Ever see *A Fish Called Wanda?* If I were you, I'd concentrate on those two little nostril holes right now."

CHAPTER 79

More tape was stripped off, and Roman's ankles wrapped together, the bones smashed against each other.

A needle stuck in his deltoid muscle, and soon he began to breathe easier.

He opened his eyes. There was no more double vision.

Stony sat in a chair facing him. He unwrapped a piece of gum, stuck it in his mouth, and smacked noisily.

"Nice place you got here." Stony said between smacks. "If I didn't know better I'd think you were a very successful doctor and probably compliment you on your practice." Stony smiled with his lips. His eyes looked bored. "You and I both know that's bullshit. I found your little cache under the stairs. You're a cold-blooded murderer."

He chewed the gum, moved his gaze slowly around the room, and sighed. "Yep, I know the rush, Doc. Nam taught me. Killing is better than heroin, am I right? Only the rush I had probably is no comparison to yours. It left me empty. Is that what you feel between… you know, *between* killings? Maybe that's why you do it, to feel full again. Helluva thing, if that's it. Me? I got a lot of rushes afterwards, trying to get rid of the killings. Drugs and alcohol worked, sort of. Okay, they screwed me up. But I finally beat them. Took a long time and some very special people."

Roman could care less about this war casualty. His eyes slowly closed.

A hard slap on his cheek. He snapped his eyes open, glared at Stony, and snorted deep breaths through his nose.

"That's better. You need to be awake so you can understand the next bit. Let's call it murder rehab one-oh-one, by Stony the guide and Jake the nice doctor. The problem is that you lack something called remorse. Most people eventually feel bad about killing another human being. You, on the other hand, seem to lack any ill effects of that rush—no come down, no retching on the big white telephone, no nothing. In fact, I think you get better at it each time because you keep succeeding without getting caught."

Damn right. Never will either. Roman tried to sneer under the duct tape, but could only feel the corners of his eyes crinkle.

Stony's head jutted forward and his eyes widened. "See. Right there. That's what I'm talking about. You think you've beat the system, and you'd be laughing at me if the tape was off."

Stony reached forward, and his fingers touched the side of the tape. Roman drew in a deep breath. As soon as the tape came off he would scream. Somebody would hear.

Stony's fingers smoothed the edge of the tape down, and he brought his face within inches of Roman's, smiling widely. "Just kidding, Doc."

Roman glared at him.

Stony pinched Roman's nostrils closed with one hand and held his head with the other.

Roman twisted his head side to side and his chest heaved against the vacuum. But Stony's grasp was unrelenting, and eventually Roman stopped struggling, though the involuntary inspiratory efforts kept his chest moving. His vision became grainy around the edges.

Stony released the hold on his head and nostrils, and Roman sucked in air so fast it whistled through his nostrils.

"Not laughing now, are you, Doc?"

Stony stood and walked around the room until Roman's breathing quieted. He sat facing Roman, his eyes a foot away. "See, that's what we call negative reinforcement. You stop struggling, and I let you breathe. Simple. But Jake and I could never come up with a good reinforcement to have you stop murdering human beings. So that's why we're doing this."

CHAPTER 80

Roman squinted hard at Stony, wondering how the hell he could get out of this. When he did, Stony would suffer. In fact, Roman had been aching to use a particular technique with a scalpel on the eyelids. Or maybe a knife instead. Yeah, Stony looked like a knife man.

"I can see by your eyes, Doc," Stony said, "that you are not accepting this very well. In fact, I'll bet you're wondering how the hell you could kill me and make it as painful as possible. Well, I have a friend who seems to have mastered the art of pain. He's been in two wars now: Vietnam and Afghanistan. Worked for the Russians. As you know, Russians usually get along pretty well with pain, as long as you give them enough vodka. We'll call this guy Victor. He pronounces it Wictor, so when he introduces himself, don't get confused. He is the opposite of no pain no gain. He believes in maximum pain for maximum benefit."

Roman's gaze flicked back and forth, searching the room. *Where was Victor?*

Not there. He turned his head a couple of times to make sure. He started to smile. Stony was bluffing.

Another slap. This one loosened a filling and turned his head back toward Stony.

"Tiny little yuk-yuk on my part. Unfortunately he's not here. He'd probably help you out a lot more than what we have planned, though.

Now that I have your attention, you should really listen to the next part and stop trying to figure a way out: there is none."

Roman wished his eyes could emit laser beams so he could burn Stony's lips off. He glared at him, willing it so.

"You have felt no remorse, no pain for all those murders. In fact, I'll bet you enjoyed every last one. I think you need a conscience. So, from now on you'll have maximum pain associated with any thoughts of murder. How are we going to know if you think about murder? You'd be surprised what we can do nowadays with PET scans and neurosurgery electrodes implanted in the brain. You remember Jake is into that, right? Deep brain implants to help with pain. He has surgeon friends who believe you need help. And I have right here a signed statement from you allowing them to make you better. And Wictor? Yeah, he's going to direct the placement of the electrodes."

Roman's eyes got very wide. He breathed so fast his nostrils collapsed on inhalation. He felt as if he would suffocate.

"Finally got your attention, huh? Figured I might. You see, Jake, that old softy, believes that if he can only rehabilitate you and keep you from murdering anybody else, you could be a great doctor and contribute a lot to society. Like me. I got over drugs and saved a few lives, so Jake wants you to be like me, a model citizen."

Stony paused, and one corner of his mouth ticked up, though his pupils had consumed his eyes: black lakes of cold.

"Imagine, you becoming like me. You and me pals."

Stony grinned. Roman's eyes were as emotionless as rocks.

"Nah. I agree with you. You'll never be a model citizen, now or ever, with or without any cattle prods in the brain. You're too good at lying, aren't you, Doc?"

Stony placed the tip of his index finger on Roman's temple. "That's why Wictor is having another electrode drilled in right here. Jake tells me it goes so deep it's in an area of your brain you can't disguise. What was the word he used? Primitive. That's it. Not just one, either. I think he said two or three—for backup, in case you get an itch to remove them.

'Course if you did that, you'd be a blubbering idiot. He didn't want me to tell you all this, but hell, you *deserve* to know. It's what you might call 'informed consent.' You doctors are big on that, I hear."

Stony glanced up at a grinding noise from outside. "Anyway, just wanted you to have an idea what the plan was before we begin. That sounds like our ride. Have to move you to a special laboratory that's been set up for this purpose by Jake and Wictor and some of Jake's associates that have, shall we say, felt the full weight of your wrath. Yes, there are other people besides Jake who have figured out you're an asshole and a very dangerous one at that. We found out over the last two days. Mr. Casper's wife suspected you a long time ago and had a private dick do some work. We can't convict you, but she was glad to contribute to this cause. It's a good one, don't you know?" Stony winked.

Roman knew, all right. He knew that he was going to get away. That quaint villa in Greece waited. Europe was still hungry for oncologists. A little plastic work on the face, a name change. But not before he ended Jake and Stony.

His eyes became heavy again. Stony's smiling face became two, and a blur.

"I can see the stimulant is wearing off. So my time with you is over, Dr. Johnson, and I'll say bye-bye. Sweet dreams. Don't forget to concentrate on breathing through your nostrils."

Roman's eyes closed involuntarily. Darkness enveloped him. In the past, darkness had been his friend. Now, a black icicle pricked at his heart. Stony's strong hands pinched under his armpits and dragged him across the carpet, his heels bumping onto the tile of the kitchen, bouncing painfully down on each stair to the garage where a motor hummed. Another pair of hands gripped his ankles, and he was flipped over onto a carpeted floor, one elbow rubbed raw and his nose slammed against the carpet so hard he almost blacked out. He concentrated hard, though. He had to stay awake to be able to breathe. Fingers gripped his face and turned it sideways, which wiped what he was sure was blood from his nose onto his cheek. A rough blanket was tossed on top of him, doors slammed shut, and the vehicle moved forward. The way his neck cranked to one side and his cheek smashed into the carpet was painful but welcome.

Pain would help keep him awake—to think and to plan.

CHAPTER 81

The vehicle turned a corner, and Roman's body shifted so his neck straightened. The relief from the pain brought immediate panic; now he had to concentrate on breathing through his nose, or not breathe at all. He tried to focus on the sounds of the wheels on the road to determine his location. But then his diaphragmatic paralysis became complete. He started to gray out and gasped, breathing as fast as a fat man after going up stairs. A woozy feeling lasted until he returned his thoughts—every thought—to breathing and re-established a rhythmic pattern. After that, his mind never wavered—breathe in, out, in, out. Besides, those he'd hired should be close on his trail. They'd better be.

Finally, the van stopped. The rear door banged open, and strong hands grabbed his ankles. His head plopped onto something hard, and he wanted to scream at the assholes for being so careless. He yearned to open his eyes and see his surroundings, his captors—memorize their features. He would kill *them* first. The blackness and straining to hear reminded him of when his mother locked him into a closet as a child. Dear Mommy had paid for that, just as his captors would suffer for this. He choked on saliva, tried to cough, forced in another breath through his nose: in out, in, out.

As someone pulled on his ankles, his shoulders started slipping into nothingness, his head on the very edge of the van floor, and he was sure they would drop him onto the ground. Another pair of hands grabbed under his armpits. They carried him to soft padding—relief from the hard, bumpy ride. He felt motion and heard squeaking wheels and steps on a hard floor; cold metal side rails pressed on one arm as they wheeled around a corner. He must be in a hospital gurney. Someone had to be very well-connected to have a gurney in a private clinic or operating room.

It was becoming more difficult to breathe, as if the paralysis were taking over his mind.

The backs of his eyelids became less dark. They must be in a lighted room. And there was a familiar and soothing smell of alcohol and antiseptics. Maybe this was a hospital. While keeping most of his concentration on breathing, he ran through a list of hospitals located about a half-hour from his house—though perhaps it had been forty-five minutes. With his constant attention upon continuing to breathe, his sense of time was terrible.

Gentle hands rolled his sleeve up, and the prick of a needle was followed by a stinging injection in his upper arm.

"Hello, Roman."

Roman opened his eyes. Bright lights—too bright to keep his eyes open, yet even the pain was good. He could move again. He twisted his head the other way and opened his eyes again. Stony sat beside him and stared at him with cold, gray eyes. "I think you might want to turn your head back over and look at Jake."

Roman glared at Stony and did not move.

Slap! It came out of nowhere.

Roman turned his head back, squinting into the bright light. Jake stood with three others, all dressed in surgical scrubs and masks. Jake's gaze seemed so kind, so forgiving. *Why?*

"You can trust me, Roman. What is about to happen to you is much better than prison or the death penalty, which you rightly deserve. However, you covered your tracks well, so it took Stony and me some time to discover just how low you were. Having that assassin murder my

Korean patients, my friends—you went too far." His voice got very soft at the end and he sounded hurt.

Oh, so they were your *friends, Jakey boy. This is too precious.*

"Unfortunately," Jake continued, his voice hard, "our evidence would not hold up in a court of law. But Stony has many interesting friends, and they have no trouble believing the evidence. One will be assisting me—Victor—I believe you are familiar with his name."

A bent man with kind, opal-blue eyes nodded at Roman.

Roman stared back. He didn't look like such a badass.

Then Victor lowered one eyelid and twisted his head ever so slightly. The slight change in his expression made Roman shudder. There was evil there. Deep.

"Oh, by the way," Jake said, "Your bald assassin friend, it seems, had debts with the CIA. And after he murdered my friends? He won't be joining you."

Roman's shoulders tightened, and he wanted to scream. Instead he closed his eyes and breathed deeply. Jake had no idea. He probably thought Roman all alone now. No help.

He opened his eyes and met Jake's gaze. *Anything else, moron?*

"One thing, though," Jake said. "I've seen your good side. You've helped so many patients. I don't really understand why you started killing. But I believe that the procedure we are about to perform will be a permanent fix for the better. When it's over, we'll watch you closely. You won't remember any of this. However, if you slip again, there's an implant that will destroy your brain. We have a nice home picked out for you if that should happen."

Jake peeled the duct tape from Roman's mouth, so careful and gentle. Jake was such a kind-hearted imbecile.

"I would like to know why you did what you did."

Roman wanted to stick a cattle prod into their hearts. He spoke loudly. His voice and his superior knowledge and powers of persuasion would convince them. "You don't understand why I did it? You think I'm selfish, that I did this for me? I would never harm anyone for my own selfish reasons. Come now, I am a doctor, like all of you. Casper, that power-hungry, money grubbing HMO idiot, only wanted what was best for his company. To hell with the doctor and forget about the patients. You can't tell me you think HMOs actually *care* about patients. I was only trying to help. You should be thankful I showed Casper the other side. If we are lucky, he was the main influence on the board of directors not paying on claims, so now that Casper is gone, perhaps they will change their idiotic payment policies on chemotherapy."

He beamed. They stared at him blankly. *The idiots needed a bit more.*

"Another ridiculous scenario that obviously needs curing are all those workman compensation patients who fake injuries in order to get compensation the rest of their lives. Surely you've seen them. They're scammers and need to feel their fake pain, don't you think?"

More blank stares. Some shook their heads.

"Gentlemen, please. I'm your savior. You just didn't know it. Now that you do, please thank me and let me go. Put down your anesthesia, your scalpels and drills, those nasty electrodes that will destroy my skilled physician's brain. Partner with me to fix medicine. You *need* my leadership, my knowledge to help medicine get back on its feet. You don't need to nationalize health care. That's what they said about HMOs. That's what they said when Medicare started. It's all a barrier between the doctor and the patient. *We* are the professionals. *We* are the smart ones, the ones that people trust to do the right thing. But instead, *we* have given that right to the HMOs, to Medicare, to insurance companies. So the patients naturally believe that we no longer hold the power. They're right. We don't. Power is information, and in this great United States of America, power is the ability to make money. It is also knowledge that others don't have about their bodies and about disease. We have been given gifts of superior minds that allow us to fathom the intricacies of the human body. With that power, that knowledge, comes a responsibility to decide life and death. That is what I've done in my career. That is what I've done in my life. If you don't believe that in your hearts, then you're not really doctors. You're mere technicians or storytellers or drug peddlers."

Jake's lips were parted and his gaze resembled that of an ape at a zoo. Gullible, trusting, and no clue, like most patients. In the next few minutes, once he let Roman go, a quick death was out.

Maybe he didn't have leukemia any more, but he would have to suffer. Oh, yes. A very, very long time.

Jake studied Roman. What Roman said rang true to him, and like all lies, the element of truth hooked him. Yet the conclusions and ultimate actions that Roman had taken were off the edge.

For the first time, Jake began to doubt that their procedure could ever help the man. "I'll give you this, Roman: you tried. How could you ever become a physician? I believe we'll get started."

Roman's voice became as dark and calm as a lake at night. "You'll never control my brain, you morons."

"Ah, your true colors. You shouldn't feel any pain, although at this point I don't give a damn."

They held Roman down and strapped his arms. One injected a sedative into his shoulder.

Roman's eyes widened and he screamed, "You are all dead. D-E-A-D!"

His struggles calmed, the sedative taking effect. They inserted an IV into his arm. As his Roman's eyes closed, the anesthetist placed a mask over Roman's face, and they wheeled him into the next room. The hiss of oxygen and anesthesia along with the puffing in and out of the anesthetist's bag intermingled with the shuffle of feet, low murmurs, and the silverware rattle of surgical instruments.

Stony went with them to the other room. As they prepared Roman for the operation, he sat and watched.

There was a scuffling sound outside the room. Stony got up and walked toward the door. Gunshots cracked, and one splintered the wood at the foot of the door.

He had no gun but pulled his knife and pushed the deadbolt. The door splintered open with such force that he fell back two steps. A wiry man with a grizzled, reddish beard and a Yankees ball cap rushed at him, swinging a baton that ratcheted and lengthened with each swing, like a black cobra striking.

Then everything went black.

CHAPTER 82

Roman had enjoyed three days of bliss.

The escape from those amateurs in the surgical suite would have been sweeter had they all been murdered. But they'd had armed help outside, and Roman's redheaded rescuer did not want to risk injury. What a shame.

But there had been rewards, very nice ones. The first day after his escape from those amateurs, he'd found Summer and taken her to where he was now, holed up in a cabin deep in the rust-colored, beetle-kill forest near Grand Lake. After all, he had friends, too. Yes, he did.

Friends like the grizzled Yankee fan who'd driven Rad's rig outside the park, the cagy man who'd somehow located Roman. The man was so thin that Roman figured he probably hadn't eaten anything but rats and beans for a year. After several angry questions about what had happened to Rad, Roman convinced the moron that Stony had killed him. That and an offer of five grand were incentive enough for the dolt to locate and hinder Stony. The redheaded bum had held out his hand immediately. A hungry man is a needy man.

Roman shivered at the narrow margin of success in the Yankee fan's rescuing him from the deep brain implants. Had Roman not feigned sedation, they would have never got out of there. The redhead had knocked Stony and the guy with the gun unconscious, kept the others at bay with a Glock while half carrying Roman to the truck. Roman had won again—superior intelligence always did. Jake and his buffoons would never control *his* mind.

Most of Roman's friends would do anything for money, though Roman's supply of that commodity might soon disappear if he didn't silence Jake. A few thousand for a couple of weeks in an isolated wilderness cabin seemed reasonable. The owner might want a tad more after Roman left. *Good luck finding me in Europe.*

Muffled cries from the basement interrupted his thoughts but reminded him of his plan. Jake would come running soon, bringing Stony and the cavalry. They'd better. Summer depended on it: at least, what was left of her did.

Roman had gotten a fortuitous call the day he escaped. Another of his paid associates had finally located Summer staying in a retired professor's home north of Boulder. A moonless night, a bit of chloroform, and her abduction had been swift and easy.

It had been odd, though. They had been about to go into the house when Summer had walked out.

"Hello, Roman. Want another kiss?" Her beaming face, the way she held her body, the confidence—Roman froze for a beat. Then she ran, but tripped going down the stairs. He was on her before she could get up again. Must be a family trait: thinking they could get away from him. The chloroform was already on the handkerchief. She was limp in seconds.

Roman went inside to silence the occupant—a Professor Steward, the door placard had read. But the woman was already dead in her bed. Must have had a stroke or heart attack, and Summer had been on her way to get the coroner.

In some ways it was unfortunate that Roman's other man had not killed Jake and Stony at the hospital. As it turned out, though, abducting Summer and having a few days with her, while at the same time making Jake and Stony sweat?

He shuddered and rolled his neck. Life had its grand moments. It was too bad the bald assassin was unavailable now. But the redhead would do. He could shoot well and would finish the job soon.

There was a bucket of water sitting in the sink he'd filled from the stream running close by the cabin. He dunked a glass inside. Must attend to his guest's thirst. Who knew what bacteria or parasites swam in those waters? Plenty of sheep and beaver upstream—giardia at the very least, E. Coli quite possible. He dried off the outside of the glass and washed his hands in the sink. *None for me, thanks.*

For three days she had performed some truly amazing feats, all to save Daddy. His heart raced and his tongue touched the corner of his mouth. He began to scratch his forearm, but immediately backed off. The pain was too much. He had taped a bandage over his whole raw forearm.

That last day, Summer had been moaning and acting as if she liked what he was doing. *Why?* He started scratching again.

"Fuck!" It hurt. He grabbed the glass of water and opened the basement door. If she'd liked the last three days, she would love what was coming.

Stony beat the hospital wall with his fist, the right hand, the one that had not been mangled by the lunatic who'd rescued Roman. The wiry, old redhead with the Yankees cap must have been on meth, he was so quick and accurate with the ASP telescoping baton. Stony fingered his forehead and winced. Another few inches to the side, a temple shot, and he'd be pushing up weeds or drooling from the side of his mouth while somebody pushed him in a wheelchair. Luckily Jake's cop friend had intervened, or the Yankees fan would have done more damage. Too bad he'd gotten away with Roman.

"Guess you're ready to leave," Jake said as he rushed into the room. Stony had pulled his jeans on and was struggling to put his casted left hand through the T-shirt.

"I should have remembered to take his phone. I forgot about them and the GPS. I'll make it up to you."

THE GUIDE

"Look, it wasn't your fault. Besides, you've helped me enough. Summer is my responsibility. I'll get her back."

"How long has it been?"

"Four days."

"Trust me on this: You need my help. If she's not already…" His voice trailed off, and he hit the wall again.

Jake squinted.

Stony frowned. "You think you can handle this guy, don't you?"

"I'm not in the wilderness anymore. I have resources."

The window cracked. A bullet hole popped into the wall a foot from Jake's head.

Stony lunged and pulled Jake behind the hospital bed. "Sure you don't want my help?"

More bullets ripped through the mattress. Pieces of sheets fluttered through the air like confetti. They crawled on hands and knees until they were out the door and well down the hallway.

A roaring sound began in Stony's head. Black smoke curled and blew through a thatched hut in the jungle. He was sitting below a window, sweat pouring off him. Someone was shooting at him from a tree outside. His left hand was freshly bandaged, the smell of antiseptic strong. Where was his gun? A smudge-faced boy tugged at his arm, and when he looked down at him, the boy's eyes were not afraid.

Someone grabbed his cheeks and shook his face. The boy disappeared. Jake's blue eyes stared at him.

"You were gone, Stony."

"Happens sometimes." He shook his head. "Been a long time, though."

"Dr. Roberts?" A portly, gray-haired nurse at the counter called to Jake. "Yes?"

She held out the phone. "It's for you."

"Take a number. I'll call them back."

She shook her head and pointed to the room they just crawled out of. "It's the guy. You know, the shooter."

Alarms blared overhead. Two hospital security guards burst through the doors of the stairwell, skidding to a stop outside Stony's room. The big one pointed at the nurse's outstretched hand with the phone. "Is that the police?" His chest heaved over a beer belly, and his chubby cheeks flared crimson.

She shook her head and blinked tears onto her cheeks. "It's for him." Her face pleaded with Jake. She held the phone as far away from her as possible. It reminded Jake of his mother holding out Summer's dirty diaper. Mom was always willing to help, though she hated dirty diapers. Although she was a lot leaner than this nurse, and never would have cried.

He stood and hurried to grab the phone. The other security guy, medium build with curly black hair, waved his hand back and forth. His voice was loud and overly confident. "No way. I'll talk with him until we get the police here."

The alarms stopped.

Jake stared at the security guys. Without the alarms, all sounds seemed magnified. The nurse sniffed; machines whirred and beeped; a loud voice crackled on the phone: "You're going to need the bomb squad if I don't speak with Dr. Roberts immediately. You and that fat sack of shit should go back to donuts and watching the security cameras."

A shot splintered the stair doors, and both security guards dropped to the floor like someone had smacked their knees with a sledgehammer. The fat one said, "Take it. Jesus Christ, Steven. Forget this." The other guard's bravado had disappeared with the rest of him, hiding behind a counter.

Jake grabbed the phone and noticed one of the hospital room doors was open next to Stony's; the afternoon sun filtered through the room from the outside window right into the hallway—a straight shot from the building across the street. *Shit!*

He rolled his body on top of the counter.

He heard a noise, insignificant really, barely audible, like someone had dropped a tiny glass Christmas ornament. A searing pain shot through his upper arm. He realized the noise had been a bullet going through a window.

The nurse cried out and grabbed her neck. Bright red, no, almost *orange* blood pulsed from around her fingers.

She fell to the floor.

CHAPTER 83

Roman shuffled around the dark basement, holding a phone to each ear: one, the cell that he'd been using to talk with the shooter; the other, the cabin's land-line portable phone. He heard a crack and rattle—like Jake had dropped the phone—then a shuffle and Jake's yell, sounding like he was in a closet. "Someone call a code. She's been shot in the neck."

Roman put the land line on mute and yelled in the cell phone. "I thought you said you had Jake in your sights. Who did you hit?"

"A fucking nurse. Hate those she-devils anyhow. Glad to take one off the planet. Last time I was in the hospital all they did was force me out of bed and—"

Roman interrupted the idiotic redhead. "I don't want to hear it! Can you get Jake or Stony?"

A form moved in the corner of the basement, catching Roman's eyes. Summer'd managed to pull off her gag.

She croaked, "Thought you wanted to kill him yourself, you wimpy coward."

Roman stepped toward Summer, then stopped. He rubbed the knot on his temple from the roundhouse kick she'd landed on his head an hour ago. Resilient little cunt. He should have starved her the first two days. But then she wouldn't have had so much energy for *him*. Resilient, athletic, and firm. Unfortunately he'd run out of sedative. No matter; he was going to enjoy the next few hours.

But first things first.

"I'm not sure I got a shot anymore, Doc." The grizzled Yankees fan said. "Besides, I hear sirens."

"I'm not paying you to kill nurses."

No reply. The cell screen said *Call ended.*

He started to fling the cell phone, then stuffed it into his pants pocket. He would need the phone later.

He walked to the box of tools he'd collected and reached for the whip. He hesitated and studied the phone. One last try. He un-muted the phone and peered into the corner. Two eyes glinted; she was crouched like a wrestler, ready for the next match to begin. With her hands still handcuffed behind her, the jutting of her breasts and her naked form made him stiff. Perhaps he should stun her, have some fun, then kill her and leave.

"What do you want?" A familiar voice issued from the phone.

"Is that you, Stony? What a delight. But I need Jake."

In the background muffled voices and clanging and *One and two and three and four and five and, one and—*

"Too bad he is so concerned about saving that bitchy old goat." Roman said. "I thought perhaps he would want to speak with his daughter one last time."

"You realize you're dead, don't you? I *will* find you. And if you harm Summer—"

"You had your chance, Stony. You're just not the man you used to be. As for Summer? She's already damaged goods. I wonder if Jake knew about that rising sun tattoo in the crack of her tight ass. Beautiful sight, and I've seen it from more than one angle. As a father, I'm sure he does not approve of that tattoo on her virgin skin. So, to make him feel all warm inside, I'll remove it—I have the tools."

He squeezed the *End* button on the phone and held it for several seconds, yearning to see Stony's face.

From the corner, her voice sounded smug despite the fear he knew his last statement must have caused. "You think you're so smart. That phone was on mute for well over a minute, plenty of time for them to trace it."

"Yes, I know."

He found the scalpel handle and attached a nice, new Bard-Parker blade. He hadn't done surgery in a while, but he had been good. No, he had been outstanding.

The multipurpose gun lay on the table. "For protection and fun," the Internet ad had said. It could shoot pepper, rubber, and paint balls, and, for the fun he had in mind, two electroshock darts. She would feel his surgery, but would not be able to move. He almost came from the thought.

He grabbed the gun, held it in one hand, the scalpel in the other.

"How about a kiss for Uncle Roman?" Then he gave her a bit of South Boston. "You love older guys like me, doncha? My Auntie and I were very close, too, ya' know. So you and me...we're wicked fuckin' weird, aren't we?"

She laughed, a cackle as crazy as her eyes.

He stepped back.

Her eyes showed large white rims, and she bared all her teeth, a demon's grin glowing in the half-light. "You have no idea, you fucking limp dick." She shook her tits. Her body glistened.

"Come on, Uncle Roman. Think you can handle a real woman?"

CHAPTER 84

Jake's hands were slick from holding pressure on the nurse's neck. Bright red arterial blood oozed through his fingers. His right upper arm leaked blood down his shirt onto his forearm—only a graze. At least a unit of blood had spurted from the nurse's neck before he got good pressure. Then her pulse disappeared, and they'd started CPR. Obese and over sixty and this stress—a heart attack was not out of the question. He struggled to hold pressure on her neck as it moved with each chest compression.

He should have pushed her out of the way. She might die because he had only thought of saving himself. Damn.

Someone dangled Silastic gloves in front of him, but he shook his head. "Can't let go. Is that IV in yet? What about the vascular surgeon?"

A medical assistant kneeled by him. "I can hold pressure, Doctor Roberts." He was gloved and had a thick wad of four-by-four gauze ready.

Jake let the assistant take over pressure.

"IV's in. Lactated Ringers 250 cc bolus going in," someone said.

Another voice came from behind him. "Dr. Schmidt's on the line, not the neurologist, but the vascular surgeon." There were two Dr. Schmidt's in the hospital.

"Wait a sec. I need to wash my hands—never mind. Hold the phone up to my mouth. Richard? Hi, sorry for the dinner call, but one of our nurses, a sixtyish white female, has been shot in the neck, and her carotid was nicked. She lost about a unit or more before we were able to get good pressure on the leak. Unfortunately she became pulseless, so we are in a full code."

He paused.

He stared at the heart monitor. "She's back in sinus rhythm. Maybe if we get enough fluids in her she may regain a pulse."

He listened. "Yes, the Ringer's is almost in, and she's typed and crossed for four units."

Someone tapped him on the shoulder and he glanced up at another physician.

"Wait a sec, Richard. Randy Dunbar just arrived. Not sure you've met him yet. He's the new intensivist. So far, what I've done—" His voice cracked, and he took a deep breath, realizing he was doing the same things he'd done in the past—work before family. "Shit! Never mind, Richard. I'll have to let Randy fill you in later. Someone's trying to kill my daughter. I have to go!"

He hung up and attempted a smile at the nurse holding the phone. "Thanks."

Dr. Dunbar, a tall, athletic bike rider, put a hand on his shoulder, confident and relaxed. "Tell me what you've got, Jake, and get out of here."

Jake filled him in.

At the nearby sink, he washed his hands and the right bicep wound. His blood-speckled watch read 5:20 p.m.—twenty minutes after the call had come in from the shooter. It couldn't be that long. Where was Stony?

The room held cops, nurses, and medical personnel, but no Stony.

Jake wrapped gauze around his upper arm and ran for the elevator, hands dripping.

A uniformed policeman with a crew cut and hooked nose stood by the elevator and pushed his hands and his uniform hat toward Jake. "Dr. Roberts?"

"Yes?"

"I need to speak to you in a quiet room, please."

"I don't have time for a statement about the shooting."

"It's not about the shooting." Something in his eyes and the tone of his voice made Jake's heart pause.

Jake peered at the cop and frowned. Then he blurted. "Did you find her?"

CHAPTER 85

The second Stony heard the shots, he knew: Roman. And somewhere inside him something burst.

He had to do it, vow or no vow.

Yet, even as he made up his mind, a deep part of him tried to rein him in, stop him using the vision of the smudged-face of Nguyen the boy. Jake's slap had brought him back to reality, and Jake's eyes had begged him to end it with Roman. Stony had to get rid of him.

When the nurse held out the phone to Jake, Stony pulled out his own cell. He'd fashioned a phone holder on the cast over his left palm: a piece of Velcro with the mate on the back of his cell. He attached the cell to the Velcro and tapped out a text message:

Roman on fone to Pdr Val Hosp. Trace it.

Stony picked up the landline phone Jake had dropped. The text came in: *Tracing.*

On the landline, Roman told him about Summer, and he nearly bashed his cell on the wall. The vibration of an incoming text stopped him. Roman hung up. Stony squeezed his eyes shut. He couldn't see. A pounding rush filled his head. He waited, breathed deep twice, then opened his eyes.

The cell screen text message read: *Hes NE of Grnd Lk. C U in 5. Hosp helo pd.*

Stony eased the landline back onto the cradle and, noting a cop coming out of the elevator, slipped out the stairwell door. He peeled the cell phone off his cast, stuck it in his pocket, and took the stairs two at a time.

At the exit, he slowed and calmly walked into the hallway.

"Where's the helo pad?" he asked a passing nurse, a tiny woman who walked with a purpose and had dark eyes.

She looked at his cast. "You mean the orthopedic clinic?"

He held up his cast. "No, I'm all fixed up. My buddy is being transferred from the Medical Center of the Rockies. We were in a motorcycle accident last week. I want to see him before I leave."

She pointed to the left. "Down that hall. There's a green sign for the ER."

"Thanks." He waved his cast and ran.

At the ER, a crowd hovered at the ambulance entrance located at the far end of the waiting room. A policeman held the door open while three or four women and a man stood outside watching the ambulance back toward the entrance. Inside, two other cops waited; one talked to two nurses.

The helo pad must be out further. How was he going to get there through these people?

He scanned the room. There was one exit to the left and, he stifled a hoot—a lighted sign hovered over another exit to his right: *Helicopter Landing Zone. Authorized Personnel Only.*

A Park ranger stood below the sign in conversation with...*Damn!* Dave. Before Stony could make a U-turn, they both eyeballed him. Dave frowned and started walking toward Stony. Stony opened the door he'd come in through and ran.

What the hell was Dave doing here? Was he here to charge Stony with keeping drugs in the fly shop?

His friend would be making an illegal helicopter landing and would need to take off right after touching down. Stony had to be on the landing pad in the next minute or his friend would fly away. Without him. He had to be there.

Stony had to get rid of Dave.

He ran, glancing down each connecting hall. From behind he heard, "Wait a minute, Stony." He turned his head. Dave loped toward him. Stony bolted around the corner. He would be out of sight but for only a few seconds. Finally what he needed appeared: a stairwell and, across the hall, several doors—including the men's restroom. He ran full tilt.

Running made him look guilty, but there was no other way. He pushed the door to the stairwell open.

CHAPTER 86

Dave rounded the corner just as the stairwell door shut. He burst through it, and the door slammed behind him. Then he quickly reopened the door and poked his head out, as if he had expected to see no one on the stairs. The hallway remained quiet. He seemed to listen closely for several seconds, then eyed the men's room, strode over to it, and entered.

Stony had been in the janitor's closet the whole time, peeking out and watching Dave. When Dave went in the restroom, Stony ran out—straight to the ER. Once he rounded the corner, he headed for the helo pad door.

But a crowd of people was blocking the door.

The faint sound of a distant helicopter filtered in. He had to do something fast. The main door to the ambulance loading dock was also packed with people. Two ambulance attendees were wheeling in a patient on a gurney.

Stony ran out the side door. It led to the ambulance parking bay.

He didn't want to do this, but if he didn't… He gripped his hands into fists. "Damn it." He had to get to Summer.

He walked past the driver's side of the ambulance. Neither the front or back was occupied. The keys were in the ignition. Everyone at the ER was preoccupied; no one was watching.

He jumped inside, started the engine, and floored the accelerator. Tires squealed and spun. He steered around the corner, out of sight of the ER.

A lamppost in the parking lot was dead ahead. It would be in clear view of the ER. Perfect. He shifted to neutral and jumped out, rolling onto the pavement, staying low and hidden. No problem. Like hitting the jungle floor in a hot LZ.

The ambulance rammed the lamppost.

Cops ran out.

The ambulance exploded. Everyone inside huddled to the windows and rubber-necked the burning ambulance.

Stony calmly walked behind them and exited to the helicopter pad. He ran and flailed his arms at the incoming chopper. The Bell BH-260 had the Channel 7 News logo on the side. In thirty seconds Stony was airborne. Down below, Stony saw Dave. He looked up at the helicopter and shook his head.

Stony donned the ear muffs/microphone and shook the outstretched hand of the pilot. "Thanks, WO." He pronounced it *woe*. Warrant Officer Wilford P. McFarland answered to "WO" from his Army friends, Mac to others. He'd flown Stony on missions in Nam, and now worked for Channel 7. His gnarled hand still gripped Stony's like a vice despite WO's ordeal with rheumatoid arthritis, which had resulted in two replaced knees and shoulders. Hazel eyes gleamed with excitement over acne-scarred chipmunk cheeks. "Damn, Stony. Takes me back. "

"Hope I don't get you fired."

"Shit, I haven't had this much fun in forever. Besides, it'll be worth it if you get the ass-wipe. You say he's a cancer doctor? Jesus. Remind me to never ask for a trade-in on my current disease."

"Yeah. Roman should be hung, right after I gut him with my dullest knife."

WO eyed Stony. He'd been in the celebration tent after Stony's Vietnam machete massacre.

Stony glanced sideways and winked. "Don't worry. I haven't got a knife. How the hell would I hold the bastard with this bum hand, anyhow?" He held up his cast.

"However," he added, "I could use a gun. You did bring the one I asked for, right?"

WO pointed behind his seat with a hitchhiker thumb.

Stony reached around and found a box of shells and his favorite handgun: a Colt 1911 .45 Autoload. In Nam it had tumbled a water buffalo before the beast had gored an army medic; in Alaska it had kept a grizzly from taking a swipe out of Sonja, though it'd jammed after that and they'd had to run. Stony didn't trust just anyone's gun. But this one was well-oiled and a damn site better cared for than his Alaska gun. It sure as hell could stop a red-headed meth maniac and a murdering doctor. He shook the box of shells open: a mixture of ACP rounds and Winchester 185 silvertip JHPs—jacketed hollow points. One side of his mouth ticked up. *Oorah.*

He checked the chamber; WO might like to keep one ready. But it was empty. He held the gun in front of him in the firing position, steadying the butt of the handle on the top of his cast. The cast was a firm platform, but the gun butt slid around like it was on ice.

He took out his cell phone and glanced at WO. "You don't happen to have a pocket knife, do you?"

WO reached in his pants pocket and pulled out a red Swiss army knife. "It's not dull, so if you change your mind…" His smile looked like a little kid with those chipmunk cheeks. He held out the knife.

Stony chuckled and grabbed the knife. "What about some super glue or tape?"

"First aid kit behind the seat. That superglue comes in handy when I cut myself with this damn thin skin I developed after the steroids."

Stony leaned over and plucked out the orange first-aid box. Once he had the superglue out, he cut a one-inch square of Velcro off the phone and glued it to the bottom of the gun's butt. He placed the butt on the cast's Velcro.

"Might have to patent that," he said to himself. Not like his real hand, but pretty damn stable.

"Thanks, WO. This should do the job. How long 'til we get there?"

"Twenty minutes, depending." He nodded at the small screen in the center of the console. "Might have to find a way between those."

Stony frowned at the weather radar. Green blots with orange centers appeared like a patchwork quilt along the radar view of the Front Range foothills. The view through the windshield confirmed it: a black-bellied thunderstorm towered dead ahead; a curtain of gray below it obscured everything beyond. He flinched at a flash of lightning.

A huge, fast-moving shape loomed in front of them. WO jerked the stick and the chopper banked hard. Stony's right temple cracked against the side window and the world went black.

CHAPTER 87

Pinpoint lights flitted through Stony's vision as he quickly regained consciousness. His right temple felt like he'd been hit by a hammer. Things were blurry. He shook his head and blinked. The headache eased and his vision cleared.

Lightning flashed again. Thunderstorms in October? What the hell? Then he remembered five years ago. He'd been drenched in rain, battered by hail, and frozen by snow, all from one fall thunderstorm in Boulder.

The dark shape had been a much larger helicopter. Why was it so close? WO had not been called Crazy Mac in Nam for nothing. He had flirted with disaster enough to not only make it through a situation like this, but to cackle at close calls.

They pitched and yawed around two more storms. One jaw-crunching downdraft, one ear-shattering crack of thunder, and they were through.

In another twenty minutes they landed on a dirt road. WO pointed to the left of the chopper. "One click north to the GPS fix."

He shut the motor down and started to get out.

Stony put a hand on his knee. "'Preciate the offer, but I got this. Best thing you can do is call in backup."

WO studied his knees, scrunched his mouth to the side, and rubbed an ear. "Yeah. You're probably right. I'll just slow you down." He put a hand out. "Oorah."

Stony shook it. "Oorah."

He tore off the headset, grabbed the gun and bullets, and jumped out. Then he remembered something. "I could use that Swiss knife, too."

WO grinned. He reached behind the passenger seat. Instead of the Swiss knife, a survival knife came out: eight-inch blade, chest belt sheath. "Thought you'd never ask."

Only one road ran north to the cabin, a fact Roman hadn't planned, but did enjoy. The thick forest of beetle-kill trees on either side of the road would be too treacherous to wander through, given the wind today. The frequent loud crashes of toppled trees only emphasized this. The dangerous obstacle course would necessitate anyone approaching to use the road or be smashed.

Normally Roman hated the wind. But today it was perfect.

Most of his life he'd been lucky. No, it wasn't luck. It was fate. A cop would drive by thirty minutes before he would enter a house. One time the power went out in a neighborhood when he needed total darkness to escape. The wind tonight once again proved it: this was what Roman was meant to do.

However, the wind was so loud that it kept him from hearing any planes or helicopters, pushing him to rush more than he preferred. No matter. Thirty minutes prior to sunset he was ready.

He squatted outside behind the large propane tank. All the curtains were open in the cabin, allowing easy viewing. A figure sat at the dining room table, head slumped, blond hair hanging forward. Stony and Jake would see that blond head, and no amount of caution would keep them out. They would have to rescue Summer. Even if they suspected a trap, they would have to come. Oh, yes. The strong always won over the weak.

In the basement, Summer had thought she could best him. A Taser was not as good as ketamine, but it had allowed him to subdue her.

For a beat he had not wanted to go on. But that was the way it always was. It passed quicker each time. This time it was gone in a breath.

The scalpel was sharp, and she bled. She screamed, though not in terror. It confused him.

The Taser wore off enough for her to say, "That was so good. I want more."

"What?"

She whispered something he could not hear. He got close to her lips. "Don't tie me so tight. I won't run away. I love this."

He choked on his spit, jumped up, and shocked her again. He stared at her and scratched at his bandaged arm, ignoring the pain. If Jake knew this it would kill him on the spot. Or was she trying to trick him into saving her?

Then a smell gagged him; her bowels had let loose with the last shock. He connected a hose to the basement sink and washed her off. The blood and feces ran down the overflow drain in the middle of the cement floor. He toweled her off from head to toe, lingering at her breasts and between her legs. A tight band stretched tighter inside him. So tight.

He combed her hair and the band relaxed. Her naked body quivered—aftereffects from the Taser. Red liquid dribbled down one butt cheek. The piece of skin was wrapped in a wet washrag in his front pocket, the wetness cool against his groin. The best souvenir yet.

He picked up the ice pick on the counter and touched the sharpened point. Her heart moved her ribs below her left breast: Lub-dub, lub-dub.

He gripped the pick, his knuckles white, the metal cool and hard against his palm. He raised the pick high, then paused.

If what she said was true, he would have a lot of fun and Jake would be destroyed. Maximum benefit.

He put the ice pick back.

Now, looking at the blond head inside the cabin bob up and down, breaths calm and regular, he was glad he hadn't killed her. The propane fireplace blazed, the TV blared, and the tea kettle puffed a weak stream of Vicks-impregnated water vapor into the air: all necessary attractants for the brave rescuers.

A south-side motion detector triggered a flood light that illuminated a dark figure trotting through the trees.

Roman crouched lower.

CHAPTER 88

Stony had jogged up the road a quarter mile, his shoes puffing dry dust with each step. There had been no precipitation on this southern part of the Western Slope for a month. The thunderstorms they had dodged on the eastern Front Range had spawned from an upslope low; none of that rain would arrive here. The tree branches on either side of the road rattled like hollow dice every time the wind gusted.

Several trees had fallen across the road. He had to stop and sidestep the large trunks; small branches snapped like balsa wood on his shoes.

He jogged forward. An odd smell filled the air. Through the trees, a cabin came into view about a quarter-mile away. One window had light streaming out, a beacon in the dark.

What was that odor? Then it came back to him: his mother rubbing Vicks VapoRub on his chest when he had pneumonia one winter. He hoped this was the right house, not some old fella's who had a chest cold.

The lighted room glared at him through the vertical lodge pole pines. A cracking sound behind him, and he rushed forward, scraping through trees in front of him as a tree crashed where he'd been. The wind feathered above him. Then it roared like a freight train. He moved faster.

He trotted toward the house, dodging trees like punches in a ring.

A bright outside light came on. He crouched low and squinted into the light, feeling like a mouse in a maze—Roman's maze, he was sure.

In Nam the jungle had held ideal cover: vines, solid undergrowth, moss-covered rocks, and easily climbed trees. Here he felt naked—exposed. The pines had been so thick before the beetle kill that there was no undergrowth, only dead trees and their needles. Even the occasional bush held no leaves. Winter was almost here.

Something caught his eye inside the cabin. Summer sat in a chair with her head hanging forward and blond hair draped over her face. Behind her, the fire in the fireplace licked over the wooden mantle. Kachina dolls sat on the mantle and would soon catch fire. The rest of the cabin would follow. The blond in the chair had to be Summer. But could it be a trap? Maybe Roman had already left and taken Summer, and this was only a ruse. The figure's head and shoulders lifted up and down in a slow rhythm. If it was a trick, it nevertheless risked someone's life. If not...

It meant Summer was still alive.

His legs tensed. He wanted to run inside. But surely Roman already had a bead on him and knew exactly where he was. "Hey, Roman," he shouted, "guess you have me and Summer right where you want us. Except you'll never get out of here. The search party has the house surrounded and they're moving in."

Inside the house, one of the Kachina dolls flared. Stony stood, using two trees to obscure his movements. He took a quick glance around the trees. The flames from the dolls licked the ceiling; the blue propane flames from the fireplace consumed the mantle. Roman would not be inside. He would not risk it.

Where was he? Stony squinted, shielding his eyes with a hand against the bright flood light.

On the east side of the house stood a large propane tank. There was no other cover close to the house. Roman would be hiding there. He could see Stony and think he was safe behind the metal.

Stony pulled out the .45 and aimed...then lowered the weapon. If he blew the tank, a fire would likely consume most of the western slope of Rocky Mountain National Park. The wind would fan the flames. Hundreds of animals would die. Many houses would be destroyed.

Rivers and lakes would clog with soot and mud erosion. An ecological nightmare from one gunshot. There had to be another way.

The flames in the house roared, obscuring the mantle. Summer's body glowed in the flickering fire. He remembered the mountain and Jake's decision to live; then in the hospital—Summer sitting by her father, both of them happy, talking, and finally embracing for a long, long time—a love so strong. She was spunky, beautiful, and seemed to have feelings for Stony. He didn't know if he could lower the wall he'd had up since Sonja, but he knew Jake needed her.

What was a human life worth? A mountain ruined? Rivers and lakes filled with ash? What about the son of a man you had killed in a fashion that gave you nightmares? What about a friend's daughter? Stony had not been able to save his own daughter, or Sonja.

He ejected the clip, stuck in two ACP rounds, and rammed the clip in.

The first shot went through the side of the tank. The second one sparked the explosion.

CHAPTER 89

As soon as the tank exploded, Roman started spreading white gas on the north side of the house. After the flood light had illuminated the dark figure so close to the house, he knew it wouldn't be long until the man keyed in on the tank, so he'd grabbed the white gas container and ran. The house shielded him from being seen.

The man's voice confirmed it was Stony. How perfect when everything came together. Stony's talk of a search party close by had to be all bluff.

Roman stopped spreading the gas and listened. In another minute, the front door crashed open. Roman sprinkled the east side of the house with the colorless, almost odorless gas, then poured a line into the woods. He looked back inside the house. Surprise lit Stony's face when he lifted up the head and stared into the hazel eyes of Mr. Yankee Doodle Dandee. *Nice.* The redhead wanted revenge worse than Roman. He and Rad went way back, so the idea of killing the man who "killed" Rad, even if he might get burned in fire... Roman had paid him an extra five grand as added incentive. Worth every penny.

Roman dropped a match on the gas-wet ground. The flames streaked and spread over the dry underbrush and up the trunks of trees. He stared at the beauty of the flames. Then he pushed against several dead trees he had pre-cut hours ago. They toppled across the road, joining others that the wind had already felled. He doused the downed trees, then tossed the white gas container in the middle of them, followed by another lit match.

He was halfway down the road to his destination when he heard a whoosh as the container erupted. He twisted his head to view the conflagration. Flames licked the tops of the trees.

If Stony survived Mr. Yankee, he would never get out. By the time he had searched for Summer he'd be crispier than burnt bacon. And of course he *would* search for her. He had to rescue her. After all, he was a hero.

Roman stared. The rhythm and dance of the orange flames soothed him. He closed his eyes to enjoy the warmth on his face. A cold wind blew on his back.

He turned around. Just in case, he waited and watched the road for Stony's search party. He'd stuffed a Glock in his back belt line. The fire's heat grew, warming the gun. No one came. He jogged down the empty road ahead. His car was not far.

Summer awoke on her side, her head pounding. Through swollen eyes she searched for light. But only a void of blackness stared back. She was cold. Goosebumps peppered her nude body. She struggled and the pain returned. Her shoulders ached. Tight plastic bands cut into her wrists, bound behind her back. But her arms were not as tightly bound as before. Roman had listened. Her trick had worked.

Her face contorted and her body shook, but no tears wet her cheeks. She laughed. It was only a croak, because her tongue felt like a piece of dried leather, thick against the gag.

She squeezed her butt cheeks together to feel the searing, fresh-burn pain where her tattoo had been.

In a way it felt good; she was alive.

But Roman would pay for that. It had taken a month for her to decide on the colors and design for her art, her painting, something that her first boyfriend had always loved. The artist had been so sensitive. And the tattoo needle over and over had almost brought her to tears. Sometimes pain was good.

Now her painting was gone.

And what Roman had done to her? A shiver ran up her entire body, as much from the cold as remembering the last days.

But he'd let her live. He had plans.

So did she.

She pushed her legs out but met resistance. The smell was different here. The basement odor was gone. No more musty mixed with the foul smell of her feces and urine. Now there was the sharp smell of gasoline and rubber. Also, she lay on carpet, not cement. She explored more with her feet and lifted her head to see outlines. She was in the trunk of a car. Wind buffeted and rocked the car. A faint burr of sound came from directly in front of her, from where the trunk must close.

Where was the emergency latch to open the trunk? She edged her swollen face forward to see. Maybe she could use her teeth.

Or her fingers.

She pulled her knees to her chest. Yes. Her bindings were loose enough for her to bring her arms around from behind, under her butt and… there. She gnawed at the plastic cuffs; rubbed them on an exposed edge of metal. They broke off.

She found a jack handle in a side pocket and leveraged it against the crack in the trunk and pushed. She slipped, and the handle clanked down. Her knuckles barked against a sharp piece of metal.

"Shit!" She tried to keep the scream to a whisper, but she sounded like a seal barking at a circus.

She tried again, this time holding on tighter and pushing the handle forward more. The metal creaked.

She pushed harder.

The trunk flew open. She jumped out and pushed trunk closed, not wanting Roman to know she was gone. With tire iron in hand, she ran into the forest.

CHAPTER 90

Stony had waited after the tank exploded, his gun firmly planted on the Velcro of his cast, aimed at the side of the tank. No Roman. The fire inside the house roared.

He tore the gun off the Velcro pad and ran. He hit the front door full tilt and it slammed open, as if it had not been latched. He rolled onto the floor. The fireplace and mantle burned so hot he shielded his face. Flames from the Kachina dolls reached high. The ceiling flickered gold and blue.

He jumped up and pulled back Summer's head. Off came a blond wig—and Stony stared into the grizzled redhead who had almost killed him two days ago. The man coughed and snarled and lifted a revolver from his lap.

Stony froze, unbelieving. Then he threw the wig in the man's face, crouched, and dodged the first bullet, then pulled out the hunting knife and buried it in the man's chest.

The redhead's eyes opened wide and his body became rigid, his other hand a claw, scratching at Stony's knife hand. Then he relaxed, coughed once, and closed his eyes. The gun rattled onto the floor. The knife grated against ribs when Stony pulled it out. He wiped the blood on the man's shirt, and slipped it back in the sheath.

He gritted his teeth and panic rose in his heart.

Where was Summer?

He rushed through the house, throwing open doors and rifling through closets. Nothing. He yanked down the attic ladder and ran up, gripping the meager railing with his right hand. Once up, he pushed the casted left hand onto the frame of the opening and balanced himself while he pulled out the pen light from his pants pocket. He searched the smoky enclosure, the penlight barely penetrating, but enough to see.

Empty.

First time through the kitchen, he'd seen a fire extinguisher on the wall. He backed down from the ladder and ran into the kitchen. He grabbed the extinguisher off the wall, ran back to the fire place, and emptied the extinguisher on the mantle and ceiling. A few flames still smoldered on the wall and ceiling, but this would buy him time. He bent to turn off the fireplace, but noticed the flames from the fireplace were gone. No more fuel.

Something caught his eye outside—a raging forest fire.

He must hurry. Only one place left. He rushed for the basement door. She had to be there.

He flicked on the light switch, and his steps creaked down the old stairs. The odor reminded him of a pit toilet that someone had forgotten to service for months. A solitary naked bulb emitted enough light to reveal every corner. One held an empty chair. Otherwise the only thing left was the smell.

Something crashed and banged behind him. He ran up the stairs. The door was jammed. He pushed hard. A tiny opening revealed a burning tree had crashed through the roof and landed against the door.

He pushed harder. No luck.

Stepping down the stairs he took a running start and hit the door with all his weight. It moved, but not enough.

He stepped back into the basement and searched each corner. A two-by-four lay in the shadows of the second corner. He grabbed it. It was sticky with a dark substance on one end and smelled of blood, probably Summer's. He clamped his jaw and ran at the door, pretending it was Roman's head. He would bash it to pieces with his two-by-four. At the last moment he stopped. If Summer was alive, he needed to get out, not break wood. He placed the two-by-four through the door crack and leveraged the tree enough to wriggle out.

He coughed and held the crook of his arm to his mouth and nose, peering through the hazy interior. The wind from the open ceiling freshened the smoke-filled air, but also fanned the flames that covered the moose-patterned couch. Another gust and the entire couch crawled with yellow, licking at every moose head.

He ran to the kitchen and turned on the faucet full force, splashing water over his body. Grabbing a dish towel, he wet it and wrapped it around his head. He lunged out the front door.

CHAPTER 91

Roman had loped down the main road until he came to a branch in it, a small two-track logging road that ran up the slope and disappeared into shadows. He stopped and danced in a circle, wanting to shout his triumph over Stony: the man who'd violated his house and his privacy, and who'd been smart enough to trick Rad and capture Roman once. A fitting adversary. Now he would burn with his revered forest. Roman's car was ahead. Thinking of who was inside the trunk, he walked faster.

What a lovely prize. He would soon see just how much she enjoyed pain. Then he would give a full report to Jake.

As he neared the car, he sensed something wrong. The beam of his penlight swept the dirt behind the car. His time with Rad had not been wasted. The tracking skills he'd learned paid off. He had not gone to the trunk before he'd left her here. Yet there were footprints in the dirt.

Had Stony already been here and released her?

No, he'd come through the woods.

Roman ran.

As he reached the woods to his left, another flashlight beam scurried after him and a voice cried out, "Police! Stop or we'll shoot."

He ran faster.

Shots peppered the dirt, and one cracked off a tree to his right.

It was difficult at a full sprint, but he managed to retrieve the garage door opener from his pocket. The Internet was a wonderful source of information on IEDs and how a garage door opener could trigger one to blow. Planning ahead was his forte.

He took the opener out of a hard clamshell sunglasses case—a precaution to prevent accidentally triggering the wad of Semtex under the car's gas tank. He pushed the button and crouched low.

Plan B.

The explosion lit the sky behind him. The shock wave and heat washed over him. He sprinted up the hill. If he made it to the top, he could cut right and follow the logging road to the closest neighbor. From his prior scouting, he knew the house was vacant, and there was an old truck in the outside garage. The truck had started with the first crank, the keys in the ignition. People were such trusting souls.

A tree fell a hundred yards in front of him. He slowed. The wind screamed through the trees. He glanced back. A curtain of flames obscured the forest behind him.

Wonderful.

They would be too preoccupied with the fire to come after him. He could afford to slow down. He didn't feel safe enough to turn on the flashlight, but the light from the fire was enough to illuminate his way.

He picked his steps and reviewed his plans for the rest of the evening. The wind would have to abate before he could fly out of the Grand County Airport. A prior patient and pilot had agreed to fly him to Mexico—in a Lear Jet, no less. Roman would call him tonight. Then, to Manzanillo, a major port city. There he could hide out for as long as he liked. Or perhaps he would fly or take a cruise to Greece after plastic surgery and an identity change. Mexico had wonderful plastic surgeons. So many options.

He stepped over a log. Ahead, smoke glowed like fog in the headlights. A thicker shadow stood by a tree trunk. Roman stopped in mid-step. That was no tree. The hard barrel of his Glock wedged between his belt and the small of his back was such comfort at times like this.

The fire roared behind him, and the wind above him, but he still heard the voice. "It's over, Roman."

Roman pulled the gun and flicked the penlight on. He aimed where the shadow had been. Only trees remained.

A sound cracked to his right. He fired at it.

An arm came under his neck, and a sharp pain stabbed between his shoulder blades.

He pointed the gun behind his back and fired.

CHAPTER 92

The wind changed, bringing the thunderstorms to the western slope. The dry trees did not need the lightning, but the two inches of sudden, drenching rain that fell over the dead wood in and around Roman's fire was enough. The fire died.

The police found Stony sitting cross-legged in soot and mud about a quarter of a mile up the logging road from where Roman's car had exploded. His hair was partially burned off, and his left hand was no longer in the cast. He held both hands limply in his lap and stared at the object in front of him: Roman's head impaled on a hunting knife, eyelids sliced off so his eyes stared back.

They had no problem moving Stony, but he never spoke. He was mute and compliant, even when they locked him in jail. The police had seen Roman run from the car, had statements from Summer and Jake incriminating Roman in deaths of patients and in torturing and raping Summer, but they didn't know what else to do with Stony.

He'd cut a man's head off, for Christ's sake.

Jake knew what to do, though. First, he got Summer medical help; she refused a shrink but got a skin graft for that ugly job Roman had done on her lower back. At least it wasn't as visible as Carla's scars.

Then Jake finally made good on his promise to help Stony. He got the best psychiatrists in town. They moved Stony from jail to a local psychiatric hospital. After a few weeks, Stony began to respond.

The official investigation termed the fire an accident. Police kept things quiet. Some of them had visited Dr. Roman Johnson for their own cancers, or a relative's. They believed Jake and Summer, but knew if the press got hold of this—no one would ever trust a doctor again.

And many cops were Vietnam veterans—some were Stony's friends. More press about a crazy veteran who cut off a doctor's head would fuel distrust of all Vietnam vets. Not a pleasant thought after forty years of taking the heat.

Investigators found the charred remains of Roman's body. They froze his head and left it in a vault at Larimer county morgue "for evidence." Officially, his death was reported as having been by the fire, so no one was surprised at the small casket at the funeral. Even though the funeral was not advertised, hundreds came to the graveside service. It snowed a half a foot that morning. Roman's office assistant, Amy, laid a wreath on his grave after the ceremony. Jake watched from under a nearby cottonwood, the dormant branches offering no cover. Summer did not come.

Later, Jake visited Stony and told him about the funeral. Jake kept one side of his face toward Stony, the side without the bandaged ear.

Stony sat in bed, his right arm casted again. He stared at some vacant space over Jake's left shoulder. "I didn't want to kill him. But he just wouldn't go away."

"I know, Stony. I know. No one believes you did anything wrong. If they do, who cares? He's dead. You're free to do what you want."

Stony nodded as if he were okay with that, but his glazed eyes were still vacant. "The thing is, I don't remember doing it. Something hit me in the head and that's all I remember until I woke up."

"That happens sometimes. You black out when something so traumatic happens."

"Maybe so."

Then Stony shook his head. "Dave probably thinks I'm a raving druggie. Bob will never take me back."

"I talked with them. They got a drug urine test on Caleb, and we got one on you at the hospital. They fired Caleb. You're free and clear. Bob said he wants you back as soon as you're ready."

"Got a piss test on me, huh? Don't recall giving permission."

"I thought—"

"Little joke from the Grumpy Guide." One side of Stony's mouth lifted as if he would smile, but that was as far as it went. He frowned. "Hey, what about you and that workman's comp guy, what was his name, Farnsworth?"

"Oh, yeah. Apparently there's a guy with MS who lives close to Farnsworth and couldn't sleep one night due to a young couple yelling and arguing on the street in front of Farnsworth's house. He'd been in a wheelchair for years and did a lot of, shall we say, binocular neighborhood watching. He was scoping out the place and noticed a man coming out of Farnsworth's house. He didn't want to report it because of his binocular habit. Felt the police might think he was a peeper. Anyway, that insurance guy, the one who came in my hospital room when you were there, he finally got around to interviewing neighbors of Farnsworth, and the MS guy identified Roman. Seems he got a real good look at his face."

Stony shook his head. "Jesus. So that was what Roman was talking about in the operating room that night, about the workman's comp scammers. He murdered that guy, too."

"Well. There's nothing direct, though they did find some of Roman's prints in an abandoned house behind Farnsworth's. Luckily for me."

"What do you mean?"

"They found a lot of evidence at Farnsworth's house that implicated me."

"What were you doing there?"

"That's the thing: I never went to Farnsworth's, but they found fibers from my carpet, along with hair and skin samples. They matched the DNA swab they took while I was in the service."

Stony mulled that over. "Roman planted it."

"They can't prove it. But with the MS guy's positive ID, that's what the police and insurance people are thinking. The rangers are also suspicious about Rad's disappearance. But nothing definite yet. With Summer's testimony, what I told them about Casper, the fact that Roman had hired Rad to find me, and now Farnsworth, I just found out great news." He paused. "They're dropping all charges against you. No one thinks a jury will convict you for what Roman did. Besides, they're glad you got rid of him."

Stony gazed off into the distance. Jake wondered if he'd lost him again. He faced Jake full on.

Stony shook his head and peered at Jake, frowning. "Jesus, buddy. What happened to your ear?"

Jake looked embarrassed. "Summer caught me with a tire iron. Pretty strong for her size. I saw her running through the woods from the fire, and when I grabbed her she must have thought I was Roman. She smacked me pretty good. The ER doc did a pretty good job sewing it up, though."

Stony smiled his crooked smile. "How's Summer holding up?"

"She's tougher than I am." Jake wanted to hug Stony for that smile; it had been too long. "I'm sure Summer will have scars, mostly psychological, though the one psychologist I finally talked her into seeing says she's doing well. Summer wants to get back to work... She's outside. She said she wanted to visit with you after me, all alone. I think she wants to thank you."

"She doesn't have to thank me."

"Right."

There was an uncomfortable silence.

"Maybe I should get back to work," Stony said.

"Absolutely. I need you to guide me next summer. I promise to bring my insulin this time."

Stony laughed, long and hard, and for the first time since their guided trip, Jake saw a spark in Stony's eyes.

Summer knocked. Jake let her in, patted her on the shoulder; she gave him a quick squeeze, a tight smile. He left. She closed the door.

The smile disappeared. She eyed Stony and he could see her jaw and shoulders were as tight as guitar strings wound too tightly. Yet her eyes held pity.

"I wanted to thank you for helping my dad in the woods, and for trying to save me from Roman."

He gazed at the floor.

"It wasn't you who killed him, though," she said.

He frowned at her. "What do you mean?"

"You didn't kill Roman. I did."

Stony squeezed his eyes closed and pushed the heel of one palm against his forehead. "Run that by me again."

"You were out cold in the forest fire; a fallen tree must have hit you. Roman was getting away. I dragged you away from the fire, took your knife and…" Her eyes were dark fire, her jaw clenched. "Look at it this way. You killed one man in the cabin in self-defense. You can rest easy that you did not kill Roman in some PTSD rage."

Stony shook his head, unconvinced. "Thanks for trying, Summer. You're like Jake, always wanting to help. But how could you have overcome Roman with only a knife?"

"I did very well in surgery; just didn't like the hours. Also, I'm a black belt."

Stony rubbed his knuckles on his cheek. He sat up straighter and squinted at Summer. "You're a surprise a minute. All right, why would *you* cut off his head and eyelids?"

She smiled. "Oh, that wasn't all I cut off." She smirked. "I started with his little head. They'll never find that, even if his body wasn't so charred up. After that I improvised. I guess I wanted him to see the flames forever. Maybe like hell."

She stopped, crossed her arms and dropped her head. "I ran after that. Forgot about you, just ran. They thought all Roman's blood on me was mine, from the shit on my back. I got a quick shower once I returned before they had a chance to rethink. Now they think you did it. *You* think you did it. Daddy told me about your vow to not kill and how you were suffering, so I thought I better come in here and let you know."

She looked at him, her eyes wet. "I'm going to tell the police everything. You shouldn't have to go to jail for this."

Stony looked out the window. He had to admit Roman deserved everything she'd done to him and more. Stony liked Summer. Hell, he felt more than that, but this was not the time.

He looked back at her. A warmth bloomed in his chest, relaxed his face, calmed his mind. No one like her since Sonja. "I can't let you do that."

"What?"

"You keep your secret, just between you and me. The police have dropped the charges. And besides, your career as a doctor would be over before it started if they thought you did it."

She moved close. He could almost feel her heart beating. "They dropped the charges?

"Yeah."

The tenseness in her face and shoulders relaxed.

"You're right. It would probably would kill my career if this ever got out. But I don't know. It can't help your guiding, either."

"Are you kidding? Much better than the Grumpy Guide. I'll bet the phones will ring off the hook. Everyone wants a guide who'll kill for them."

He chuckled. One corner of her mouth raised, and she shrugged.

"Besides," he continued, "the police have hushed this up. No one will know. They don't want it out that there was a serial-killing doctor in the community, or that he was killed by a Vietnam vet in a PTSD rage."

She moved closer still, so close he could smell the fresh soap smell. Her eyes were moist but held his gaze gently. "Are you okay with this?"

Stony closed his eyes, took a deep breath in, and let it out as slow as if each morsel was something he needed to feel leave. "Oh, yeah. More than okay."

A tear dripped down one of her cheeks. "I'm so sorry you had to suffer for what I did."

She hugged him. Her body was warm and shook gently with sobs.

He wrapped his bad arm around her and rubbed the other palm over one of her shoulders, and said nothing. He was afraid he might say the wrong thing. She was Jake's daughter. She had just been sexually abused. This feeling he had would not happen. Could not.

Not yet.

After a minute her sobs quieted and she broke the embrace. She pursed her lips, dragged the back of her hand across her nose, and peered at him.

She smiled. "Dad was right."

"'Bout what?"

"You're the best." She kissed him on the lips.

He held her close and kissed her back.

She broke their embrace, grabbed his hand and pulled him toward the door. "You don't need to be here anymore."

"Could I at least put on a t-shirt? Blue jeans are okay, but this hospital gown…"

She opened the door and glanced back at him. "Kinda sexy, really. Besides what do we care what they think?"

They walked out the door together, hand in hand, into the long hallway toward Jake.

Stony murmured close to her ear, "I guess this means we're telling your dad."

She giggled, pulled a bit harder and they began to run.

—The End—

DAN'S WAR

Dan's War is about the end of world oil…in two weeks. Abdullah El-Hamain, a high-roller OPEC member, hates Big Oil for polluting earth and killing his wife. His solution: sink or swim—end global warming by destroying the entire world's oil supply in two weeks, using spiders and nanobacteria. Drawn into his apocalyptic scheme is Dan Trotter, a CIA computer savant without equal, but with an Asperger's-like syndrome that makes him a social goof. If Dan can only become a field agent in a real war he will become a hero like his father, breaking out of his geek job, and gain the respect from his wayward son and roaming wife. Dan soon finds himself in the middle of an oil war, a war that his own computer program helped start.

ABOUT THE AUTHOR

 Although Luther Milton (Milt) Mays grew up and now lives in Colorado, he spent most of his adult life as a Navy doctor, caring for those at the forefront of many conflicts, including Vietnam. He graduated from the Naval Academy and Creighton Medical School. His medical career included tours with the Marines, a Navy Security Group in Scotland, and now at the Veteran's Hospital in Cheyenne, Wyoming. He has been a fly fishing guide in Rocky Mountain National Park, and continues to ply these waters with a long stick and pieces of fur and feather.

Other published works by Milt include a novel, *Dan's War*, and short stories, "Thanksgiving with Riley" and "The Dry-Land Farmer." He is married with three children and a grandson who will soon be learning the joys of flinging a fly.

Don't miss Milt's soon to be released book, an irreverent poem on the wisdoms and frustrations of fly fishing, *Take the F##king Fly*, beautifully illustrated in colors straight off the river by Mike Friehauf.

For more information, please visit Milt's website at www.miltmays.com.

www.ingramcontent.com/pod-product-compliance
Lightning Source LLC
Chambersburg PA
CBHW050908250626
47155CB00001B/150